You may think you know the story. It goes like this: once upon a time, there was a sixteen-year-old girl named Jane Grey, who was forced to marry a complete stranger (Lord Guildford or Gilford or Gifford-something-or-other), and shortly thereafter found herself ruler of a country. She was queen for nine days. Then she quite literally lost her head.

We have a different tale to tell.

Pay attention. We've tweaked minor details. We've completely rearranged major details. Some names have been changed to protect the innocent (or not-so-innocent, or simply because we thought a name was terrible and we liked another name better). And we've added a touch of magic to keep things interesting. So really anything could happen.

This is how we think Jane's story *should* have gone.

Also by Cynthia Hand

The Last Time We Say Goodbye

Unearthly

Hallowed

Boundless

Radiant: An Unearthly Novella (available as an ebook only)

Also by Brodi Ashton

Diplomatic Immunity

Everneath

Everbound

Evertrue

Neverfall: An Everneath Novella (available as an ebook only)

Also by Jodi Meadows

The Orphan Queen

The Mirror King

The Orphan Queen Novellas

(available as ebooks only)

The Hidden Prince

The Glowing Knight

The Burning Hand

The Black Knife

Incarnate

Asunder

Infinite

Phoenix Overture: An Incarnate Novella (available as an ebook only)

MY

CYNTHIA HAND

LADY

BRODI ASHTON

JANE

JODI MEADOWS

HARPER TEEN

An Imprint of HarperCollinsPublishers

For everyone who *knows* there was enough room
for Leonardo DiCaprio on that door.

And for England. We're really sorry for what
we're about to do to your history.

HarperTeen is an imprint of HarperCollins Publishers.

My Lady Jane
Copyright © 2016 by Cynthia Hand, Brodi Ashton, and Jodi Meadows
All rights reserved. Printed in the United States of America.
Library of Congress Control Number: 2015948301
ISBN 978-0-06-239176-6

Typography by Jenna Stempel
18 19 20 21 PC/LSCC 10 9 8 7 6 5 4
❖
First paperback edition, 2017

What is history but a fable agreed upon?
—Napoleon Bonaparte

The crown is not my right. It pleaseth me not.
—Lady Jane Grey

PART ONE

(in which we revise a bit of history)

Prologue

You may think you know the story. It goes like this: once upon a time, there was a sixteen-year-old girl named Jane Grey, who was forced to marry a complete stranger (Lord Guildford or Gilford or Gifford-something-or-other), and shortly thereafter found herself ruler of a country. She was queen for nine days. Then she quite literally lost her head.

Yes, it's a tragedy, if you consider the disengagement of one's head from one's body tragic. (We are merely narrators, and would hate to make assumptions as to what the reader would find tragic.)

We have a different tale to tell.

Pay attention. We've tweaked minor details. We've completely rearranged major details. Some names have been changed to protect the innocent (or not-so-innocent, or simply because we thought a name was terrible and we liked another name better). And we've added a touch of magic to keep things interesting. So really anything could happen.

This is how we think Jane's story *should* have gone.

It begins in England (or an alternate version of England, since we're dealing with the manipulation of history), in the middle of the sixteenth century. It was an uneasy time, especially if you were an Eðian (pronounced eth-ee-uhn for those of you unfamiliar with the term). The Eðians were blessed (or cursed, depending on your point of view) with the ability to switch between a human form and an animal one. For instance, certain members of the general public could turn themselves into cats, which greatly increased the country's tuna-fish consumption, but also cut down on England's rat population. (Then again, other individuals could turn into rats, so nobody really noticed.)

There were those who thought that this animal magic was terrific, but others who saw it as an abomination that needed to be eradicated immediately. That second group (known as Verities) believed that human beings had no business being anything other than human beings. And because Verities were largely in charge of everything, Eðians were persecuted and hunted until most of them died out or went deep into hiding.

Which brings us to one fateful afternoon in the royal court of England, when King Henry VIII, during a fit of rage, transformed into a great lion and devoured the court jester, much to the audience's delight. They clapped enthusiastically, for no one really liked the jester. (Later, the courtiers discovered the incident was not a rehearsed act of artful deception, but indeed an actual lion masticating the jester. When the audience found out the truth they no longer clapped, but they did remark, "That clown had it coming.")

That very night, King Henry, once he'd returned to his human form, decreed that Eðians weren't so bad after all, and henceforth should enjoy the same rights and privileges as Verities. The decision to sanction the ancient magic made waves across Europe. The head of the Verity Church was not pleased with King Henry's decision, but every time Rome sent a missive denouncing the decree, the Lion King ate the messenger.

Hence the phrase, *Don't eat the messenger.*

When Henry died, his only son, Edward, inherited the throne. Our story begins in the middle of tense times, with an increasing animosity brewing between Eðians and Verities, a teenage king with a tenuous grasp on the throne of England, and a young lord and lady who have no idea their destinies are about to collide.

Totally against their will.

ONE

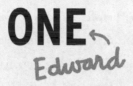

Edward

The king, it turned out, was dying.

"When?" he asked Master Boubou, the royal physician. "How long do I have?"

Boubou wiped his sweaty brow. He disliked giving bad news to royalty. In his line of business, sometimes it led to the stockades. Or worse.

"Six months, perhaps a year," he croaked. "At best."

Bollocks, thought Edward. Yes, he'd been sick for several months now, but he was sixteen years old. He couldn't be dying. He had a cold, was all, a cough that had been hanging on longer than it should, perhaps, a tightness in his chest, a recurrent fever, some headaches, sure, frequent dizzy spells, a funny taste in his mouth sometimes, but dying?

"You're certain?" he asked.

Boubou nodded. "I'm sorry, Your Majesty. It's 'the Affliction.'"

Oh. That.

Edward suppressed a cough. He instantly felt worse than he had only moments before, like his lungs had overheard the bad news and were shutting down already. He'd known of others with "the Affliction," always hacking into nasty blood-spotted handkerchiefs, acting all faint and trembly, then eventually excusing themselves from court to die a horrible, wheezy death out of view of the ladies.

"You're . . . certain?" he asked again.

Boubou fidgeted with his collar. "I can give you tonics for pain, and make sure you remain comfortable until the end, but yes. I am certain."

The end. That sounded ominous.

"But . . ." There was so much he wanted to do with his life. First off, he wanted to kiss a girl, a pretty girl, the right girl, possibly with tongue. He wanted to throw grand, lavish balls to show off his dancing skills to the nobles. He wanted to finally best the weapons master at swords, because Bash was the only person he knew who forgot to let him win. He wanted to explore his kingdom and travel the world. He wanted to hunt a great beast of some sort and mount its head on his wall. He wanted to climb to the top of Scafell Pike, get as high up as a person could possibly go in England, and look over the lands stretching below him and know that he was king of all he surveyed.

But apparently none of that was going to happen.

Untimely was the word people would use, he thought. *Premature. Tragic.* He could practically hear the ballads the minstrels would sing about him, the great king who had died too soon.

Poor King Edward, now under the ground.

Hacked his lungs out. They've yet to be found.

"I want a second opinion. A better one," Edward said, his hand curling into a fist where it rested on the arm of the throne. He shivered, suddenly chilled. He pulled his fur-lined robes more tightly around him.

"Of course," said Boubou, backing away.

Edward saw the fear in the doctor's eyes and felt the urge to have him thrown into the dungeon for good measure, because he was the king, and the king always got what he wanted, and the king didn't want to be dying. He fingered the golden dagger at his belt, and Boubou took another step back.

"I'm truly sorry, Your Highness," the old man mumbled again toward the floor. "Please don't eat the messenger."

Edward sighed. He was not his father, who indeed might have assumed his lion form and devoured the man for bearing this dreadful news. Edward didn't have a secret animal inside of him, so far as he knew. Which had always secretly disappointed him.

"You may go, Boubou," he said.

The doctor breathed out a sigh of relief and darted for the door, leaving Edward alone to face his impending mortality.

"Bollocks," he muttered to himself again. "The Affliction" seemed like a terribly inconvenient way for a king to die.

Later, after the news of his upcoming royal demise had spread around the palace, his sisters came to find him. He was sitting in his favorite spot: the window ledge in one of the south turrets of Greenwich Palace, his legs dangling over the edge as he watched the comings and goings of the people in the courtyard below and listened to the steady flow of the River Thames. He thought he finally understood the Meaning of Life now, the Great Secret, which he'd boiled down to this:

Life is short, and then you die.

"Edward," murmured Bess, her mouth twisting in sympathy as she came to sit beside him on the ledge. "I'm so sorry, brother."

He tried to smirk at her. Edward was a master of smirking. It was his most finely honed royal skill, really, but this time he couldn't manage more than a pathetic halfhearted grimace. "So you've heard," he said, trying to keep his voice light. "I do intend to get a second opinion, of course. I don't feel like I'm dying."

"Oh, my dear Eddie," choked out Mary, dabbing a lace-edged handkerchief at the corner of her eye. "Sweet, darling boy. My poor little dove."

He closed his eyes for a moment. He disliked being called Eddie, and he disliked being talked down to like he was a toddler in short tights, but he tolerated it from Mary. He'd always felt a bit sorry for his sisters, what with his father declaring them bastards and all. The year that his father had discovered his animal form—the Year of the Lion, the people called it—King Henry VIII had also decided that the king got to make all the rules, so he'd annulled his marriage to Mary's mother and sent her off to a convent to live out the rest of her days, all so he could marry Bess's mother, one of the more attractive ladies-in-waiting. But when Wife #2 failed to produce a male heir, and rumors started to circulate that Queen Anne was an Eðian who every so often transformed into a black cat so she could slip down the castle stairs into the court minstrel's bedchambers, the king had her head chopped off. Wife #3 (Edward's mother) had done everything right; namely, she'd produced a child with the correct genitalia to be a future ruler of England, and then, because she was never one to stick around to gloat, she'd promptly died. King Henry had gone on to have three more wives (respectively: annulled, beheaded, and the lucky one who'd outlived him, ha), but no more children.

So it had just been the three of them—Mary, Bess, and Edward—as far as royal spawn went, and they'd been their own brand of a mismatched family, since their father was possibly insane and definitely dangerous even when he wasn't a lion, and their mothers were all dead or exiled. They'd always got on fairly well, mainly because there had never been any competition between them over who was meant to wear the crown. Edward was the clear choice. He had the boy parts.

He'd been king since he was nine years old. He could only faintly remember a time when he wasn't king, in fact, and until today he'd always felt that monarchy rather suited him. But a fat lot of good being king was doing him now, he thought bitterly. He would have rather been born a commoner, a blacksmith's son, perhaps. Then he might have already had a bit of fun before he shuffled off this mortal coil. At least he would have had an opportunity to kiss a girl.

"How are you feeling, really?" Mary asked solemnly. Mary said everything solemnly.

"Afflicted," he answered.

This produced the ghost of a smile from Bess, but Mary just shook her head mournfully. Mary never laughed at his jokes. He and Bess had been calling her Fuddy-Duddy Mary behind her back for years, because she was always so cheerless about everything. The only time he ever saw Mary enjoy herself was when some traitor was beheaded or some poor Eðian got burned at the stake. His sister was surprisingly bloodthirsty when it came to Eðians.

"'The Affliction' took my mother, you know." Mary wrung her handkerchief between her hands fretfully.

"I know." He'd always thought Queen Catherine had died more of a broken heart than any physical malady, although he supposed that a broken heart often led to a broken body.

He wouldn't have a chance to get his heart broken, he thought, a fresh wave of self-pity washing over him. He was never going to fall in love.

"It's a dreadful way to die," Mary continued. "You cough and cough until you cough your lungs right out."

"Thank you. That's very comforting," he said.

Bess, who'd always been a quiet one next to her solemnly loquacious sister, shot Mary a sharp look and laid her gloved hand over Edward's. "Is there anything we can do for you?"

He shrugged. His eyes burned, and he told himself that he was definitely not going to cry about this whole dying thing, because crying was for girls and wee little babies and not for kings, and besides, crying wouldn't change anything.

Bess squeezed his hand.

He squeezed back, definitely not crying, and recommenced pondering the view outside the window and the Meaning of Life.

Life is short.

And then you die.

Shortly. Six months, a year at best. Which seemed like an awfully small amount of time. Last summer, a famous Italian astrologer had done Edward's horoscope, after which he had announced that the king would live forty more years.

Apparently famous Italian astrologers were big, fat liars.

"But at least you can rest assured knowing that everything will be all right once you've gone," Mary said solemnly.

He turned to look at her. "What?"

"With the kingdom, I mean," she added even more solemnly. "The kingdom will be in good hands."

He hadn't really given much thought to the kingdom. Or any thought, truthfully. He'd been too busy contemplating the idea of coughing his lungs right out, and then being too dead to care.

"Mary," Bess chided. "Now is not the time for politics."

Before Mary could argue (and by the look on her face, she was definitely going to argue that now was always the time for politics), a knock sounded on the door. Edward called, "Come in," and John Dudley, Duke of Northumberland and Lord President of the King's High Privy Council, stuck his great eagle nose into the room.

"Ah, Your Majesty, I thought I'd find you up here," he said when he spotted Edward. His gaze swept hurriedly over Mary and Bess like he couldn't be bothered taking the time to really see them. "Princess Mary. Princess Elizabeth. You're both looking well." He turned to Edward. "Your Majesty, I wonder if I might have a word."

"You may have several," Edward said.

"In private," Lord Dudley clarified. "In the council room."

Edward stood and brushed off his pants. He nodded to his sisters, and they dropped into their courtly curtsies. Then he allowed Lord Dudley to lead him down the stairs and across the palace's long series of hallways into the king's council chamber, where the king's advisors normally spent hours each day filling out the appropriate royal paperwork for the running of the country and making all the decisions. The king himself never spent much time in this room, unless there was a document that required his signature, or some other important matter that required his personal attention. Which wasn't often.

Dudley closed the door behind them.

Edward, winded from the walk, sank into his royal, extra-cushy red velvet throne at the head of the half circle of chairs (usually occupied by the other thirty members of the Privy Council). Dudley produced a handkerchief for him, which Edward pressed to his lips while he rode out a coughing fit.

When he pulled the handkerchief away, there was a spot of pink on it.

Bollocks.

He stared at the spot, and tried to hand the handkerchief back to Dudley, but the duke quickly said, "You keep it, Your Majesty," and crossed to the other side of the room, where he began to stroke his bearded chin the way he did when he was deep in thought.

"I think," Dudley began softly, "we should talk about what you're going to do."

"Do? It's 'the Affliction.' It's incurable. There's nothing for me to do but die, apparently."

Dudley manufactured a sympathetic smile that didn't look natural on his face, as he wasn't accustomed to smiling. "Yes, Sire, that's true enough, but death comes to us all." He resumed the beard stroking. "This news is unfortunate, of course, but we must make the best of it. There are many things that must be done for the kingdom before you die."

Ah, the kingdom, again. Always the kingdom. Edward nodded. "All right," he said with more courage in his voice than he felt. "Tell me what I should do."

"First we must consider the line of succession. An heir to the throne."

Edward's eyebrows lifted. "You want me to get married and

produce an heir in less than a year?"

That could be fun. That would definitely involve kissing with tongue.

Dudley cleared his throat. "Uh . . . no, Your Majesty. You're not well enough."

Edward wanted to argue, but then he remembered the spot of pink on the handkerchief, and how exhausting he'd found it simply walking across the palace. He was in no shape to be wooing a wife.

"Well, then," he said. "I suppose that means the throne will go to Mary."

"No, Sire," Lord Dudley said urgently. "We cannot let the throne of England fall into the wrong hands."

Edward frowned. "But she's my sister. She's the eldest. She—"

"She's a Verity," objected Dudley. "Mary's been raised to believe that the animal magic is evil, something to be feared and destroyed. If she became queen, she'd return this country to the Dark Ages. No Eðian would be safe."

Edward sat back, thinking. Everything the duke was saying was true. Mary would not tolerate the Eðians. (She preferred them extra-crispy, as we mentioned earlier.) Plus Mary had no sense of humor and was completely backward thinking and would be no good at all as ruler.

"So it can't be Mary," he agreed. "It can't be Bess, either." He twisted the ring with the royal seal around his finger. "Bess would be better than Mary, of course, and both of her parents were Eðians, if you believe the cat thing, but I don't know where Bess's allegiance lies concerning the Verities. She's a bit shifty. Besides," he said upon further reflection. "The crown can't go to a woman."

You might have noticed that Edward was a bit of a sexist. You can't blame him, really, since all his young life he'd been greatly exalted for simply having been born a boy.

Still, he liked to think of himself as a forward-thinking king. He hadn't taken after his father as an Eðian (at least, he hadn't so far), but it was part of his family history, obviously, and he'd been raised to sympathize with the Eðian cause. Lately it seemed that the tension between the two groups had reached a boiling point. Reports had been coming in about a mysterious Eðian group called the Pack, who had been raiding and pillaging from Verity churches and monasteries around the country. Then came more reports of Verities exposing and subsequently inflicting violence upon Eðians. Then reports of revenge attacks against Verities. And so on, and so on.

Dudley was right. They needed a pro-Eðian ruler. Someone who could keep the peace.

"So who do you have in mind?" Edward reached over to a side table, where there was always, by royal decree, a bowl of fresh, chilled blackberries. He loved blackberries. They were rumored to have powerful healing properties, so he'd been eating a lot of them lately. He popped one into his mouth.

Lord Dudley's Adam's apple jerked up and down, and for the first time since Edward had known him, he appeared a tad nervous. "The firstborn son of the Lady Jane Grey, Your Majesty."

Edward choked on his blackberry.

"Jane has a son?" he sputtered. "I'm fairly certain I would have heard about that."

"She doesn't have a son at the moment," Dudley explained patiently. "But she will. And if you bypass Mary and Elizabeth, the Greys are next in line."

So Dudley wanted Jane to get married and produce an heir.

Edward couldn't imagine his cousin Jane with a husband and a child, even though she was sixteen years old and sixteen was a bit spinsterish, by the standards of the day. Books were Jane's great love: history and philosophy and religion, mostly, but anything she could get her hands on. She actually enjoyed reading Plato in the original Greek, so much so that she did it for fun and not just when her tutors assigned it. She had entire epic poems memorized and could recite them at will. But most of all, she loved stories of Eðians and their animal adventures.

There would be no doubt that Jane would support the Eðians.

It was widely rumored that Jane's mother was an Eðian, although no one knew what form she took. When they were children Edward and Jane's favorite game had been to imagine what animals they would become when they grew up. Edward had always imagined he'd be something powerful and fierce, like a wolf. A great bear. A tiger.

Jane had never been able to decide on her preferred Eðian form; it was between a lynx and a falcon, as he recalled.

"Just think of it, Edward," he remembered her ten-year-old

voice whispering to him as they'd stretched out on their backs on some grassy knoll, finding shapes in the passing clouds. "I could be up there, riding the wind, nobody telling me to sit up straight or complaining about my needlework. I'd be free."

"Free as a bird," he'd added.

"Free as a bird!" She'd laughed and jumped to her feet and run down the hill with her long red hair trailing behind her and her arms spread out, pretending to fly.

A few years later they'd spent an entire afternoon calling each other names, because Jane had read in a book that E∂ians often manifested into their animal forms when they were upset. They'd cursed at each other and slapped each other's faces, and Jane had even gone so far as to throw a stone at Edward, which actually did rile him, but they had remained stubbornly human throughout the whole ordeal.

It'd been a great disappointment to them both.

"Sire?" Lord Dudley prompted.

Edward shook off the memories. "You want Jane to get married," he surmised. "Do you have someone in mind?"

He felt a twinge of sadness at the idea. Jane was easily his favorite person in this world. As a child, she'd been sent to live with Katherine Parr (King Henry's Wife #6), and so Jane and Edward had spent hours upon hours in each other's company, even sharing many of the same tutors. It had been in those days that they'd become fast friends. Jane was the only one who Edward felt truly understood him, who didn't treat him like a

13

different species because he was royalty. In the back of his mind he'd been holding on to the idea that perhaps someday he'd be the one to marry Jane.

This was back when it was slightly less frowned upon to marry your cousin.

"Yes, Sire. I have the perfect candidate." Dudley began to pace back and forth across the room, stroking his beard. "Someone with good breeding, a respectable family."

"Of course. Who?" Edward asked.

"Someone with undeniable Eðian magic."

"Yes. Who?"

"Someone who wouldn't mind the red hair."

"Jane's hair isn't so bad," Edward protested. "In some lights it's slightly less red, and rather pretty. . . ."

"Someone who could keep her in line," Dudley continued.

Well, that made sense, thought Edward. Jane was notoriously willful. She refused to be pranced around court like the other girls of noble birth, and openly defied her mother by bringing a book to certain court functions and passing the time in the corner reading instead of dancing or securing herself a future husband.

"Who?" he asked.

"Someone who can be trusted."

This was starting to seem like a very tall order indeed. "Who is it?" Edward raised his voice. He disliked having to ask a question more than once, and this was four times now. Plus Dudley's pacing was making him feel a bit seasick. Edward pounded his fist on the side table. Blackberries went flying. "Who is it? Blast it, Northumberland, just spit it out."

The duke stopped. He cleared his throat. "Gifford Dudley," he muttered.

Edward blinked. "Gifford who?"

"My youngest son."

Edward took a moment to absorb this information, adding up all of the criteria Dudley had given him: someone from a respectable family: check; someone who could be trusted: check; someone with undeniable Eðian magic . . .

"John," he blurted out. "Do you have Eðian magic in your family?"

Lord Dudley lowered his gaze. It was a dangerous thing to admit to Eðian blood, even in today's more civilized age, where you might not get burned at the stake for it. While being an Eðian wasn't technically illegal any longer, there were still so many people throughout the kingdom who shared Mary's opinion that the only good Eðian was a dead one.

"I'm not an Eðian, of course," Dudley said after a long pause. "But my son is."

An Eðian! This was too good. For a minute Edward forgot that he was dying and marrying off his best friend as some kind of political strategy. "What creature does he become?"

Dudley reddened. "He spends his days as a . . ." His lips moved as he tried to form the right word, but he failed.

Edward leaned forward. "Yes?"

Dudley struggled to get the words out. "He's a . . . every day he . . . he . . ."

"Come on, man!" Edward urged. "Speak!"

Dudley wet his lips. "He's a . . . member of the equine species."

"He's a what?"

"A steed, Your Majesty."

"A steed?"

"A . . . horse."

Edward fell back, open mouthed for a few seconds. "A horse. Your son spends his days as a horse," he repeated, just to be sure he'd got it right.

Dudley nodded miserably.

"No wonder I haven't seen him in court. I'd almost forgotten you had another son besides Stan! Didn't you tell us that your other son was a half-wit, and that's why you deemed him inappropriate to appear in social settings?"

"We thought anything was better than the truth," Dudley admitted.

Edward scooped a blackberry off the table and ate it. "When did this happen? *How* did it happen?"

"Six years ago," Dudley answered. "I don't know how. One moment he was a boy of thirteen, throwing a bit of a tantrum. The next he was a . . ." He didn't say the word again. "I do believe that he'd be a good match for Jane, Sire, and not simply because he's my son. He's a solid boy—excellent bone structure, able-bodied, reasonably intelligent, certainly not a half-wit, anyway—and obedient enough to suit our purposes."

Edward considered this for a few minutes. Jane loved all things Eðian. She wouldn't have a problem with marrying one. But . . .

"He spends every single day as a horse?" Edward asked.

"Every day. From sunrise to sundown."

"He can't control his change?"

Dudley glanced at the far wall, which bore a large portrait of Henry VIII, and Edward realized how foolish he sounded. His father had never been able to control his lion form. The anger would take him and then the fangs would come out, literally, and he would remain a lion until his anger abated, which often took hours. Sometimes even days. It had always been uncomfortable to watch. Especially when the king decided to use somebody as a chew toy.

"All right, so he can't control it," Edward acquiesced. "But that would mean that Jane would only have a husband by night. What kind of marriage would that be?"

"Some people would prefer such an arrangement. I know my life would be a lot simpler if I only had to attend to my wife in the hours between dusk and dawn," said Dudley with a weak laugh.

It would hardly be like having a marriage at all, thought Edward. But for someone like Jane, such a marriage could afford her a sense of privacy and the independence she was accustomed to.

It could be ideal.

"Is he handsome?" he asked. Dudley's other son, Stan,

had suffered the misfortune of inheriting his father's eagle nose. Edward hated the idea of marrying Jane off to that nose.

Dudley's thin lips tightened. "Gifford is a bit too easy on the eye for his own good, I'm afraid. He tends to attract . . . attention from the ladies."

Jealousy pricked at Edward. He gazed up once more at the portrait of his father. He resembled Henry; he knew that. They had the same reddish-gold hair and the same straight, majestic nose, the same gray eyes, bracketed by the same smallish ears. Edward had been considered handsome once, but now he was thin and pale, washed out from his bout with the illness.

" . . . but he will be faithful, of that I can assure you," Dudley was blathering on. "And when he and Jane produce a son, you will have your Eðian heir. Problem solved."

Just like that. Problem solved.

Edward rubbed his forehead. "And when should this wedding take place?"

"Saturday, I think," answered Dudley. "Assuming you approve of the match."

Edward had a coughing fit.

It was Monday now.

"That soon?" he wheezed when he could breathe again.

"The sooner the better," Dudley said. "We need an heir."

Right. Edward cleared his throat. "Very well, then. I approve the match. But Saturday . . ." That seemed awfully soon. "I don't even know what my schedule looks like on Saturday. I'll need to consult—"

"I've already checked, Your Majesty. You're free. Besides, the ceremony must take place after sundown," added Dudley.

"Right. Because in the daytime, he's . . ." Edward made a faint whinnying noise.

"Yes." Dudley produced a scroll of parchment and unrolled it on the desk upon which all the official court documents were signed and sealed.

"I bet you spend a fortune on hay," Edward said, finding his smirk at last. He inspected the scroll. It was a royal decree—his permission, technically speaking—that Lady Jane Grey of Suffolk be wed, on this Saturday hence, to Lord Gifford Dudley of Northumberland.

His smirk faded.

Jane.

Of course it had been a fantasy, this notion he'd had of marrying Jane himself. She had very little in the way of political capital—a rich family, to be sure, a title, but nothing that would truly strengthen the position of the kingdom. Edward had always known that he was supposed to marry for England, not himself. All his life he'd had a constant stream of foreign ambassadors trotting out the portraits of the daughters of the various European royalty for him to peruse. He was meant to marry a princess. Not little Jane with her books and her big ideas.

Dudley put a quill in his hand. "We must consider the good of the country, Your Highness. I'll ride for Dudley Castle tonight to fetch him."

Edward dipped the quill in the ink but then stopped. "I need you to swear that he will be good to her."

"I swear it, Your Majesty. He'll be a model husband."

Edward coughed again into the handkerchief Dudley had given him. There was that funny taste in his mouth, something sickly sweet that mixed badly with the lingering blackberries.

"I'm marrying off my cousin to a horse," he muttered.

Then he put the quill to the paper, sighed, and signed his name.

Jane

TWO

"And the blessed event will take place Saturday night."

Lady Jane Grey blinked up from her book. Her mother, Lady Frances Brandon Grey, had been speaking. "What's happening Saturday night?"

"Stand still, dear." Lady Frances pinched Jane's arm. "We need to make sure these measurements are perfect. There won't be time for alterations."

Jane was already holding her book as still as possible, and at arm's length. A feat of strength for someone who could wrap her own fingers around her upper arm.

"Note the bust hasn't changed a smidge," said the seamstress to her assistant. "Probably never will, at this rate."

In another feat, this one of self-restraint, Jane did not smack the woman's head with her book. Because the book was old and valuable: *The Unabridged History of the Beet in England: Volume Five.* She didn't want to damage it. "All right, but what's happening Saturday night?"

"Arms down now," said the seamstress.

Jane lowered her arms, marking her place in her book with her index finger.

Her mother plucked the book from her hand, tossed the precious tome of beets onto the bed, and adjusted Jane's shoulders. "Stand straight. You'll want this gown to hang correctly. You won't be carrying your books during the wedding, after all."

"Wedding?" Mild curiosity edged into her tone as she leaned to one side to look at her mother around the seamstress. "Who's getting married?"

"Jane!"

Jane snapped straight again.

The seamstress noted the final measurements of Jane's hips (poor for childbearing—another of Jane's failures) and gathered her supplies. "We're finished now, my ladies. Have a good afternoon!" She fled the sitting room in a flurry of cloth and needles.

Lady Frances pinched Jane's shoulder. "*You're* getting married, my dear. Pay attention."

Jane's heart immediately began to beat faster, but she told herself not to worry. It was only an engagement, after all. She'd been engaged before. Four times, as a matter of fact.

"To whom am I engaged this time?" she asked.

Lady Frances smiled, mistaking Jane's reaction for acceptance. "To Gifford Dudley."

"Gifford who?"

The smile turned into a frown. "The younger son of Lord John Dudley, Duke of Northumberland. Gifford."

Well, Jane knew of the Dudleys. Though the family itself was fairly minor as far as noble houses went, known more for the prize horses they bred and sold, there was one other interesting fact: John Dudley was the president of the High Privy Council, the right hand of the king, a trusted advisor and perhaps the most powerful man in England, aside from Edward himself. And some might argue that point, too.

"I see," she said at last, though she had never encountered this Gifford fellow at court. That seemed suspicious. "Well, I'm sure he'll be just as wonderful as the other fiancés were."

"Do you have any questions?"

Jane shook her head. "I've heard all I need. It's only an engagement, after all."

"The wedding is on Saturday, darling." Her mother looked annoyed. "At the Dudleys' London home. We leave tomorrow morning."

Saturday. That . . . was soon. Much sooner than she'd expected. Of course she'd heard *Saturday* before, but she hadn't actually thought about how soon it was, or internalized what that might mean for her.

This wedding might actually happen. Her heart started to beat fast again.

"It is my greatest wish for you to be happily married before you're too old for it." Lady Frances didn't clarify whether "too old for it" meant happy or married. "Anyway, I think you'll like this one. I hear he's a handsome creature."

So Lady Frances hadn't seen him, either. Jane felt a chill. And with the likelihood of him inheriting the Dudley nose—

Jane recalled the seamstress's comments about her bust. And the fact that she had unsightly red hair and was so slight of stature that she was sometimes mistaken for a child. Maybe she shouldn't judge. Looks, after all, should not decide the worth of a person. But that terrible nose . . .

"Thank you for warning me, Mother," she called as her mother swept out of the room.

Her mother didn't answer, of course. Too much to do before Saturday.

Saturday. That was four days away.

Jane got dressed quickly. Then she grabbed her book about beets, chose a second and third book (*Eðians: Historical Figures and Their Downfall* and *Wilderness Survival for Courtiers*) just in case she finished the first, and headed out to the stables. If this Gifford person was going to be her husband (but a lot of things could happen between now and Saturday, she reminded herself), then she had a right to know exactly what she was getting herself into.

Over the years, Jane had studied every map of England, both historical and modern, and that included more localized maps of the kingdom. And so she knew that Dudley Castle, where the Dudleys resided when they weren't in London, was a little more than a half a day's ride from Jane's home at Bradgate. She could have simply ridden her horse to Dudley Castle, but violence was on the rise in the kingdom and the countryside was reportedly dangerous to travel alone and unguarded. (The household staff said Eðians were responsible for the disorder—some group called the Pack—but Jane refused to believe these awful rumors.) The last thing she needed on top of this sudden marriage announcement was to get caught in some kind of scuffle. So in the interest of safety (and not enraging her mother), she ordered a carriage to drive her to Dudley.

All she needed was to check on the nose situation.

It was a lovely day. The rolling hills that surrounded Bradgate were bright with early summer. Trees were in bloom. Sunlight glimmered off the stream that burbled alongside the road. The red brick of the manor gleamed invitingly behind her on a small rise. Deer leapt away as the carriage rattled along, while birds sang pretty songs.

Jane liked London; there were benefits to staying there, of course, one being close proximity to her cousin Edward. But Bradgate Park was her home. She loved the fresh air, the blue sky, the old oak trees standing on distant knolls. Her grandfather had intended the park to be the best deer-hunting ground in all of England—and it was, so it frequently received prestigious royal visitors, but that hardly mattered to Jane. (She didn't hunt, though Edward was quite good, she'd heard.) To Jane, walking through Bradgate

Park was the second-best way to escape any problem of Real Life.

The first-best way, of course, was through books. So as she left Bradgate behind, she allowed herself to become enraptured by the unabridged history of beets. (Did you know the ancient Romans were the first to cultivate the beet for the root, rather than just the greens?)

Jane, as we mentioned earlier, loved books. There was nothing she relished more than the weight of a hefty tome in her hands, each beautiful volume of knowledge as rare and wonderful and fascinating as the last. She delighted in the smell of the ink, the rough feel of the paper between her fingers, the rustle of sweet pages, the shapes of the letters before her eyes. And most of all, she loved the way that books could transport her from her otherwise mundane and stifling life and offer the experiences of a hundred other lives. Through books she could see the world.

Not that her mother would ever understand this, Jane thought after she finished the last page of her beet book and closed it with a sigh. While Lord Grey had encouraged her studies when he'd been alive, Lady Frances had never accepted Jane's hunger for knowledge. What could a young lady possibly need to know, she'd often said, besides how to secure herself a husband? All that Jane's mother ever cared for was influence and affluence. She loved nothing more than to remind people that she was of royal blood—"My grandmother was a queen," she was fond of saying, over and over and over again. Too bad that the late King Henry had written Lady Frances out of the line of succession years ago. Probably because he just didn't like her attitude.

Power and money. That was all that mattered to Lady Frances. And now she was selling off her own daughter the way one barters a prized mare. Without so much as asking her.

Typical.

Jane shook away the familiar resentment toward her mother and put her book aside, cringing at a bend in one corner, likely sustained when Lady Frances had abducted the book and hurled it to the bed. The poor book. It didn't deserve to be hurt just because Jane had to get married.

Married. Uck.

She wished people would stop trying to marry her off. It was such a bother.

Jane's first engagement had been to the son of a silk merchant. Humphrey Hangrot had been his name, and since Hangrot Silk had been the only silk merchant in all of England, they controlled the prices. Humphrey's parents were not shy about reminding the Grey family of their exciting new wealth. Most notably this was done by draping their stick-figure son in layers and layers of their most expensive brocade available. Jane had lost count of the number of balls she'd been forced to attend at the Hangrot family home; she'd survived by always having a book in hand.

As for Humphrey, he'd introduced himself to her as the "future king . . . of silk," and instructed her to touch his sleeve. No, really touch it. *Feel* it. Had she ever beheld such fine cloth? She'd asked him if he realized the worms were boiled in their own cocoons in order to degum the silk, and he refused to speak to her after that. The engagement had dissolved thanks to the sudden arrival of a second silk merchant, one who was willing to undercut Hangrot Silk's prices enough to take all of their business, which led to the immediate destitution of the family. No one, it turned out, wanted to pay Hangrot Silk's outrageous prices, and the family retreated to a small home in the country where they faded from the public memory.

The second engagement had been to Theodore Tagler, a virtuoso violinist from France. He'd been touring England with the Oceanous Orchestra when his family came to visit London. Several highborn families had heard about the Taglers' desire to find a wife for their son—a lady of refined taste and good family, and who wouldn't mind her husband's long absences, should she decide not to accompany him on tour. Lord and Lady Grey had immediately suggested Jane—they were still trying to recover from the Hangrot scandal—and the match was approved.

Jane had a fair ear for music and enjoyed many sonatas, minuets, and symphonies. She even liked the occasional opera—her favorites being the tragedies in which the lovers both died in the end as punishment for a small act of mercy—but she hadn't been fond of her new fiancé's style of playing, which she found rather boisterous. Theodore himself turned out to be rather boisterous as well. The saying "bull in a china shop" came to mind. How he'd been able to handle such a delicate instrument had been a mystery to her, and it had been the instrument that dissolved this engagement as swiftly as the last.

The violin, a one-of-a-kind Belmoorus from the late violin maker Beaufort Belmoor, had been stolen. Snatched. Thieved. Taken from its place in the home of Beaufort Belmoor's children. It had been tracked across France and through Spain, all the way to England. The "owner" who'd loaned the violin to Theodore Tagler—as all non-musician owners of instruments do to ensure their possessions are played regularly—had been arrested and, in spite of Theodore's innocence in the matter, he and his family had also gone into immediate destitution.

The third engagement had been to Walter Williamson, the grandson of a famous but reclusive inventor, though what it was he had invented was said to be a state secret. If it hadn't been for the whole marriage thing, Jane wouldn't have minded Walter; he appeared intelligent and well read, and spoke often of the legacy his grandfather had left. He, too, had aspirations of invention. It was in his blood, he said, not that he had ever shown a hint of creativity.

Only a month into the engagement, papers were released revealing Walter's grandfather had been a thief, imprisoned these last fifteen years. Public regard of the Williamson family plummeted, and (as you can surmise) the result was immediate destitution.

And the fourth engagement—well, the young man turned out not to exist. Jane's mother (for Jane's father had died between the third and fourth engagements) had received a miniature painting of a handsome fellow, not realizing it had been a sample work— an advertisement for the artist's skills. And while Jane's mother was typically intelligent, she'd been desperate to marry Jane off to someone by now, and had misunderstood the note accompanying the miniature. "I present to you an opportunity fit for someone of Lady Jane's rank" had meant the skill of the artist, not the imaginary—though incredibly handsome—fellow in the painting. Her mother had announced the acceptance of the proposal before the artist could write back to inquire about travel for Jane's portrait and a reminder that his fee was non-refundable.

In a fit of anger and embarrassment, Lady Frances told a revised story in which she was the victim of a vicious prank—and so soon after her own husband's tragic death. This time it was the artist who fell into immediate destitution.

It seemed that agreeing to marry Lady Jane was a very risky business.

If her track record with fiancés was anything to go by, Gifford Dudley's days—and the days of his family's prosperity—were numbered.

She almost felt sorry for him.

Jane picked up the second book, the one about Eðians, and traced the word with her forefinger. What she wouldn't give to have an animal form. Something no one would dare to bother or force weddings upon, like a bear. But if being an Eðian was hereditary, as many people insisted, then the trait had skipped her. (No one was supposed to know, but Jane had once overheard her parents arguing about her mother's Eðian magic.) And if the gift was bestowed on the worthy (another popular hypothesis, though less scientific), all her efforts to be so deserving had fallen woefully short.

In the distance, a castle jutted into the sky at the top of a steep hill. A bustling village huddled at the base, the villagers stopping to gawk as the carriage passed through the town gates and began the slow climb up. Jane admired the castle's towering keep (built in the eleventh century, if she knew her architectural history, which of course she did) with its beautiful white stone and narrow, slitted windows. It looked like a very defendable place, she thought, almost ominously so. Like the owners expected an attack at any moment.

The carriage had to pass through three more gates and over a moat before they reached the central courtyard, where the driver stopped outside the elegant castle apartments. These were a new, more modern addition, clearly, with peaked roofs and many windows. The whole place seemed like the look-don't-touch kind of home. Perfectly manicured. Never enjoyed.

Jane scanned the dozens of windows for movement, but all was quiet, save the horses loitering in the wide field on the far side of the castle.

So these were the prize horses Lord Dudley bragged about so much.

She hopped out of the carriage and walked toward a closed gate to look at them.

All the horses were fine creatures with sleek coats and spindle-thin legs. But the best among them was a beautiful stallion on the other side of the field. His muscles rippled as he thundered across the grass, his head high and ears alert. He thrashed his head so his mane streamed back in the wind, the sun gleaming off his chestnut coat. He was simply magnificent. While, true, her experience with horses was generally limited to the gentle and well-mannered geldings appropriate for a lady, Jane thought she had never seen a horse more worthy of the constant bragging.

How amazing it would be, she imagined then, to live as a horse. The ability to run like that, to fly across the ground on those strong, powerful legs. No one nagging her, pinching her, commenting on what a small, insignificant person she was.

What she wouldn't give for the ability to change into a horse and escape not just this engagement, but everything that was wrong with her life.

"My lady," came a man's voice from behind her. "May I help you with something?"

Jane turned and craned her neck, first noting that the gentleman who stopped beside her was a well-dressed fellow. Then she finished looking up.

There it was.

The nose.

Truly, it was a great, arching eagle nose that would enter a room five whole seconds before the rest of him did. (It may help the reader to recall the long-nosed plague doctor mask that would appear in the next several decades. It is said the design of those beaked masks was actually inspired by the Dudley nose, though never within a Dudley heir's hearing.)

God's teeth! What if this was Gifford?

"I'm here to visit Lord Gifford Dudley," she said hesitantly, catching herself as she addressed the nose. But it was right over her. It was hard to avoid. She took a measured step backward in hopes she'd be able to meet his eyes.

"Ah." The man smiled knowingly. "You're here to visit my brother."

Whew. This nose—rather, this man—wasn't Gifford, but Stan Dudley, the older brother who sometimes accompanied his father to court. (Not that Jane paid much attention at court; she had too many books to read.) But what if Gifford's nose was worse?

She clutched her books to her stomach and considered prayer. Would praying for a decent-size nose be considered sacrilege?

"Yes. I'd like to see Gifford now."

"I'm afraid he's unavailable. He's, uh, busy with the horses." Stan glanced at the pasture, but if Gifford was out there, Jane couldn't see him. The only creatures were the horses, who'd moved to a new spot of grass.

"He won't receive me?"

"Not right now."

This was infuriating. She wanted to at least lay eyes upon her intended before they were to be wed. Was that so much to ask?

Stan turned his head, momentarily blocking the sun with his nose. "I see you're upset. I'm terribly sorry, but you know my brother never has time for ladies until after dark."

Ladies . . . plural?

Sir Nose went on: "You must be . . . Anne? Frederica? Janette?"

33

Jane blinked at him. "I'm sorry? Who?"

Stan crossed his arms and inspected her more closely. "Red hair. That is unusual. I can't recall my brother mentioning one of his ladies was a redhead."

"One of his ladies?" she managed to squeak.

"Surely you didn't think you were the only one. But I'd thought he usually preferred brunettes. Taller. With more . . . shape."

Jane gasped. This was outrageous. Who did this Stan fellow think he was? Why, Jane was of royal blood (her great grandmother was a queen, after all), cousin and friend to Edward VI. She had the king's ear, and it would not be long until that royal auricle heard all about the rude, impolite, presumptuous, rotten man—

She was saying none of this out loud, she realized. Instead she was standing there, slack-jawed, while the mouth beneath the Dudley nose continued to guess her name. There were so many names. At least one for every letter of the alphabet. Did Gifford have relations with all of these women? Or was Stan simply being mean?

"All right," Stan said. "I give up. I'll tell him you came by, if you tell me who you are."

She mustered the strongest tone she could. "I am Lady Jane Grey. His fiancé."

Stan went still for a moment, and then hurried into a bow. "Oh, I see. My lady. I'm so sorry. I didn't realize. I should never have said all those things. It's just you have such red hair for a highborn. I mean . . . I would never have mentioned the other ladies. Because there are no other ladies. Anywhere. In the world. Except my wife.

And you. Gifford will be a faithful and loyal husband to you. Like a dog! Well, not like a dog." He sighed. "I'm sorry, I shouldn't have said anything—"

Jane just glared at him. Well, at his nose. It was hard to see much else.

"Please accept my sincerest apologies, my lady." Stan Dudley made several feeble attempts at reparation, mumbled something about leaving her to her thoughts—which were surely as pure as the whitest blossoms of the most virginal tree—and then he was gone.

So. Her husband-to-be was a philanderer. A smooth operator. A debaucher. A rake. A frisker. (Jane became something of a walking thesaurus when she was upset, a side effect of too much reading.) No wonder no one had seen him, since the libertine was too busy with the horses during the day—allegedly—and too busy with the strumpets at night.

This was not acceptable.

Jane stomped back to her carriage. She imagined all the things she would say to Gifford, Edward, her mother, and whoever else had arranged this marriage for her. Angry, angry things.

She'd thought this engagement would ruin Gifford's life. But for the first time (in, perhaps, ever), she'd been wrong: the engagement to Lord Gifford Dudley would ruin her life.

Unless she put a stop to it.

Jane straightened her spine. She was not going to marry Gifford Dudley. (And what kind of name was Gifford Dudley, anyway? Honestly!) Not Saturday. Not ever.

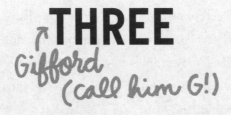THREE

The worst part about waking up when the sun went down was the distinct grassy taste of hay in his mouth, an unfortunate side effect of actually having hay in his mouth. But the affliction of unwanted-hay-in-the-mouth-itis (or "hay-mouth" as his mother referred to it, like someone else would refer to morning breath) was not to be avoided when one ended each day as an undomesticated horse and began each night as an undomesticated man.

Almost man, his mother would say. At nineteen years of age, he was almost a man. Definitely undomesticated.

As he pushed himself into a crouching position, and then into a standing position, G (please call him G, and avoid referring to him by his terrible given name, Gifford Dudley, the second—and therefore insignificant—son of Lord John Dudley, Duke of

Northumberland) stretched out his haunches, which were now hips.

He reflected on this morning's jaunt across the countryside. He'd gone northwest this time, running at a flat-out canter over green hills and lush forests for hours before he had to search for water. There was nothing, he imagined, that could compete with the feeling of a life without boundaries or borders, and the wind running through his hair. Mane.

He hadn't asked for this power. (If he had, he definitely would've requested the ability to control it as well, even though it would be rather missing the point for a curse to come with an on/off switch.) Still, there was an upside to it. He belonged to no one. (Who would want a half horse/half man?) He could pick a spot on a map and then go there the next time the sun was up. (Provided his horse brain remembered the way. G would argue that horses were not known for their sense of direction, instead of the likelihood that he—even as a man—could get lost in his own closet.) Best of all, he had no human-ish responsibilities.

After the freedom he enjoyed during his days, nightfall was usually a bit of a letdown. G searched out the pail of water his servant always left for him in the corner, and once he spotted it he galloped over (in a human way, but probably resembling a horse more than any other human could) and ladled a cupful of water into his mouth.

The transformation always left him dehydrated, and tonight he needed his wits about him. Due to an entirely nighttime existence, there were only so many activities in which the human G could participate. With the casual, often brash way G spoke, and his general rambunctious demeanor, it was easy for his parents to assume he spent his human hours in the boudoirs of questionable ladies or getting tipsy in brothels. Lady Dudley was often overheard lamenting, "That boy and his dalliances . . . What are we to do?"

G let them believe that; in fact, he often boasted of his conquests with different ladies in order to play along. If they thought he was something of a Casanova (although they of course couldn't equate him to the literal Casanova, who wouldn't be born for another two hundred years), it left G the freedom to do as he pleased. Besides, the truth of how he spent his nights was far more humiliating. He would rather his parents believed he was carousing with the ladies.

A sharp knock sounded on the stable door.

"My lord?" Billingsly called from the other side.

"Yes," G said, trying to shake the whinny out of his voice like someone else would clear his throat in the morning.

"Your trousers."

The stable door opened just wide enough for an arm covered in the blue of the steward uniform to extend through, holding a pair of trousers.

"Thank you, Billingsly." G took the pants and stepped into them as Billingsly set the rest of his clothes on a wooden table so the hay wouldn't besmirch the young lord's ensemble.

"And, my lord, your father would like a word with you when

you are appropriately attired."

"My father?" G said, alarmed. "He's returned to the castle?"

"Yes, my lord," Billingsly said.

G fastened the buttons on the front of his jacket and pulled on his tall leather boots. "Please tell my father I am otherwise occupied. I have . . . plans."

Billingsly cleared his throat. "I'm afraid, my lord, your father was rather insistent. You'll have to reschedule your . . . um . . . po—"

"Billingsly!" G cut off his servant as the heat rose in his cheeks. "I thought we had an agreement that we would never mention the . . . thing . . . outside of . . . the place."

"I'm sorry, my lord. But I couldn't recall your requested code word for it."

G closed his eyes and sighed. Billingsly had only recently discovered the true nature of G's secret night outings and had been convinced (cough, bribed) not to tell G's parents. "Dalliances, Billingsly. My dalliances."

"Right, my lord. Your dalliances will have to wait, because your mother requests your company as well. She is with your father in the drawing room."

His father and his mother both here at the estate, in the same room, and summoning him? This sounded rather serious. Yes, his father occasionally requested G's company to discuss his future, his equestrian curse, his inheritance (or lack thereof, considering he was the second son), his desire for more comfortable hoof-wear and a blacksmith who could keep his mouth shut. But his mother rarely participated in these discussions. She was more at ease in a nurturing role, like giving him sartorial advice or fixing his hair (or mane, depending on the position of the sun in the sky).

G looked at Billingsly. "It's not Christmas, is it?"

"It's May, my lord."

"Somebody's birthday?"

"No, my lord."

"Somebody died?" For a moment, he let himself believe it might have been his perfect older brother, Stan, who had died, leaving behind his perfect wife and their perfect son, but then he realized Stan never made mistakes, and leaving behind a family due to an untimely death would most certainly be considered bad form. In addition, then G would be responsible for marrying and heiring. He shuddered at the thought.

"Not that I am aware of, my lord," answered Billingsly.

G pressed his noble lips together and blew, a sound that was all horse.

"Shall I translate that to mean you are in compliance?"

G closed his eyes. "Yes."

"Very good, my lord."

What G wouldn't give at this moment to be able to change into a horse at will. Then he could put fifty miles between himself and his father's nose. (He would probably need forty-nine of those miles just to get out from under the sniffer.)

Twilight transformed into deep dusk as G made the trek up from the stables to the side door of the apartments. His mind was galloping at breakneck speed wondering what his parents wanted to speak to him about.

From the time he was old enough to sit at the supper table, he'd been aware of his inferior position in the family. Stan always got served before G—the main course and all the side dishes. When their father introduced the two of them, it was always, "This is Stan, the next Duke of Northumberland, heir to the Dudley fortune." Long pause. "Oh, and this is my other son, Stan's brother."

Here, your narrators will point out two facts that may have contributed to the Duke of Northumberland's embarrassment surrounding his second son. One: the Eðian power was widely considered to be hereditary, and neither the duke nor his supposedly devoted wife had the magic. Two: the duke had an epic nose, the proportions of which were legendary; Gifford's nose was the perfect size, and the shape could've been the inspiration of sonnets.

The combination of these two details made the duke often glance sideways toward his wife, and repeatedly treat Gifford as if he wasn't there.

That was why at the age of thirteen, Gifford had requested his name be reduced to just G, since nobody seemed to care what his name was anyway.

Billingsly led G from the side entrance down the third main hall, where G caught a glimpse of himself in a hanging mirror and paused to fish a stray piece of hay out of his chestnut-colored hair. His mother had strict rules of civility inside the castle, the most important of which was, "All signs of equestrian escapades are to be left in the stable, where they belong."

His mother had always approached his curse as if G wanted to spend his days as a quadruped. As if it were just another way for a privileged teenage boy to rebel. She often forgot that he didn't ask for this curse, and that if he could find a way to control it, he would give Billingsly's right arm for that information.

As if he could hear G's thoughts, Billingsly pulled his right arm in front of his body, and away from G's line of sight.

"In here, my lord," he said as he swung open the doors of the drawing room, using his left arm.

Inside the room, his father sat behind an ornate wooden desk, his mother, Gertrude, standing behind him. Her hand rested on Lord Dudley's shoulder as if they were posing for a portrait. His little sister, Temperance, was on the couch, playing with her knights-and-ladies doll set.

"Giffy!" she said when she saw him enter the room. Tempie was the only one in the world who could get away with calling him Giffy.

"Hi, Curly," G answered, for Tempie had the curliest blond tresses in all of England.

"Ah, son," Lord Dudley said. He motioned to a woman standing in the corner, Tempie's nurse, who immediately took hold of the little girl's hand and led her from the room. Tempie waved awkwardly as she balanced her dolls and held her nurse's hand. "Thank you for joining us with such haste."

"Father," G answered with a slight bow of his head, although now he knew something must be wrong, because "joining with haste" was the best compliment his father had given him in two years. (His previous compliment had been in recognition of "keeping to the background" when Rafael Amador, the emissary from Spain, was visiting.)

"We have some excellent tidings for you," his father continued. Gertrude stood a little taller at this. "And for your future happiness."

Uh-oh, thought G. Future happiness was always code for—

"You have grown into a fine young man, and a stout, er, stallion," his father said. "We may not have a handle on controlling the equestrian situation, but this minor daily divergence from humanity does not preclude you from leading a relatively normal life, nor will it strip you of the rights and privileges afforded any nobleman."

First of all, G was annoyed that neither of his parents could tell it like it was and use the phrase "horse curse," instead referring to it as his "equestrian condition" or a "minor daily divergence from humanity" or some such nonsense. But the more worrisome part of his father's speech was the bit about the "rights and privileges afforded any nobleman." Because this could only mean—

"Marriage, son," Lord Dudley said. "Marriage to a well-vetted and—as far as can be anticipated without being tested—fertile young lady, of excellent lineage and equally verifiable family connections."

G's worst fears come true. "Wow, Father. Fertile and well vetted? You make it sound so very romantic."

At this point, Lady Gertrude moved her hand from her husband's shoulder and placed it on the back of his neck, as if to prove a showing of such ardent affection was indeed possible in forced marriages. "Darling boy, if left to your own devices, I fear you would never marry."

"I thought that fact was already established and agreed upon," G said. A month after he'd first begun to turn into a horse, he'd overheard his mother lament to his father that no self-respecting lady would want a half horse for a husband. And then his father had said his chances would've been better had he been a horse both day and night, and skipped the human part entirely. Then perhaps his parents could sell him and receive some compensation for all their trouble.

G had gone out and slept in the barn after that.

Now, in the drawing room, Lord Dudley shook off his wife's hand as if he were shooing away a pesky insect. "It is my wish for all of my children to marry."

"Why? You don't need heirs from me," G said. "I'm second son."

"Which is why I have invested the last fortnight securing your happiness—"

"You mean, arranging for me to wed a perfect stranger," G interjected. "Well, thanks but no thanks, Father."

A vein G had never noticed before popped out on Lord Dudley's forehead. "I am securing your happiness and thus ensuring your future and your own estate and a fortune for future generations of Dudley men and you will get married and father a son or two or seven before you turn into a horse forever, *is that understood?*"

G backed up a step, partly to avoid Lord Dudley's increasingly airborne spittle and partly because he did not know turning into a horse forever was even a possibility, although he had to admit the freedom of galloping far away and blending in with the wild horses of the Cornwall region sounded tempting when compared to impending nuptials. It wasn't like he wanted to spend the rest of his life alone. Marriage had its merits, he supposed. But what kind of husband could he make? His parents' own marriage had taught him that when there is no great love in the beginning, better acquaintance would only lead to more contempt.

Besides, what woman would marry him once she found out the truth?

"But Father— "

"You're getting married, or I'll have you gelded, so help me, I will," Lord Dudley ground out.

"And what is the name of my dearly intended?" G asked.

This response seemed to calm Lord Dudley a degree. "Lady Jane Grey."

"Lady Jane Grey?" G hoped he had heard his father wrong. He hadn't been present in court for several years now, but he knew of Jane. Her reputation preceded her.

The book girl.

"Lady Jane Grey. Daughter of Lady Frances Brandon Grey. First cousin once removed to King Edward."

Lady Gertrude leaned forward. "What do you think, my boy?"

G took a deep breath in and exhaled slowly. "I'm thinking lots of things. Like the fact that the lady's face has rarely been seen because it's usually buried in a book."

"You've never opposed the education of a lady before," his mother said.

"And I am still not opposed to it. But what if she is merely using the *Second Volume of the Political History of England* to cover up some hideous malformation on her face?"

"Gifford!" his father said.

G's mouth snapped shut at the sound of his given name.

"Your sharp wit will get you nowhere." Lord Dudley flared his nostrils and exhaled—a move that nearly produced a windstorm. "My boy. It sounds as if you are under the delusion that this match is merely a suggestion." His lips disappeared into his beard, as they did when Lord Dudley was upset. "Believe me when I tell you the negotiations behind this match have been arduous and delicate, and your romantic notions of lifelong bachelorhood will not be humored." He stood and put his fists knuckle-down on the desk, the top of his head reaching the mouth of the stuffed bear carcass hanging on the wall, caught in mid-roar. "Let me repeat. YOU WILL MARRY THE LADY JANE GREY!"

His voice echoed off the walls. Nobody moved for fear of disturbing the beast further.

Lord Dudley unclenched his fists and walked over to G.

"Congratulations on your upcoming nuptials, son. I'm sure you will be very happy."

"Thank you, Father," G said through clenched teeth. "One last thing. Does Lady Jane know about . . . the equestrian situation?" G couldn't believe he'd resorted to using a phrase his father would use, as if the upcoming marriage had suddenly made him more ashamed of his curse.

Lord Dudley put his arm around his son, but it is was only so he could escort him from the room.

"It matters not," he said, and closed the door in G's face.

It matters not. What was that supposed to mean? That she knew about it and it was of no concern to her? Or she didn't know, and it wouldn't matter just as long as she repeated her vows before sunup?

Billingsly met G near the side entrance of the great estate.

"Your overcoat, my lord. I have your horse waiting to take you to your . . . dalliances."

G rolled his eyes. Every time Billingsly used the code word *dalliances*, it sounded so suspicious. Maybe he should have come up with a different word. And yet, *dalliances* had a certain cadence to it. If he thought about it hard enough, he was sure he could incorporate it into his performance tonight.

Dalliances. Dalliances. What rhymed with *dalliances*? G concentrated as he put his left foot into the stirrup and hoisted himself onto the back of his horse, Westley. *Valients . . . es? Balances?*

He was lost inside his own head, searching for rhymes, when

Stan passed him on his way down the road from the castle.

"Brother," Stan said by way of greeting.

When G had asked Stan to call him G instead of Gifford, Stan had resorted to calling him the even more generic "brother."

"Good evening, Stan," G said.

"Where are you off to?"

G's heart rate increased. His brother was rarely curious about G's comings and goings. Maybe Stan knew about the wedding, which would give G more consequence in Stan's mind. Or maybe he was just making small talk. Either way, the scrutiny wasn't welcome.

"Um . . . I'm off to . . . dalliant."

Stan tilted his head.

"To do the dalliant. To be dalliant." God's teeth. He'd never really investigated how to use the word, and the only times he'd heard it uttered were in the form of one or both of his parents saying something like, "There he goes again. That boy and his many dalliances . . ."

"I have plans," G said. "That may or may not involve dalliancing."

Stan nodded. "Perhaps it will be a redheaded girl this time. A short one. With brown eyes. Would you fancy a girl like that?"

"I'm not generally picky," G answered cautiously. "It's just a dalliance, after all."

"Right. Well, carry on."

"Thank you," G said. "Good night, Stan."

He put his head down and urged his horse into a smooth canter. At this point, he could not afford any more distractions or impediments. He held his lantern as steady as he could, but he didn't need much light for this journey. It was simply a turn to the right, then to the left, then two rights, then a slight right, then a hairpin left, then up the hill, then over the bridge, then a sharp left, and you were there. G could've done it with his eyes closed.

By the time G tied his horse outside the Shark's Fin Inn, the moon was high. He could already hear the raucous crowd inside cheering and hissing and shouting oaths and clanging goblets. He checked in with the barkeep, signing his name as John Billingsly, and then took a stool at a table with four other men, who had clearly already downed multiple flagons of ale.

"Back again for more, are ye?" said the man with the bushiest beard.

G ignored him and placed his hand over his vest pocket, feeling for his latest work, "The Ecstasy of Eating Greenery." Then he reached down and felt for the dagger at his hip.

Public poetry readings were known to be a rough business, especially when presenting new material. A man could lose a lot more than just his pride.

FOUR

Edward

When you were dying, Edward quickly discovered, people would
let you do pretty much whatever you wanted. So he made some new
unofficial decrees:

1. The king was allowed to sleep in as long as he wished.

2. The king no longer had to wear seven layers of
    elaborate, jewel-encrusted clothing. Or silly hats with
    feathers. Or pants that resembled pumpkins. Or
    tights. From now on, unless it was a special occasion,
    he was fine in just a simple shirt and trousers.

3. Dessert was to be served first. Blackberry pie, preferably.
    With whipped cream.

4. The king would no longer be taking part in any more
    dreary studies. His fine tutors had filled his head with

enough history, politics and philosophy to last him two lifetimes, and as he was unlikely to get even half of one lifetime, there was no more need for study. No more lessons, he decided. No more books. No more tutors' dirty looks.

5. The king was now going to reside in the top of the southeast turret, where he could sit in the window ledge and gaze out at the river for as long as he liked.

6. No one at court would be allowed to say the following words or phrases: *affliction, illness, malady, sickness, disease, disorder, ailment, infirmity, convalescence, indisposition, malaise, plight, plague, poor health, failing health, what's going around,* or *your condition.* Most of all, no one was allowed to say the word *dying.*

And finally (and perhaps most importantly, for the sake of our story)

7. Dogs would now be allowed inside the palace. More specifically, his dog.

Edward had always loved dogs. Dogs were uncomplicated. They loved you without expectation. They were devoted and loyal, not because you were the king and you could have their heads chopped off if they displeased you, but because it was in their nature to be so. Most of the time he greatly preferred the company of dogs to the company of men.

Edward's favorite dog was named Pet, short for Petunia. She was the best kind of dog, a large Afghan hound with flowing, wheat-colored hair and long, silky ears. Pet was warm and soft and goofy and always good for a laugh. And so for the past few days, simply because Edward said so, Pet had been allowed in the throne room, the dining hall, the council chambers, and his newly arranged bedchamber in the turret. Wherever the king went, so too went Pet.

His sister Mary, for the record, did not approve of dogs in the castle. It was undignified. It was unsanitary.

Bess was allergic. (Plus she was more of a cat person.)

But neither one of them could really protest, because their brother was dying, and how does one deny the wishes of a dying king?

So it was that on Friday morning, after breakfasting on black-berry pie and whipped cream, Edward was lounging on the throne in a shirt and pants, not even wearing his crown, with Pet's head resting on his lap. He was scratching behind one of her silky ears, and Pet's hind leg was moving in time to his scratching, because she couldn't help herself. Mary was in the corner, muttering something about fleas. Bess was sniffling into a handkerchief. Lord Dudley, having just returned from his trip to his country estate to fetch his son, was sitting in a much smaller chair on Edward's right, reading over some official-looking document, a pair of spectacles (or the early predecessor of what we think of as spectacles) perched on the landscape of his nose.

That's when Edward heard the indignant footfalls ringing on the stone in the outer corridor and the familiar, high-pitched voice demanding, *"No, I must speak with the king, now, please,"* but before the steward even had a chance to announce, *"Lady Jane Grey, Your Majesty,"* which was protocol when someone was about to enter the king's presence, the doors to the throne room burst open and in rushed Jane.

It was Friday, as we mentioned. If all went according to Lord Dudley's plans, Jane and his son Gifford would be tying the knot tomorrow night.

Edward smiled, happy to see her. He hadn't seen much of her lately on account of his illness, but she was just as he always pictured her, albeit a little travel-worn.

Jane, however, did not seem happy to see him. There were two bright pink spots in the middle of her cheeks and wisps of her ginger hair sticking to her sweat-dampened face, as if she'd run all the way from Bradgate. And she was frowning.

"Hello, cousin," Edward said. "You're looking well. Why don't you sit down and have a nice cup of—"

Tea, he was going to offer. Because he was English and that's what the English do under stress: they drink tea.

"No tea," Jane interrupted, waving away the royal tea mistress who was approaching her with a teapot in one hand and a saucer and teacup in the other. "I need you to talk to you, Edward. It's urgent."

The throne room, which was full of courtiers, fell silent for a few seconds and then broke out into a rumble of scandalized murmurs, although whether the lords and ladies present were more scandalized by Jane's casual use of Edward's first name or her very rude refusal of his offer of tea, we can't say. Lord Dudley cleared his throat.

"All right," Edward said a bit nervously.

Jane's gaze darted around the throne room, as if she had just noticed that she had an audience. Her face reddened even more. "I need to speak with you about, um . . . the reign of King Edward Plantagenet the Second. I've been reading this very important book about that period of English history, and I wanted your opinion on the subject."

Alone, her eyes said. *Now.*

Concerning the wedding, of course.

Edward was quiet for a moment, trying to figure out how best to handle the logistics of seeing Jane in private.

"It is of great historical importance!" Jane insisted.

"Ah . . . yes," Edward stammered. "Very well. I would be delighted to talk to you about the reign of King . . ."

"Edward Plantagenet," Jane provided.

"The First."

"The Second," she corrected.

"Yes, of course. Why don't we go for a walk and you can tell me all about it?"

Jane's small shoulders sagged in relief. "Thank you."

Edward stood up. His eyes met Dudley's. The duke looked decidedly disapproving, but Edward ignored him.

"I'm going to walk with Lady Jane in the orchard," Edward announced. "Carry on without me."

"But, Your Majesty," protested Mistress Penne, rushing forward. She was his nursemaid, a plump, kind-faced old woman who had looked after him when he was a baby and been called back to his side during his illness earlier in the year. Lately she was always hovering, fretting that he wasn't dressed warmly enough, worrying that any small exertion might be too much of a strain on his now-delicate constitution. "Are you sure that's wise, in your condition?"

That was one of the forbidden words, but Edward decided he would allow it from Mistress Penne because when he'd get his fevers she'd sit next to his bed and put a cool cloth on his forehead, and stroke his hair, and sometimes even sing to him.

"Yes, Sire, perhaps you should rest," agreed Dudley.

Edward waved them off. "What's the worst that could happen? I could catch my death?"

He was trying to be brave and jovial in the face of it all, but in this he obviously failed. Dudley looked disappointed in him. Mary appeared more solemn than usual. Mistress Penne put her hand over her wrinkled mouth and shuffled away, sniffling.

Brilliant, he thought. *Just brilliant.* But should dying people have to apologize?

Jane looked at him, suddenly taking in his plain clothes and lack of crown and the wag-tailed dog at his side. "Edward? What's going on?" she asked.

"Come," he said, stepping down from the throne and offering Jane his arm. "Let's get out of here."

And so they walked, dog and girl and king, out of the palace and across the grounds and down through the entire length of the orchard, where they settled under the white blossoms of an apple tree.

"All right," he said, once they were certainly out of earshot of anyone from court. "What's the matter, Janey?"

"I can't get married tomorrow," she burst out. "You've got to call it off."

"But why?" Edward picked up his scratching of behind Pet's ears, and she made a happy dog noise deep in her throat.

"I simply cannot marry him, that's all. Not him."

"But I hear he's a fine young man, Jane," Edward said. "Lord Dudley assured me that Gifford will be a model husband."

When he wasn't busy galloping around the countryside, Edward thought a tad guiltily.

Jane picked at the brocade on her gown. "That's what they all say, isn't it? A fine young man. A good match. How fortunate I am, indeed. Well. I went to Dudley Castle a few days ago, for I thought I might get a chance to see him or speak with him before we're to be wed, and . . ."

Ah, so she must have seen Gifford in his steed-like state. Which must have been rather a shock, if nobody had told her that Gifford was an Eðian beforehand. "What happened?" he asked.

"It was awful. It turns out, Gifford Dudley is a . . . he's a—" She couldn't even finish the word. "Please, Edward," she said, and to his horror, her voice wavered and broke. "You don't understand. He's a hor—"

"I know," he said.

She stared at him. "You know?"

"Yes. Lord Dudley told me."

"But then why did you agree to the match?" she cried indignantly. "How could you wish me to marry such a—"

"I didn't think you'd mind," Edward said.

Her brown eyes widened. "What?"

"I thought you'd be intrigued by his condition."

"No, I can assure you, I am not intrigued by anything to do with him." Jane's nose wrinkled up in distaste. "And I wouldn't exactly say he has a condition."

"Then what would you say?" Edward was starting to feel as though he'd missed something.

"He's a horrible skirt-chaser!" she exclaimed. "A stud, a ladykiller, a womanizer!"

Oh.

So she didn't know about Gifford's steed-like state.

"Well, Janey," he said with a cough. "That's hardly surprising, is it? They say he's handsome."

"Do they?" she said, with an edge of hysteria. "Do they say that?"

"Yes," Edward affirmed. "And rich, handsome young men with titles can generally have their pick of the ladies."

Unless you were a teenage king with a coughing problem.

Jane's mouth pursed. "I can't marry him. Please, Edward, you must put a stop to it."

Edward couldn't stop this wedding, he knew, not in his country's present political climate. But he sensed that if he explained the true reason for her rushed nuptials (that they were in a great hurry for her to produce an heir who would inherit the throne of England after he died), it would only upset her further. Instead he tried to think of something soothing to tell her, but nothing especially soothing came to mind.

"I'm sorry, Jane," he tried. "I can't. I . . ."

"If you care for me at all," she said then, "you won't force me to marry him."

Edward experienced a tightness in his chest. He coughed into his handkerchief until purple spots appeared on the edges of his vision. Pet raised her head from his lap and cast an accusatory glare in Jane's direction.

"Are you all right?" Jane murmured. "Edward. Are you . . . ill?"

"I'm dying," he confessed.

He watched the color drain from her face.

"I thought it was only a chest cold," she murmured.

"No."

"Not 'the Affliction'?" she guessed, and closed her eyes when he just gazed at her sadly.

"I do intend to get a second opinion," he said. "A better one."

"When?" she asked in a small voice. "When do they think . . ."

"Soon enough." He took her small ink-stained hand in his. "I know this marriage is not what you want. Believe me, I understand.

Remember when I was engaged to Mary Queen of Scots?" He shuddered. "But you have to marry somebody, Janey, because that's what young ladies of high birth do: they get married. You can't hide in your books forever."

Jane bent her head. A lock of runaway red hair fell into her face. "I know. But why him?" she asked. "Why now?"

"Because I trust Lord Dudley," he said simply. "And because I'm out of time. I need to know that you'll be taken care of. After I'm gone, who knows who you'd be matched to? There are worse fates than ending up with someone young and good-looking and rich."

"I suppose," she said.

He knew he should tell her about the horse thing. This was a detail she should be aware of. But he couldn't find the appropriate wording for what was essentially, *and by the way, the guy you're marrying actually is a stud. Literally.*

He should tell her.

He'd get someone else to tell her.

"Do this for me, Jane," he said gently. "Please. I'm asking as your king, but also as your friend."

She remained silent, staring down at their clasped hands, but something changed in her expression. He saw there the beginnings of acceptance. His chest felt tight again.

"All will be well, you'll see." He squeezed her hand. "And, if it will make you feel better, I'll speak to this Gifford fellow about his carousing problem. I'll make him swear to be a picture of fidelity.

I'll threaten him with the rack or something."

She looked up. "You could do that?"

He smirked. "I'm the king. Anything else you'd like me to do to him? The stocks? The cat o' nine tails? Thumbscrews? The Spanish tickler?"

He was relieved to see the hint of a smile that played across her lips.

"Well," she said thoughtfully, sliding her hand from his to bury her fingers in the fur at Pet's scruff. "He might be in need of a good foot roasting."

"Done," he agreed.

She let out a little sigh. "I suppose there is one other thing you can do for me, cousin," she said after a moment.

"Whatever you desire," he said. "Name it."

Her warm brown eyes met his. "Walk me down the aisle?"

His heart squeezed again. "Of course," he said. "It would be my pleasure."

After he'd seen her off in a carriage back to Chelsea (where the Grey family stayed while they were in London) Edward sought out Lord Dudley, who he found in the council chambers engaged in what appeared to be a very serious conversation with Mistress Penne. On the subject of his failing health, no doubt.

"So," the duke said as Edward drew near. "Did you persuade her?"

Mistress Penne felt his forehead with the back of her hand.

At his side, Pet let out a low growl, and the nurse withdrew her hand.

"I'm fine," he said.

The nurse gave him a look that conveyed that she was still offended by his earlier flippancy, and retreated with a rustle of skirts. He watched the door swing closed behind her. Then he dropped into his red cushy chair and reached for the bowl of blackberries.

"Sire," Lord Dudley began. "You must take care to—"

Pet stuck her long nose into the blackberries and snuffed, sending the bowl clattering to the floor and berries rolling in every direction.

Edward gave the dog a stern look as servants rushed in to clean up the mess.

"Bad dog," he said.

She wagged her tail.

"Sire, you mustn't overexert yourself," Dudley said.

"I'm fine," Edward insisted. "The fresh air did me good. And yes, Jane has agreed to marry your son. But why did no one tell her about the horse . . . situation?"

Dudley shook his head as if the issue was entirely unimportant. "I've found that women do not need to be burdened with such minor details."

Well, that makes sense, thought Edward. "Even so, I'd like to speak with your son."

Dudley's mouth disappeared into his beard. "My son Gifford?"

he asked, as if he hoped Edward might inexplicably need to parlay with Stan.

"Yes. Send for him immediately."

"I'm afraid that's impossible, Your Highness." Dudley gestured to the window, where sunlight was streaming in from the west. There were still hours before sunset.

"Oh. Right," Edward said. "Well, as soon as night falls, then."

Dudley still looked uncomfortable. "But, Sire, there are so many preparations that need to be made before tomorrow's ceremony. It will be difficult to get my son away from—"

"I desire to speak with him," Edward said in his I-Am-the-King voice. "I will speak with him tonight."

"Yes, Your Majesty," Dudley conceded. "As soon as the sun is down."

Suddenly Edward was tired, so very tired. He sagged against the back of his chair. Pet whined and licked at his hand.

"Are you all right, Your Highness?" Dudley asked.

"I. Am. Fine." Edward straightened. "I'll be in my chambers," he said, although he had no idea how he was going to manage the stairs. "Send Gifford there when he arrives."

"Yes, Sire," the duke said tightly, and then he left Edward to catch his breath.

It was less than an hour past sunset when, as expected, there came a knock on the door to Edward's room. Pet started barking but stopped immediately when Gifford Dudley stepped inside.

The two boys stood examining each other. Gifford was predictably tall, broad of shoulder, and boorishly square of jaw. He was as comely as his father had described him, and for a moment Edward actually hated him for looking so decidedly strong and able-bodied. But then Gifford dropped into a bow, and Edward remembered he was king.

"You sent for me, Sire?" Gifford murmured.

"Yes. Please sit down." They both sat awkwardly. "I wish to discuss Jane."

"Jane?" Edward couldn't tell if Gifford meant this as a statement or a question or if he even knew who Edward was referring to.

"Your future wife."

Gifford nodded and scratched at the side of his neck, bearing an expression very similar to one that Jane had been wearing earlier today: the staring-into-the-face-of-doom look.

"Jane is a special person to me," Edward began. "She is . . ." There really wasn't a good enough word to describe Jane.

"I have yet to meet her," said Gifford delicately. "But I'm sure she's very . . . special."

"She is." Edward sat forward in his chair. "What troubles me, Gifford—"

"Please, call me G," Gifford interjected.

Edward frowned. "What troubles me, er . . . G, is that you haven't been at court these past years, and while I understand why"—he cast Gifford a significant look that said, *I know all about the horse thing*— "and I know your family to be perfectly respectable

63

and worthy of someone as . . . special as my cousin Jane, I feel that I don't know you."

Then he stopped talking for a minute because Pet, with her tail wagging, had plopped herself down right next to Gifford's chair—Gifford's, not Edward's, mind you—and was staring up at the young lord adoringly. Gifford smiled down on her and reached out to scratch what Edward knew was just the right place behind Pet's chin.

She sighed and put her head in his lap.

Even she couldn't resist this fellow's charms.

Edward started coughing, and then coughing, and then coughing some more, so hard that his eyes watered. When the spasms subsided both Pet and Gifford were looking at him with concern.

"Anyway," Edward wheezed. "I want to know, G, that as her husband you will take care of my dear cousin."

"Of course," Gifford said quickly.

"No," Edward clarified. "I mean that there will be no one else that you're going to take care of. Ever. Only Jane."

Comprehension dawned in Gifford's eyes.

"Jane deserves a devoted and virtuous husband," Edward continued. "So you will be a devoted and virtuous husband. If I hear even a whisper of anything otherwise I will be very unhappy. And you would not like to see me unhappy."

Gifford looked decidedly alarmed, which pleased Edward. He might no longer be strong, but he was still powerful. He smiled. "Do you understand?"

"Yes," Gifford said. "I understand, Your Majesty."

"Good," Edward said. "You're dismissed."

Gifford was on his feet, already nearly to the door, when Edward called after him, "Oh, and one more thing."

Gifford froze, then turned. "Yes, Your Majesty?"

"Jane is unaware of your condition. Your . . ."

Gifford sighed heavily. "Horse curse. My horse curse."

"Yes. No one has informed her yet. I want you to be the one to tell her."

Gifford's eyes flashed with something resembling panic. "Me?"

"She deserves to hear it from her husband," Edward said. As he spoke the words he thought that this sounded like a very wise idea. A kingly idea. Inspired. "You probably won't see her before the wedding, I understand, but before the night is through, before you and she . . ." He stopped. He didn't want to think about the end to that sentence. "You should tell her."

There it was again, the doomed look, on Gifford's too-handsome face. "Have I a choice, Sire?"

"Do any of us have a choice where destiny is concerned?"

Gifford lowered his head. "A man may fish with the worm that hath eat of a king, and eat of the fish that hath fed of that worm," he said, his voice building in intensity.

Edward stared at the young lord for a few long minutes. "I assume that means you'll tell her."

"Yes, Sire," the young lord mumbled, and took his leave.

Edward watched from the window as, below in the courtyard, Gifford mounted his horse and galloped off the palace grounds. Edward felt good about how the conversation had gone. Then he crossed to his bed and slung himself down into it.

Pet came over to lick at his face.

"Off with you, traitorous dog," he said, pushing her away playfully, but then he scooted over to make room, and she jumped up beside him.

Jane
FIVE

The wedding day was upon her.

The ceremony was being held at Durham House, the Dudleys' London home, which meant on Saturday afternoon Jane was taken across the city by carriage and deposited, along with her mother, the seamstress, and Adella, her lady-in-waiting, into the Dudleys' family library, which was to serve as a dressing chamber. (Only it didn't seem as much of a library as it did an unused storage room, somewhat cleared in hasty preparation for the wedding.) Light streamed through the windows, thrown open to let in the breeze. There were bookcases (Jane could almost feel them calling out to her), a stack of wooden trunks, and The Gown waiting on a wire frame.

"This is so exciting," chirped Adella as she fluttered around the sunlit room, touching everything as though it were all good luck. Puffs of dust flew up at her fingers. "You're finally getting married!"

"Finally," Jane said, staring at The Gown. It was gold-and-silver brocade, embroidered with diamonds and pearls. (Recall that these were the days before Queen Victoria famously wore a white gown for her wedding and forever changed matrimonial fashion.) It really was a lovely creation, and expensive, no doubt. Perhaps she'd even hear just how expensive if she were to protest this match even further.

But Edward had asked her, and she would do this for him.

A knot tightened in her stomach when she thought of Edward.

Once, when she'd lived with Katherine Parr, when she and Edward had been hiding in the back of the library of Sudeley Castle all afternoon, which they often did, and after she'd started complaining about her many terrible engagements, which she often did, Edward had poked her in the ribs and said, "Such high standards, Jane. Well, I suppose you could always marry me."

Back then marriage had seemed to her like a silly game rather than a cage to be locked in, as it was starting to feel now. "That'd be quite a risk you'd take, getting engaged to me," she'd replied. "You know I bring about the ruin of all of my potential suitors. Besides, I don't think I'd like to be queen. Too many rules."

"Oh, come now, it wouldn't be so bad." Edward had tapped her upturned nose and smiled. "We'd have a jolly time together."

They'd both laughed like it was a joke, and never spoken of it further, but Jane had thought about it later. That he might have meant it. She'd suspected for a while that Thomas Seymour and her mother were plotting that very thing—sending her to live with the dowager queen to be educated and refined, on the off chance that one day she'd marry Edward and become queen herself.

He was right, too. It wouldn't have been so bad, even if it was difficult to think of Edward as anything more than her friend. She'd read about romance, about how your heart was supposed to pound in the presence of your beloved, your breath was supposed to catch, etcetera, etcetera, and she'd never felt anything like that around Edward. But she could think of worse things than marrying her best friend. Far worse things.

But then Katherine Parr had died in childbirth, and Thomas Seymour had committed treason and lost his head. Jane had been sent back to Bradgate, and her mother had started looking for eligible husbands again.

And now Edward was dying, and Jane was getting married tonight. Probably.

Unless some kind of miracle happened.

Afternoon transformed into evening, and it seemed less likely that a horrible catastrophe would befall the Dudley family and save Jane from her fate. The Gown went on, the green velvet headdress went up, and Jane's hopes went down.

The worst part?

No books.

Between all the hair plaiting and gown adjusting, Jane let her fingers drift across the book spines on the shelves of the library.

History, philosophy, and science: her favorite things. Things that would save her if the wedding got boring.

"No books." Lady Frances smacked Jane's hand away from the gilt-lettered spines. "I will not have my daughter say her vows from behind a dusty old book."

"They'd be less dusty if the Dudley family took care of them." Jane gazed longingly at the literary cornucopia. Indeed dusty, but certainly still in fine enough shape to read a hundred times. "Maybe you'd prefer I brought my knitting."

"Watch your mouth. No one likes a sarcastic wife." A strand of Lady Frances's brown hair turned gray, as if by magic. (Not actual magic, mind you, but the magic that daughters possess over their mothers. As we all know, the only actual magic is Eðian magic.)

At least the wedding meant Jane would no longer live with her mother.

After a bit more tugging and twisting and distress over Jane's general flatness of bosom, there was a knock on the library door. "It's time."

A glance at the window revealed dusk had fallen. It was night.

"What kind of man insists on getting married after dark?" she muttered as she was ushered from the room. *A boorish brute,* Jane thought. *That's who.*

She shot one last longing look at the neglected books. Maybe, at least, they would come with the husband. They could make a trade. The books for— Well, she would figure out what he wanted. Besides women. Edward had said he would speak to him. Even someone like Gifford couldn't say no to his king.

Jane couldn't seem to catch her breath. (And it wasn't just that her corset was too tight, although it was. Extremely.)

She'd always known she'd have to get married, of course. The string of destitute ex-fiancés could not continue forever.

But to someone who'd spent time with dozens—maybe hundreds—of women, how could she compare? To Gifford, what would she be but another woman and the end to his debauchery? He'd resent her every day of their marriage, and not just because of her narrow (unsuitable for childbearing) hips and her odd red hair.

Jane tried to drag her feet on her way to the great room, but her mother hurried her along and sooner than seemed possible, they stood near the wide double doors, both thrown open to release the sound of music and voices. Flickering candlelight cast a haunting glow over Edward, who was waiting for her. He smiled and stood when she arrived, using the armrests for support as he did. "You look beautiful, Jane."

"You look—" Jane didn't finish her thought. Today he was wearing the royal regalia, the crown and coat and gold dagger, all the fashion required of a king about to give away his cousin at the altar, but underneath the layers of brocade and fur, he still looked thin. Sick. Dying.

"I know." He plucked the end of his fur-lined coat between his white-gloved fingers. "I look as handsome and regal as ever. But don't stare. You'll embarrass me."

Jane mustered a smile.

"Now, Jane," Lady Frances said after all the appropriate greetings and genuflections to the king were made, "try to be happy. This is your wedding day!"

Jane exchanged a look with Edward and rolled her eyes as her mother and lady-in-waiting went into the great room to take their places. Jane made sure to stay out of the line of sight from the guests. As soon as she appeared, people would expect her to begin the long trek to her betrothed.

"Jane," Edward said when they were alone. "I wouldn't ask this of you unless it was important."

"I know." She didn't need a repeat of yesterday's conversation.

"I did speak to him," Edward said. "His nights of carousing are over."

"The nights of carousing that have already occurred can never be undone." She tried to cross her arms, but the embroidered gems caught so she left her hands at her sides. If she ruined The Gown before she'd even said her vows, her mother would never let her forget it. "He's a dissolute man, a reprobate, a—"

She'd run out of synonyms. That was disappointing.

"Janey—" Edward coughed into a handkerchief that was already speckled with pink.

She waited a moment, unsure whether to help or say something about his condition, but as he stuffed the handkerchief back into a pocket, his face was red with the exertion or embarrassment or both. Instead, she jumped on to the next subject that would help take both of their minds off his affliction. "So, you saw Gifford.

Prepare me: how bad is the nose?"

A general flurry of motion came from the great room, and Jane realized that she'd moved within view of the wedding guests.

Edward's eyebrows raised. "I guess you're about to find out."

With a sigh, Jane picked up her bouquet—White Roses of York and cowslips—and took her place by the king's side. Arm in arm, they entered the great room. It was filled with people, all of them staring at her. What she wouldn't give for a book to hide behind. She'd have brought a spare book for Edward, too, though perhaps he was more used to the attention, what with being king.

Hundreds of candles lit the great room, a line of them illuminating a path to the altar, where a priest and the groom waited. There were even more candles behind them, which made it impossible to really get a good look at her betrothed.

Together, Jane and Edward made a slow, stately march down the aisle, ignoring the murmurs about how the king seemed sickly, and how the color of her gown made her hair look court-jester red, and how odd and hasty this wedding was. Jane tried to shrink into The Gown.

Then, much too soon, they'd reached the altar and Edward took one of Jane's hands. "To you, Lord Gifford Dudley, I give my cousin and dearest friend, Lady Jane Grey." Before Jane's hand was passed from one man to the other, she gave Edward a light squeeze and blinked away the tears prickling at the backs of her eyes. This couldn't be happening. Not really.

"Thank you." Gifford's voice was deep, but his tone completely bland as he took Jane's hand and helped her up the step where she stood before him at last.

She looked up. And up. And nearly crushed her wedding bouquet.

Gifford Dudley was unfairly handsome: impressively tall and well shaped around the neck and shoulders, with glossy chestnut hair tied into a short ponytail, and expressive brown eyes. And his nose. His nose. It was perfectly shaped: not too long or short, not too plump or skinny, and even the pores were discreet. There was no trace of the Dudley Nose Curse.

Praise all the gods and saints, Lord Gifford Dudley may have had an unfortunate name, but he did not have the nose. She wanted to sing. She wanted to spin around to where Edward was taking a seat in the front and tell him all about Gifford's perfect nose.

It was a miracle. A marvel. A wonder. A relief. After all, she would be expected to kiss this man by the end of the ceremony, and the last thing she needed was to lose an eye. Then again, she might have expected he'd be free of the curse, or there would be a lot of one-eyed women in England.

The elation drained out of her.

Well, so he was handsome. Good for him. It wasn't as though there weren't other handsome men in the world—men who didn't spend every night with a new woman. His perfect nose did not excuse his poor behavior.

For his part, Gifford did not seem to find her appearance

remarkable. Of course not. Few did, unless they were commenting on the hair.

The wedding continued, and Jane dared a glance at the guests. Edward sat stiffly in his chair, his mouth drawn tight like he was in some kind of pain. Her mother sat with the groom's family; Jane recognized Lord Dudley and his wife, who leaned away from each other, which did not bode well for the marriage Gifford must have grown up observing. Lady Dudley sat close to a young girl, who clutched a doll in one arm and gave a shy wave. Then there was Stan and his wife, both with stiff postures and haughty faces, and a young child between them, toddling on the pew. If Stan remembered his crass assumptions about Jane the other day, he gave no indication, but Jane allowed her eyes to narrow at him slightly as the priest began declaring the all wonders of holy matrimony.

First, true love. No danger of that here. Gifford was staring over her shoulder, a bored, put-upon look on his face. Still bitter about what he and Edward had talked about, undoubtedly.

Second, virtue. Jane snorted, drawing Looks. From her mother especially, who developed another gray hair.

Third, progeny. Jane blanched and went cold. She'd almost managed to forget about that part of marriage. Children. The making of. She would be expected to produce a child. Children. Plural. After all, Jane had no brother, which meant it would be her job to conceive heirs for the Grey estate. The fact that women often died having babies, or shortly thereafter—she was thinking of Edward's mother, who'd lived only a few days before departing this world—was alarming enough, while having multiple children was just tempting fate multiple times. Especially considering her deficiency in the childbearing-hips department.

But even that was a worry for another time. Because as the priest droned on about the joy of children, how every child would strengthen the bond between the parents, Jane realized that tonight there would be . . .

That was, she—they—would have to . . .

Gifford looked rather stricken, too, as though the idea of the two of them . . . creating offspring had not yet occurred to him, either.

Jane clenched her jaw. So she had red hair and he preferred brunettes. Was she that unattractive that even someone as questionably virtuous as Gifford the Carouser would not want to— She couldn't even think it. Not now. What had her mother called it?

The very special hug.

When she'd been engaged to Humphrey Hangrot, her mother had tried to prepare her for the wedding night.

"The very special hug might be unpleasant," Lady Frances had said. "But it's part of the wedding night, and part of your duty as a wife. You'll need to produce as many heirs as you can manage. The event itself will be over quickly, at least. Don't think too much about it."

Jane had just stared at her mother, mortified, and later tracked down every book on anatomy that had ever been written. There were the obvious differences between a man's body and a woman's body, ones anyone could notice. And then, she'd discovered the not-so-evident differences. It hadn't taken long to figure out what went where, and what a terrifying thing the very special hug must be for a woman.

And now, as the priest announced it was time for the vows, Jane's stomach knotted and the bouquet slipped in her sweaty hands.

Gifford's tone was paper dry as he said his part. "I, Gifford Dudley, hereby declare my devotion to you. I swear to love you, protect you, be faithful to you, and make you the happiest woman in the world. My love for you is as deep as the ocean and as bright as the sun. I will protect you from every danger. I am blind to every woman but you. Your happiness is paramount in my heart."

From the first row of guests, Gifford's mother dabbed at her eyes with a handkerchief, and the girl fought a small fit of giggles. Edward was stoic faced, his blood-dotted handkerchief crumpled in his fingers.

Gifford took her damp hand and pushed a ring onto her finger. "I give myself to you."

"I receive you." It sounded more like a croak. "And I, Jane Grey, hereby declare my devotion to you. I swear to love you, parley with you, be faithful to you, and make you the happiest man in the world."

The original version of the vow her mother had suggested had said "obey you" but that simply would not do. It was enough that Jane had agreed to keep the word *love* where she had tried to insert

77

the phrase "feel some sort of emotion," but with *obey* she could not bend. She would consult him regarding decisions. She didn't have to listen to him after that. And she would be faithful. She might try to make him happy, unless he insisted on being unreasonable.

She continued: "My love for you makes the wind appear a mere breath, and the sea a mere drop. I will consult your wisdom. I am deaf to the call of temptation. Your happiness is my northern star." She took his hand and shoved on the ring awkwardly, her bouquet still clutched in her fingers. "I give myself to you." Never had she dreamed of uttering such words.

"I receive you." He, at least, looked equally miserable.

The priest beamed. "Is there anyone who would like to contest this match?"

Please please please. Jane risked a glance at Edward, who had not moved at all. There would be no last-minute rescue. No awful coincidence. Nothing to keep this from going any further.

"Then," declared the priest, "I name you husband and wife. You may kiss."

Jane squeezed her eyes shut and waited. Entire seconds fell by, and then a touch warmed her chin and lifted her face, which she'd turned down to her shoes. The kiss came quickly. It wasn't anything more than a touch of his lips to hers, so light it might not have happened at all. But the guests were cheering and when she and Gifford turned to face everyone, Edward's eyes were shining, her mother wore a triumphant smile, and the girl with Gifford's parents was kissing her doll.

"Now to survive the feast." Gifford's words were low, perhaps not even for her, but they were the first real words he'd spoken since they'd met.

"Perhaps there will be a buxom serving girl to help you pass the time," she snapped without thinking.

Gifford met her eyes coldly. "Perhaps there will be a book for you to hide your face in."

They moved down the aisle together, to lead the way to the wedding feast, and the last shred of hope in her shriveled and died. He was as awful as she'd expected, and now she would be spending the rest of her life with him.

And suddenly the rest of her life, stretched out before her with the marriage bed and children and seeing each other only when was absolutely necessary, seemed like an exceedingly long time.

SIX

Maybe he had been a bit rude.

But to be fair, he'd had his reasons. One reason. Which was: he hadn't been prepared for the fairness of the maiden who had met him at the altar.

Until the ceremony, he had, in jest, been vocal about the possibility that Jane was hiding behind books because she was trying to conceal the hideousness of her face. But deep down he'd hoped it was true. Because that would've made it easier to tell her the truth about his horse curse. If she had been less attractive, there might've been the chance that a half horse/half man was the best she could do. But Jane Grey could certainly do better than Gifford.

Not that she was a stunning creature. She did have that fire-red hair, after all. But G had to admit that not one in twenty men would find her unseemly. Her eyes were the color of varnished oak flecked with deep mahogany—perceptive eyes that seemed to drink in everything around her. Her skin was creamy and unblemished. Her figure had all the expected parts in all the right configurements. But it was the supple pout of her lips—and they had pouted a lot during the ceremony—that could inspire poetry.

Like kissing cherries, he thought, but that wasn't a very good comparison.

And now, he had to tell those lips about the curse. He'd promised the king he would share the news with his bride before he and she . . . before they . . . what was the official term for it?

Ugh. *Consummated,* G thought. What was it with this obsession with consummation of a marriage? As if the "I do"s weren't enough. At least the nobility of England no longer required live witnesses to the event.

But right now, at the wedding supper, a bigger problem was emerging. Every time G thought about how to break the news to her, he gulped down a cup of ale. And he thought about it a lot. Every time he looked at his new bride. And he looked at her a lot.

As a side note, he decided her frown would not inspire poetry. Because the poem would read: *Her frown made him desire they be better strangers.*

And what was Jane's relationship with the king anyway? When Edward had summoned G expressly to tell him how "special" Jane was, Gifford had gotten the distinct impression that perhaps the king would have preferred to have Jane for himself. Yes, she was Edward's cousin, but perhaps they were "kissing cousins," judging from the way Jane had clutched the king's arm as they'd walked down the aisle together. And the way she'd kept glancing in Edward's direction during the ceremony.

Perhaps his wife was in love with another man.

The thought left a bad taste in his mouth. He washed it down with more ale.

He turned away and scanned the crowd. Billingsly was coming toward him, threading his way through the tables. "My lord," he whispered in G's ear. "Your father has asked me to gently urge you to switch from ale to cider."

"Billingsssssssly," G said, marveling how long one could sustain the *s* in Billingsly's name. Perhaps he had consumed more ale than he'd thought. "Billingsssssssssssssssssssly." He leaned away from his bride. "I wonder if you might do me a favor."

"Yes, my lord."

"I wonder if you might tell Lady Jane about the whole . . ." G waved his hand in a circle as if to say, "Fill in the blank about the horse stuff."

Billingsly looked from Jane back to G. "My lord, under other circumstances, I would gladly assist you. But I believe the lady would prefer to hear such news from you."

"Coward." G took another swig from the goblet of ale in front of him. Where was the honor among servants these days? He caught a hard glance from his new wife, and judging from the narrowness of her eyes, he assumed she disapproved of his ale consumption. He wished his ale consumption was all there was to cause disapproval.

G raised his glass toward her, and said loudly, "To my beautiful bride!"

The entire assembly hall raised their goblets in response. "To the Lady Jane!" they said in unison.

G took another gulp, and thought about the best way to break the equestrian news.

My dear, you know those four-legged majestical beasts of the land? Well, you married one!

No. That could not be the right approach.

My sweet, have you ever had a difficult time deciding between man or beast? Well, now you don't have to!

Again, he thought better of this tactic.

Sweet lady, there are those of us who sleep lying down, and those of us who sleep standing up. I can do both.

No.

You know how some men claim to have another, perhaps hairier side?

Have you ever cursed the fact that your loved one has just the two legs?

Did you know that horses have incredible balance?

Hey! What's that over there? And then he would gallop away.

G shook his head and could almost feel the ale swirling in his brain. It was at that moment he reasoned to himself that the assembly hall was not the place to tell his wife about his alter ego. Too many people.

Hours later, when G was practically sloshing with ale, he came to the conclusion that the walk to their bedchamber was not the place to tell his wife, either. Too many mounted deer heads on the walls.

Minutes later, as his wife stomped into the bedchamber, and G then mimed the action of a man carrying a woman across the threshold, he decided that the bedchamber was not the appropriate place to disclose his secret. Too quiet.

After that, the only other possible time to tell her would've been the few seconds between the act of stripping off his boots and then falling downward, and he happily would've told her then, only his lips were smashed against the wooden slats of the floor before he could get the words out.

But he'd promised the king he would tell Jane, and a promise was a promise. So just before the world went dark, he said, against the floor, "Mah Lavy? I ammmm a horrrrrrffff."

"Pardon me?" Jane's voice came from somewhere in the black clouds behind his lids.

He could not repeat himself. Besides, it wasn't his fault his wife couldn't understand plain English.

G wasn't sure what awakened him. Perhaps the distant sound of servants beginning breakfast preparations in the kitchen. They always started so early.

Or maybe it was the sound of soft breathing coming from the bed above him. G was not used to sharing a bedchamber with another person, although at the moment, because of his hazy brain, he couldn't remember exactly who it was.

Or perhaps it was the gray tones of the impending dawn.

Dawn.

DAWN!

G threw off the blanket covering him (his new wife must have draped it over him at some point during the night) and using the fringe hanging down the side of the headboard tapestry, he pulled himself up.

Jane was asleep, her red hair splayed out over the pillow like a halo of fire. G paused for a moment, admiring the soft swell of her cheekbones, and wondered why he had not previously noticed that her neck curved in a very delicate and appropriate way as it connected to her shoulder. He would have to include that particular body part in his poem about her pout.

Dawn, he reminded himself. It was moments away.

G reached out and jostled her shoulder. The change was so close, he could feel it. Jane moaned and shook off his hand.

"My lady, wake up!" She didn't respond. "Jane!" he shouted louder, nudging her.

She turned toward his voice and her eyes fluttered. "It is not morning," she said.

"Yes, it is. What do you think that light through yonder window is? I must warn you of something, and it really is not extraordinarily consequential, but it can be rather alarming if you're not prepared for it——" Why was he using so many words? Why hadn't he practiced this speech? He'd barely ever said two words to her in a row, and now suddenly he was using *all the words.* "You've heard of that ancient, some would say beautiful, magic of our ances-tors—" Uh-oh. It was too late. In one swoop, he was standing over her, much taller than he'd been a moment ago.

Jane's eyes went wide. She scooted to the farthest edge of the bed and brought her fingers to her lips. "Wha—?"

G stepped backward, his hindquarters smashing up against the wall. This bedchamber was certainly not made with a horse (on his wedding night) in mind. Originally he had planned on shar-ing his equestrian news, gently excusing himself just before dawn, and trotting down to the stables. Of course, that plan would have required significantly less ale.

Jane furrowed her brows. "Gifford?"

It's G, he thought, but then he remembered he hadn't had the time or the mental acuity to tell her to call him G. He threw his head back and let it drop again in what he hoped would look like a nod.

She raised a gentle hand toward his face. G leaned down and sniffed her palm and then the curves of her fingers, his equestrian instincts taking over. He caught a whiff of wine on her wrist, surely left over from the night before, and used his horse lips to try to draw out the remnants.

Oh, no, he thought. *I just nibbled on her wrist.* He couldn't help it, though. The wine had been particularly aromatic last night. (He would have to ask the servants which year was used.) But before he did anything else, he had to force himself to stop nibbling her wrist. He needed a distraction from the smell of wine, so he lowered his head to the table next to the bed, and promptly ate the bridal bouquet. There. That would satisfy his nibbling for the time being.

When he was finished, Jane sighed and gathered up the torn stems of what was once a bundle of White Roses of York and a dozen cowslips. G remembered because his mother had picked them out specifically, having pledged her troth holding a similar bouquet when she'd married G's father.

"You are an Eðian?" Something between awe and yearning appeared on Jane's face.

G gave his best nod.

Jane set the stems down on the table and turned back to G. "You must tell me everything. How did you get the magic? When did it first appear?"

G tried to follow her questions, but a sensuous odor wafted into the bedchamber, filling his large nostrils and making his mouth water.

He sniffed loudly and whinnied.

"Gifford? Are you listening to me?" Jane's voice cut through his preoccupation with his olfactory senses.

He wanted to answer that of course he wasn't listening to her. She obviously wasn't the source of the scent.

He stamped his right hoof on the wooden floor, hoping the lady would understand the simplest of horse signals.

"Change back so you can speak to me," Jane said. "Please."

But to G, it sounded like *wah wah wah* and *wah wah wah*, for all he could focus on was the smell in the air.

Apples, G thought.

He closed his eyes and shook his mane.

With a helping of . . . hay.

The door to the bedchamber squeaked open an inch, and the aroma intensified. G turned away from the lady, who was apparently still talking because her mouth was moving, and toward the door.

"Lady Jane?" It was Billingsly's voice coming through.

Jane pulled the bedcovers up to her neck. "Yes?"

"It's Billingsly, my lady. I believe Lord G is still within the room? I am here to help."

"Please come in," Jane said.

Billingsly entered carrying an apple in one hand and clutching stalks of hay in the other. G released a full-blown neigh at the sight.

Billingsly held out the apple and G latched on to it with his teeth, the succulent juices dripping onto his tongue.

"There's a good boy," Billingsly said, scratching G's neck.

Before he could consider how it would look to Jane, G nuzzled Billingsly's cheek in response. He quickly pulled back and shook out his mane, in what he hoped was a very dignified manner. Yes, he was a horse, but he was still a man. Except anatomically. And he would be treated accordingly, with the utmost respect.

"Here, boy," Billingsly said, dangling the hay in front of G's nose and then tossing the bundle into the far corner of the room. "Fetch!"

G sauntered over to the corner and began chewing.

"I asked him to change back to talk to me, but he won't," Jane said. "It's disrespectful to remain a horse in the bedchamber, I should think."

Considering what had to have been a monumental shock, she seemed to be taking the equestrian news rather well.

"My lady, Lord G does not have the ability to change as he pleases. He is a horse from sunup to sundown."

"Does not have the ability? I've read about Eðians who undergo their initial change in moments of great emotion, but the ability to control it can be learned through focused training. All it requires is determination and discipline. Perhaps Gifford simply lacks that, but I would be pleased to help. I've quite a knowledge of Eðians."

And, good feelings gone. He blew a raspberry toward her and she flinched.

"I'm sorry, did I offend the beast?" Jane said.

"My lady, you might consider leaving the bedchamber to Lord G for the day."

Her lips pressed together. "Why should I be the one to leave?"

"Because Lord G, in his present state, cannot fit through the door."

(This was true, for the average size of a human being during this age was much shorter than it is today, and the doorframes reflected that.)

At this, G looked frantically about for escape options. The window was nearly large enough for him to leap through; however, they were at least fifty feet above the ground, and horses were not known for their ability to absorb the impact of a fifty-foot free fall.

G scraped his hoof along the floorboards, as if he were a bull looking to charge. The only problem was, he had nowhere to go. He snorted. With no place to run, the curse was feeling very much like a prison as opposed to its usual feeling of freedom.

"My lady, Lord G has an affinity for running when he is in this condition. And now that he is trapped here for the day, and he has eaten . . ."

Jane held her hand up. "Say no more, Billingsly." She turned toward the horse. "Lord Gifford. It seems fitting that you be relegated to your room all day, considering your behavior last night. Perhaps the confinement will provide the impetus you need to develop the ability to control your gift."

Gift. G's nostrils flared. *There's no controlling it,* he thought. *And call me G!*

He spent the day pacing. He knew this situation was only temporary, and that he would not be trapped in this room forever, but for G, running across the countryside, tethered to nothing, was an essential part of his soul. He often wondered if that was how he got the curse in the first place. Something deep inside of him yearned to run, to break free of the disappointment his parents displayed toward him. Not only was he the second, and therefore unimportant son—the one without the esteemed nose—but as he grew up, he was always "wasting" his time reading poetry and plays. Rubbish, his father had called it. As a boy of thirteen, he'd skipped out on his fencing classes to read under a tree behind Durham House. When his father caught him and threatened severe punishment, G had run across the field, down the road leading away from London, and didn't stop until he reached the edge of the dark forest.

G lived to run. And ran to live.

And now, after the humiliation of turning into a horse in front of his new bride, he was trapped in this room like a caged . . . *beast* was the word she'd used. A wife was simply a new person to disappoint.

And since this was supposedly the first day of his happily-ever-after, he could only conclude that marriage consisted of four solid walls, a door too small to squeeze through, and a window too high to jump from

The lines of a poem formed in his head.

The stifling air, damp and dank for want of release,
The horse, too still and stuck, in need of a little grease,
To shimmy his frame through a door too small,
But even then, he'd be stuck in the hall . . .

Not his best work.

SEVEN

Edward

"Edward, dear," Mistress Penne said from her chair beside his bed. "Eat your soup."

She lifted the spoon to his lips, and he allowed her to feed him a few swallows, but then he turned his face away.

"Just two more bites," she coaxed.

"I'm not hungry." He would have liked to remind her that he was the king and not some little boy she could boss around, but getting all those words out seemed like a lot of effort. Instead he fell back against the pillows and pressed closer into the steady warmth of Pet's body where she was stretched out beside him. The dog's tail thumped against the blankets. She licked her lips and gave him a yearning look expressing that if he didn't want to eat his food, she'd gladly undertake such a task for him.

He was too tired to give her any.

"Sire," the nurse tried again. "You must eat if you are to regain your strength."

He knew this was true, but it didn't make it any less humiliating. He was mortified when he thought about last night. How, as he'd walked to the carriage after the wedding feast, his legs had abruptly given out underneath him and he'd tumbled to the muddy ground. How one of his stewards had lifted him easily in his arms like the king had no more substance than a woman, and carried him the rest of the way. How he'd also had to be carried up the stairs to his bedchamber, and how he'd spent every moment since then in bed. He'd slept for the entire night and most of the morning, but had awakened to a feeling of bone-deep exhaustion, as if he had not slept a wink. And now he was being spoon fed like a toddler.

He was dying, he finally admitted to himself.

He'd known this before, of course, but now the idea seemed real. His strength had abandoned him, and he doubted it would ever return. The coughing fits were coming more frequently, and there was a lingering pain in his joints and spine. Even his head felt diluted, as if his thoughts had to work their way through a bank of clouds to reach him.

He was dying.

Already. Hadn't it been less than a week ago that Master Boubou had given him six months to live? A year at best.

He was dying, he thought numbly. Sooner than expected, apparently. Soup was of no consequence.

"Sire," the nurse prodded.

"Leave me," he muttered, and when she did not move away quickly enough, he barked, "Leave me!" and Pet raised her head and bared her teeth at the old woman.

Mistress Penne bustled away. Edward soothed Pet by resting his hand on the smooth space at the crown of her head and stroking. Her tail thumped again. He closed his eyes.

Behind his eyelids he replayed Jane's wedding. He remembered her standing in her wedding gown, all gold and silver and jewels, her red hair shining. He recalled the way Gifford's gaze had swept over Jane as they had approached him, the flicker of surprise and definite male interest in his eyes before he'd forced his expression back into perfect blankness.

When Edward had seen that flicker, he'd felt hope for Jane. That maybe this would be more than a marriage of convenience. That maybe she'd find love.

He thought, *I will never find love.*

He remembered the touch of Jane's small, cool hand in the crook of his arm as he'd walked with her.

He thought, *I will never feel a woman's touch.*

He remembered the way Jane's cheeks had flushed when Gifford had tilted her face up to be kissed.

He sighed. Pet scooched up on the bed and licked his chin. He pushed her head away, but resumed stroking her behind the ear.

His last moment with Jane had been at the end of the night, when Lord Dudley had announced that it was time for the young couple to "turn in," as he'd phrased it, and Jane had come to him to say good-bye. He'd known by the gleam in her dark eyes and the ramrod straight way that she was holding herself that she was both furious and terrified at what came next.

The consummation.

"Jane," he'd leaned to whisper in her ear. "Don't fret. You'll be all right."

"He's drunk," she'd hissed. "So now we can add 'inebriant' to the list of his charms. A boozer. A lush. A tippler. A souse."

"You will find something to like about him," he'd answered, and kissed her cheek. "Be happy, cousin. For me."

Then Gifford had led her away. To their bedchamber.

Edward thought, *I am never going to consummate anything. I'm going to die a virgin.*

And he'd felt more sorry for himself than ever.

The floor beside his bed creaked, and he opened his eyes. Master Boubou was hovering over him, and behind him Edward could make out the outline of Lord Dudley's nose.

The doctor took Edward's hand and felt for a pulse at his wrist, then frowned.

"So it's good news, is it?" Edward smiled at his own joke and was immediately overtaken by coughing.

"I'm afraid not, Your Majesty," said Boubou, when the coughs subsided. "You appear to have taken a turn for the worst. Your heart is very weak. Perhaps the wedding was simply too much exertion."

Edward resolved that he would never, ever, no matter how bad things got, regret being there for Jane at her wedding. "So what's to be done about it?"

"I've brought a tonic." Boubou helped Edward to sit up as Lord Dudley handed him a goblet of a dark liquid that tasted as bad as it smelled, like rotted leaves with a touch of fennel. But almost immediately after the tonic touched his tongue, he felt slightly better, clearer of mind, less exhausted.

"I should probably bleed you at some point," Boubou continued delicately after Edward had dutifully downed the tonic.

Edward tried not to cringe. He'd been bled once before, when he'd first become ill. He thought that if anything, the bleeding had only made him feel weaker. Plus it was unsettling watching his blood drain into a bowl.

"No," he said. "No bleeding."

Boubou didn't argue, but the doctor didn't seem to be afraid of him any longer, which Edward found disappointing.

Lord Dudley shuffled forward hefting a writing tray, which he placed carefully across Edward's lap. Then he produced a large parchment scroll and unrolled it on the tray.

Revised Decree on the Line of Succession, the scroll read, followed by a lot of very fine print that swam before Edward's eyes.

"What is this?" Edward asked.

"Your royal will, Your Highness," the duke said, motioning for Boubou to bring him a quill and a pot of ink. "We discussed how you would name Jane Grey's male heir as your successor. Remember?"

Edward had a vague recollection of this

"But considering this most recent turn in your health," Dudley continued, "I thought it might be prudent to revise the line of succession."

For a moment Edward was confused. Then he realized. "Because you don't think I'll live long enough for Jane to have a son."

Dudley said nothing, but his gaze lingered on the parchment. Edward squinted to read the flowery calligraphy. At the top was his title: Edward the Sixth, by the Grace of God, King of England, Ireland, and France.

(Back then the English monarchy liked to claim ownership of France, even though France had a perfectly suitable king of its own. The relationship between the two countries was obviously strained as a result.)

"'For lack of issue of my body,'" he read, then stopped to take a breath. "'Upon the event of my death, I bequeath my kingdom and the entitlements and protections thereof, to the Lady Jane Grey and the male heirs who follow her.'" He glanced up at Dudley. "You want me to make Jane herself the queen?"

Dudley nodded sagely, his eyes gleaming above his great nose.

Edward didn't know why he felt surprised at this news.

"But she's a woman," he murmured. "The crown can't go to a woman, right?"

"Jane would have my son to guide her," Dudley said. "And me."

Well, that made sense, thought Edward. Lord Dudley had been one of his most faithful and trusted advisors over the years. The duke had never led him astray.

Dudley handed him the quill.

Edward hesitated. He ignored Dudley's protests and rose shakily from his bed, crossed to the window to stare down at the courtyard. For just a moment he thought he actually saw Jane down below him, the jewels of her golden gown catching the sun, her hair a gleam of red. But when he looked again she was gone.

Jane was on her honeymoon, he told himself. Not here.

Then he allowed himself to truly consider the idea of Jane as queen. His little, stubborn, and bookish, utterly sweet cousin Jane. Queen of England.

She wasn't going to like that. She'd even said as much once. Too many rules.

But what was his alternative? Mary was still a Verity and a royal stick in the mud. Bess was still of an uncertain opinion when it came to her stance on Eðians. Jane was the only decent choice left from the royal line, unless you factored in Mary Queen of Scots.

He shuddered.

"Queen Jane," he whispered to himself. "Queen Jane."

It had a nice ring to it, he thought. Jane would be a kind queen, for one thing. She was well educated—some would even say too well educated, for a woman. She was clever. She had backbone, wouldn't let the counselors make all the decisions. She could make a good ruler, an excellent ruler, even, in spite of the whole female problem. He allowed himself the sentimentality of picturing Jane in the palace, living in his chambers and taking her meals at his table and reading the books from his library.

Wearing his crown.

"Is there a problem, Sire?" Dudley prompted. "Do you need to lie down?"

"Give me the document," Edward said. Dudley moved the parchment to a nearby side table, and Edward signed his name carefully. The duke leaned over him to drip wax onto the bottom of the paper and helped Edward to press the ring with the royal seal into the wax. After that was finished, Dudley signed the paper himself, as a witness, along with Master Boubou. Then Dudley rolled the scroll up and whisked it out of sight.

Weariness tugged at Edward again, and he got back into bed, sinking against his plethora of pillows. He closed his eyes.

He had just made Jane the most powerful woman in England.

He liked the idea, but there was still something nagging at him. A doubt. A whisper of worry.

He tried to ignore it. His stomach rumbled, and he decided that any misgivings he might be feeling were due to how hollow and exhausted he was. He really should eat something, he thought. He wished Mistress Penne had left the soup.

He opened his eyes to ask Dudley to send for her but fell silent when he saw the duke and the doctor standing close together, staring out the window where he had been standing a few moments before.

"So. It is done," the duke said in a low voice.

"It is done," Boubou affirmed almost mournfully. "And it will be done, as I promised."

A chill trickled down Edward's spine. He must have made some kind of noise, because both men turned to look at him. Edward quickly closed his eyes and tried to steady his breathing.

"It won't be long now," he heard Boubou say from the far side of the room, then the creak of the door's hinges. "A day or two, at most."

Edward felt a shadow fall over him. "Sleep well, Your Majesty," came Lord Dudley's voice, almost tenderly, and the duke's clammy fingers brushed a strand of hair from Edward's feverishly hot face. Edward didn't move, but next to him he felt Pet's body tense, the beginnings of a growl working its way up through her chest.

He flexed his fingers where they were buried in her fur, trying to put her at ease.

Lord Dudley turned and hurried out, the sound of his footsteps falling urgent on the stairs. Edward opened his eyes. Pet let out a soft, angry bark.

"It's all right, girl," he said to Pet.

She turned over to have her belly rubbed. He obliged her absent-mindedly, trying to clear his thoughts enough to interpret what he'd just heard.

It is done. Well, he'd signed the document, so that was probably the *it* they'd been referring to.

But then Boubou had said, *It will be done,* and something about a promise. And Edward had no idea what that meant.

And, then, most troubling of all: *It won't be long now. A day or two at most.*

It won't be long now.

He was fairly certain that the *it* in this instance was his death.

He slept until the nurse returned a few hours later. This time she carried a plate of blackberry pie, piled high with whipped cream.

Edward's mouth watered.

He had the fork in his hand, a piece of delicious pie nearly to his lips, when Pet snarled. Not growled. Not barked. Snarled. Then she lunged toward the pie.

Edward was so surprised that he dropped the fork.

Mistress Penne was so surprised that she dropped the plate. It clattered loudly to the floor.

He expected to see Pet dash to lick up the pie (he really should have given her some of the venison from his soup earlier), but the dog ignored the food completely. She leapt to the floor between Mistress Penne and Edward, teeth bared, hackles raised, hair standing up all over her body. The sounds coming from her throat belonged to a much bigger animal.

The nursemaid's watery eyes bulged. "The dog has gone mad," she gasped.

Edward was inclined to agree. Pet looked truly terrifying.

"Back away slowly," he advised. "Once you get to the door,

run and get Peter Bannister. He's the kennel master. Send him here. He'll know what to do."

"I can't leave you here."

"Pet won't hurt me," Edward said with more confidence than he felt. He was about seventy-five percent certain, at least, that Pet wouldn't hurt him.

This was all it took to satisfy Mistress Penne. She took three hasty steps back and then was gone.

Pet's snarl faded. She sat down. She still did not seem even remotely interested in the pie. She reminded Edward of a statue of a stone lion that his father had commissioned for the royal gardens, standing at attention, back stiff, head high, ears forward.

She was guarding him, he realized. But from whom? Mistress Penne?

Soon he heard footsteps on the stairs again, and Pet stood up, her tail wagging.

Peter Bannister came bursting in the door. His eyes went first to Edward, taking in the monarch's rumpled bedclothes and pale, strained face, but when he found that the king was unharmed, the kennel master dropped to his knees beside Pet. The dog licked his face, then whined deep in her throat and sat down again near the foot of Edward's bed.

"There now, my girl," Peter soothed in his rough peasant's lilt. "It's all right. You can come out."

Come out? thought Edward. *Come out of what?*

Pet whined again.

Peter crossed to the door and bolted it from the inside, then turned back to the dog. "Fine. Come on, then."

"What is it that you wish her to do?" Edward asked, out of breath. "Shake hands?"

Pet snorted.

"I know I told you never in the palace," Peter said, as if he were actually having a two-way conversation with Edward's dog. "But now I'm telling you that it's safe."

Another whine.

"Petunia," Peter scolded. "For the love of Pete. Focus."

Pet stood up, then lifted her front paws onto the edge of Edward's bed, her neck thrown back like she was stretching. There was a flash of light, as painful as if Edward had accidentally glanced into the sun, and he closed his eyes.

When he opened them again there was a naked girl standing at the foot of his bed.

His mouth dropped open.

Peter wordlessly lifted one of Edward's fur blankets off the bed and wrapped it around the girl, who looked a bit dazed herself.

"Give her a minute," Peter said.

Edward still had his mouth open.

"It always takes time, after the change," explained Peter, as if Edward was supposed to know what he was talking about. "Especially after spending so long out of human form."

The girl shook her head as if to clear it, sending her long blond hair cascading around her shoulders. Then she said, "What is a second opinion?" She asked the question slowly, as if she were carefully choosing each word.

"A second opinion?" Peter repeated.

The girl turned to look at Edward with soft brown eyes, and in that instant he knew unequivocally that this girl was Pet. Pet, his dog. This girl. An Eðian, clearly. A naked Eðian girl.

He closed his mouth.

"What is a second opinion?" she asked again, shifting closer. She didn't seem to be at all concerned that she was only draped in a fur blanket.

"I just rubbed your belly," Edward blurted out.

She cocked her head to one side. "You want to rub my belly?"

"She's been out of human form for a while." Peter's face reddened.

"You keep saying that you're going to get a second opinion," Pet-the-girl said.

Edward wasn't really listening. He was too busy thinking, *I have been sleeping with this dog for a week. Her body against mine. My dog is actually a naked girl. Naked. Girl. Naked.*

"A second opinion is when one doctor tells you something bad, so then you get another doctor to tell you what he thinks. To make sure that the first doctor was right," Peter said.

Pet nodded. Then she was silent for several heartbeats before she said, ever so carefully: "It is my opinion that Your Majesty is being poisoned."

That shocked Edward out of his my-dog-is-a-naked-girl reverie.

She bent to scoop a handful of the pie from the floor, holding the blanket around her with one hand and the pie cupped in the palm of the other. She brought it to her face and sniffed.

"There's a bad smell," she said. "In the berries. A wicked smell."

She held the palmful of pie out to Peter, who also sniffed it and then frowned.

"Yes," Peter said. "That doesn't smell right. Well done, lass."

Pet-the-girl smiled, the kind of smile that Edward sensed was the equivalent of a tail wag. He was beginning to feel like he was dreaming, the strangest and most inappropriate dream he'd ever experienced.

"So you're saying that someone poisoned my blackberry pie," he said.

"Not someone," Pet-the-girl said matter-of-factly. "The nurse."

"Mistress Penne?"

She nodded. "Her body is stiff with lying. The scent of fear is all over her. I watched her. She puts the bad smell in all Your Majesty's berries."

She was accusing the woman who had changed his diapers and kissed his boo-boos and sung him to sleep of poisoning his beloved blackberries. It was unbelievable, but Edward believed it nonetheless. He believed Pet. Perhaps only because he couldn't imagine this plain-spoken creature capable of telling a lie.

"But why would she do that?"

"Because the bad man pays her," Pet answered.

"What bad man?" Peter frowned.

"The one with the big sniffer."

Edward rubbed his hands over his eyes. Lord Dudley. Which meant the doctor was probably in on it, too. It was all falling into place. The *it* they'd been talking about. Assassinating him. So Jane would be crowned queen and then Dudley could rule the kingdom.

He sighed. It was a bit cliché, really. A familiar story, even for back then. The evil, power-hungry duke, grasping at the crown. The villain.

Which made Edward the naïve, unsuspecting fool.

And he'd married Jane off to the villain's son.

They were both pawns in a political game.

He wanted to stand up. He wanted to pace and scream and break things. He wanted to send somebody to the dungeon. Torture. The executioner's block. He wanted to become a lion and roar down the stairs and find the duke's throat. But even the thoughts tired him, and instead, as if to remind him of his body's current frailty, he was wracked by a violent coughing fit, which held on to him so long that his vision dimmed and he was afraid he was going to pass out.

"Your Majesty is still breathing?" Pet-the-girl said softly, when he could hear anything outside of his own noise again. He felt her head upon his shoulder, her body against his, offering comfort the way she would in her other form. She still smelled like dog: her breath, a woodsy musk emanating from her skin, mixed with a scent he recognized as his own cologne.

He tried to sit up. "I'm fine."

She pulled away and smiled at him. "Fine. Yes. You are a fine person. My favorite."

Peter cleared his throat. "You must excuse my daughter, Your Majesty. As I said, she's been out of human form for a very long while." He took Pet-the-girl by the hand and tugged her off the bed.

Her brow furrowed. "Have I displeased Your Majesty?"

"No, Pet." Edward turned toward Peter. "She's your daughter?"

Peter nodded.

"Are all the dogs in my kennels E∂ians?" Edward wanted to know.

"No, Sire. I have three sons and two daughters in the kennel, is all."

"Oh, is that all?" Edward said wryly, but he couldn't seem to find his smirk.

"My family has served your family in this way for generations," Peter said. "We have guarded your palaces and your lands. Sat at your feet. Protected you on the hunt and in the home."

Pet-the-girl's chest swelled with pride at her father's words (not that Edward was noticing anything about her chest), as if the man was reciting an ancient oath.

"I didn't know," Edward said. "Why did no one tell me?"

It seemed that he'd been in the dark about so many things.

Peter shook his head. "No one knew, Your Majesty. Not even your father."

Pet-the-girl was smiling at Edward again. "Your Majesty chose me, out of all the others, to come inside the palace. Your Majesty likes me best."

"Indeed," he agreed faintly. This was becoming too much for him. He felt dizzy. The cloudiness was obscuring his thoughts again. He fell back against his pillows and took several deep breaths. His stomach gurgled loudly. He was still hungry, but how could he trust anything anyone offered him? Mistress Penne. Dudley. Boubou. The people he had counted on most were trying to kill him.

He was angry, of course, but more importantly, this just really hurt his feelings.

His eyes burned. "What am I going to do?" he murmured.

He felt Pet-the-girl's hand come down on his shoulder. "I will keep Your Majesty safe," she said.

He felt something like a warm breeze on his face, and when he looked up he saw Pet was a dog again. She jumped up on the foot of the bed and lay across his feet.

Edward didn't know whether or not he should object.

Jane EIGHT

So. Her husband was a horse.

And no one had told her.

Not her mother, not Edward, and certainly not Gifford. She'd had to find out as it happened and get the details from a servant. Outrageous.

Jane paced the hallway outside Gifford's bedchambers, listening to the horse clomp around inside. She squeezed the broken stems of her poor, mauled bouquet. It wasn't that she was opposed to marrying an Eðian. On the contrary, she found that rather exciting. But there was the small matter of Gifford seeming to despise her, and the larger matter of *no one telling her*.

Well, she couldn't be sure her mother had known about the equestrian aspects of her husband, and Gifford was a drunken

109

debaucher so of course he couldn't be expected to tell her the truth. But Edward! Edward had known. He'd said he thought she would find Gifford's condition intriguing, but where she'd assumed he meant Gifford's nighttime women habits, now she knew he'd actually meant Gifford's history of daily horsehood.

From others, that omission would have been forgivable, because others sought only to use her in their schemes and politics. But Edward was her best friend. She had never kept any secrets from her cousin, and his silence on this matter was unpardonable.

And he deserved to know that.

Inside Gifford's bedchamber, the clomping paused and something decidedly wet sounding plopped on the floor. A rank odor came from the room.

Unacceptable.

Jane hurled her bouquet stems at the door, marched out of Durham House, and ordered a carriage to take her to the palace.

The whole ride there, Jane practiced what she would say to Edward. She would lay out the points for him: the breach in trust, the disappointment, the hurt, and the reminder that she had married this horse boy because he had asked.

Only as she stomped up the palace steps, receiving raised eyebrows from members of the esteemed noble class, did she realize she was still wearing The Gown and all her wedding attire. The Gown rested askew on her chest and hips, and the headdress listed to one side. The plaits in her hair had come undone in her sleep.

Well, it had been very late at night by the time the wedding was over, and there'd been no spare clothes for her in that wretched room, not even a nightgown. Certainly she wasn't going to sleep naked in the presence of that—that—horse boy.

"My lady." A nose appeared, Lord Dudley following close behind. "I'm surprised to see you."

She smoothed back her hair as the duke approached her. "As I'm sure you've guessed, my new husband is indisposed right now."

Lord Dudley grimaced. "Ah, yes. Of course you know about my son's . . . condition." Embarrassment flashed across his face, and Jane had the sense he wasn't used to discussing the equestrian affliction with anyone, and therefore wasn't used to disguising his feelings on the subject.

She smiled and threw back her shoulders, anxious to take out her frustrations on someone. "Of course I do. He's quite a magnificent creature, don't you think? Very strong. Regal. I can see you only purchase the finest quality hay for him. What sort of diet does one feed a beast like that? Horses are herbivores, if I'm not mistaken. But human men can be quite carnivorous. I assume you considered the logistics of a meat diet on a horse stomach years ago, though. I'd be interested to see your research, my lord."

Her husband's father turned pale.

"You know, I've been meaning to acquire a horse of my own. I thought I might get outside more and enjoy some exercise. Imagine the benefits of riding a horse that truly can understand your every command, and spot potential danger not just on an instinctual level, but a human level as well. No more shying at wheelbarrows or cows or other harmless things."

The duke's frown was turning into a glower. "Gifford is my son, not an animal."

"Given his Eðian existence and his rather promiscuous nocturnal activities, I would think you'd have realized long ago that being your son does not preclude him from also being an animal. The two states are not mutually exclusive."

Alarmingly, Lord Dudley gave her an oily smile when he should have shriveled further. "Promiscuous perhaps, my lady, but you appear to have thoroughly enjoyed the benefits of his experience."

Jane immediately turned red.

"Can we expect happy news soon? I have been looking forward to the idea of more grandchildren."

Her face felt like it was on fire, but as the duke turned away, a superior set in his expression, she called out, "I'm surprised you don't have a hundred already!"

Then she realized that was not quite the stinging quip she had intended, and actually dug her deeper into the losing side of their verbal battle. As the duke vanished around a corner, she crossed her arms and shifted her course to a small powder room where she could begin to make herself presentable—not that Edward ever cared how she appeared, but she didn't want everyone in the palace to assume she'd had a rambunctious night with her new husband.

She spent several minutes adjusting The Gown as best she could, and then she went to work on her hair, first carefully removing the headdress. Untangling the mess took a bit more work, followed by some finger combing, and then she pulled her hair into a low bun and pinned it into place.

After she inspected herself in the framed silver mirror, she proceeded to the turret room where Edward spent all his time lately.

A pair of guards stood watch at the base of the stairs.

"I'm here to see the king," she announced.

The two men glanced at each other, and the one with a big, bushy unibrow said, "His Majesty is asleep. If you'd like to wait in the library, someone will be along to tell you when he's ready to receive you."

Jane frowned. Edward had never been a late sleeper before. Then again, he'd never had "the Affliction" before. He'd looked so pale and worn last night that it was a wonder he'd even been sitting straight by the end of the feast.

Well, there were worse places to wait than the library.

"Inform me as soon as the king awakens. I want to know the instant he's available."

"Of course, my lady." The guard stood at attention once more and resumed looking through her.

Jane headed for the library, a familiar place filled with memories of time spent with Edward. Often, they would choose a topic and whoever produced the most facts about it by the end of an hour would win. (Jane had won a lot, a fact she loved to remind Edward about. Those few times she'd lost still haunted her nightmares.)

It was here she'd first learned about Eðians, how they'd been persecuted for centuries, and that the gift typically ran in families, though neither she nor Edward had been blessed with an animal form. Edward, and everyone else, might have been frightened of his father's second form, but Jane had always been jealous of her mother's (very secret) magic.

Did Lady Frances know about Gifford? She was outspoken in her dislike of Eðians (in spite of being one herself), so maybe no one had told her, assuming she wouldn't approve the match otherwise. (Few people realized just how desperate Lady Frances was to marry off her daughter. She'd have married Jane to a tree stump if it had been allowed.)

Jane sighed and wandered toward the selection of books on horses: feeding, caring for, history, anatomy, potential illnesses, and how to braid a tail.

She spent a few hours lost in old texts describing the process of driving the nail through the shoe and hoof, the importance of equine companionship, and the necessity of grooming not just the fur, mane, and tail, but picking rocks out of the hooves as well. Furthermore, what to do if the hoof was split.

Fortunately Billingsly was probably responsible for all that, and maybe Gifford didn't need shoes, as he likely didn't want iron nailed into his bare feet when he transformed every evening. She'd have to ask.

By noon, Edward had not emerged from his chambers and Jane was getting hungry. She put away the books and returned to the stairwell. The same two guards were on duty. "Has the king awakened?" she asked.

"I'm afraid His Majesty is not taking visitors today." Unibrow Guard didn't break his stance.

Jane scowled. "He will see me. Tell him that Lady Jane—" She stopped. Her name was Lady Jane Dudley now. Jane Dudley. Terrible. She swallowed hard. "Tell him that his cousin Jane wishes to speak with him."

"The orders are that he sees no one today."

"Go up and ask if he will see me. Because he will." Jane crossed her arms and leaned her weight on one hip. "I'll wait right here."

"No one is allowed to see the king today, my lady. If he wants to see you, he'll send for you."

Jane bristled. "This is ridiculous. You must allow me to see him immediately. There won't be any problem, you'll see."

"My lady, if you continue to insist, we will call for someone to escort you out of the palace."

Her face was hot with anger. How dare they block her from seeing her cousin?

Unless . . .

Unless Edward was getting worse and had ordered himself into isolation, but why would he isolate himself from her?

As she left the palace—without an escort—she decided to write a letter to him.

She stopped just before entering her carriage and glanced up at the turret.

A silhouette filled the top-floor window for a moment. Edward? Before her return to Bradgate Park, she'd have recognized the shape of her cousin anywhere, but now he'd grown so thin she couldn't tell if the shadow had been him or not.

She stepped into her carriage and drove away.

Jane spent the afternoon in Chelsea, avoiding her mother's questions as Adella and a handful of maids packed for the honeymoon. She'd written a few notes, had the letter to Edward sent out, and then took an hour to decide which fifty books she would bring to the country. They'd be there for weeks, and she wanted to be prepared for a lot of quality alone time. Apparently Gifford would be spending his days as a horse, and thus useless for company.

Maybe that was all right.

A little before dusk, she took a carriage back to Durham House and returned to Gifford's bedchambers. He was still in horse form, sleeping, as far as she could tell. The bed had been moved to one side, and in the corner sat a cold pile of, well, the expected result of a large animal being trapped inside a room all day. She pressed a handkerchief to her nose and opened the window to air out the stink, then went to the wardrobe, where she found a shirt and trousers.

She lit a few candles, and then sat on the bed to wait while the sun fell toward the horizon.

Last time, the change had been sudden, just a burst of light she hadn't expected, and when she'd finished blinking away the sparks, her husband had been a horse.

Now that horse stood there sleeping, his sleek coat shining in the last rays of sunlight. It seemed incredible that those slender legs could carry the entire body, and not just carry, but run and jump and prance. She hadn't been exaggerating when she'd told Lord Dudley that his son was a magnificent beast. If only he could *control* it. Well, it was fortunate he'd married her, as she knew quite a lot about Eðians. If anyone could help him learn to govern his gift, it was Jane. And her books.

Then it happened. Light flared and the sleeping horse became a sleeping man, lying naked on the floor.

His eyelids fluttered and his nose wrinkled at the stench of his own manure. Jane leaned over the side of the bed and lowered his trousers in front of his face.

"Thank you, Billingsly." His voice was groggy.

"You're welcome."

Gifford's eyes went wide as he snatched the trousers and shoved the wad of fabric over his nether region. Jane sat back on the bed while her husband scrambled to his feet.

"My lady, please! I am indecent."

"You are," Jane agreed. "Not to mention the fact that you are also unclothed." She slipped off the opposite side of the bed, away from him and his nudity, but also away from the pile of unfortunate smells. "Is there a reason, Gifford, that you didn't tell me about your condition?"

"Please call me G." He adjusted his grip on the trousers,

letting the legs hang in front of him as though he were wearing them. Almost. "Everyone calls me G."

"I've never heard anyone call you G. Besides Billingsly, but he is a servant. He would call you Josephina if you ordered. Anyway, you haven't given me an answer as to why I spent my wedding night attending an ale-stinking sot, and the morning after sharing a bed-chamber with a horse."

"Well, when you put it that way . . ."

"I'm sorry, but how would you put it?" She refused to grin, even though his discomfort was delicious. After the utter mor-tification of earlier, both with Lord Dudley and the guards, she reveled in this feeling of power over him. It was about time some-thing went her way.

"I would say you spent our wedding night with a charmingly tipsy gentleman who was hesitant to pressure an obviously virtuous lady to rush into . . ."

Oh. That.

Jane blushed and glanced out the window toward the busy street. She chose a passing cart full of apples to find fascinating, but it was quickly gone.

"And as for the equestrian awakening, I fail to see a downside."

"You mean the thing no one warned me about? It seems like a subject that might come up. For example, 'Oh by the way, your future husband changes into a horse as soon as the sun rises every morning.'"

He shrugged.

"Do you even try to control it?"

"It's a *curse*, my lady. Controlling it would defeat the purpose."

"And what is the purpose?" Perhaps if she knew the nature of it, she could better help him solve this pesky problem.

"I don't know."

"Gifford, you never get to see the light of day." Yet he *failed to see* a downside. "I *fail to see* an upside, except for the possibility that I will one day need a quick escape, in which case it will be useful to have a fast horse."

Gifford grunted. "There will be no riding the horse! In fact, I believe this is an opportune time to set some ground rules for this marriage."

"Like what? Hay preferences?"

"Number one." He went to tick off the number on his forefinger and subsequently dropped the trousers. She took a moment to admire the ceiling. Then Gifford retrieved his trousers and continued without the visual aid. "Number one: there will be no riding the horse. Number two: there will be no bridling the horse. Number three: there will be no saddling the horse."

"Well, then what is the point of owning a horse?"

"You do not own me!" He closed his eyes and exhaled slowly. "My lady, would you mind exiting the bedchamber while I dress?"

She tilted her head. "No, I don't think I will, because I have a few rules of my own."

He slumped a little. "All right."

"Number one: no touching my books. Number two: no

chewing on my books."

He snorted indignantly. "I would never chew on your books."

"You ate my bridal bouquet."

He looked surprised, as though he'd forgotten. Then he nodded. "So I did. Continue."

"Number three: I will never find hay in my books."

"Do all of your rules pertain to books? I suppose I understand why, since your social shortcomings mean books are your closest friends." He momentarily seemed taken aback at his own rudeness.

Jane narrowed her eyes. "Are you sure your true Eðian form isn't a jackass?"

"Very funny, my lady. And that reminds me"—he pointed a finger at her—"no horse jokes."

He was making it too easy. "Ah, my lord, why the long face?"

"That's it!" After a frantic look around the room, he grabbed a book from the nightstand. The trousers hung dangerously to one side as he let the book flop open. "I don't recall you mentioning anything about bending the spine of a book."

Alarm filled her. "Put down the book." She wanted to look away, as he seemed distracted from holding the trousers in place, but she couldn't take her eyes off the book. What if he hurt it? What if he followed through with his threat?

"No horse jokes," he said.

"My lord, I apologize for the horse joke. If you put down the book—unharmed!—I will give you a carrot."

He brandished the book at her. "Was that a horse joke?"

"Neigh."

"Was *that* a horse joke?"

Before she could respond, a maid barged into the room to turn down the bedcovers, only to find Gifford with his trousers pressed against his waist, Jane with her face flushed, and a pile of shredded clothes (from this morning's transformation) on the floor. The maid gasped and held her hands to her mouth, then fled the room with an embarrassed cry.

A slow smile pulled at Gifford's mouth. "She thinks we consummated."

Jane's face burned as she snatched the book to the safety of her arms. "My lord, I will leave you to properly attire yourself. A carriage is waiting to take us to our honeymoon." (The word *honeymoon* was quite new at this point in history, and actually involved a month's supply of mead for the newlyweds rather than a romantic getaway, but for the sake of delicate sensibilities, we'll pretend *honeymoon* meant then what it does now.)

Gifford held the trousers over his hips once more. "I anticipate your books are waiting for us as well."

"Don't worry. I left space for you." She took her book and fled.

Jane wasn't sure when Gifford had packed, or if Billingsly had done it for him, but her new husband's trunks were in the stowage area on top of the carriage. There hadn't been room for her books up there, so she'd been forced to construct a small wall of religious, scientific, and philosophical texts between herself and Gifford.

"Is all this really necessary?" he asked when he arrived and spotted her fortress of books.

"Considering that this country house they're sending us to belongs to the Dudleys, and I've seen the way your family treats books, I couldn't be sure there would be enough to keep myself occupied during the day." She stroked the spine of the nearest book: *An Analysis of Eðians' Paintings and Their Impact on Society: Volume Three.*

"How many of these will you finish by the time we arrive?" He eyed them warily, as though the books were some sort of army of knowledge. Some of the corners were rather sharp, she supposed.

"None." She sniffed and indicated the lantern, which cast only a dim glow over her side of the carriage. "It's not bright enough to read by and I don't care to ruin my vision. Instead I'm going to knit until I'm too tired to care that I'm trapped in a carriage. I didn't have the luxury of sleeping all day. If you were truly a charmingly tipsy gentleman, you'd have insisted we rest tonight and make the journey in the morning."

"But I'd be a horse."

"And infinitely more useful for pulling the carriage."

"That would violate rule number two: no bridling the horse."

"Carriage horses use halters."

"Did you learn that from a book?"

The carriage jolted and they were carried down the long drive.

"I learned it," she said, "from being observant." That wasn't half as cutting as she'd have preferred, but he wasn't paying attention anyway. (Thus making her point.) He'd tied his hair into a tail and had his head leaned back on the high seat. As they drove past a street lantern, his profile was silhouetted: it was the perfect blend of soft around his mouth and sharp over his (curse-free) nose. The fan of his unfairly long eyelashes flashed as he opened his eyes and glanced at her.

She lowered her gaze to the knitting on her lap, hiding her flush behind a veil of hair. He was attractive. She was married to him. She could look. She *should* look.

As long as he didn't know about it. The last thing she needed was for his ego to get any bigger.

They rode in silence while she knitted, but when at last she held up her work, the scarf was far from scarf-like. The tragedy of wool was short, and skinny in the wrong places. It almost resembled some sort of fat rodent.

"What is it, may I ask?" Gifford asked, squinting at her handiwork.

"None of your business." She lowered her work and began unknitting an entire row of stitches one at a time, erasing their tangled existence with much more finesse than she'd created them. (She had a lot of practice unknitting things. She could unknit entire wardrobes. You'd imagine that lots of practice unknitting would mean lots of practice—and improvement—knitting, but your imagination forgot to account for Jane.)

Jane tried again, this time making sure to count the knits and purls, and pull every ply through the stitch. By the end of the row, the scarf had grown fat and twelve stray plies stuck out in little loops. "I think you're getting better." Gifford leaned one elbow on her books. "I'm still not sure what it's supposed to be, but it looks more like something than it did a few minutes ago."

She scowled and jabbed his elbow with the point of her free needle. "No touching my books, remember?"

Gifford withdrew, and Jane put aside her knitting.

"So there is something you aren't good at," Gifford mused. "You don't seem like the kind of person to continue something she's not immediately perfect at, so why knitting?"

"Practice makes perfect," she answered primly. "And I wanted to make something for Edward. He gets cold sometimes now. . . ."

Gifford was frowning. "I take it you and the king are close," he said quietly.

"Yes. Quite."

"But how close are we talking, here? Old-childhood-chums close, or former-paramours close, or still-can't-live-without-each-other . . ."

Jane had no idea what he was going on about. Fortunately, the sound of screaming ahead saved her from having to figure it out.

"What is that?" Jane thudded the heel of her palm on the side of the carriage. "Driver, halt!"

"Screams mean danger, my lady." Gifford reached for her, but the book wall prevented him from getting very far, and then the carriage had stopped moving and Jane was out the door, into the night.

She picked up the hem of her dress and ran toward the sound, stumbling over the rutted dirt road, which ran on a hill above a long stretch of farmland.

"My lady!" called the driver, echoed shortly by Gifford.

But Jane didn't stop running until she was well ahead of the carriage, and standing on a prominence overlooking a wide field where, on the far side, a single cow lowed in bovine terror.

The moon was high and full enough to illuminate the events unfolding on the outskirts of the field below: a handful of people brandished sticks and pitchforks and various other farming tools, attempting to block the path of a pack of wolves.

"Jane, what are you doing?" Gifford caught up with her, and he saw what she saw. "God's teeth."

"Gifford, you must do something."

"Do what?" His face was drawn and pale in the moonlight. His eyes hadn't shifted from the wolves below.

"Save those people. The wolves are trying to attack their cow!" Most of the people below were adults, both men and women, but a few couldn't be older than eleven or twelve. "The wolves will go through the people to get to the cow."

"And how do you propose I make this daring rescue? Shall I hurl books at the wolves? Throw myself in front of the cow to save it?" He looked at her askance as one of the children screamed and began to flee from the wolves. The pack leader yipped, and two of its pack mates leapt toward the child, who crumpled into a ball to protect his head and neck as the wolves nipped at his arms. A man broke the blockade and ran to help the child, and the wolves took advantage of the chaos. A couple of wolves lunged toward the whole group, forcing them to defend themselves while the rest of the pack moved around and began a steady lope toward the mooing cow.

"If you won't help them, I will!" Jane scrambled back toward the road and scanned for a place with a shallow enough incline to descend, but there was nothing easy, aside from a series of protruding rocks she could climb down.

Gifford was running after her, and the driver looked uncertain whether to leave behind the carriage.

Jane reached the outcroppings of rocks and stretched to find footing on the first one. Below, the wolves had reached the cow on the far side of the field. The cow's scream rang across the night. A man shouted, "This is what you get, if you mess with the likes of us!" Jane realized then that this man was not one of the farmers, but a better-dressed fellow who was running alongside the wolves. And there were three more men with him, armed with swords and bows.

Why were there *people* with the wolves? It made no sense.

Tears blurred Jane's vision as her foot finally touched the first rock, and she crab-crawled downward. But before she made it very far, two strong hands plucked her up by her underarms, and lifted her away from her mission.

The villagers were still screaming, though the wolves had abandoned the child and the other farmers. The cow was dead. The four men with the wolves were dragging it away.

"It's over, Jane." Gifford didn't release her; his hands were hot on her ribs.

She stared beyond him, where the peasants were regrouping, consoling one another. Their voices drifted up from the field. "Third cow this week," someone said.

"The Pack will take everything unless we hunt them down," a man replied. "The children will starve."

A small *meep* came from Jane. The poor children.

"Is he going to be all right?" someone called, looking toward the people surrounding the child who'd been attacked. Jane held her breath. Even Gifford turned to listen.

"The bites aren't deep. As long as they don't fester . . ." Their conversation grew too quiet for Jane to hear.

Gifford stepped back, releasing his grip on her. "This way, my lady. Let's go back to the carriage."

"But we have to help them—"

"It's over now. What would you do for them? They'll take care of one another." He gestured toward the carriage, where the driver shifted from foot to foot. "Don't you have an ugly scarf to finish?"

How could he joke at a time like this? Clearly Gifford Dudley had no sense of responsibility or honor.

Jane hugged herself and gazed toward the farmers once more. Some were taking the injured child away, while others stayed to discuss ways to make the fields more secure. Gifford's question had been fair: what would she do for them? The attack had happened. The wolves and strange men were slinking out of view, the cow carcass loaded onto a cart.

"Very well."

"Thank you." Gifford offered his arm as though he actually thought he was a gentleman. Jane jerked away and walked on her own, though her whole body trembled with adrenaline and panic at how close that child had come to dying, and how the peasants might go hungry now.

When she sat in the warm carriage, surrounded by her books and her pathetic knitting, the only thing she felt was cold.

Those people were in trouble. In need of help. And Gifford had done nothing.

NINE

Gifford

There was nothing he could've done. If he hadn't stopped Jane, she would've been hurt. G was a strong man, at least he thought he was, but under no circumstances did he have the ability to dispatch an entire wolf pack.

And those had been no ordinary wolves. They were part of the E∂ian Pack, G was sure of it.

He would not have stood a chance against them. The Pack was well known all over England. For E∂ians, they represented a kind of Robin Hood figure—taking back what for so long had been denied to them. For the rest of the country, they were terrifying bandits. Ruthless. Cunning. And even if G had managed to stop the attack while remaining alive, saving one small village would've done nothing to abate the numbers of the desperate and starving.

He sighed and scratched at the gold-leaf windowsill of the carriage, and a few flecks of gold flaked off into his palm. What those peasants wouldn't do for a handful of the shiny metal. But for G's father and the other nobles like him, gold was a mere decoration. G had never known hunger, not really, but he had seen it. He'd been all over the countryside as a horse, and it seemed to him that the entire kingdom was going hungry. But what could one person do?

Nothing, he thought. One person could do nothing. So there was no point being noble about it.

The driver hit a bump, causing one of Jane's books to topple. G cut a glance toward Jane, expecting her to stage a dramatic rescue of the fallen tome, but her face remained a blank mask. Her chest heaved, perhaps still out of breath from the tumult of the attack. Just below her collarbone, her skin was red and splotchy.

G grabbed his flask of water, splashed a bit on a handkerchief, and handed it to her.

She looked at it warily for a moment, and then took it and pressed it against her delicate neck, along her collarbone, and just under her hairline in the back. She did it so gracefully that G decided he would include a description of the motion in his poem about her pout and the curve of her neck.

Oh that I were the handkerchief in that hand, that I might touch that neck. . . .

"Thank you," she said, handing him back the kerchief.

Her silhouette against the moonlit window was lovely. This creature was his *wife,* he thought again with a kind of disbelief, and no matter what her (incorrect) perspective was, he'd saved her back there. At this instant, he could feel a pull toward her, a desire to protect her always. For the briefest of moments, G considered the romantic notion of secretly shoving the handkerchief inside his shirt, against his heart. He caught himself leaning ever so slightly toward her.

Jane turned to him, a blush on her cheeks. "My lord, if you'd be so kind as to remain on your own half of the seat. My books are crushed as is."

Ah. There she is. The aloof and disappointed lady. G mentally slapped his own cheek, over and over until it burned red under his imaginary hand and he was sure he'd slapped out every romantic notion. He wanted to tell her she'd have more room if she'd just get rid of her books, but he supposed that in her case, it would be like telling a mother she'd have more room if she threw out her children.

So instead, he took the handkerchief, smiled sweetly at his lady, and let it fly out the window.

As the carriage pulled into the country house, his concerns about the Pack were momentarily replaced by his exasperation with Lady Jane.

The house staff was there to greet the happy couple, usher them into the parlor, and offer them water and wine—no more ale for G. They moved the copious amounts of luggage inside and then, in the tradition of servants faced with honeymooners (especially after news of ripped clothing in the marital bedchamber had reached their ears) they disappeared, leaving the couple alone. To do whatever it was that newlyweds did at night. On their honeymoon.

Which, judging by Jane's behavior, consisted of staring out the window, counting the stars.

She hadn't yet forgiven G for when he'd stopped her from hurling herself at the wolves, but seriously, what was her plan of attack? Drown them in petticoats? Crush them with her bulky knowledge of *Herbs and Spices Indigenous to the Spanish Highlands: Volume Two*? Maybe he should just call it a night. He opened the door to exit the drawing room, but was met with two servants.

"Your bedchambers are being prepared," one of the men said.

G rolled his eyes as the servant closed the door in his face. Perhaps his father had instructed the staff to promote as much couple time as possible. "Don't let one leave the room without the other," he could imagine his father saying.

Jane was still staring out the window. He wasn't sure she had even noticed his attempted departure. G was pretty certain there'd be no persuading her to the bedchamber at this point, but they had one month in this house, and the only way to survive the honeymoon would be a congenial companionship, rather than the scornful disdain of the present. So he tried to be affable.

"Can I get you anything, my lady?"

She didn't turn around. "I have servants for that."

G sighed loudly and sank onto a sofa. "What, exactly, have I done to you? Besides the offensive act of existing, and being forced to marry you?"

Jane turned around. "Those two grievances are beyond your control, and I would never hold you accountable for things beyond your control."

"What then? What have I done to offend thee?" he said in a mock-formal tone.

She made a fist so tight, her knuckles turned white. "You are a drunken lothario who . . . who . . . cannot keep his horse in his pants!"

G tilted his head at this. "To be fair, my pants are not where I keep my horse."

"Don't try to deny it!" Jane said. "I heard it all from Stan, who mistook me for one of your . . . dalliances."

G held a hand up. "My lady, if you please, let's take these offenses one at a time." He gestured toward a chair. She folded her arms. "Please," he added.

She sat down, albeit in a chair he had not motioned to.

A peace offering, in the form of the truth, would be the best course of action at this point. "First, the charge of drunkenness. I will admit that on the night of our blessed union I was inebriated, but that was a solitary—or let's say unusual—occurrence based on the fact that I was reluctant to bind my life to a lady about whom I'd heard much, but experienced very little."

"And 'binding your life' would hinder your nightlife, would it not?"

"Ah, which brings us to your second charge. That of my being a lothario." G paused and considered telling her about the poetry readings, but he thought better of it. He'd already endured humiliating horse jokes and derision about his lack of ability to control the power. How loudly would she laugh if she knew this "lothario" spent his days composing poems and plays, and his nights writing and performing them? "Yes, I have enjoyed the company of ladies."

"Ha!" Jane pointed at him as if through her own verbal cunning she'd just gotten Alexander the Great to admit he was overly ambitious.

"Yes, yes," G said, placating. "I crack under your withering stare. If I may continue?"

She nodded triumphantly.

"I spend my days as a horse. I haven't been to court in years. I haven't felt the sun on my skin for just as long. I wasn't sure I could ever be fit to be a husband, since I'm only living half a life and it's the half when most people sleep. You can't imagine how lonely that can be. So yes, up until the night of our heavenly merger, I took comfort in relationships of the fleeting variety—"

"Otherwise known as prostitutes," Jane interrupted.

"Despite my history with ladies of negotiable affection, I gave my word to your king to be a faithful husband of the utmost standing."

Jane's face softened the tiniest bit.

"And I have kept my word."

She raised her eyebrows. "For two days."

"Yes. Look, I've led a solitary existence. It's hard to make friends. And despite the efforts of the Lion King, Eðians are still feared and mistreated."

Her face grew tight again. "Let's discuss that. You have this magical ability, this ancient honor, passed down from our ancestors, destined to be bestowed upon the champions among us. And yet you call it a curse."

"My lady, you have a distinctly naive and hopelessly optimistic view of E∂ians."

"It is not naive," Jane said. "My opinion has been cultivated over years and years of study."

"Studying histories that glorify their legends."

She pressed her lips together and shook her head. "Have you ever read one single book about them in your life?"

"No." He preferred poetry and fiction to informational books. But he wasn't about to admit that. He stood and walked over to her, towering above her. "I don't have to read about it. I've lived that life. Tell me, lady, what would your beloved history books say about that E∂ian attack on those poor peasants earlier this evening? Where was the glory, the honor, in tearing apart an entire community for a few measly bits of meat? Where are those stories in your precious books?"

"Those were not E∂ians," Jane said softly.

"Indeed they were," G said. "Real wolves would not allow a feral dog into their ranks, nor would they work with men to raid a village. That, my dear, was the infamous Pack."

Jane frowned. "The Pack is just a rumor. E∂ians would never do such despicable things."

"You are mistaken. To think such is to be naive."

"I don't understand you. You're Eðian, yet you speak of Eðians with as much loathing as Verities."

G poured two goblets of water from a pitcher on an end table. He was determined to keep his composure, despite the general irritating nature of conversing with his wife.

He handed her one of the goblets. "I do not loathe them. I just believe that random magical abilities do not constitute the honor of a man."

"Or a woman," Jane provided.

He closed his eyes and breathed deeply. "Or a woman," he acquiesced. "I didn't choose to be what I am. One moment I was fighting with my father and daydreaming about running far away. The next moment, I was a horse, and literally running far away. Ever since, if the sun is up, I'm a horse. And if the sun is down, I'm a man. If it is a gift, I do not deserve it. If it is a curse, I do not deserve it."

He took a sip of his water and then continued. "Evil will exist among Eðians, just as goodness will exist among Verities. I believe Eðians deserve protection from persecution. The scales need to be righted in the direction of equality. And if it were the other way around, and Verities were persecuted, I would still fight for equality. Not dominance. Dominance leads to tyranny."

There was silence in the room for a long time.

"I did not know your feelings about the subject matter ran so deep, G," Jane said.

She had called him G. That had to be a good sign if there ever was one. And her full lips were curved up ever so slightly.

"I didn't know I felt so strongly about it, either," he said. And that was the truth.

She glanced away demurely. "Perhaps if you didn't waste away your human hours on drinking and whoring, you'd discover more things to give a shilling's worth of thought about."

G put his hand to his forehead and rubbed hard. He thought again about telling her he was a poet. But when he lowered his hand, he saw that she was smiling. Then she smiled wider. And her red hair, which moments before had looked like a den of scarlet snakes wrangled together in a prudish bun, now resembled beams of sunbursts around a fiery center. She was radiant.

"Do you know how I think we should spend the first night of our honeymoon?" she said in a soft, low voice.

For the first time since the announcement of their betrothal, G knew exactly how he wanted to spend the night. A pit of anxiety and anticipation formed in his stomach. He raised his eyebrows expectantly.

Her eyes got brighter, if that was possible. "I think we should raid our food cupboards and take some smoked meat down to the peasants who were attacked earlier!"

G worked hard to keep his face from falling. "My lady, you read my mind," he said, grateful that his lady could not read minds.

In addition to the meat, dried fruit, and hard-rind cheese from the larder, G and Jane also gathered up an assortment of herbs, strips of linens, and tea leaves.

As Jane put it, "Yarrow tea helps with the pain. I learned that from reading *The Proper Treatment of Wounds on the Battlefield During the War of the Roses: A History*."

G watched in awe as she used a pestle and mortar to grind three different herbs and two spices. She then removed an innocuous-looking wooden slat from the wall in the corner of the larder, reached inside, and produced a corked bottle.

"Is that liquor, my lady?" G raised one eyebrow.

"I messaged ahead and had the servants hide it," she said as if she believed strong marriages started out by hiding the liquor. She'd probably read it in a book somewhere.

G didn't know whether to be impressed or really, really annoyed. Either way, he agreed that now was a great time for a drink. Except Jane poured a couple of ounces of the stuff into the mortar and then re-corked the bottle and returned it to its hiding place.

G made a mental note of where the wooden slat was.

She mixed the liquor with the powder and then poured it into a jar and sealed it shut. "They can let this tincture steep for eight days, and then it will help with those wounds that are difficult to heal."

G nodded, understanding very little of what she had just said. They had dressed in their plainest clothing, and now they draped their most mundane cloaks around their shoulders, so as not to appear highborn. G wrapped their supplies in a sheet and hoisted it over his shoulder.

"Shall we?" he said.

Jane lit a lantern and held it high. "We shall."

They didn't want to bother the servants or the coachman with details, which made what they were about to do seem slightly illicit and possibly the most exciting thing either of them had done.

G told only the stable boy of their plan, so that he could help prepare a simple horse and wagon. Jane hoisted herself up in a very unladylike manner, which made G smile, and then they were off.

There was no guard or lookout to stop them from entering town. G led the horse and wagon to the center of the small village, where light glowed in the windows of the largest structure. As the wagon came to a stop, the soft moans of the wounded met their ears.

G climbed down. "Wait here," he told Jane.

Apparently, "wait here" meant "hurry along" to Jane, for she scrambled down the carriage before G had taken one step.

He rapped at the door, and when no one came to open it, he turned the latch himself.

"Who are ye?" a tired-looking man said.

"We are a husband and wife who heard of your misfortunes, and we bring food and supplies for the binding of wounds."

The man narrowed suspicious eyes.

Jane stepped forward, took the man's hand softly in her own, turned the palm up, and placed a piece of bread there. "Sir, I have bread and dried beef and mead."

G glanced at his wife. "Where did you get the mead?"

She ignored him. "Please let us be of service."

A portly woman—who had been tending a boy's leg—came forward. "We would be grateful for it, my lady."

"Oh, I am not a lady," Jane said, although she couldn't hide her elegant manners and way of speaking.

The woman didn't argue. "Let 'em through, ye stubborn man," she said.

The old man stood aside while G and Jane distributed food, strips of linen, tinctures, and salves to the people. G grabbed for the bottle of mead, but Jane said she would be in charge of its distribution.

His wife, he realized after all of two minutes, was magnificent. She was not afraid to wipe away blood, and patiently taught the villagers how to properly dress a wound and how to prepare more tinctures.

"I could use some meat," an old man said to G.

"Quiet, please," G said. "I'm watching the lady." (This was obviously G's first foray into helping the needy, or anyone beyond himself, for that matter, and he was not used to the protocol of service.)

"Do you think she was ever employed as a healer?" G said.

"I don't know. She's your wife," the old man said.

Jane looked up and caught G staring at her. She smiled and tossed him some linen strips. "Get to work," she said.

As the two of them tied and cleaned and washed and fed and comforted, they began to hear rumblings of complaint, but not about them. About the king.

"The Pack grows in power, and yet the king does nothing."

"The previous king would never have let it get to this point."

"The previous king was a lion. King Edward is a mouse."

At this, Jane looked grievously offended, and G wondered anew about the nature of her feelings for the king.

The murmurs continued. "It's all the fault of those filthy Eðians."

"How are we to protect ourselves when they can transform into such cunning creatures? They should be rounded up and locked away, for the safety of the country."

Jane flashed G a worried expression. He smiled in what he hoped was a comforting way and tossed her some fresh bandages.

After a couple of hours, every wound had been bound, every cut washed and cleaned and wrapped. As Jane and G made their exit, grateful lips kissed the knuckles of the two anonymous benefactors.

Jane had not recovered her good humor after hearing the people's grumblings about Eðians and the king, so G tried to rouse her spirits by talking about what he would do if he ran the country, and eventually Jane joined in. Pretty soon they were shouting decrees they would implement if only they were the rulers of England.

"No more hungry people!" Jane said.

"Accessible medicine for all! Including steeping tinctures! And more tinctures that need to steep!" G said.

"Prosecution of those who prey on the weak!" Jane said.

"An unlimited fountain of free ale!" G said.

At which Jane frowned.

"And . . . the funding of higher education for women!" G said.

That seemed to satisfy his lady for the time being.

When they arrived at the house, G had only a couple of hours before horse time. In their bedchamber, Jane set a pillow and blanket on the floor next to the bed.

"Jane, I cannot allow you to sleep on the floor," G said gallantly.

She smiled. "The pillow and blanket are for you, my lord."

"Ah. Of course."

G lowered himself onto the hard wooden floor, and Jane climbed into the bed, blowing out the candles as she pulled the covers tight around her.

Neither of them said another word. But each fell asleep to the sound of the other's breathing.

TEN

Edward

Dearest Edward,

I hoped to visit you this morning, but when I arrived at the palace I was informed that you are not receiving visitors. I must confess my surprise and disappointment that you would not see even me, but I know there must be a good reason, and I suspect that this self-imposed isolation means that your illness is taking its toll. For this I am so very sorry, cousin, and I wish there was something I could do to make you well again.

I'm sure you must be wondering what it is I came to see you about this morning, mere hours after my wedding. My dear cousin, the wedding is precisely the topic I wanted to discuss with you. Or rather, my newly acquired husband.

Gifford is a horse.

I'm certain you knew this, what with your referrals to "his condition" and assumptions that I would find it intriguing. What I cannot fathom is why you chose not to tell me. We've always told each other everything, have we not? I consider you to be my most trusted confidant, my dearest and most beloved friend. Why, then, did you neglect this rather critical detail? It doesn't make sense.

But perhaps in this, too, I wonder now, you felt you had a good reason.

I hope that we will be able to speak more on this subject when I return from my honeymoon in the country.

All my love,

Jane

Edward sighed. He carefully folded the letter and laid it on the bedside table. Over the past three days he had read Jane's letter no fewer than a hundred times, and each time he felt as though she were sitting beside him, chastising him of course, but there all the same.

He closed his eyes and mentally composed a letter back to Jane. It went something like this:

Dearest Jane,

Sorry I made you marry a horse. Your father-in-law is trying to kill me. Send help.

But Edward knew that he could expect no help from Jane. Any message he might write to inform her of his predicament or warn her of Lord Dudley's insidious intentions for both Jane and the kingdom would surely be intercepted by the duke. Even if the message did somehow manage to make it out of the palace, it would likely fall into Gifford's hands, and Edward could only assume Jane's husband was in league with his father.

So. The king was in trouble, or, as they would have phrased it at the time, up ye olde creek sans ye olde paddle.

He sighed again. The night Pet had turned out to be a girl, Edward and Peter Bannister (and Pet, too, but she wasn't much help with strategy, bless her heart) had come up with a plan to get Edward out of the castle. It was a good plan. First, Edward should stop ingesting poison. Then, when the poison he had already unwittingly taken had worn off, when he had regained some of his strength, when he could at least walk again without falling, he would request to be taken out to the gardens for fresh air. (Because it's a well-known fact that fresh air has magical healing properties.) Then, on one of these walks through the gardens, Peter Bannister would happen by with a horse and help Edward onto said horse. And then Edward would flee.

But things weren't going according to plan.

For the past three days Edward hadn't eaten anything that didn't pass a sniff inspection from Pet. Which was tough, because in order to obtain a sniff inspection from Pet, one had to wait until someone wasn't hovering over him (which these days was proving to be difficult) and then quickly lower his plate to the floor beside his bed (because he wasn't allowing Pet to sleep in the bed anymore, because, well, that would be inappropriate) and then wait for her to wag her tail. Code for: no wicked smells here; feel free to chow down.

At first the poison had only been offered up once a day, in his berries and berry-related pastries, but then Mistress Penne had noticed that the king seemed to have lost his passion for blackberries, and the wicked smell began to infiltrate the rest of his food. And then his wine.

So now he was down to water and hunks of bread and cheese that Peter Bannister sometimes slipped him. At this rate he was looking at dying of poisoning or dying of starvation.

The word *famished* had taken on a whole new meaning for Edward. He found that most of his dreams were now centered around a vision of himself sitting at a table laden with minced meat pies and roast legs of lamb and bowls and bowls of sweet, ripe blackberries.

Oh, how he missed blackberries.

But in spite of the fact that not a drop of poison had crossed his lips in over three days, Edward was not getting better. He could barely stand on his own, let alone walk, and had to be helped to the chamber pot. The coughing had not subsided; if anything, it was getting worse. His handkerchief was more pink than white now. His thoughts were still so cloudy most of the time.

And Dudley was becoming suspicious. "You must eat, Sire," the duke was admonishing him at this very moment, as Mistress Penne offered him a bowl of chicken broth and Edward pushed it away. At least chicken broth didn't appeal to him that much, but even the oily brown substance was making his mouth water.

Edward was trying very hard not to smell it, lest he be overcome by his hunger and grab the bowl and drain it, poison or not.

"You must at least try, Your Majesty," Dudley said.

Edward's teeth clenched for a few seconds before he reined in his temper. "Why must I try?" he replied. "Will this bowl of broth keep me from dying?"

Dudley's lips thinned. "No, Sire."

"Then why bother?" Edward raised himself up slightly. "You've got your precious document signed now, don't you? You don't need me anymore. So if I'm going to die, I'm going to do it on my own terms."

If this was a political game then he was showing his hand, he realized. He should be more cautious, but he didn't care. He was tired of feeling helpless.

The duke stared at Edward with narrowed eyes, studying his face. Then in a cold voice he said, "As you wish, Sire," and slunk away, closing the door behind him.

Mistress Penne, still holding the bowl of broth, clucked her tongue in disapproval.

Edward imagined the nurse's less-than-slender form stretched on the rack while he dropped poisoned berries into *her* mouth.

From beside the bed, Pet gave a low growl. Mistress Penne eyed her warily and then exited the room, taking the broth with her.

Edward's stomach rumbled. He groaned.

Pet whined and licked his hand. He couldn't quite bring himself to pet her.

He picked up the letter from Jane and read it again.

"My confidant," he murmured to himself. "My most beloved friend."

He wondered if he would ever see her again.

That afternoon, his sisters came to visit him, without Dudley or Mistress Penne or even a servant to accompany them.

He couldn't believe his good luck. He had almost forgotten his sisters in this whole mess, but here they were, Mary and Bess in his room, each holding a box, a present of some kind, both averting their eyes from him as if they couldn't bear to see how wasted away he had become.

Help had arrived at last, he thought.

His sisters, Mary especially, had connections. Mary's uncle was the Holy Roman Emperor, who Edward usually counted as a bit of an enemy, but desperate times called for desperate measures. Mary could rally an army for him, a few soldiers, at least. She could oust Lord Dudley, if it came to that. And Bess was tremendously clever. She'd studied books on herbs and medicines, he thought he remembered. Perhaps she could find an antidote for the poison.

"I am glad to see you both," he breathed, smiling weakly.

"Oh, Eddiekins, we're so sorry this has happened to you." Mary put her box on the little table in the corner and moved to sit at the edge of his bed, sending Pet scrambling out of the way of her voluminous skirts.

Mary ignored the dog. She took Edward's hands in hers and

leaned toward him earnestly. Her breath smelled of wine. "I want you to know that I will look after England," she said, her voice overly loud, like she was making a speech to the masses. "I will restore our country to its former glory. There will be no more of these blasphemous reformational ideas that Father spread in order to justify his own sinful lifestyle. We will root out this Eðian infestation, starting with that horrible Pack that everyone's talking about. I'll see them all burn. We will be free of Father's impurity. I swear it."

Well, Dudley had been right on that count, Edward thought. Mary hated Eðians. But he had bigger problems at the moment.

He glanced at Bess, who was staring at him intently, then back to Mary. "Listen, both of you." He took a deep breath. "I don't have 'the Affliction.' Lord Dudley has been poisoning me."

Mary pulled free of Edward's grasp.

"Eddie," she said soothingly. "No one's trying to harm you. Lord Dudley least of all."

He scrambled to sit up. "No! He is! You must arrest him!"

Mary's brow rumpled. "Eddie, my dear boy. The duke has been your trusted advisor for years."

"He wants the country for himself," Edward insisted. "He wants me dead."

There was a moment of heavy silence.

"Why do you think Lord Dudley is attempting to poison you, Edward?" Bess queried then, softly.

"My dog," he said breathlessly, winded from all this excited talking he was doing. "My dog could smell the poison in my black-berries."

Both ladies turned to look at Pet, who was sitting on her haunches across the room. The dog rose to her feet uncertainly.

Mary's nose wrinkled in distaste. "Eddie, please. Now is not the time for jokes."

"I'm not joking," he protested. "I've never been more serious in my life. My dog will tell you. Won't you, Pet?"

He looked pleadingly at Pet.

She cocked her head at him quizzically.

"Come on, Pet. It's all right. Show them," he urged.

They all stared at the dog.

"You think your dog can talk?" Bess said slowly.

"Yes. She's . . ." *An Eðian,* he was about to say, but the word died on his lips. Mary had just been talking about how she wanted to purge Eðians from the country.

Pet whined and lay down on the floor, her brown eyes worried.

Mary shook her head. "Edward," she said even more solemnly than usual. "You're not well." She stood up and went to the table where she'd laid the box. She undid the ribbon and opened it. "Lord Dudley thinks of you as a son, you know. He is devastated by what's happening to you."

Edward fell back, flummoxed. He could not think of anything else to say that would convince them.

"He said you haven't been eating," Mary said, as if this entire outburst of Edward's was forgotten. "So I brought you something."

She reached into the box and lifted up , . . . a blackberry pudding.

"Your favorite," she said brightly.

The sweet smell of the berries filled Edward's nostrils. His stomach clenched. "Haven't you heard anything I've said?" he gasped.

"Now, Eddie, don't be difficult." Mary produced a little silver knife and a china plate and cut him a hefty portion. She sat down next to him and lifted the fork to his mouth.

"Have a bite, Eddie," she said. "For me."

He met her eyes, hers glittering with some dark determination, his glossed by a sheen of tears. In that moment he understood the truth.

Mary was in on it.

"Be a good boy, Eddie." She pushed the fork forward.

"Don't call me Eddie," he returned in a low voice. He gathered his strength and reached up to take the fork. He turned it around slowly, balancing the precarious morsel of pudding. His hand wavered, trembled, but he managed to hold the tines to her lips. "You first, sister."

His heart ached with the betrayal of it. She was his sister. She was a terrible, humorless, traitorous, bloodthirsty, dowdy spinster of a woman, twenty years his elder, but she was still his sister. His own flesh and blood.

Silence.

Mary stared at him. Bess still was standing across the room

like she'd been frozen in place, her expression unreadable.

Mary smiled quickly and took the fork back from Edward, set it on the plate. "I couldn't possibly," she said. "I'm watching my figure."

"You're watching your figure do what?" he asked.

Her eyes closed for a moment. Then she smiled again, tensely. "Oh, Edward, always joking, aren't you?" She stood up and brushed imaginary crumbs from her skirt. "At least your illness hasn't robbed you of your sense of humor."

He wanted to tell her that he'd given the throne to Jane and see if she'd find that so funny. He couldn't imagine that Mary would be in collusion with Lord Dudley if she knew that particular detail of the duke's plan.

But telling Mary about the newly revised line of succession would only put Jane in danger. So instead he said, "The duke will turn on you, too, you know. Just as soon as he's done with me."

She stiffened. "You are confused, brother. You're not thinking clearly. And I am sorry for you." She touched his shoulder like maybe she even meant it. "I am sorry."

He waited for her to leave before he turned his attention to Bess. He'd never seen his other sister's face so pale and drawn. Her freckles stood out against her nose. He remembered a time when he was a child, when she'd let him count her freckles. Twenty-two of them, he thought.

"Do you think I'm confused, too, Bess?" he asked.

She shook her head almost imperceptibly. Her gray eyes were

fierce and shining. They were her father's eyes. His eyes.

She walked over to place her gift for him on the bedside table, then leaned down to kiss his cheek.

"I believe you," she whispered against his ear. "I will help you. Trust me, Edward."

"Rest, brother," she said more loudly, as if there was someone else in the room.

After she'd gone, he opened her present. It was a smaller box than Mary's, but inside he found a jar of honey-soaked apricots and a flask of cool water.

Trust me, she'd said.

The day his father died, he and Bess had been sitting together when they'd received the news. Edward was a boy of nine and Elizabeth thirteen, but both of them were keenly aware in that instant that everything had changed. "The king is dead. Long live the king," his uncle Seymour had announced, which meant that Edward was king. He'd been overwhelmed by sorrow and terror, and started to cry.

"I don't want it," he'd said, trembling all over. "I don't want to be king, Bess. I'm not like Father. Don't make me be king."

Elizabeth had turned to him and kissed his hand.

"It's going to be all right," she'd whispered. "Trust me."

Trust me.

Edward ate the apricots and drank the water without a second thought. If Bess was also poisoning him, then he supposed he would happily die. When he was finished he felt more refreshed than he had in weeks, good enough to sit up and examine the rest of Bess's box, where he found a small scrap of parchment with Bess's flowery writing on it. *You're in danger. I'll return tonight.*

And in spite of all the trouble he was in, he felt better. Because there was still someone he could trust.

He woke in the middle of the night to Pet snarling. Before he was even fully awake, rough hands were upon him, forcing his arms up painfully. Hooded men loomed all around his bed. Someone lashed one of his wrists to the bedpost. He kicked and struggled, but to no avail—he had no force behind his blows, no strength.

He did, however, have Pet. She lunged over him with her teeth snapping. He heard a muffled curse, followed by a thump and a yelp as one of the men tossed the dog aside. Then came the noise of a sword leaving its sheath.

They were going to kill Pet.

Edward stopped struggling. "Wait!" he called out. "I relent." He coughed for a minute. He couldn't get air in his wretched lungs. "I relent," he gasped again. "Don't hurt my dog."

Pet whined. One of the men grabbed Pet by the scruff and tied a rope around her neck. Suddenly she surged forward and buried her face in Edward's shoulder.

He put his free arm about her and whispered against her long silky ear. "Don't worry about me, Pet. Find Jane. Tell Jane what's happened."

She whined again, and the man yanked on the end of the rope, dragging her across the floor and then out of the room.

Edward's heart thundered in his ears. He coughed again, into the air because his free hand was now being tied to the other bedpost. A man with a candle stepped toward the bed. Boubou. Edward glanced around at the other figures surrounding him.

"Honestly," he managed to rasp. "You need three armed men to subdue me? I'm already dying."

The man who was tying up his wrist grunted and jerked the rope tight.

"Oh," Edward said, with sudden clarity. "Because you think I might transform into a lion and devour the lot of you?"

If only he could.

When he was secured, the men melted into the shadows, leaving him alone with Boubou. The old doctor looked tired and gruff, like he was unaccustomed to being awake at this hour, and it irritated him. He set the lantern down and slung a dark satchel from his back, from which he unrolled a set of rather sharp-looking knives.

Edward hardly felt the pain when the doctor cut his arms and drained the blood into a large pewter bowl. He was nearly senseless, hovering just outside some balmy unconsciousness, when the door creaked and through his half-open eyelids Edward thought he saw Lord Dudley's nose. Which in his semi-delirious state struck him as hilarious.

"Excellent," he slurred. "So glad you could join us, John."

"Always so petulant," the duke replied. "Foolish boy."

Now Boubou was holding a goblet to his mouth. Unlike the

tonic they'd given him last time, before he'd revised his will, this one tasted so sweet it made his teeth ache.

Wicked, he thought.

He tried not to swallow, but Boubou held his head back and kept pouring the poison down his throat, unrelenting until he was forced to swallow. The doctor wiped Edward's lips with a napkin.

"So this is it," Edward hardly had the strength to say. "Bravo, Boubou. You've successfully committed regicide."

Boubou's eyes crinkled at the corners. "It was a pleasure serving you, Your Majesty."

Edward laughed. He was floating out of himself. Boubou was untying his hands but he couldn't feel them. He drifted between light and dark. The last thing he remembered before he spun away entirely was the sound of the door closing, and a key turning in the lock.

There was a scratching sound. Once, and then again. Edward sucked in a lungful of air. He was alive. *How* was he alive?

The scratching came again, more insistently.

"Pet?" he called hoarsely.

Now he heard a sharp, bright noise from the direction of the door. The mew of a cat. Which made no sense.

He sat up. The wounds on his arms from the bloodletting throbbed, but his head felt remarkably clear. He threw off the blankets and swung his legs over the side of the bed. Tested his strength.

Maybe he could stand.

He tried. He stumbled to the door and attempted to open it.

Locked.

The meow came again. There was a flicker of light under the doorway.

He swayed and put his hand against the rough oak of the door to steady himself.

"Hello?" he whispered.

"Edward," came a faint, familiar voice on the other side of the door.

"Bess," he breathed.

"I can't stay," she said, so softly he could barely hear her. "They'll come back. They assume you'll be dead by now, but they'll come back to check. They wanted to make it look like you died of 'the Affliction,' but if they find you alive now, Edward . . ."

"Get me out of here."

"I can't. I don't have the key. You have to go out the window."

"Bess, it's a fifty-foot drop."

"You could climb it," she suggested. "When you were a boy you were always such a climber. You were never afraid of heights."

He snorted. Right. Climb down. But carefully, step by deliberate step, he walked to the window and pulled back the drapes. It was morning, the sun just breaching the palace walls. Below him, so far below, the courtyard stretched toward the river. Guards were posted at regular intervals.

No good.

"Bess?" he murmured.

"I'm here."

"I can't climb down. There's got to be another way."

She didn't answer.

He moved back to the door and leaned against it. He felt stronger now, but he was also so tired that he almost couldn't stand.

"I gave you a draught in the apricots to counteract the poison, but it won't last," Bess whispered. "You have to get out, Edward. Then go north. To Gran at Helmsley. She can help you. I'll join you if I can."

"How did you know they were going to come for me tonight?" His knees wobbled, but he fought to stay upright.

"There's no time to explain," she said. "You need to go. Now."

"I would love to," he said. "There's only one problem. I'm currently locked in a tower."

She sighed. "You'll have to climb . . ."

"I'm too weak," he said. "It's too high up."

". . . or you will have to change yourself. You have to find your animal form."

He would have laughed, but he was too shocked at the idea. "My animal form. You're saying I'm an Eðian."

"Your father was an Eðian," she said matter-of-factly.

"Yes. I remember." His hand formed into a fist against the door. "I'm not my father."

"Your mother was an Eðian, too."

His breath caught. "My mother?" He'd only ever seen a

painting of her, fair and golden-haired and smiling a secret smile.

"I saw her change once," Bess told him. "I was a child, but I never forgot. She could turn into a bird, Edward. A beautiful white bird."

He held back a cough. "My mother."

"It's in your blood, brother. Both of your parents were E∂ians, and so are you."

How he wished that were true. But it had never happened. No matter how much he'd wanted it. "How do you know?"

"There's no time," she hissed. "They're coming. Just do it, Edward. Find it inside yourself. I have to go."

There was that flicker again, at the crack in the bottom of the door.

"Bess?" Edward whispered.

No answer.

He heard heavy footsteps at the bottom of the stairs.

"Bollocks," he muttered to himself.

He staggered again to the window. The sky was pink against the horizon, growing brighter with every passing moment. A puff of wind touched his face, lifted his hair, filled his aching lungs with coolness. He closed his eyes.

I could change, he thought.

He wasn't a lion. Deep down, he knew that. He'd always known it.

The footsteps were drawing closer.

He had a sudden thought. He crossed quickly to the bedside

table, took out a quill and ink, and scrawled a message on the back of Jane's letter.

She would think he was dead.

Maybe he would be.

Behind him, a key scraped into the lock.

He turned to the window.

This time, they would kill him. They would make sure of it.

He had to go.

He let his fur robe slip from his shoulders and onto the floor. He stepped up onto the windowsill.

Find it inside yourself, Bess had said.

He closed his eyes again. He thought of all the times he and Jane had tried to change themselves, to find the animal inside, and how it had never worked.

He thought of his mother, a beautiful white bird. His mother, whom he had no memory of. But perhaps she'd left him a gift in his blood.

Perhaps he could be a bird.

The door crashed open, but he didn't hear it. He didn't see Dudley burst into the room. He didn't hear the duke's shout.

Because he was falling.

And then he was flying.

And then the wind lifted him, filling his wings, and he left the palace behind.

Jane ELEVEN

Jane was alone. At least, as she awakened the morning after her rather eventful night with Gifford, she didn't hear the sounds of his breathing. Horse breathing or otherwise.

She checked over the side of the bed to find his blanket nest empty. He must have crept out just before dawn.

She leaned back on the pillows and closed her eyes, thinking about the adventure they'd shared, the gratitude they'd witnessed, and the laughter that had come from both of them. He'd made her laugh. She'd made him laugh. And the cutting little remarks that had defined their relationship thus far had possessed an almost friendly quality.

A thrum of pounding hooves sounded outside. Her heart thundered in response, anxious. Last night had been so — She searched for just the right word. Not magical. Not pleasant.

Satisfying. They'd done something. They'd helped those people. But now it was light out and Gifford was a horse once again. The magic (maybe it had been a little bit magical) of last night was over, burned away with the sun's heat.

Jane rolled out of bed and found her trunks had been unpacked. Her dresses hung in wardrobes, all perfectly arranged. For a moment, she considered calling in a maid to help put her together, but she changed her mind and chose a simple dress to wear today. When she was presentable, she took a book—*The Formation of Mountains and the Balance Achieved in Valleys: a Theory of Eðian Magic in the Mundane World*—and a small sack of breakfast foods outside.

Gifford was running in the meadow, head tossed back and mane streaming in the wind. His tail was flagged, dark and glossy in the early summer day. In motion, he was a creature of complete beauty: his legs stretching out before and behind him, lifting him, carrying him across the grassy land.

As Jane approached a broad-trunked apple tree, Gifford switched directions and trotted toward her, snorting. She bent to place her book and breakfast on a large, protruding root, and when she straightened, Gifford stood a few feet away, watching her with those dark horse eyes.

"Good morning." She held out a hand and approached him.

He sniffed, soft whiskers brushing her palm, and allowed her to pet his smooth, flat cheek. It was easier to touch him when he was a horse. As a horse, he, one, couldn't talk back, and two, seemed less human and therefore was less intimidating. Which made her preferring him like this more awkward, considering they were married, but having a preference at all seemed like a step in the right direction.

"There's something I wanted to tell you."

He adjusted so that she rubbed between his ears, then gave a little shake as if instructing her to scratch.

She obliged. "I was thinking about the Eðian attack last night, and your actions. Or, rather, what I perceived as your inactions."

Gifford angled his head so she'd scratch at the base of one ear. Was he even listening? Could he really listen, in this form?

That made it easier to keep going.

"When I saw those people in trouble, I wanted to help them. I had no idea what I'd do, though. I couldn't have fought off the Pack. I couldn't have saved their cow. And if I'd gone in all high-born, as you put it, they might have been offended. I hadn't even considered that, but you did.

"I thought you were trying to prevent me from taking action, but the truth was that you were protecting me from myself. You prevented me from climbing down rocks I had no business try-ing to climb, and prevented me from confronting Eðians I had no power to stop."

Gifford didn't appear to be listening. Finished with the ear scratching, he'd wandered toward her breakfast and was nosing through the bag.

Jane sighed. "What I'm trying to say is that I appreciate what you did, but don't expect me to ever say it again. I hope you're paying attention."

The stallion snorted in triumph as he pulled an apple from the bag, the red fruit pinned between his teeth. He tossed it into the air, caught it, and gobbled the whole thing down within seconds.

"I was going to eat that," she said, not that Gifford even bothered to look ashamed. She shooed him away—"Go run"—and sat down on the tree root to read and eat her breakfast, but instead, Gifford lowered himself to lie next to her, his front legs tucked to one side. He watched while she propped the book on her knees and started to read, carefully keeping crumbs away.

She was halfway through *The Formation of Mountains and the Balance Achieved in Valleys: a Theory of Eðian Magic in the Mundane World* when Gifford nipped at the corner of the page she was turning.

"No chewing the books," she reminded him, and offered him another apple, which he inhaled immediately. But when she dropped her face to read again, he nudged the book with his nose and stared at her. She glanced up. "What? Use your words."

He blinked and nudged the book again.

"You want me to . . . read to you?"

He nudged the book.

Warmth bloomed in her chest. "All right. But pay attention. I won't reread something if you miss it."

His ears flicked back at a squawking bird on the far side of the meadow, but faced her again when she began reading aloud. After a while, he rested his chin on the root next to her, and while she held the pages open with one hand, she placed her other hand on his nose, stroking the soft fur every so often.

A few days passed in this manner, with Jane reading to Gifford while the sun was up, and the two of them spiriting food and medicine to nearby villages at night. If the house staff noticed that the lord and lady appeared to be going through the food stores unusually quickly, they never complained.

In the parlor, Jane finished reading the last pages of *The Jewels of the World: Man-made Marvels and How They Were Built* just as the sun touched the horizon. She watched the orange and red burn across the sky, shining through the large windows. Outside, Gifford-the-horse stopped running as his own light overtook him, and the silhouette of a horse became the silhouette of a man. As soon as he regained a sense of his humanity, he'd come inside for dinner/breakfast. Anticipation stirred deep in her stomach.

She placed her book on the shelf and buzzed around the parlor lighting candles for a few minutes, trying to appear busy.

Twilight had deepened when at last the door opened and Gifford stepped inside, clad in the clothes she'd laid out for him. His hair was combed and tied in a tail again, and there was the usual bounce to his step, as though running for half the day didn't affect him whatsoever. "Good evening, my lady. How many books did you read today? Anything about horses?"

"You have hay in your hair."

He smoothed his hand over his hair before he caught her smile. "No horse jokes."

"Never! But I wanted to ask: are you catching a chill? You sound hoarse."

Gifford snorted and shut the parlor door behind him. "And you look flushed. I hope you're not burning from the sun."

"If I didn't spend every day reading to a horse whose only thoughts were for the apples I provide—"

"I never asked you to climb the tree to fetch more apples. And while we're on the subject, I am a horse, not a stool."

"Will you add that to the rules?"

"And risk another rule regarding your books? I think not." He came toward her, subtly checking his ponytail for hay. "My lady, there's something I wish to discuss."

His tone had changed, the ever-present playfulness shifting into something more serious. It was the same tone he'd used when he'd described his feelings on being an Eðian and how he believed the scales needed "to be righted in the direction of equality" for Eðians and Verities alike.

"All right." Truly, he'd been more handsome than ever during his speech that night. It had been the first time she'd ever thought there might be more to his mind than women, ale, and the wind in his mane.

"I wasn't sure whether to tell you." He closed his eyes and turned his face away from the candle she'd just lit. "It seemed like it might be easier for you to assume I hadn't the wits to comprehend what you were saying, but I've given this a lot of careful thought and I've decided I wanted you to know."

Jane gazed up at him.

"The other day when you came out to the meadow and told me that you appreciate what I did during the Eðian attack, I heard. I understood."

So he'd gone off in his horsey-like behavior simply to put her at ease. How unexpectedly kind of him.

"But I also wanted you to know that what you tried to do—that was very honorable, if ill-advised. I'd been so busy studying the Pack I'd hardly thought to do something, having already decided there was nothing I could do. And while I will never regret preventing you from being foolishly brave, I do regret that I had not been willing to even try."

Jane said nothing. The words were nice, but this was a man accustomed to wooing women. He was adept at appealing to whatever side of them would move him closer to the bed. Married or not, Jane refused to be so easily swayed. She needed proof.

Gifford's eyes were still closed, his face still in shadow. She touched his jaw and turned him until he looked at her. He was earnest and serious.

"As much as it pains me for you to know yet another of my flaws," he said, "I wanted you to know that I heard every word you said that day, and I've heard every word since. Sitting under the tree with you, listening to you read, has become one of the best parts of my day."

"Second only to apples?"

The tension in his shoulders relaxed. "I know there is more to you than your apples."

Jane blushed and said, "Sharing my books with you has been one of the best parts of my days here, as well."

His gaze was steady on her, and though they stood very close together, neither of them moved.

Would he kiss her? Part of her hoped he would. A big part, maybe. Multiple parts: her butterfly-filled stomach, her thudding heart, and her lips, which remembered the gentle breath of a kiss during their wedding. Not meant to be sweet then, just swift, but now proof that he was capable of such tenderness.

She shifted toward him. "G . . ."

"My lady?" He touched her arm, and if he was surprised about her use of his preferred address, he didn't show it. There was a hopeful note in the way he said, "Jane?"

A knock sounded, and a maid entered without waiting for permission. Jane and G jumped apart as if they'd been caught in a compromising position. Which they had, almost, but they were married so it was allowed.

Jane's heart pounded and she couldn't seem to catch her breath, though G's recovery appeared much smoother. Perhaps he was more used to being discovered like this—or worse.

"Yes?" Gifford's voice was rough; maybe he wasn't as recovered as he appeared. "What is the meaning of this?"

The maid stepped aside to admit two burly men in royal guard uniforms. "Lady Jane must return to London immediately," it was Unibrow Guard, the same man who'd prevented her from seeing Edward the day she left London.

Jane went cold. No good news came in the middle of the night. "What is wrong?"

"We're not at liberty to say, my lady, but you must come with us. Your belongings will follow. A carriage is waiting."

"Perhaps you should tell her what it is you want from her first," said G, stepping closer to Jane. "There's no need to keep her in suspense."

"I'm afraid we're under orders to do nothing but deliver Lady Jane straight to the Tower of London."

"By whose orders?" G pressed.

"Your father's." The guard turned to the maid. "Pack their belongings and send along everything later tonight. Ensure the lord and lady have something to eat for the journey. . . ."

Jane's mind whirred as the guards continued giving orders and she was taken from the house. Why would she be needed at the Tower? Was Edward there? Had he sent for her? Had his illness grown worse?

Before she realized, she'd been packed into the carriage, with a book shoved into her hands. G sat beside her murmuring something that might have been comforting, but all she could think of was Edward: how pale he'd looked at the wedding, the hollows under his eyes, and even the way he'd stopped wearing the daily attire befitting a king.

Unibrow Guard sat in the carriage with Jane, the only one who seemed to know how to speak, though nothing he said was particularly useful for assuaging her anxiety. It was only as the carriage burst into motion that Jane noticed the rest of the guards: almost a score of men on horseback riding alongside her and Gifford as they bounced along the road. They were armed with swords, and all wore the Dudley crest.

"Please," she tried again. "What is the reason for this?"

"You'll find out as soon as we arrive."

This man was a fortress.

She looked over at G from the corner of her eye. His jaw was set, and he fidgeted with his hands in his lap.

Guilt or worry?

Gifford couldn't have anticipated this, could he? Unless he'd planned something with his father ahead of time, but to what end? While Lord Dudley didn't seem to like Jane very much, there could be no benefit to cutting short the honeymoon.

Perhaps she was suspicious of him simply because she didn't like his nose.

And suspicious of G because she *did* like his nose.

Perhaps Edward had recovered and he wanted to speak to her directly about her letter. Perhaps he was summoning her in order to apologize. Just because no one had ever recovered from "the Affliction" didn't mean he couldn't be the first.

Jane lowered her eyes to the book in her hands. *Famous Steeds of England in the Fourteenth Century.*

"You looked like you needed a book," G said. "It was on top of the pile."

"Thank you." But the words were automatic, and Jane spent most of the ride staring out the window as a knot of worry tightened in her stomach.

It was late when they arrived in the outskirts of London, so a certain stillness of sleeping was to be expected. But tonight, either because of her mysterious summons or because there was truly something off about the city, there was a subtle almost-paralysis in the streets. As if everything were a painting. Even the wind had died.

Their carriage clattered unnaturally loudly down the road. A few people appeared in doorways, staring.

The Tower of London, too, held that stillness when they arrived. That feeling of a held breath.

(We'd like to take this opportunity to point out that, in spite of the name, the Tower of London is actually a castle with many towers. The White Tower, Bloody Tower, the Flint Tower . . . It's all very impressive.)

There were few reasons that might explain why Jane was being taken to the tower in the middle of the night, and none of them were good.

"This is all so ominous," G muttered as the carriage jerked to a halt while the first portcullis was raised. One of the horses whinnied and tossed its head. "My friend up there agrees."

They started moving again, now crossing the bridge over the

moat. There was a foul odor rising from that cesspool, but Jane hardly cared, and didn't even bother to cover her nose, or tell Gifford the impressive—if disgusting—history of the Tower of London moat.

When the second portcullis was raised, they moved through the outer ward, under another portcullis (there were a *lot* of portcullises, Jane observed somewhere in the back of her mind), and then made their way toward the majestic White Tower.

The carriage stopped right before the door to the keep. Jane glanced across the Tower Green, toward the chapel. Torches burned on walls, but there was no movement, save the rustling of raven wings above. "Please just tell me what this is about," she said.

But her guard only took her book and left it on the seat. She was ushered into a great hall where a crowd of council members waited, and though everyone turned to look at her when she entered, flanked by her husband and a troop of guards, hardly anyone spoke.

Jane looked to the throne for Edward, but her cousin wasn't there. "What is all this?" she asked again. "Why was I brought here? Where is Edward?"

Lord Dudley strode forward, his nose an arrow that pointed straight at her. "Lady Jane. I'm relieved you could return so quickly."

It wasn't as if she'd been given a choice.

"There is news."

Obviously.

Jane glanced at G, whose face had grown impassive at his father's appearance. "Please," Jane said at last. "Tell me."

Lord Dudley's voice was somber, but it sounded across the throne room like a gong. "King Edward the Sixth is dead. Long live Queen Jane."

TWELVE
Gifford

The words "Queen Jane" rang in G's ears, but the more pressing matter was the sudden and extreme paleness of his wife's face. He felt that familiar urge to protect her, the one that had manifested during the Pack attack.

"Edward is dead?" Jane said, her voice almost inaudible.

Oh right, G thought. The king's death should've been the most pressing issue. It was only Jane's close relationship to the king that stopped him from saying, *Yes, my lady, but did you hear the second part? About the whole queen thing?*

Lord Dudley nodded solemnly. "He succumbed to 'the Affliction' this morning."

Jane's gaze went vacant. She stared at nothing for a long moment. G edged toward her, and then back, not sure what to do.

Was she going to faint? Or would she consider that a very cliché thing for a woman to do? Desperate to console her, he almost considered shouting, *Quick, someone, get her a book! Any book!* But he wasn't sure if she was the stubborn Jane of the "I have servants for that" variety, or the Jane he'd almost kissed earlier, and he didn't want to be humiliated in court by having his attempts to help his wife rebuked.

Especially if she was to be queen.

A flurry of activity broke out at one end of the throne room as Jane's mother swept in.

"Darling Jane," she said, swooping over to her daughter, taking her in her arms. "I am so sorry about your dearest friend and cousin, the king."

She spoke louder than necessary, but G suspected she wanted everyone to hear.

Jane limply returned her mother's embrace, and then all at once seemed to notice that the throne room was bursting with people and every single one of their faces was focused on her.

"I think I'd like to be excused for a moment," she said, a little louder and to no one in particular. "I'm sure the rest of you need time to mourn as well."

G glanced at Lord Dudley, who seemed surprised by Jane's declaration.

"Um . . . I'm sorry, my lady, but you need to stay for the coronation," the duke said.

"Oh?" Jane said. "Is the new king to be crowned immediately?"

Lord Dudley frowned. "No. A new queen."

"Ah," she said. "Princess Mary?"

"No. It is you, my lady." Lord Dudley bowed in her direction.

Jane turned to her left, then to her right, seeming to search for the lady to whom he was referring.

And then recognition dawned upon her face.

Her mouth opened slightly. "But . . . but . . . I don't want to be queen. It's not my right. Mary is the rightful heir."

A squire stepped forward and unrolled a scroll of paper. "By royal decree, from His Majesty King Edward. A Revised Line of Succession. 'Upon the event of my death, I bequeath my kingdom and the entitlements and protections thereof, to the Lady Jane Grey and the male heirs who follow her.'"

Lord Dudley raised an elbow. "May I escort you to the throne so we can commence with the coronation?"

"So quickly?" She stepped back.

"We need a queen. Now, my lady," Lord Dudley said.

Jane's mother bowed deeply before her. G could tell from Jane's face that this act was perhaps the most disturbing gesture of support she could have received. Her brows knitted together, her hands stayed firmly at her side, and she gazed pleadingly at G. He was pretty sure if she could turn into a Brown Carpathian bull she would stampede out of the castle and never return.

Horse, she mouthed. He then realized she wanted him to become a horse, and carry her far away. G wished he had the ability to comply.

Here was his lady, shaking ever so minutely under the heavy stares of every member of court. This was the Jane with the brilliant red hair and radiant face. The one who didn't pretend everything was under her control. The one who was most accustomed to a book staring back at her, not a person. Not a roomful of people. The one who, realizing what a formidable task ruling a country was, would never lunge for the crown when given the chance.

This was his lady. His wife. And he would take care of her.

G stepped forward, took her hand, and draped it over his arm. They stood, nose to nose, for a very long moment, the hum of murmurs in the throne room dimming to near silence.

"You can do this," G whispered.

Her voice was ragged. "I can't."

He shrugged. "Okay, we'll tell them thank you so much for the very kind offer of running the country, but no thank you. I have no desire to honor my cousin, the king's, wishes. Now where are my damn books?"

Jane cracked the tiniest of smiles. "That sounds about right."

"Or, perhaps, as an alternative, and merely a suggestion"—G ran his fingers lightly over her knuckles—"you could accept the throne, and do everything you said you would do if you ever ran the country."

She looked up. He took her face in his hands.

"Remember the people we helped? Now you could help an entire kingdom, from giving the highest born a new perspective and lending aid to the lowest peasants. We could help them, together. I'll be right here with you. Except when . . . I have to be outside. But I'm with you, Jane."

"Is it possible?" Jane said. "That we could help others and rule?"

G gave her a look of eternal optimism. "Let's not forget the free fountain of never-ending ale."

Jane threw her arms around G, taking him and the entire court by surprise. The more conservative ladies in the throne room daintily held lace handkerchiefs to their bright cheeks. The servants in attendance gave one another knowing looks, as though to say, *With such a forward lady, no wonder there were shredded clothes in the wedding bedchamber.*

Lord Dudley, on the other hand, beamed as if the couple were producing a male heir right then and there.

A chill went down G's spine at the sight of his father's smile. His father never smiled. Which made G wonder just what the duke was up to.

Lord Dudley led Jane to the throne, but she would not let go of G's hand. In fact, she squeezed his fingers until he winced, increasing the pressure as the Archbishop of Canterbury lowered the crown onto her head. She let go only to hold the scepter and the orb, the final symbols of the monarchy.

The hand with the orb shook, and Jane's eyes narrowed enough that G thought she might chuck the ball toward Lord Dudley's eagle nose. He had to admit it provided a very tempting target. But she refrained, and placed the orb and scepter back on the pillow.

"Long live Queen Jane!" Lord Dudley announced.

"Long live the queen!" the members of court replied.

And it was over. Just like that. Hours ago, they were alone in their country house, possibly about to kiss, and now Jane was queen. Although G had missed the last few years of court, and therefore any sort of changes to royal protocol, he distinctly remembered the coronation of King Edward. There'd been three days of celebrations in anticipation of the event, and the coronation itself had lasted hours. And it had taken place in the opulent Westminster Cathedral, not this less formal throne room. King Edward had been nine at the time, and seemed barely able to stand under the weight of the crown and the royal robes.

But Jane's coronation had lasted ten minutes. There were no street-side celebrations to welcome the new queen. None of the pomp and splendor that should accompany a coronation. Even now, as G glanced around the throne room, the expressions on faces ranged from forced smiles to worried glances, excepting the mother of the queen and G's own still strangely beaming father.

Lord Dudley stood by the throne, assuming a position of power a little prematurely, by G's assessment. A line had formed to receive the queen, and vow allegiance to her, but G was no longer watching the line. Instead, movement at the entrance caught his attention. A messenger entered the room—cautiously, as all messengers did after the reign of the Lion King.

When Lord Dudley saw the messenger, he casually stepped

away from the throne and met the boy, who handed over a sealed envelope. G tilted his head to get a better view around a particularly portly lady-in-waiting. Lord Dudley broke the seal, but not before G noticed a royal imprint in the red wax that sealed the letter.

As the duke read the parchment, he frowned and then frowned deeper. He refolded the letter, stowed it in his pocket, and hastened away.

No one else took note of the transaction. The once uncertain atmosphere around Jane had turned into excitement for the new Queen of England.

G leaned down to whisper in Jane's ear. "Your Majesty."

Her eyes flashed. "Don't you dare 'Your Majesty' me."

He smiled. "My lady, please excuse me for a moment."

Worry sparked in Jane's eyes, but she nodded. "Hurry back."

G quickly and quietly followed his father to a far corner of the room. Lord Dudley pulled his most trusted advisor inside a small alcove. He produced the envelope and handed it over. The advisor read the contents, frowned, and dropped the hand holding the letter to his side.

"It is as I feared," Lord Dudley said. "Despite our best efforts, word of Jane's ascension has reached Mary before our men could apprehend her. Someone must have sent warning."

G ducked a little farther behind a pillar.

"Where is she?" his advisor asked.

"They do not know. She has most probably fled to Kenninghall. But more importantly, she refuses to accept Jane as rightful queen."

G felt his heart beating through his ribs at this news. But what his father said next was even more frightening.

"Find her. Arrest her. Do it before nightfall tomorrow. If we fail, Mary could retain the backing of the army. And then we will lose the throne."

G's skin went cold as the advisor rushed toward the exit, presumably to execute Lord Dudley's orders. How had Mary not known about the revised order of succession? Maybe the king had not gone so far as to consult with his sisters, but surely he'd at least told them about his wishes before his death. Hadn't he?

G watched as his father pulled down on the ends of his jacket and straightened his back, all the while shifting his face from a tense expression to one of practiced optimistic decorum. G strode over to him.

"Father," he said.

Lord Dudley startled but recovered quickly. "Gifford, you should be attending to the queen."

"Father, I saw the messenger."

The duke made a swatting motion with his hand. "Oh, that was nothing. A trifle about your new living quarters. So many things to arrange."

G took a deep breath, hesitant to reveal his eavesdropping, but he had to know more. "I heard what you said to your advisor. About Mary."

Lord Dudley took hold of G's arm and yanked him behind one of the ornate royal banners hanging from the ceiling.

"Be careful, son. Do not speak of such things. They are not your concern."

"If they are a threat to my wife, they are very much my concern," G said, trying hard to keep from raising his voice.

"I beg to differ. A queen and her consort do not need to be informed of every little detail of running a kingdom. That's why I have a job."

"Little detail? I heard you say—" G spoke too loudly and his father cut him off with a scathing glance.

"I heard you say," G continued quietly, "that you . . . that we could lose the throne if Mary is not captured."

The duke placed a heavy hand on G's shoulder and threw his nose to the air as he inhaled sharply. G was surprised he didn't inhale half the court along the way.

"Son, I am only going to explain this once. Your wife is queen. The late King Edward provided for this succession, and received the ratifying signatures from all thirty-one members of the Privy Council. You are the queen's consort, and very soon you will make a powerful king."

G? As king?

Well, that was a terrifying idea, but he and Jane had talked at length about what they'd do if they ruled the country. Together, they could make a difference. Besides, he'd look great in a crown.

"Still, you have much to learn," G's father went on. "Leave these matters to me. Trust me, I will not allow a foot-stomping illegitimate hag to get in my way!"

"You mean, to get in the queen's way," G said slowly. "Right, Father? The queen's way?"

"Yes, yes, the queen's way," Lord Dudley said dismissively.

"But Mary is rather popular among the people despite being a bit duddy. If she rallies support—"

G's father put a hand up. "Gifford, I have put forth great effort to secure your future, and the future of our country. I have done things you would never be brave enough to do. Focus on becoming king. Until then, keep your expert opinions limited to things you understand. Like apples."

With that, his father ducked out from behind the banner, leaving G with that fallen expression that can only come from the harsh rebuke of a father. He stepped out from the chapel. When Jane saw him, she didn't smile. Maybe his father was right. Until he was crowned king, he shouldn't worry about things that didn't concern him.

THIRTEEN

Edward

The king (the actual king, we mean), through no particular fault of his own, was lost.

During the first few hours in his newly acquired Eðian form, he'd been caught up in what he could only describe as a kind of beautiful bird joy—the sweet euphoria of flight, of riding the wind, testing the strength of his wings, encompassed in the soundless serenity of the world as seen from so high above. He'd lost himself in how good it felt to no longer be . . . well, dying.

Edward didn't know this at the time, because he had no way of looking at himself and assessing what kind of species of bird he actually was, but he had transformed into a kestrel, which is, for those readers who are not bird-enthusiasts, a small falcon—*Falco tinnunculus*—with very handsome brown-speckled feathers.

Edward simply knew that he had wings and a beak and two legs that ended in talons, which made him some kind of bird. And he knew that up there, against the sky, he was free in a way that he had never been free before.

But after a while—who knows how long, really, as kestrels aren't known for their ability to keep track of time—he began to have a nagging human thought in the back of his brain, and it was this:

I should be doing something.

Which led to: *I should be going somewhere.*

He strained to remember more. *It's not somewhere that I should be going to, so much as someone,* he thought. *Someone who will help me.*

Then he remembered that he was not just a bird, but a king, and someone had attempted to assassinate him and steal his throne, and he had a sister named Bess who had told him —what had she told him? That his mother had also been a bird, a beautiful white bird, and wasn't it divine to be a bird, to rule the air, to dive and lift so, to hover, and then the bird joy had him again.

Some time later he thought, *No, that wasn't all Bess told me. She said to go to Gran*—his grandmother—although he hadn't seen the old lady in years.

At Helmsley. Which was an abandoned, half-fallen-down old castle.

North, somewhere.

Now which way was north?

As a sixteen-year-old human boy, Edward had never possessed

the keenest sense of direction, since most of the time when he wished to travel to a place he was taken by carriage and did none of the driving. As an only-a-few-hours-old bird, he didn't know north, either. He knew there was a river in one direction, and a series of low hills in another direction, an expanse of green field below him, and in that field he somehow knew there was a little brown field mouse, just coming out of its hole. Without consulting him at all, his body plummeted toward the defenseless creature, wings tucking in, talons reaching, until Edward-the-bird struck the mouse with tremendous force and snatched it from the face of the earth. The poor thing gave a rather awful shriek, which was understandable, and then went quiet. Edward-the-bird flapped off to a nearby tree branch, still clutching the mouse, and then, to Edward-the-boy's horror . . . he ate it, bones and fur and all.

Edward stayed in the tree for a while, disgusted with himself on the one hand, and on the other wanting to go out and find another delicious mouse, or perhaps a tasty garter snake. A growing bird has to eat. But he needed to get control of these bird impulses, he decided. He needed to get moving. The sun was going down. Hadn't it just been morning?

North. I need to find my way north, he told himself sternly.

Which way was north, again?

The sun goes down in the west, he recalled vaguely. He subsequently pointed himself toward what would be, by extension, north. But once he was in the air, it was only a few minutes before the wind charmed him again, and the bird joy overtook him, and when he came back to himself more hours had passed and it was dark and there was no way to know which direction he'd been flying in, and which way he should go.

So, as we said before, the king was lost.

For a while he followed a carriage that was making its way slowly down a road. The carriage must be carrying someone important, he concluded, because there were mounted guards riding on all sides of it. Then he figured that someone with so many men—perhaps twenty—could be heading toward London, and that was the last place he wanted to go, so he turned around and flew in the opposite direction.

The road led him to a shabby-looking village. At the edge of the small cluster of buildings there was a large oak tree, and he settled into the upper branches and looked around. His eyesight, he found, was quite marvelous in the dark.

The village was comprised of a scattering of cottages with thatched roofs, and a smoke-bellowing building that must be the blacksmith, a small stable, and a large ramshackle wooden building in the center that seemed to loom over all the others, with lit windows and a sign over its door with a horse head carved into it. He could hear bawdy music from inside, and men laughing and talking loudly. An inn.

He could become human again, and go inside. People would surely recognize him—after all, his face was on their coins. His subjects loved him, didn't they? He was their beloved king, deigned by God to be their ruler. That was what he'd always been told.

But how did one return from bird to human, exactly? There were no magic words that he was aware of, no series of gestures, no spells to transform him. He wasn't entirely sure how he'd managed to go from human to bird, before. He'd simply jumped from the window and wished for wings and hoped he wouldn't die.

He glanced at the inn again. In an inn, there'd be food. Real food, not mice. And dinner rolls. And tall glasses of ale. All of which would almost certainly not be poisoned.

There'd be stew—maybe rabbit stew, so tender it almost melted in your mouth, with onion and a bit of carrot and potato, something that would warm his empty belly, at last.

There might even be blackberries.

Edward fell out of the tree. Since he was in the highest branches, his crash down made a spectacular amount of noise, branches breaking and Edward cursing and then thumping hard onto the ground. He landed on his left ankle all wrong, which alerted him to the fact that he had ankles again. He had done it somehow. He had wished to be a human eating human food, and here he was.

The door to the nearest cottage was flung open, and a large, red-faced woman wearing an apron stepped out. She was holding a rolling pin. From behind her wafted the smell of baking bread, which instantly made Edward's stomach grumble and his mouth began to water.

Lord, he was hungry.

He struggled to his feet. His ankle hurt so much his eyes watered.

"Madam," he wheezed.

The woman looked him up and down, which is when Edward realized a second important bit of news about himself.

He was, apparently, naked.

Edward tried to respond to this humiliating situation in as kingly a way as possible. Kings didn't cower down holding their hands in front of their private parts like simpletons. He stood up straight. Tried to look her in the eye.

"Er . . . madam, I know this looks . . . less than ideal, but I can explain. I'm—"

"Pervert!" she screamed.

"No, no, you've got it all wrong."

"You're one of those filthy Eðians, aren't you?" she yelled, her face growing even redder in hue.

Or maybe she didn't have it all wrong.

"This was a decent village, you know, before your kind came around spoiling it. Thieves and murderers, the lot of you. Like those dogs that watch me get dressed through the window and then run away. Perverts!"

"No, I can assure you, I never—"

The woman's mouth opened and she brandished the rolling pin over her head like a Highland warrior. "PERVERRRRRRRT!" she screamed, and then she ran at him, clubbing him wherever she could reach.

Edward tried to run. His ankle didn't cooperate, and he was out of breath within a few steps, so he didn't get away as quickly as he would have liked, but the woman wasn't in the best of shape, herself. After she'd beat him about the head with her rolling pin a few times, she seemed satisfied to fall back, screaming "Pervert!" after him as Edward stumbled on nakedly through the night.

He tried to steal some clothes that were hanging to dry outside of a farmer's house, farther down the road, but the farmer had a dog, who wound up giving him a nasty bite on his right leg—the uninjured one, of course. Finally he ended up at another farm in the hayloft of a large barn, hiding under a horse blanket in a pile of prickly hay.

I'm better off as a bird, he thought miserably. He tried to turn himself back—to imagine himself with wings again, but nothing happened. The hay made him sneeze, and then cough, and then cough some more. The poison was still inside of him, working its evil. He was so weak. And now his ankle throbbed. His calf burned from where the dog had bit him. There was a goose egg rising near his temple where the woman had beaned him with the blasted rolling pin, and bruises forming up and down his thin, shivering arms, which bore scabbing cuts from Master Boubou's bloodletting.

Plus he was cold. And hungry. And horribly, horribly lost.

He buried his face in the blanket and blinked back bitter tears. What he wouldn't give for his dog right now, her warmth and her protection, even though the thought of Pet as a girl continued to unsettle him. Now Pet was lost to him, too. Everything was lost. Jane. Bess. His crown. The kingdom.

What was he going to do?

Then, because he was exhausted on top of being poisoned and injured and starving, the king—or we suppose that Edward was technically no longer the king at this point, because the carriage he'd seen earlier had contained Jane and Gifford on their way to the castle, and Jane had, only moments before, been crowned the official Queen of England—the boy who had been king, then, dropped off into a fitful sleep.

He woke up with a lantern burning bright next to his head, and a knife at his throat. Because this was the kind of night he was having.

"Hello," said the owner of the knife.

A girl.

A girl about his age—no older than eighteen, surely, although it was hard to tell in this light—a girl with startling green eyes.

He didn't dare to move. Because knife.

"Well," she said after a long moment, "what do you have to say for yourself, then?"

Only Edward didn't understand what she said, because what he heard was, "Wull, whadja hev to see fer yeself, thun?"

"You're Scottish," he murmured. "Am I in Scotland?"

She snorted.

"I'll take that as a no," he said.

The green eyes narrowed. The knife didn't leave his throat.

"Who are you?" she demanded, and he caught her meaning this time. "What are you doing here?"

He didn't know how to answer her questions. If he told her who he really was, chances were that a) she wouldn't believe him, and she'd cut his throat, or b) she'd believe him, and because he was the ruler of England and she was Scottish and this was the year 1553, she'd get even more pleasure out of cutting his throat. Neither option ended well for him.

She was looking at him expectantly, and the knife against his neck was cold and decidedly unpleasant, so he decided he'd better start talking, and he'd better make it good.

"My name's Dennis," he burst out.

"Dennis," she repeated. Still with the knife. "Is that your first or last name?"

"I'm an apprentice for the blacksmith in the village," he said quickly, to cover that he didn't actually know whether Dennis was his first or last name. "And I was set upon by thieves on the road."

At this, the girl's mouth turned up in a charming—or Edward would have found it charming, if she hadn't been threatening his life at the moment—little smile. She was pretty, and the green eyes were the least of it. A riot of headstrong black curls cascaded all around her face, which was pale and heart shaped with a delicate, pointed chin and a small red mouth.

"You're a poor liar, is what you are." With the hand not holding the knife she suddenly pulled back the horse blanket that was covering him and gave him a quick once over, neck to toes and everything in between.

Edward was too shocked to protest.

"Just checking to make sure you didn't have a sword under there," she said with a smirk. "But I don't see anything particularly dangerous." She removed the knife from his neck and sat back. "Poor wee thing. You're a bit of a mess, aren't you?"

Edward grabbed the blanket back from her and pulled it to his chest. He wasn't sure what she could be referring to as a poor wee thing. Certainly no part of him. His face was hot as a branding iron. "I was set upon by thieves, as I told you," he stammered finally. "They took everything."

"Oh, wearing fine silks, were you? Poppycock. Who are you, really?" She grabbed his hand and turned it over in hers. "Because you don't have the hands of a blacksmith, that's sure."

He jerked his hand away and rose unsteadily to his feet, still clutching the unwieldy blanket around him. The girl stood up, too, and brushed hay off her trousers. She was wearing *trousers*, he realized. Black trousers and a white tunic and a black cloak, with black boots that came nearly to her knees. He'd never seen a woman in trousers before. It was improper. And unnerving. And surprisingly attractive.

"Who are you?" he fired back. "Because I don't think you're the farmer's daughter."

The green eyes flashed, but she smiled again. "Do you know what I think?"

He couldn't begin to guess.

"I think you're an Eðian on the run," she said. "And when it started raining you ran in here for shelter, in your animal form, of course, so now you're stuck here without a stitch of clothes." She *tsk*ed her tongue sympathetically. "So what animal form do you take?"

"It's raining now?" he said, and then he became aware of the pounding of water against the roof. Because, again, this was the kind of night he was having.

"Are you part of the Pack?" she asked. "You seem a bit green for that."

He was about to say something like he didn't know what she was talking about with the Pack, and of course he wasn't an Eðian. But before he could get this out, the girl's head cocked slightly to one side, listening, and then she snuffed the lantern. The hayloft was plunged into inky blackness.

"Wha—" he started, but she stepped close and put a finger to his lips to quiet him, and he lost his train of thought.

Below them, the barn door opened. A man bearing a lantern shuffled in. He spent a few minutes feeding the animals, all the while grumbling about the rain. The entire time Edward and the girl stood frozen in the hayloft, a breath away from each other, her finger still against his lips.

Even in the dark, her eyes were green. Like the emeralds in the crown jewels.

He was holding his breath. He wanted to kiss her, he realized, which was ludicrous. She'd been holding a knife at his throat moments ago. She was a stranger. She was a woman who wore pants. She couldn't be trusted.

Still, there she was, her finger against his lips, making him think of putting his lips on her lips. And when his gaze dropped from her eyes to her lips, a girlish flush spread over her cheeks. Which made him want to kiss her even more.

The farmer went out.

The girl stepped back, the humor gone out of her expression. She cleared her throat and fingered the knife in her belt nervously.

"I should go," she said.

For some reason, this was the last thing he expected—for her to leave now, after she'd woken him and threatened him and questioned him so relentlessly. *Now* she was leaving? And he didn't want her to go.

"But it's raining." This sounded lame even to him. "And you haven't found out who I am yet."

She shrugged. "Sadly, I don't care that much."

She moved toward the ladder that would take her down to the barn floor. In another minute she'd be gone, and he'd be here in the same situation he'd started in—no clothes, no money, no plan. Alone.

"Wait," he called.

She started down the ladder. She'd just reached the bottom when the barn door swung open, and there was the farmer again, this time holding a rusted old sword. The girl moved like she would run, but the farmer thrust the business end of the blade right at her chest. She froze.

"I knew you was in here," the farmer growled. "Couldn't stay away from my chickens, could you? Had to come back for the rest."

She lifted her hands in a kind of surrender, but that aggravating smile tugged at her mouth. "They were very tasty chickens. I couldn't help myself."

The farmer snorted in disgust. "I ought to run you through right here and be done with you. But I'll turn you over to the magistrate in the morning, and he'll cut off one of your hands. That'll teach you."

I should do something, Edward thought. *Save her, somehow.* But he was naked and unarmed. Not exactly a knight in shining armor.

The girl stood up straighter. "Or what about this? You let me go, and I'll steer clear of your chickens in the future." Without waiting for an answer to her proposal, she feinted to one side and then darted to the other, but the man caught her by the hair. He dragged her away from the door. She struggled, reaching for her knife, but he grabbed it first and tossed it onto the dirt floor.

I really should do something, Edward thought. *Now would be good.*

"Or maybe," the farmer said. "I'll cut off your hand myself. . . ."

Okay, that does it, Edward thought.

There was a flash of light in the hayloft. The farmer looked up, startled, and then the bird that was Edward descended on him, talons clawing at the man's face. The farmer screamed and released his sword. The girl took this opportunity to knee the farmer in the acorns. He dropped to the floor. She kicked him. She paused then, as if she might say something, one of her smart little lines, but she seemed to think better of it. She just grabbed up her knife and ran.

Edward followed her as best as he could from above. It was a good thing that as a bird he had sharp eyes, because she had a skill for melting into the shadows of the forest. It was difficult for him to navigate the trees. The rain was letting up, at least, a drizzle now, and the moon peeked between the clouds. The girl ran on and on, light on her feet, pacing herself, as if she were accustomed to taking such outings in the middle of the night.

She went for more than a mile or two before she stopped in a small grove to rest. Edward fluttered to the branches in the tree above her. She glanced up.

"Should I be worried about bird droppings on my head?" she laughed at him.

He gave an indignant squawk.

"Come down. You can change back now." She swung her cloak from off her shoulders. "Here."

He dropped to the ground, but then he stood there for several minutes in bird form without anything flashy happening.

"You really are a greenie, aren't you?" she asked. "Do you not even know how to change back, then?"

He changed. Still naked. The girl looked at the ground with a stifled smile and held out the cloak. Edward grabbed it and put it on, which was loads better than the horse blanket, but still left him feeling exposed and drafty.

"Thanks for your help." The girl tucked a stray black curl

behind her ear. "I'd have gotten clear of him myself, but it would've been messier."

"So you're a chicken thief," Edward said.

"Among other things," she admitted.

He'd never met a common criminal before. He would have found the whole thing wildly exciting if he wasn't so tired of things being so wildly exciting.

"I'm Gracie," she said, meeting his eyes.

"Is that your first name or your last name?" he said.

She grinned. "Grace MacTavish," she clarified, and gave a little bow. "At your service."

"Edward," he replied simply.

"Not Dennis?" She had dimples, he noticed, not when she smiled so much as when she was trying not to smile.

"Not Dennis."

"Good. I would have felt sorry for you with a name like Dennis. Shall we go?"

"Where?" he asked.

"Somewhere safer."

Safer sounded good. Out of habit he held out his arm. She looked at him incredulously, but then she took it and they started walking.

"I would have turned back there," she said as they made their way through the trees. "But then I would have lost my clothes as well, and it's a half day's hard run to the next place I've got clothes stashed. And I adore these boots," she added.

"Turned? So you're an Eðian?" His heart thudded stupidly in his chest. What was it about this girl that flustered him so?

"Yes, an Eðian," she said. "I've never seen a kestrel Eðian before. You make an attractive bird."

His stomach turned over. "I'm a kestrel? Are you quite sure that's what I am?"

"I'm not much for bird watching, but I know my birds of prey," she said. "Why should that bother you?"

He didn't answer, but the truth was that in the rules of falconry, which Edward had been practicing since he was a boy, there were certain birds suited to certain stations. The king's bird was the gyrfalcon, the largest and most majestic bird of them all. As a prince he had worked with falcons (only slightly lesser in grandeur), while his father's knights had used sacrets; the ladies, merlins; the squires, lanners; and so on and so on.

The kestrel was the smallest and weakest of the falcon species. Only the servants worked with kestrels.

He stifled a cough. "What animal are you?"

Dimples. "I suppose you'll have to wait and see."

His legs suddenly felt weak, and it wasn't from the effect of the pretty girl. All of this exertion had been too much for him. His head was cloudy. He stumbled.

She tightened her grip on his arm.

"You're not well," she observed. "Do you want to stop?"

He nodded. She led him under a tree with a large root sticking out of it, where he could sit. He spent several minutes coughing weakly into the cloak. She stood a few paces away, studying him.

"Do you have 'the Affliction'?" She looked a bit worried at the prospect of having strolled arm in arm with a diseased man.

"No." Edward looked up at her. "No, I was being poisoned."

Those mischievous eyebrows of hers lifted. "Poisoned? By whom?"

"By Lord Dudley," he said, too tired now to try to think up an answer besides the truth.

"Why would someone want to poison you?"

"Because . . ." This was it. The moment he'd tell her who he was, and she'd have to decide what to do with him. "Because I'm . . ." he tried again.

"Out with it," she urged. "I'm not sure I can stand the suspense."

Well, if she was going to decide to cut his throat after all, at least it'd be over quickly. Best to be done with it.

"I'm Edward Tudor," he answered. "And I need your help."

Jane FOURTEEN

Well. She was queen. That was unexpected.

Jane gave a half-panicked, disbelieving laugh. How could Edward do this to her? *Why* would he do this to her? He didn't even believe that women belonged in leadership positions. If Edward had been in his right mind, he never would have chosen to make her queen.

That must have been it: Edward hadn't been in his right mind. He'd had "the Affliction" boiling his brain and ruining his decision-making skills—which had until recently, in her opinion, been quite reasonable. But what could Edward possibly expect her to do with his crown?

She laughed again, although it came out as more of a sob. She was the queen. The ruler. The monarch. The sovereign. The leader.

The head of state. The chief. The one wearing the proverbial pants. The person in charge. The boss. The. Queen. Of. England.

Jane had always resisted the notion that women were weaker than men, not just physically, but intellectually. Her education had been as good as Edward's—they had even shared some of the same tutors for a time—and Jane had always excelled at whatever she put her mind to. She could speak eight languages, for heaven's sake, and was considered by some of her instructors to be a marvel at rhetoric and reasoning. She understood the complexities of philosophy and the nuances of religion. She devoured books several times a day, the way ordinary people took their meals. She memorized poetry in Latin simply to pass the time. All this she could do as well as any man.

But could she rule a country?

Jane paced her new bedroom—a chamber in the royal apartments of the Tower of London fit for (what else?) a queen. Last night, after receiving her subjects (the thought made Jane's stomach lurch) she'd been sent to her chambers to rest, Lord Dudley citing that a queen should not be kept up so late, and she'd need to be refreshed for a long day of queenly activities that awaited her in the morning.

Jane had been exhausted, so she'd complied, but she'd made certain everyone knew she wasn't being *sent to her room like a child*. She'd shot Gifford a quick look—was he coming?—but Lord Dudley pulled Gifford aside to speak with him. So Jane had grabbed a book without checking what it was (it turned out to be *Afterlives: The Hundred-Year Debate of Eðians and Reincarnation*), and hurled it onto the gigantic bed when she realized it was about death.

Then it had truly hit her: Edward was dead.

She would never see him again.

He was gone.

After a long, angry cry, she hadn't been able to sleep, so as the sun lifted and somewhere (hopefully outside) Gifford turned into a horse, she explored her chambers. The decor was annoyingly opulent. Long, silk brocade drapes framed the windows, while several wardrobes lined the walls, filled with more gowns than she could imagine wearing. In the two places along the wall not occupied by wardrobes, there was a door that presumably joined the queen's rooms with the king's, and a vanity with a large glass mirror, just in case she wanted to look at herself and admire how very queenly she wasn't.

No, there were circles under her eyes from last night's journey and devastation. Her skin, previously flushed from days in the sun, now looked sallow and drawn. Her eyes were raw from crying, itchy and red and as puffy as a pastry. Not to mention all her normal flaws.

She looked nothing at all like a queen.

The worst part about her new chambers was that all these wardrobes and vanities and drapes meant there was no space—none at all—for a bookcase. Who on earth could feel comfortable enough to sleep in a room with no books?

Edward would never sleep again, she reminded herself tearfully.

He would never read a book again.

A knock sounded and she ignored it, choosing instead to flop down in the center of her bed, surrounded by pillows and blankets, and compose a mental list of all the things Edward would never do again. Obvious things, like eating and breathing, she skipped. She was on number twenty-seven: scratching his dog behind the ears, and number twenty-eight: eating ridiculous amounts of blackberry pudding, when her visitor knocked again, then entered anyway.

"Good morning." Her mother swept into the room, followed by a troop of ladies-in-waiting. At Lady Frances's instruction, some of the ladies drew a bath, scenting the water with rose oil until the smell filled the room and Jane's eyes watered. Others opened the vanity, selecting a frightening array of cosmetics. Still more put tray after tray of food on a table: sausages and eggs, bread drizzled with honey, and fruit with rivers of cream.

As all this activity unfolded around her, Jane remained on the bed, unmoving and unmoved.

"Well?" Lady Frances snapped her fingers at Jane, drawing startled glances from the maids. After a moment, she seemed to realize what she'd done, and softened her voice as she dropped her hand to her side. "Jane, my dear. Your Majesty. It's time for a bath and breakfast. You must prepare to meet your people."

Jane had met her people last night. "I'm mourning my cousin."

"I know, my dear, but you must— That is, I think it would be wise to show yourself strong and capable immediately. Don't wait for a crisis before you take action."

"You think I should take action?" Jane asked.

"Indeed." Her mother's mouth twitched into a smile. "I think you should immediately prove yourself a capable ruler."

Capable. Right. Jane fidgeted with the corner of a woven blanket. (Another thing Edward would never do.) "There are some issues I feel should be addressed. Minor issues." Huge issues. When Gifford had taken her face between his hands and reminded her about their conversations in the country house, he'd made her remember the people. That was the only reason she'd agreed to take the throne. The people. The poor. She would do anything to help them.

"Good." Lady Frances offered a hand and tugged Jane from the fortress of blankets. "Then we'll bring those items before the Privy Council and begin solidifying your reign. You know Lord Dudley desires to aid you in the same manner he aided King Edward—may he rest in peace—as well as many others in the court. Including myself. We all want to help you become the queen you were meant to be."

"I was never meant to be queen."

"And yet you are."

"Do you think I'll make a good one?" Jane's voice was unintentionally small. The words weren't what she'd aimed for, either, but as soon as they were out, she was overcome with the desire for her mother's approval and support.

Lady Frances narrowed her eyes and gazed at Jane the same way she scrutinized the servants at their housework. "If you can focus on ruling the kingdom instead of reading those silly books, you'll be a queen always remembered."

Apparently even Jane's ascension to the throne wasn't enough to make her mother proud of her. She swallowed down her disappointment. It didn't matter, she told herself. She didn't need her mother anymore.

She had Gifford.

Jane didn't know if she could rule a country. She wasn't meant for a life on the throne. She wasn't even remotely prepared to be queen. But she did know one thing: Gifford would be there with her, he would help her, and she was going to give it her very best try.

"I want to see Edward's body," Jane announced later. "To say good-bye."

She was walking through the hall with her mother, Lord Dudley trailing a few steps behind. They were on their way to the first of the day's activities, not that anyone had bothered to tell her what it was. She supposed she'd find out soon enough, and in the meantime, the silence between the three of them was ripe for making demands.

"I want to see his body today. This morning."

"I'm afraid that's simply not a good idea, Your Majesty." Dudley's tone was gruff. "He was quite ill. It's best to remember him as he was before."

Jane choked back a wave of hot grief. "I want to see him. Where is he?"

"It's simply not appropriate, Your Majesty—"

Jane clenched her jaw, then deliberately unclenched it. "I am the queen, and I demand to see my cousin's body."

"There's simply too much to do today."

If Lord Dudley said *simply* once more, she'd *simply* have his head chopped off.

No, that wasn't true. She wouldn't. He was Gifford's father.

"Lord Dudley." She addressed only him on this, since her mother had been silent on the matter so far. "As queen, it's my duty to see to my predecessor's funeral arrangements, and I wish to pay my respects to him first. Privately."

He was silent as they turned into a more crowded hall. People glanced at her and whispered. A few bowed. "Very well," Dudley said. "I will make arrangements for you to visit him. I'm afraid it won't be today, though. There's too much to do."

If they waited much longer, she'd be visiting a rotting corpse. According to *The Glorious and Gruesome Stages of Death: A Beginner's Guide*, bodies began deteriorating very quickly, bloating and stinking and decaying until all that was left was a horrifying echo of the people they had been before. Jane had seen her father and Katherine Parr shortly after they'd died, and that had been horrible enough.

She didn't want to see Edward in the rotting stage. The thought made a shudder run deep through her.

"Arrange it as soon as you're able," she said sharply, a terrible thought springing to her mind.

Dudley didn't want her to see her cousin's body.

Something was wrong here, outside of the obvious wrongness of Edward being dead and Jane being queen. Something was very wrong, and she intended to find out what it was.

The rest of the day was a whirlwind of first-day-as-queen moments:

Standing in front of the Privy Council as the members introduced themselves.

Sitting on the throne as some of the more prominent merchants of London came to visit her.

Signing documents about palace staff, various lords' holdings, and marriage requests. The last bit made her feel a little guilty, but evidently the first several requests on the pile were for people who wanted the arrangement approved, so she decided to think of it as giving her blessing. Still, it was disconcerting to have that kind of power in her hands.

Those were a string of more actions that Edward would never again take: signing his name, picking at a thread on the throne cushion, and hearing every council member talk about how great and terribly important they were. (Maybe that wasn't something to be missed.)

There were also a handful of invitations to preside over state events, visit various nobles' country homes, and attend something called the Red Wedding. Jane checked the "will not attend" box without giving this last invitation a second thought. As if she wanted to go to any more weddings.

None of it seemed very important, though. Nothing significant or helpful to the people. It was all busy work. She was given time to eat, but otherwise kept occupied. There was little opportunity to think about Edward or ask questions about Dudley's motives, or do much of anything but wonder if she couldn't put in an order for a new throne—she felt like a child sitting in this one, her feet barely touching the floor.

And annoyingly, Lord Dudley insisted on accompanying her everywhere. Like he was afraid that the moment she was out of his sight, she'd be out the window and heading for the hills.

Which didn't sound like such a bad idea at this point.

"There was much Edward wasn't able to do in his final days," he was saying to her now mournfully. Dusk was falling. They were both waiting for Gifford at an exit near the stables, with amber sunlight falling through the open door and casting long, dark shadows down the hallway. "Our late king was so very ill. One of his last acts was to name you as his successor. It was his only thought, his only goal in those hours, naming the one person he trusted above all others."

Above even the duke himself? He was trying to flatter her, certainly.

"Yes. Well, I still wish to see his body," she said.

"Perhaps tomorrow," Dudley agreed faintly.

"I'd also like to travel to the palace at Greenwich, as soon as we're able, to see to his room and his books. And what has happened to his dog, Petunia? I should like to see her as well. Can she be brought here?"

"Of course," Dudley said, but she could tell by the look on his face that he had no real intention of seeing to her requests. But why deny her? What was he hiding?

She turned to gaze out at the sun, which was slowly falling below the horizon. She wished it would move faster. She'd feel better with Gifford here. "I also want all but one of the wardrobes moved out of my room," she said, as if that were the conversation they'd been having the entire time. "There's no need for every single one of them. Store them someplace else if you feel I need that many garments."

Dudley's lips thinned with a frown. "Your room would be quite bare without them, Your Majesty."

"We'll replace the wardrobes with something else, obviously."

"What else could a queen possibly want in her chambers?" Lord Dudley managed to look genuinely flummoxed. "A large mirror, to make the room appear bigger? A golden stand to rest your crown upon each night?"

Jane wasn't even wearing the crown now. She had no idea where it was.

Dudley continued. "A loom? Paintings? A spinning wheel? A chair for knitting in?"

He clearly didn't know her at all. "Oh, my knitting skills are the foundations of textile legend," she said, resisting the urge to roll her eyes.

Dudley brightened, as though relieved to have figured out something that would occupy so much of her time. "A chair for knitting you shall have, then! And all the yarn and needles a beautiful queen could desire."

Ha.

"Father, don't be daft." Gifford approached, a tall shadow against the twilight sky. "What my wife desires—and what you should have guessed, had you paid attention—is bookcases. And books, of course, to fill them. Not more decorations or useless items. She wants books."

Jane's heart jumped as Gifford paused next to her, the sleeve of his jacket brushing her elbow. He knew about bookcases. He'd called her his wife. A tiny thrill managed to burst through the grief and confusion she'd been swamped in all day. "My husband is correct," she said, smiling. "Bookcases. Books. There's nothing I like more."

"Except me." Gifford winked at her, though; they both knew that wasn't true.

Dudley clapped his hand down on Gifford's shoulder. "Ah, son. I'm glad to see you return from your daily deviation from—"

"Yes." Gifford cleared his throat. "Same as I do every evening."

Tension snapped between the men. Jane's skin prickled at the sudden memory of Gifford slipping away last night to go speak with his father.

What had Gifford and Dudley talked about? Gifford had said nothing to her about Dudley since her coronation. He had been unusually quiet, actually, about everything. Uncharacteristically quiet. One might even say suspiciously quiet.

Well, he'd been a horse all day, of course. He hadn't had time to confide everything.

Jane sighed. She didn't trust Lord Dudley, but why? There had to be more to her misgivings than her dislike of the man (and his nose).

"Come." Gifford offered his arm, and she took it. "Let's go in to supper. I'm starving for something other than hay."

Dinner was insufferable. First she had to dress in layers and layers of foolish finery: furs and silks and velvets, jewels on her fingers and neck and hair, and worst of all, a type of platform shoe that she was forced to wear so that her dresses, which hadn't yet been hemmed to her slight frame, wouldn't drag the floor. Then she and Gifford were paraded into the great hall, where a hundred courtiers waited. At her arrival, they all stood until she took her place at the head of the table. Everyone was watching her, and she dearly would have liked to shrink or crawl under the table, neither action befitting of a queen.

Gifford sat on her left, Lord Dudley on her right, throughout the various courses of the meal: soups and soufflés, pies and pastries, and veal and venison. There was so much food, Jane thought she might explode. So much food, the people in the villages she and Gifford had visited could have lived on it for a week. The thought of so much extravagance and waste while there were Englishmen suffering and starving made her feel a bit sick.

They were halfway through the meal—eating some kind of meat pie—when Lord Dudley turned to Jane. "Your Majesty," he said quietly, so that the other people at the table besides Gifford might not hear. "I thought we should discuss when to hold my son's coronation. Not tonight, as I'm sure you're exhausted, but tomorrow night would be appropriate, and then we'd have the day to prepare. I've already got his crown picked out."

Jane stilled, her fork lifted halfway to her lips. "His crown?"

"Yes. To make Gifford the king."

Gifford the king.

Jane's hand trembled as she set her fork down.

The king. That was it, then. This whole mess made sense. The hasty wedding. The generosity of using the country house. The way he'd insisted she be crowned queen only moments after she learned of Edward's death, foregoing all of the traditional procedures.

It was so obvious she felt stupid for not seeing it before. Through her, and through crowning Gifford king, John Dudley meant to rule England.

"No." The word burst out of her. She darted a glance at Gifford. Shock flickered across his face, and then was snuffed out as quickly as a candle.

Dudley's nose turned red. "And why not?"

She hardened her expression. Maybe she should have worn her crown today.

"Your Majesty," he added.

She lowered her voice to just above a whisper. "There are

several reasons, none of which I am obligated to divulge to you. But I will give you the most obvious reason, which is that Gifford is a horse."

Dudley's jaw practically dropped, which only encouraged Jane to go on.

"Consider it," she said, leaning toward the duke. "How can your son help me rule the kingdom when he's present only half the time—and during the half when most people are asleep?"

Gifford signaled for the serving boy to bring him more wine.

"Your Majesty, please reconsider," Lord Dudley pleaded. "Your position will be much stronger with your husband as king. The people will see it as a sign of strength—"

She took a deep breath. "They need signs of my strength, not my reliance on the men around me."

"But every queen needs a king," Dudley sputtered.

She shook her head. "If you feel he needs a title, I can make him a duke. Duke of Clarence, perhaps. How's that?"

Gifford snorted (a noise that was remarkably horse-like), lifted his goblet, and drank deeply.

"Your Majesty, I must implore you to change your mind." Dudley paused and came at the subject in a new, calculatedly kind way. "This is understandably a difficult time for you. Let's not be hasty with this decision."

"Indeed," she said coolly. "I would undoubtedly feel more at ease if I could visit my cousin's body. Perhaps after that we can discuss the prince consort."

Lord Dudley rubbed his chin, nearly losing a finger to the dagger of his nose, and nodded. "We should delay this discussion until a more suitable time presents itself."

"Yes," Jane agreed. "A more suitable time."

She dared another look at her husband. Gifford's cheeks were flushed and his eyes were bright as he drained yet another goblet of wine. A servant rushed forward to refill.

"No more," Jane said, much too loudly. She reached across her husband's plate and laid a hand on the rim of his goblet just before the servant began to tip the pitcher of wine. "You've had enough."

Chatter in the dining hall softened, and then made a full stop. Everyone looked at Jane with her hand over Gifford's goblet, and the servant standing there awkwardly, and Gifford sitting between them with his face slowly turning red.

Belatedly, Jane realized what she had done.

Under the stares of shock and amusement, Jane pulled away from Gifford and his still-empty goblet, and slowly stood up.

Everyone else followed immediately.

"I've had a long day," Jane announced. "I'd like to retire for the evening. Darling husband, do you wish to join me?" Maybe if they talked, he'd say all the things she wanted to hear: that he agreed with her, that he found the idea of being king silly and unnecessary, that this was all his father's idea, his father's scheming, not his.

She turned to Gifford. The turn of his mouth said something like, "I don't know, what do you want me to do? I am, after all, yours to command." But he held out his arm for her to take.

"Nothing would delight me more than to spend time in your magnificent company."

They walked in tense silence. When they reached their chambers she strode into her bedroom and threw off her outer robe like she couldn't bear its weight any longer, then started plucking the jewels from her throat and hair.

Gifford lingered in the doorway.

"Are you coming in?" she asked, pausing to hurl her platform shoes into the corner. "There's nowhere to sit, but feel free to pull up a wardrobe."

He came in and let the door shut behind him.

"What would you like to discuss with me, Your Majesty?" Gifford's tone held none of his typical friendliness. His brown eyes were cold. A muscle ticked in his jaw.

"You're angry," she observed.

Gifford raised an eyebrow. "What right have I to be angry? I am merely your subject, Your Majesty."

Jane scowled. "Don't be silly. You aren't merely my subject."

"Then what am I, Your Majesty?"

Jane clenched her fists and paced faster. "You're my husband. My prince consort."

"Yes, Your Majesty. And your prince consort I shall remain."

He was being so childish.

"Stop saying 'Your Majesty'!" Jane tore a pillow off her bed and hurled it at him. He sidestepped it quickly. "I told you not to call me that."

216

He blinked slowly, as though trying to give an impression of guilelessness. "Then what should I call you, Your Majesty?"

"Use my name."

"Yes, Your Majesty." He bowed and swirled his hand a few times in an overly dramatic display of courtesy. "Anything you say, Your Majesty. And not to question Your Majesty, but shouldn't you be using the royal we? You are all of England now." He paused a beat. "Your Majesty."

"Why are you even angry about this?" She hurled another pillow, which he again artfully dodged. "You hate politics. You've been avoiding court for years." She gave a bitter laugh. "The idea's so ridiculous it's almost sad. Can you imagine yourself prancing around the throne room, having carrots fed to you between petitions? What use could you possibly be as the king?"

"So you think I'm ridiculous. You think I'm useless."

"I didn't say that." She brandished another pillow.

"You didn't have to say it. Just because I don't spend all my time with a book attached to my nose doesn't mean I can't infer what you meant." He still hadn't moved, aside from dodging pillows. His hands were behind his back. His chin was lifted. Even his hair was perfect. "Admit it. You're ashamed that I'm an Eðian."

"No! But this is still a dangerous place for Eðians, and it's already causing talk that dinner is held after dark—just like our wedding—even in high summer."

"Tell them I'm a vampire," he said. "That should give them something to talk about. Anyway, what about all those decrees we discussed? Making the kingdom safe for Eðians? Protecting the innocent? Helping the poor? What were you doing all day if not securing the safety of your people, Your Majesty?"

"A hundred things you couldn't begin to understand since you spent your day galloping about the fields and eating apples. I didn't ask for any of this, you know. I haven't had a moment's peace since we came here. First I'm told that my best friend is dead, and oh, by the way, that means that I'm the queen now—surprise!—a position I'm not remotely prepared for and I only agreed to accept because you encouraged me. Then, instead of being allowed to mourn for my cousin, I'm shuffled from place to place, signing insignificant documents and picking the color of the new table linens and meeting people I hate, all the while wondering why your father clearly wants *you* on the throne so badly."

"Why wouldn't he want me on the throne?" Gifford asked.

"Well, you have to admit, this is awfully convenient for you, a quick marriage to someone who's suddenly in line for the throne. After all, I know you didn't marry me for my hair."

"I married you because I was given no choice," he said.

"And of course you had no idea that your father was planning on making you the king of England. Didn't you hear him, Gifford? He's already got your crown picked out."

"What makes you afraid to share power?" he said hotly. "Why couldn't I be king?"

So there it was. He wanted to be king.

Perhaps that was what he'd wanted all along.

The pillow dropped from her hand. She took a step back, the betrayal of it piercing her through. All her life, she'd known that she was being used as a pawn in other people's political games—by her father, by Thomas Seymour, by her own mother, and now by Lord Dudley. But she hadn't wanted to imagine that she'd be used by Gifford.

"Is that all I've been to you?" she asked, struggling to keep the tremor from her voice. "A means to an end?"

He stared at her, hurt flashing in his eyes. "You don't trust me."

"I don't trust anyone!" she cried. "How can I when it's clear that this is all a game?"

"Jane . . ."

"I saw you and your father speaking after the coronation. He put his hand on your shoulder, like he was proud of you. What were you even talking about?"

Gifford didn't answer.

"See. You're doing exactly what he wants!" Her face was hot. Boiling. She'd never been so wounded and so angry in her life.

"I am not!" Gifford scooped up a pillow from the floor and threw it at her, though his aim was wide and he missed by quite a bit.

"You're even terrible at throwing!" she yelled.

"I missed on purpose!" He marched to the door connecting her room and his. "Now if you'll excuse me, Your Majesty, I've had enough accusations for one evening."

"Fine! Go away. I don't want to see you."

He hauled open the door on her side, finding another door on the other. It had no handle. He pushed at it, rattling the door in its frame a few times before he realized it wasn't going to let him through.

"What makes you think you're qualified to be king when you can't even open a door?"

With an indignant snort, he slammed her door shut again and marched out the front door.

Slam.

A few seconds later: *slam.*

He'd gone into his room.

Well, good. "I never want to see you again!" she shouted through the adjoining door.

"Just read your stupid books!"

"My books aren't stupid. You're stupid." Jane threw a pillow at the door. An answering thump signaled another pillow or maybe even a shoe.

Jane sank to her bed, the fire draining out of her.

She choked on a sob.

She wouldn't cry. She wouldn't. She refused to cry about Gifford.

But then she did. She was a sixteen-year-old girl, after all, and sometimes a sixteen-year-old girl needs to throw herself into a pillow and let the tears come as they may.

FIFTEEN

Gifford

G had never wanted to hit someone with a pillow so much before in his life. He couldn't believe how the evening had gone. Nor could he believe how his wife really perceived his usefulness: as a half man, incapable of ruling over his own wine goblet, let alone the country.

Jane didn't want him to be king.

It wasn't like he had ever yearned for the crown. (Being royalty looked like too many people telling a person what to do, if you asked him.) And yet, when one's wife wore the crown, one got to thinking maybe a follicular adornment like a crown wouldn't be so bad. It made sense. Otherwise, how would the introductions of the royal couple go?

"Ladies and gentlemen, presenting Her Majesty, the Queen of

England! Escorted by . . . this fellow."

Really, he should blame his father. Dudley had been preparing him to become king, speaking of the coronation as if it were inevitable. Saying things like, "We'll discuss that when you're king. . . ." and "When you're king, you should really have a changing room built closer to the stables."

He'd never wanted the crown.

But he hadn't thought his wife would deny it to him. And with such voracity. Granted, they had only been married for a little more than a week, so it shouldn't have been surprising that she didn't trust him. But how could she not trust him?

G spent the early morning of day five of Queen Jane's rule cantering through the grassy lowlands to the north and east of the castle. He kept trying to think of all the reasons why it was good not to be a king.

First, it would be hard to gallop with a crown.

Second, if he were king, he would rarely be alone, and would hardly be allowed to jaunt about the countryside on his own. He'd probably have an advisor on his back. How degrading.

Third, he had to admit, his lady was the more knowledgeable one. He was sure that somewhere along the way, Jane had read a book with a title like, *How to Rule a Kingdom, Even if You're Thirty-Second in the Line of Succession and Chances Are You'll Never Actually Rule: Volume One of Three.*

And finally, being a king was exactly the kind of responsibility G liked to avoid. If he were king, people would expect great things of him. His every action would be judged and weighed against the monarchs of the past. And if he made mistakes, well, a king's mistakes had consequences. It was a lot of pressure.

Uneasy lies the head that wears the crown, G thought. Which was a pretty good line. He wished he had ink and paper. And hands with opposable thumbs, so he could write it down.

G snuffed (the horse's equivalent of a sigh). He'd never wanted to be king. And his lady presented some logical reasons for her decision, although at the time, he would've appreciated the logical reasons being delivered in a less hostile way. Preferably with fewer pillows whooshing past his head.

Still, the rejection burned.

G slowed from a canter and leisurely trotted over toward a brook winding its way through the valley. He lowered his head and slurped water. It tasted cool on his tongue, and helped calm his burning ego.

What did a life as prince consort look like? He couldn't help picturing it as some sort of personal valet, who attended the left side of the queen with astute devotion and when the queen said, "I'm thirsty," he would reply by jumping to his feet and saying, "Your Majesty, if I have to search out the magical Carpesian Waters of Romania myself, killing loads of bandits along the way, you. Shall. Have. Your. Water."

G shook his mane and whinnied, the sound definitely coming across as a whine, even to his own ears. He realized that in reality, he would not be a personal valet, and even if he were, there would most likely be a pitcher of water nearby.

The sun shot across the sky much faster than he liked. He could almost see the streak marks.

Sometimes he dreaded turning into a horse and leaving his humanity behind, but today, he dreaded the setting sun and the fact that he would soon have to face his wife. He wanted to be supportive and caring, and he wanted to talk about how they were going to change the kingdom, and he didn't want to feel inferior and powerless, because he knew Jane—at least he thought he knew her—and he knew she would not make him feel inferior and powerless.

G had always thought of himself as a rather enlightened sort of fellow, especially compared to the other men of the day. When his brother Stan's wife had questioned Stan during a family dinner, she'd been locked in her room for three days. G would never react so harshly. Jane loved books, and that had never scared him like it did other men. Yes, it had irritated him in the beginning—a perfectly reasonable reaction—but that was because her books were bulky and space-consuming and seemed to be more important to her than he was. Or people in general. Then Jane had read to him underneath the tree, in that soft lilting voice of hers, so sure in the pronunciations of all the big words. Like *sesquipedalian*. Which Jane said meant "big word."

He had never blamed her for reading. Or for thinking. Or for stating her opinion so often. And God's teeth, she stated her opinion often.

He would never have lorded his "lord and master" title over her.

But now, she was his queen. His sovereign. His ruler. The night of the coronation, he had pledged his allegiance to her, and her alone.

How was he supposed to be a husband after that? Was he to be lord and master of his household, as long as his household, the queen, agreed?

The sun continued its speedy trajectory toward the horizon, and G turned back toward London and hastened his trot.

His thoughts didn't sound like his own. They sounded more like his father's or his brother's. G had never fully formed his own opinions regarding the roles of men and women in the world. His partnership with Jane had always naturally felt like that: a partnership. Not a dominion. Not a master/servant situation. Even when they didn't particularly like each other, they treated each other with disdain equally.

She tried to throw herself into a Pack attack, and he prevented it.

He tried to drink himself into an ale-induced stupor, and she hid the stuff.

She educated him about herbs and . . . that other plants that grew in . . . that one place she was reading about. He educated her to accept that not all Eðians were good.

She knew about tinctures. He knew about alfalfa.

She had the soft skin and the delicate cheekbones and that

strange way her lips moved along with the words when she read a particularly intriguing passage. . . .

G closed his eyes. Her soft skin. Her lips.

Those lips that Love's own hand did make, he composed wistfully.

As he approached the Tower stables, he wondered who would be there to greet him tonight. Her Majesty the Queen of England . . . or his lady?

He walked into the dining room, prepared to find a lavish supper full of servants and silverware and food befitting a queen, but what he saw utterly surprised him.

Two place settings, two candles, and a platter holding a small roasted duck, surrounded by root vegetables and garnishes, as well as a small bowl of fruit. And the Queen of England sitting at the end of the table.

He looked wary. "Your Majesty," G said.

"My lord," she said, nodding her head.

"Where is everybody?"

"Who?"

"Your . . . court? Your ladies? Your servants?"

She shrugged. "Being queen comes with several advantages, one of which is that if I order everyone out of the dining room, they obey."

"Even my father?" G said.

Jane winced at the mention of his father, but she recovered quickly and replaced the wince with a blank expression. "Even him.

You should've seen the look on his face, but yes, even him."

G's father was obviously a tense subject between them, but right now, everything seemed to be a tense subject between them. G grabbed a flask of wine from the end of the room and two goblets, even though he was pretty sure only one would be used. He sat himself down at his place on her right-hand side. He filled his goblet, raised the flask toward her in a questioning gesture (she declined of course), and then he set the flask on his right, out of reach of the queen. She did not object.

If anything, tonight he would prove he could handle his own goblet. He would be king of his cup.

They served themselves from the dishes before them, and then G steered their conversation to safe topics. They discussed her day of navigating her queenly duties, and his day of navigating the north-eastern hills. Her day of picking out the color of her ladies' brocades, and his day of picking hay out of his teeth with his tongue.

She said his father was at her side all day long and she was quite annoyed with his ever-presence, and she would be glad he was to be gone from the castle the following day.

"My father is going somewhere?" G said. Great. They were back on the subject of his father.

"Yes. I thought you knew. Oh, no, of course you wouldn't, because he received the message while you were in your . . . four-legged state. He was called away urgently to the countryside. He wouldn't say why, so I assumed it was a personal matter." She brought a hand to her lips. "Oh, I'm so sorry. I should've been concerned that the matter might be of import to you as well, since you are Dudley's son."

She said it as if blood ties to the man directly spoke to his own character. G fought the urge to engage in the territory they'd already covered and raised a hand. "My lady, I am sure everything is fine with my father." And the truth was, G wasn't worried about any sort of family emergency. He could only think that the urgent business calling his father away had more to do with the same business that had occupied the entirety of his father's mind for the past several years: the business of controlling the throne.

G guessed this latest message had to do with the hunt for Mary. And if his father was personally answering the call, it meant things were not going well.

"Gifford? Are you all right?" Jane asked.

"To be sure," G answered, shaking away the thought. Several times, he'd considered telling Jane about what he'd overheard the night of her coronation, but he thought better about it. She had been so distressed about becoming queen in the first place, and if she were to know Mary didn't accept her as sovereign . . .

No, he would hold back the rampant speculation and wait until his father returned with actual news. Although if she found out he'd withheld information, she would have a real reason to not trust him.

"I am merely concerned with our . . . I mean . . . *your* first decree as sovereign ruler."

"Oh. Right. I've been contemplating that today, while I was

reading in the book *Drafting Decrees, the Ancient Language of Binding Arbitration*." She reached under the table and pulled up a messy stack of parchments, many covered with her handwriting, phrases scrawled, words crossed out. "I've been practicing how I could phrase it, so that I don't mention Eðians directly, or Verities for that matter, but so that it covers them and also covers other people who might be unfairly. . ." Her voice trailed off as she looked at G.

She had used the word *I*, not *we*. (He'd wanted the Jane and Gifford We, not the Royal We, which she still refused to use.) This was definitely the Queen of England, and not his lady, sitting at the head of the table. G leaned back and poured himself another cup of wine.

"Am I boring you?" Jane said.

"No," G responded, "but that's only because I stopped listening ages ago."

"Ah," Jane said.

She looked down at her plate, her cheeks tinged with pink, and G wondered if he had been too straightforward. But really, did she even need him here for this conversation? She obviously didn't need him by her side, ruling the kingdom. Why did she want him around for the drafting of decrees?

They ate the rest of their dinner in silence, being that there appeared to be no safe topics left to discuss, and then they went to their separate adjoining residences, the door between them never opened.

* * *

They didn't see much of each other for the next few days. G's day-light hours were spent wandering farther and farther from the castle, to the point where on the eighth night of the reign of Queen Jane, he had gone so far from the castle that when the sun set, he was still miles away. He made it to a cluster of trees outside one of the villages surrounding London just as the transformation took place, and he hid himself in a patch of bushes. Why hadn't he fig-ured out to control this blasted curse yet?

He guessed because he hadn't really tried.

What he wouldn't give to be at Dudley Castle right now, with its remote location and the roads he knew in the dark of night.

Yes, he'd run into this problem a few times when he'd gotten carried away at his home, and he'd discovered that the best course of action was to find a tavern attached to a brothel. There it was easy to grab clothes strewn about, the owners of which would be too sloshed to care. And these kinds of taverns were easy to find. Just follow the noise.

G wrangled up a few of the leafier vines, positioned them in all the right places, and ventured out of the trees and into the vil-lage, keeping to the shadows and following the noise to the nearest tavern, which was called The Three Ladies. Judging by the "ladies" standing outside, G had found his place.

There are two rules to finding clothes when you need them and are currently without: the first, act like you know what you're doing; the second, do it all in one continuous motion. G took note of the nearest darkened window, inhaled deeply, and dropped the back cluster of leaves. (He would need an empty hand.)

He threw open the window and climbed in, incurring feminine gasps and another figure drunkenly clamoring for light. But it was too late, because G was already out the bedroom door wearing someone else's trousers, and pulling his arms through shirtsleeves.

To the inhabitants of said room, G would be dismissed as a ghost. Until the following morning, when the owner of said trousers discovered their absence.

G walked to the adjoining tavern, holding his trousers up to account for the ale belly of the previous owner. He made the decision then and there to cut back on his ale consumption.

The coronation of the queen was so recent that G was fairly certain people wouldn't be able to recognize Her Majesty Queen Jane, let alone her consort. Nevertheless, G kept his head down as he crept from the back rooms and toward the bar. He was so focused on reaching the front door without assault, he almost missed the faint whisper.

"Long live Queen Mary."

G stopped and whipped about. Two red uniforms caught his eye. The soldiers were standing at the bar, the bartender handing them brown bags full of something bulky.

Perhaps G had misheard the declaration. But no, the names Mary and Jane sounded nothing alike. Then he heard another declaration, whispered again, this time from one of the soldiers at the bar, and in a response.

"Long live the true and rightful queen."

G froze in step. His heart tried to escape up his throat. He swallowed it back down. He knew that he must keep a low profile, although that was more of an automatic response before it was based in logical reasoning. Reason would tell him he was the queen's consort, after all. The soldiers should be under his wife's control.

And yet, here were the rumblings of treason in this random tavern just outside of London. Several more soldiers dotted the seats in the great room of the place, but they had no ale in front of them. Only food and water. G had a moment to be grateful he wasn't dressed in his usual finery, and therefore did not look out of place.

He strode to the front door, an urgency in his step that wasn't there before, and as he exited the tavern, he noticed points of light dotting the hillside.

Campfires. Tents. An encampment. Within marching distance of London. He needed to get back to the Tower, and fast. Curse his damn curse. Why couldn't he just change at will? He was a horse minutes ago. Minutes ago! He got down on all fours right there in the dirt road and squeezed his eyes shut and—

"Stand up, ye daft beggar," one of the wobbly tavern patrons said.

G waved him off and tried to focus on the feeling of the wind in his mane, his haunches springing from the—

"Had too much to drink, that one," another man slurred. "Thinks he's an arse!"

Realizing it wasn't going to work, G shot up from the ground. "A horse," G said sharply to anyone who would listen. "A horse! My wife's kingdom for a horse!"

A group of drunken men looked at Gifford as if they were disgusted someone could consume so much ale.

"Peace, ye fat guts!" The largest and sweatiest of the men spat at G. "No one's gotchyer horse."

"No, I *need* a horse."

The large man belly laughed. "Of course ye do. Hey, Mason, get the beggar man a horse!"

The whole group belly laughed, and G thought better of telling them it really wasn't that funny, and that the man who had spoken really had the fat guts, and instead he just took off running toward the castle.

G ran flat out for a good minute, minute and a half, before he realized he would have to pace himself, and as a man, he didn't have the endurance he enjoyed as a horse.

It was going to be a long trip back to the castle.

Hours later, when he reached the gates, and spent extra time convincing the guards he really was the prince consort, he staggered into the main hall and through the series of stairways that would lead him to the queen's chamber. It was well after the queen would've given up on him for supper and turned in.

He used his fist to bang on her chamber door.

"Jane!" he shouted. "Jane, open up."

After a few long moments, she opened the door, the vestiges of sleep still in her gaze, a long robe draped over her shoulders. At the sight of G, she pulled the robe even tighter.

"What is it?" she said primly.

He pushed his way inside and shut the door behind them.

"This is very—" Jane started to say, but G cut her off.

"My lady, Your Majesty . . . Jane. You need to call a meeting of the Council Privy."

"It's the Privy Council, Gifford."

"Yes. That. Call a meeting." He sat her on the bed and told her a brief version of events, continuing even after her raised eyebrows at the part where he was in the bedroom of a brothel, all the way to seeing the troops. When he was finished, Jane took hold of one of the posts of her four-poster bed.

"But . . . but your father assured us we were fine."

"Where is my father?" G asked. "Have you seen him today? Is he back?"

"No. I haven't seen him since he left a few days ago."

G took a deep breath. "Look, I haven't been as forthright with you as I should, but please believe me. I thought I was acting in your best interests, and I will explain it all, but we need to call a meeting of the Privy Council now."

She nodded, and G went to the door and shouted for the servant outside to gather the council members, and then he went back in and explained everything to his lady. The message his father had received about Mary. The fact that Mary would never accept Jane as queen. The emergency missive he'd received that had called him away. After he was finished, Jane's face had drained of color, if that were possible for such a pale creature.

"But . . . surely we would have heard of soldiers encamped so close, especially if they were hostile to the crown."

G nodded. "That's why I wanted to call the meeting of the Privy Council. They all ratified the king's change to the line of succession, but I feel that they have been keeping things from you, and me as well, because they didn't think we could handle it yet."

Jane's face grew even paler, so at this point her skin was a gray color.

G took her hand. It was the first time they'd touched in days. "It will be all right. I'm sure the council knows of the advance, and has made preparations."

Jane went to get dressed while they waited for the council to be gathered. G offered to leave and have one of her ladies come in and help her, but Jane begged him to stay (chair turned, of course) and insisted she could dress herself, because she'd been dressing herself for all these years and she certainly hadn't forgotten—

G begged her not to explain.

She finished getting dressed. G went through their adjoining door, quickly put on trousers that fit and a simple tunic, and then returned to Jane.

And they waited.

And waited.

And waited.

Hours passed. There was no hint of dawn in the sky, but it couldn't be far off.

Jane had taken to pacing her room, and G had the fleeting thought that they would have to reinforce her floor for all the pacing she had done in, what was it? Almost nine days of being queen.

Finally, there was a knock on the door.

G opened it, and there was the original messenger they'd sent. "Your lordship, I sent word to the members of the Privy Council, and well, most of them have quarters nearby, and some don't, so some had to be tracked down . . . and . . . well . . ."

"Well what?" G said. "Are they all gathered yet?"

"No, my lord."

"That's all right. We will meet with the ones who are gathered so far." It was getting late, after all, and he wanted to meet before the hour of horse.

"But, sir, there are . . . none."

"None?"

"I do apologize, sir. There are none. I don't know where they are. I've asked the queen's guard to look, but I don't know how hard they tried. . . ."

Suddenly, the messenger just stopped talking and ran away.

"G?" Jane said. "What is it?"

"Stay here. I'm going to check on something."

G stepped out into the passageway, and Jane followed close behind. He'd known she wouldn't stay.

The hallways were strangely quiet, even for the predawn hour.

At the very top of the White Tower, they stopped at a window that overlooked the direction of the encampment. G peeked his head out and saw the soldiers and the banners with an embroidered pomegranate on a bed of roses.

And then his mouth turned down. And his shoulders sagged. And his heart sank.

"What do you see?" Jane asked in a hushed whisper.

"An army at the gates." G tried not to look as terrified as he felt. "Mary's army."

SIXTEEN

Edward

"Are we there yet?" Edward asked for the umpteenth time.

"We're five minutes closer than the last time you asked," answered Gracie.

"Well, when are we going to get there?"

"Another day," she answered. "Perhaps two if you keep stopping to ask me silly questions."

Edward sighed. After day upon day (upon day) of trudging north through the woods in the seemingly endless rain, always wet and chilled to the bone, the king was tired of walking. His feet hurt, his head ached, his injured ankle bothered him, and fits of coughing and dizziness regularly overtook him.

The poison was still killing him, he supposed.

Right now the poison was the least of his worries. A few days ago there'd been soldiers on the road. The sight of them had filled Edward with dread, because the banners the soldiers marched under were not of the red roaring lion that marked Edward's reign, but a pomegranate on a bed of roses. Mary's insignia.

They'd been marching toward London.

Which meant things were about to get really bad for Jane.

"Can't we find a way to get there any faster?" he asked, also for the umpteenth time.

Gracie smiled over at him with false sweetness. "You know, this journey would be far quicker if you'd turn yourself into a bird and ride upon my shoulder. Quicker and quieter."

They'd had this argument before.

"No." Edward didn't think it proper to be carried by a woman—how would she ever be able to see him as a man if she was the one bearing him to safety? "If we could just travel on the main road . . ." he suggested.

This was also something they'd argued about.

"No," she refused flatly. "The last thing we need is to come upon more soldiers, or even worse, members of the Pack. We have to stay out of sight."

"Then perhaps we could acquire a horse. . . ."

She stopped walking and turned to look at him. "Acquire a horse, you say? Do you know of any nice, friendly farms just giving away their horses?"

He quirked an eyebrow at her. "You're a thief, aren't you?" At least that was what she claimed as her occupation: stealer of chickens, professional bandit, highwayman when the need arose, cat burglar, occasional pickpocket. She admitted easily to her loose association with the law. Edward wondered how one came by that particular skill set at the tender age of seventeen, which is how old she told him she was, but Gracie didn't answer a lot of questions when it came to her past. She was somewhat evasive about her present situation, as well.

"Stealing a horse is punishable by death," she reminded him.

"Unless you happen to know a king who could pardon you."

She set her hand against her hip and he instantly regretted bringing up who he was. Ever since he'd confessed to being king, the girl had been moody. Oh, she seemed to like him well enough most of the time; she was kind and often merry of soul, and sometimes even wonderfully, confusingly flirtatious, but every now and then she'd remember that he was not just her travel companion but the King of England, and then she'd go quiet. Or even worse, she'd get annoyed with him.

Like now, for instance.

"Well, Sire," She loved to call him Sire, but the way she said it made him suspect she was making fun of him. "You might not have noticed, but you're not exactly a king around here. We can't snap our fingers and have a coach with golden wheels and four fine white horses to carry us wherever we wish to go. We have to make do with our own two feet."

Edward tried to think of a clever reply, but then he had to stop to lean against a tree, because he was out of breath.

Gracie saw the haggard look on his face and turned to squint toward the west, where the sun was quickly descending. "We should stop for the night." She slung her pack against a nearby stump and started to set up a quick, makeshift camp.

"I could keep going," he wheezed as she bustled around gathering kindling. "I'm perfectly capable of continuing."

She ignored him.

"All right, then," he conceded graciously after she got a fire started. "We can stop, if you feel you can't go on." Even as he spoke his traitorous body sank to the ground beside the fire, craving its heat. He closed his eyes. Just to rest them for a moment.

"Are you going to be all right?" Gracie asked.

He opened his eyes and cleared his throat. "Of course. I'm perfectly fine. I only agreed to stop because I know women need to rest more often, on account of your delicate constitutions."

She snorted. "All right, then. Wait here. My delicate constitution and I will be back soon." She bent to remove her boots. Edward tried not to ogle her shapely feminine ankles (a sight that would have been indecent in the royal court, as a woman's ankles were considered scandalously provocative at this time), but he couldn't help staring.

She had lovely ankles, he thought. Very nice.

Gracie glanced up like she'd felt his gaze. "Would you like to paint my portrait, Sire? It will last longer."

He flushed and looked away, which was a good thing, because then she turned her back to him and quickly removed the rest of her clothes and was therefore completely naked for all of three seconds, which he just caught a glimpse of in his peripheral vision before a light flashed, and where Gracie had been standing there was a small red fox, complete with pointed ears, whiskers, and a bushy, white-tipped tail.

Yes, Gracie was a fox. No, really. She was. Literally. (We know. It's too good.)

The fox slipped away into the underbrush, silent as a shadow.

Darkness fell. He watched the stars come out. The rain had finally stopped, and a gentle breeze was blowing, cooling his face. An owl hooted from somewhere in the trees. It was a beautiful night. The kind of night that makes you pensive. And Edward was alone.

It should be mentioned that Edward wasn't accustomed to being alone. In his life before, it'd been exceedingly rare for him to have even fifteen minutes to himself. He'd been the glorious sun with an orbit of men revolving constantly about him. Men to watch that when he ate he did not choke. Men to help him onto his horse. Men to teach him Latin. Men to comb his hair. Men to refill his glass when it was empty, which it never was, because he had men to fill it. Even while he slept there'd been men standing just outside his door to guard him.

And now here he was, completely alone. He found this situation both euphoric (he could scratch himself and no one was looking; no one was judging him—no one!) and unsettling. (What if he choked?)

Edward could have used this time to think about many things: to consider his next move in finding Helmsley and his grandmother and a cure for the poison, to reflect on the nature of trust and betrayal and how hard it was even as king to find good, reliable help these days, to plot a way to regain his kingdom, or at the very least to worry about how his little cousin Jane was doing at that very moment, facing down Mary's army. But Edward didn't think about any of that.

He thought about Gracie. How she was a fox (but Edward was not aware of this little irony, as to our knowledge the term *fox*, used to convey the attractiveness of a woman, was not invented until Jimi Hendrix sang "Foxy Lady" in 1967). How she was, undoubtedly, a thief (but it was all too clear to Edward that although Gracie was definitely a criminal, there was nothing common about her). And how he very much wanted to kiss her.

This last part he found astounding. Gracie was the least appropriate girl in the world for him to receive his first kiss from; he knew that. He was the King of England. She was a Scottish pickpocket. But still, impractically, impossibly, he wanted to kiss her.

She was the one, he'd decided. The lucky girl he was going to kiss.

Now all he had to figure out was how to make said kiss happen.

Usually, when Edward wanted something, he simply had to ask for it. He had no doubt that back at court, if he'd wanted a woman to kiss him, all he would have had to do is say, *Lady Suchandsuch, I wish you to come over here right now and press your lips to mine,* and his wish would have literally been her command. He wouldn't have even had to say please.

But this was different. First off, as Gracie had so generously pointed out, he wasn't much of a king around here. Secondly, if he came right out and asked Gracie to kiss him, he had a feeling that she would laugh in his face. And thirdly, he didn't just want to kiss Gracie. He wanted her to *want* him to kiss her.

But how could he make her want him to kiss her? It had seemed to Edward that she'd been at least slightly interested in the prospect of snogging back in the barn. She'd looked at him *that way.* He shifted uncomfortably in front of the fire. But after that she'd immediately tried to get away from him. But then she'd been helping him. But then she was always leaving him alone.

Women were complicated creatures.

The bushes rustled and Gracie-the-fox stuck her head out and gave a funny little bark, the cue for Edward to turn away again so that she could dress. He stared down at his feet as the Eðian light flashed and Gracie-the-girl snatched up her clothes and disappeared again into the forest.

When she finally emerged, she was carrying a dead rabbit and a bundle tucked under her arm. She tossed him the bundle.

Edward unfolded it eagerly. Whenever she left him for a time, she always returned with something they needed: a pair of pants, to start with (because that had been Edward's biggest shortcoming), followed by a battered cloak, a linen shirt, and a warm woolen blanket. A loaf of bread here. A flask of water there. A slightly rusted but otherwise decent sword. And, the pièce de résistance—boots. A fine, supple pair of boots in exactly his size. How she had pulled that off, he had no idea. He thought it best not to ask.

This particular bundle turned out to be a pair of mismatched socks.

"Thank you," he said, immediately kicking off his boots to put them on.

"You're welcome." She didn't look at him, but sat down on a stump across from the fire and drew from her belt a hunting knife with a beautiful pearl-encrusted handle. Edward felt a bit sick as she made a cut in the rabbit's belly and then pulled its skin off in a single smooth motion. Before this, most of his food had been served to him already dressed and prepared and looking like food, not like some poor defenseless animal.

He remembered the field mouse he'd eaten as a bird. His stomach grumbled unhappily. He turned his attention back to the socks.

"Oh, there's a hole in the toe," he discovered.

"Is there?" She didn't glance up from where she was now gutting the rabbit. "I suppose you'd like me to mend it for you?"

"Yes, that'd be nice," he said, pleased. "When you get time."

"And you've let the fire go down, so you'll be wanting me to stoke it up again."

"Whatever you need to cook the rabbit," he answered.

"And should I press your shirt while I'm at it?"

"It *is* a bit wrinkled," he admitted, although he wasn't sure how she would manage it.

There was a gross plop at his feet—rabbit innards. He gasped and looked up to find her standing over him, feet apart, green eyes furious.

"I'm not your serving wench!" She shook the skinned rabbit under his nose. "I said I'd help you, and I will, but I won't be ordered about. You're not my king, and I'm not your subject. So don't you be telling me what to do."

He blinked up at her, taken aback.

"I wasn't—I didn't mean to give you orders, or make you do all the work. It's just that I . . ."

She folded her arms across her chest.

"I've never had to look after myself before," he muttered to his feet. "I don't know how."

She was still for a moment, and then he heard her move away. When he dared to look up again she was roasting the rabbit on a stick over the fire, her black curls all tumbled about her face and shoulders, her expression grave as she stared into the flames.

His heart sank. She hated him. She was probably thinking about what was the fastest way to be rid of him.

"I'm sorry," he said softly.

She lifted her head and met his gaze, her face aglow with firelight. "I'm sorry, too," she said at last. "I shouldn't have bitten your head off. I'm just touchy on the subject, I suppose."

"The subject?"

"Of English kings."

"Oh." He gave her a weary smile. "Well, that I've noticed. But I think my head is still attached. Last I checked, anyway."

Her dimples appeared; she was trying not to smile back. Hope flooded back into his chest. Maybe she did like him.

"I suppose it's not your fault," she said. "You must be used to people waiting on you hand and foot and tripping over each other to serve you."

"Yes." But he hesitated to tell her about how often he'd felt trapped in a gilded cage by all of that attention. How he'd yearned to accomplish things on his own.

"And you spent your days passing royal decrees, not working to keep yourself warm and fed," she added.

He shrugged. "I left most of the decree making to my counselors." He'd always found the running of the country to be about as interesting as watching grass grow, so he'd mostly delegated it to others. It's what they were there for, he reasoned.

"So what did you do?" she asked. "Eat, drink, and be merry, all the livelong day?"

"No." He scoffed, but he was thinking of the way he'd started each day as king being dressed by his servants, his morning meal taken in his private chambers on a literal silver platter, then off to his hours of lessons with the most impressive tutors of the realm. Then lunch. Then he'd spent the afternoons (before his illness had struck him, anyway) playing tennis or practicing at archery and swordplay. He was fairly good with the lute, too, and sometimes he'd perform little plays with his grooms. And sometimes he'd gone hunting. For deer. And bears. And (gulp) foxes.

It occurred to Edward then that in some ways he'd always been preparing to be a king, instead of truly being one.

He cleared his throat. "So, how old were you," he asked, to change the subject, "when you discovered you were an Eðian?"

"Oh, I've always known it," Gracie answered. She turned the rabbit slowly to its other side. "My ma and da were, and all my aunts and uncles and cousins and such. It would have been a great disappointment to me if I'd turned out differently."

"But when did you know you were a fox?" he asked.

She shrugged. "Many Scots are foxes. And harts and hinds, martens and roes, the beasts of the chase, we are. Why else do you think the English have taken such pleasure in hunting us?"

Gulp. The English, aka Edward. Although he considered the bad blood between England and Scotland to be completely his father's doing, certainly not his own, except for all that business with Mary Queen of Scots. He shuddered. "So why are you helping me, if you're Scottish and I'm English and we should be trying to kill each other?"

She lifted the roasting stick from the fire and drew out her knife again to divide the rabbit. To answer his question, she said, "I've always had a weak spot for the truly pathetic creatures of this world."

"Thanks," he said wryly, and promptly burned his tongue on the rabbit. "God's teeth, that's hot!"

Gracie handed him a flask of water, which he took gratefully.

"So tell me about this granny of yours who's going to save the

248

day." She had the sense to blow on the meat before she began to eat it, and for a moment Edward just watched her. "Your granny at Helmsley?" she prompted.

"Oh. She's the old Queen Mother," Edward explained. "My father's mother, Elizabeth. She was supposed to have died half a century ago, even before my father became king. But they only told the people she'd died, when in truth they spirited her to Helmsley, where she's been ever since."

"Why?"

"Because she's a skunk."

Gracie snorted with laughter. "A skunk?"

"An E∂ian, in the time when it was illegal to be an E∂ian," Edward continued around a more careful mouthful of rabbit. "But my grandfather loved her, he truly loved her, so rather than burn her at the stake he decided to stage her death and send her away. We'd take a trip out to the country to see her every few years, Mary and Bess and I, and my cousin Jane a few times, too, since Gran is her great-grandmother. She's so old—she's got to be nearing ninety now, I'd say—and she has no decorum whatsoever. Once, she made Father so angry that he turned into a lion, and we were afraid he'd devour her, but then she turned into a skunk and sprayed him right in the face. It took weeks for him to be rid of the smell."

"Sounds like I'm going to like her," Gracie said with a grin.

"Jane and I adored her. She loved to play games with us. It's her face on the cards, you know, whenever you draw the queen of hearts."

"Is that so?" Gracie was already done with her rabbit, and flung its bones into the brush. She always ate quickly, without anything resembling manners, as if she might have to flee at any moment. Edward, on the other hand, was taking time to savor his rabbit. He was finding this fire-cooked food better than anything he'd been served in the palace, because now when he ate he was always so hungry, and he could feel the food giving his body strength that he desperately needed. This food was giving him life.

"So is it really only a day left before we arrive at Helmsley?" he asked when he was finished.

"If we don't run into any more problems." Gracie sucked at a bit of rabbit grease on her fingers. "But, like I've said time and again, we could get there much faster if you'd only—"

"And I've told *you* time and again," Edward interrupted. "I'm not going to become a bird and ride on your shoulder like your pet. If it were so simple as that, I could change and fly straight there, couldn't I? I could leave you behind."

"Well, don't be staying on my account." She leaned back on her arms and gazed up at the stars. "Fly, then."

"I can't," he admitted. "I don't know the way."

She made a sound like a chuckle.

"Besides," Edward continued lightly, "I suppose I've come to enjoy your company."

It could have been hopeful thinking, but the Scot seemed pleased at this announcement. "Have you, now? Well, I suppose I like your company as well, when you're not being a spoiled brat."

"Oh, thank you very much," he muttered.

"You're quite welcome. But you should fly away, if you can. Helmsley wouldn't be very far as the kestrel flies."

He shook his head. "When I'm a bird, I forget myself. I forget everything but the wind and the sky. I'm just flying, floating above it all, and it's the best feeling in the world. I'm not sick. I'm not king. I'm free."

She'd moved closer to him when he spoke of flying, her expression pensive. She gazed up at the stars, and he tried not to be distracted by the alluring arc of her neck. "It does look lovely up there," she murmured. "I've often dreamed of flying."

"But I lose all sense of time and purpose when I do," he continued. "Does that happen to you when you change? Does the animal take over?"

She looked thoughtful. "I do have foxy thoughts, sometimes. A love of holes. Of running. The squawk of a chicken just before my teeth sink in—" She blushed and showed her dimples again, eyes dancing in the firelight.

He pretended to stretch his arms, in order to shift even closer to her. (This isn't in the history books, of course, but we'd like to point out that this was the first time a young man had ever tried that particular arm-stretch move on a young woman. Edward was the inventor of the arm stretch, a tactic that teenage boys have been using for centuries.)

Gracie didn't move away. The kiss might have happened then, but at that exact moment the wind shifted, sending a cloud of smoke from the fire into their faces. They both coughed, of course, but Edward coughed and coughed until his vision blurred. *Curse Dudley and his poison and his plan and all this wretched coughing,* he thought. No way she'd kiss him after he just hacked up half his lungs.

Gracie jumped to her feet and made herself busy tending to the fire. "Anyway, you're a greenie," she said as she strategically arranged more pieces of wood. "You've just discovered your Eðian form. You'll learn to control it, in time."

He sighed. "How do you do control it?"

"It's not so hard. When I want to change, I take a deep breath to clear the head, and I think something like, *To be a fox now would be to find our supper, and to find our supper would be to help the young king,* and then the fox rises to the occasion. Speaking of which," she added, turning to her pack. "I've brought us some dessert."

She took out a handkerchief and unfolded it, and there, glistening in the firelight, was a handful of blackberries.

Edward didn't know what happened. One minute he was fine, pleased, even, at the prospect of having the taste of blackberries on his tongue again, and then the next he was thrashing in a violent series of seizures, his eyes rolling back in his head, his mouth foaming. He could barely discern Gracie's face over him, her eyes wide with worry.

After several moments the shaking passed. He lay for a while curled on to his side, exhausted and panting, then coughing again, always coughing, then vomiting up rabbit. When he was done Gracie laid her cool hand against his forehead.

"You're hot," she murmured.

He wished he could take that as a compliment. "I'm sorry," he said. "I don't have one or two days to get to Helmsley, do I? I'm still dying, apparently."

Her jaw set. "You need to change. It's the only way."

All that was left of his pride seemed to have deserted him. "How?" he whispered.

"I'll wrap you loose, so you won't be injured, and bind you to me, and carry you."

"Bind me to you?" he croaked, struggling to keep his eyes open.

"Like a mother would carry her bairn," she said, grabbing his hand. "You'd be safe, and we'd go quickly. I can run like the wind, even when I'm not a fox." She pulled his hand into her chest, where he could feel the strong beat of her heart. "I promise you. I can get you to your granny."

"All right," he whispered, a hint of a smile appearing on his lips. "I can't very well say no to spending the night resting against your bosom, can I?"

She snatched his hand away. "Don't be fresh."

He gave a soft laugh, and then he was a kestrel. Gracie sighed and pulled the cloak around him, and it was dark, and warm there against her, and good. Really, really good.

He became slowly aware of a faintly bad smell. He stretched and was surprised to find himself in his human body again, on a real bed, it felt like, covered in furs. He opened his eyes. A single candle burned in the darkness, and as his eyes adjusted he could make out a figure sitting by his bed. A woman.

"Gracie? Where are we?"

"You're at Helmsley," said a voice, but it wasn't the Scot's voice. It was Bess. She smiled at him and caught his hand. "I was beginning to think you wouldn't make it."

"I was beginning to think so, too," he admitted.

"Here." She brought a cup to his lips. He drank and then hissed at the taste. It wasn't water, but a concoction so foul it made his eyes tear.

"It will snake the poison from your blood," Bess told him. "Gran made it."

"Gran's here?"

"Of course I'm here," came a gruff old voice from the doorway. "Where else do you suppose I would be?"

"Hello, Gran."

"You've got yourself in quite the pickle, haven't you, my boy?" Gran said. She went to the window and drew back the heavy velvet curtains. Warm midday sunshine poured in.

"Gran," Bess admonished warmly. "You shouldn't address him as *boy*. He's still the king."

"He's a birdbrained boy, as far as I can tell," the old lady cackled. "I mean, getting himself poisoned. My word, child. People tried to poison me ten times a day, when I was queen. None of them ever succeeded."

"Yes, Gran," he said. "It was in poor form to get myself poisoned."

"Now get up," she ordered. "You need to get the blood moving through you, to give the antidote a chance to work."

He still felt light-headed and wobbly, but he didn't argue. He let Bess support him as he sat up and swung his legs out of bed. That's when he discovered he was wearing only the white linen shirt Gracie had stole for him, which hit him mid-thigh.

"Um, where are my pants?"

Gran scoffed. "Oh, please, it's nothing I haven't seen before." She got on the other side of him and poked him in the ribs. "Up with you."

He stood. It did not escape his notice that Gran was as unpleasantly fragrant as ever, but the skunk smell was actually working to clear his head. He felt weak and hollowed out and half-naked, of course, but decidedly better.

Maybe he wasn't going to die.

Gracie appeared in the doorway. Her gaze went straight to his white, white legs.

"Your Majesty," she said with a grin, and curtsied impertinently, which looked all wrong because she was still wearing trousers.

Or maybe he wanted to die, after all.

Still, as Gran had said, it was nothing she hadn't seen before.

Gran and Bess were both looking from Gracie to Edward and back again with amused expressions. Then Bess snapped out of it and fetched his pants. He tried to ignore his burning face as she helped him put them on, one leg and then the other. Once they were fastened, he stood up straight and said, "I can manage," shook Bess off as she tried to help him, and walked slowly but steadily across the room to the window. It looked like a summer day outside: birds singing, green grasses swaying in a half-tended garden below, sky so blue you would doubt that it had ever rained.

"How long have we been here?" he asked.

"You arrived early this morning," Bess provided.

Less than a day, then. Gracie had run them here in less than a day. He glanced back at her. "You can run pretty fast, for a girl."

"Well, I may have held up a nobleman on the road and borrowed his horse," she confessed.

A crime punishable by death, he remembered. "I owe my life to you," he said.

Her dimples appeared. "A girl does what she can, Sire."

"Oh, I like her," Gran announced. "Can you play cards, my dear?"

"A bit. And I hear you're the queen of hearts," Gracie answered, which clearly pleased the old lady even more.

"There's no time for cards, Gran." Bess's expression was so solemn that she vaguely resembled Mary for a moment. Which made Edward remember Mary. And her soldiers, marching toward his castle.

Gran sighed. "True enough for you, but not so for me. Come along, you," she said to Gracie, grabbing the girl's arm and towing her toward the door. "I'll show you how to play trump."

"Keep an eye on her sleeves," Edward called after them. "You never know what she might be hiding up there."

Gracie made a face that said, *Do I look like an amateur to you?* and he was tempted to warn Gran, too, that the Scot was more than what she seemed. But then they were gone.

"We need to talk," Bess said in a low voice.

He crossed back to the window and leaned against the sill. Bess closed the door, then pulled a chair up beside him. "All right, Bess," he murmured, suddenly tired again. "Tell me what's happened."

"Jane became queen, as you intended."

"As Dudley intended," he corrected darkly.

"The duke also attempted to capture Mary and me and throw us in the Tower, so we would pose no threat to Jane's rule," Bess continued. "But I slipped out when I heard them coming, and Mary caught wind of it through one of her craftier spies, and escaped to her estate at Kenninghall, and from there she went to Flanders to enlist help from the Holy Roman Emperor. She raised an army, of course, and from what I understand, she took back the throne this morning."

"We need to go," Edward said. "I need to be there, now."

Bess shook her head. "Mary wanted this—for you to be dead and the crown upon her own head—to rid the kingdom of Eðians and return to the purity of the old days. She will stop at nothing."

He remembered the bite of poisoned pudding that his sister had pressed firmly to his lips. To ensure that very thing.

"So she was in on it all along?" he asked. "With Dudley."

"No." Bess's mouth tightened. "It was by chance that Mary and I found out about Dudley poisoning you. One day, on our way to see you, we happened to overhear a conversation between the doctor and the nurse concerning an extra ingredient they were adding to your blackberries. When Mary confronted Dudley about it, he claimed that he was paving the way for Mary to take the throne, although I think he always intended for Jane to rule, and for Gifford to rule over Jane, and Dudley himself to rule over Gifford. But Mary bought his story, and played along, as did I, although all the while I was trying to find a way to save you."

"Like with the jar of apricots," he remembered. "You did save me."

She nodded and smiled at him tenderly. "You're my little brother. I could not stand by and let any harm come to you."

"But Mary is my sister, too," Edward said. "She's my godmother, for heaven's sake. How dare she try to steal away my birthright! I am the rightful king!" He was overcome by another wave of fatigue, so much that Bess rose to offer him her chair, and he couldn't help but accept.

"I am the king," he muttered.

"Not to Mary, you're not," Bess said, putting her hand on his shoulder. "Not anymore."

SEVENTEEN

Jane

There was no battle for the kingdom.

Within minutes of Mary's arrival, red-coated soldiers had swarmed in, wrested Gifford's sword away from him (not that he really attempted to use it), and bound Jane and Gifford's hands with ropes. In short order they were marched down the stairs and through the Tower at sword point.

"I'll try reasoning with her," Jane said as they made their way to the throne room.

"Do you think it will do any good?" Gifford was pale, but she could see he was trying to be brave.

"I don't know. Just let me do the talking. Everyone knows that Mary hates Eðians."

"She can't tell just by looking at me, you know. It's not like I have a tail hidden in my trousers."

"Even so. Now would be a fantastic time to learn to control your gift."

They reached the throne room, which was packed with soldiers and nobility alike. Her ladies-in-waiting were all there, a few looking faint on account of all the excitement, while others had their noses turned up like they'd never thought Jane made a good queen, anyway.

Her mother was there. She looked up as Jane and Gifford entered, but didn't meet Jane's eyes. A guard poked Jane in the ribs to get her moving toward the throne.

Where Mary waited.

Edward's eldest sister reclined in the throne, Jane's crown already gracing her brow. She wore a voluminous gown of crimson damask, with roses embroidered along the blue background of the hems. She looked regal, as though she'd known her whole life that this was what she was meant to do.

"Jane." Mary's tone was sweet as she leaned forward. "You haven't been harmed?"

Jane stood before her own throne. She kept herself as straight and tall as possible and let her eyes sweep over the assembly near the throne: dukes, members of the Privy Council, and standing at the front, John Dudley, Duke of Northumberland.

"You," Jane murmured. "Whose side are you on now?"

His only answer was a slippery smile.

"Jane." A note of irritation snapped in Mary's voice. "You

haven't been harmed?"

Jane turned her eyes back on Mary. "You're sitting in my chair."

A few people in the crowd gasped, but Mary only smiled. "Jane. Dear one. Surely you know that it was only through the plots of others that you managed to sit here at all. The throne was always meant to be mine until Edward"—her voice cracked at the late king's name—"produced an heir. Unfortunately my brother never had that opportunity. He was taken from us too quickly. The law states that I am next in the line of succession."

"Edward amended his will. It was his final act before he died." Jane didn't look at Lord Dudley again, but hadn't that been exactly what he'd said? Now he was just standing there, accepting Mary as queen?

"I feel sorry for you, Jane." Mary nodded to herself. "You were caught in this game without the smallest hint how to play it."

"Edward left the throne to me." Jane kept her voice soft but firm. "He revised the line of succession."

"My brother was ill and persuaded to do nonsensical things by certain parties who had everything to gain." Mary looked pointedly at Lord Dudley. "Those parties were given a choice—the same choice I'm going to give to you."

"But the crown is not your right," Jane said, in spite of feeling— just days before—that it wasn't her right, either. Jane at least knew it, while Mary seemed to feel entitled to the throne.

"The Privy Council disagrees."

The Privy Council had voted to give the crown to Mary? Jane prickled. How dare they turn on her? She could not believe it. After listening to them brag about themselves for hours on her first day as queen, she rather felt she'd earned their respect and loyalty.

"As I said," Mary went on, "I want to be fair. I'm giving everyone a choice to bow to me."

Gifford, who had been quiet all this time, suddenly leaned toward Jane until his mouth was against her ear. "I have to get out of here," he said urgently. "It's almost morning."

He was right. She could sense the glow of dawn behind the windows. And Mary was not turning out to be very reasonable.

"Give us until tonight," Jane pleaded. "We need time to consider—"

"There's nothing to consider," Mary said. "It's a simple yes or no."

Gifford shifted from foot to foot. "Jane—"

"I haven't slept or eaten," Jane argued. "Before I make such a decision, I need to rest. To think. Please, if we could just—"

It was too late. The first ray of sunshine breached the window. Next to Jane, another kind of light flared. There was the sound of clothing tearing and hooves clapping against the marble floor.

The crowd let out a collective gasp of horror. Guards rushed forward, swords in hand.

Mary surged up from the throne.

Jane's heart sank.

Gifford was a horse.

Jane had the wild thought of leaping onto Gifford's back and riding away as quickly as they could. (Of course, that would violate Horse Rule 3: no riding the horse.) But it would be difficult for him to navigate the narrow, winding stairs in his current state, and even though Gifford was pressing close to Jane as if to protect her, there was no way to climb atop him. Her hands were still bound behind her back.

"Seize them," Mary commanded.

Soldiers yanked her away. She tried to wriggle free, and Gifford snapped and kicked, but then one of the men held a sword to Gifford's long neck. Someone else pressed a knife to Jane's throat.

Girl and horse met each other's eyes, and that was when they stopped fighting.

"Well." Mary settled back onto the throne. She spoke with that sweet voice again, but now Jane couldn't miss the edge of contempt. "How surprising."

One of the guards looped a rope around Gifford's neck. He didn't resist. A guard came up behind Jane, cut the ropes binding her wrists, and clasped on a pair of metal shackles. Which seemed like overkill.

"Dearest Jane," Mary said. "My late brother had such fondness for you. It is in his memory that I make this offer. That, and as I said earlier, I've always felt a little sorry for you. Not just because you couldn't comprehend the game being played around you, but because of that unfortunate red hair of yours. It's just— Well, I don't want to be rude."

No, Jane thought, *you just want to take my throne and kill my husband.*

She turned to look at Gifford, who didn't stir. He'd only been her husband for a little while, such a very little amount of time, relatively speaking. She didn't know his favorite color or the food he liked best—outside of apples, which seemed like a horse preference. She'd assumed he'd been part of this game, trying to manipulate her like everyone else, but that didn't matter to her now. What would happen to him? What would happen to them both?

"My offer is fair, and I urge you to accept," Mary was saying.

"I'm still waiting to hear what it is," Jane said numbly.

"Ah. Dear. I'm sorry. I thought it must have been obvious what I want from you. What everyone else has already done." Mary gestured at Lady Frances and Lord Dudley. "Accept me as your rightful queen and denounce evil. Denounce heretics. Denounce Eðians."

Of course.

"Sweet little Jane. You like to prattle on about Eðians and heroes and other such nonsense. You are young and those sorts of things seem attractive to you, but you must grow up now. Renounce the Eðians, including your husband, and live out the rest of your days in exile. I've arranged for you to be sent to a monastery, even. You'll be quite safe and comfortable there."

"And if I don't agree?"

Mary made a swift slice of her hand over her throat. "I didn't think that needed to be said, either, what with the extensive reading you've done, but I suppose I've overestimated you."

Jane glanced at her mother, who nodded. Urging her to give in. As she herself must have done.

The throne room was silent as everyone waited to hear Jane's answer.

"What will happen to my husband?" she asked.

Mary shook her head with false sadness, but her eyes were sparkling. "In the morning, he will be burned at the stake."

Jane's hands flew to her mouth—or rather, would have, but she was still shackled. The metal bit deeply into her wrists as she strained against it. "No," she breathed. "Don't hurt him. He can't help what he is."

Mary tilted her head. "So you knew that he is an abomination?"

Jane's eyes cut to Dudley.

The duke said, "Of course *I* hadn't the faintest idea, Your Majesty. If Gifford was in and out of the house at all hours and refused to go to court, I assumed my son was merely acting out like any normal boy. Why would I assume he had something darker to hide?"

"That's a lie," Jane said, but no one cared.

"This is about you, dear. Did you know your husband was a beast?" Mary pressed.

"I found out on our wedding night. Everyone who knew"— she glared at Dudley—"neglected to tell me."

"And were you surprised?" Mary's tone was honey sweet.

"Certainly."

"And do you reject his vile magic? Do you renounce your ties to him?" Mary leaned forward. "It's simple. Name yourself a Verity and your life will be spared. Or deny me, and I'll have your head."

Jane closed her eyes. Her shoulders ached. Her wrists stung, and liquid heat dripped down her hands—blood. Never before had she been so mistreated, and a desperate part of her wanted to say yes, she denounced him and she'd go live in a monastery, exiled for the rest of her days.

But Gifford would die.

He hadn't abandoned her. A former womanizer and drunk and (current) horse he might be, but he'd just proven himself to be the most loyal person in her life. In spite of the way she'd treated him, her accusations and her hurled pillows and her scorn, he'd tried to warn her. He hadn't fled when the army arrived. He hadn't switched sides.

Could she abandon him now?

Gifford-the-horse had kept his head down throughout this entire interrogation, his nose almost brushing the floor, the very picture of docility. But now he lifted his head. His eyes, at once both human and horse, met hers. *Do it,* his eyes urged. *Renounce me. Save yourself.*

Memories of their time in the country floated back to her: their banter, reading beneath the tree, helping those in need, and most of all, that almost kiss as the sky was deep with twilight and candles burned around them. There was no denying the truth:

Gifford Dudley was a good man, Eðian or not. And he was her husband. For better or worse.

The answer must have shown on her face.

"Little Jane, be reasonable." Mary pressed her hands together. "What purpose will your death serve?"

"It will serve to prove that you do not control this kingdom. It will serve to prove that not everyone will bow down to you. You think to rule us with fear, but you cannot. I will never renounce my beliefs, or my husband."

Mary's face darkened with anger. "Take her away! And do something about this . . . animal!"

Soldiers grabbed at Jane. She couldn't resist, not with her bleeding wrists cuffed behind her back, but she continued speaking.

"Eðians are people, too. You only hate them because you fear them!"

Mary's guards dragged her away, and no one lifted a finger to help her.

Jane had read about despair.

The hopelessness of Socrates, who'd felt no recourse but to poison himself rather than facing a life in a cave prison. The terror of Anne Boleyn, Bess's mother, who'd been beheaded just years before, after being tried for adultery. The resignation of Cleopatra, who'd taken her own life with the bite of an asp after she and her husband lost the Battle of Actium.

The despair in books was a distant, safe thing. She'd thought she understood the depth of the emotion as she read through the pages of her beloved books, her life touching those of men and women long dead. She'd felt for them, cried for them, tried to breathe for them when they no longer breathed. And then, she'd been able to close the book and place it on its shelf, the words trapped between the leather covers.

Oh, sometimes it had taken her hours or days to recover from a particularly emotional book, but there'd always been another to take her mind off the anguish.

There were no books here.

Nothing could distract her from the forced march up the stairs of the Queen's House (built at the bidding of Anne Boleyn, and then ironically the place of her captivity before she was executed), into a bare room where Jane was to live out the remaining hours of her life. Nothing could distract from the four brick walls surrounding her, the cold and the darkness, or the searing pain in her wrists and shoulders even after the shackles had been removed.

Too sore and tired to pace, Jane slumped in the middle of the floor. There was no furniture; it had been removed so she couldn't spend her last night in a bed. Such decency, she inferred, was above her, an Eðian-loving heretic.

"I am sixteen years old," she told the empty room. "And tomorrow I will die."

That's what the guards had told her. Tomorrow she'd be beheaded.

Who would go first? Her, or Gifford? Would they be able to

see each other? Perhaps Jane would be made to watch as her husband burned alive, and then her head would come off before she could even shed a tear. Or the other way around, maybe. Gifford might see the axe swing and a flash of red hair flying, and then they'd light the pyre beneath him.

Jane hugged her knees and shuddered. Her imagination was too vivid.

Night fell. She knew only because the faint light from the windows faded, not because her body gave her any useful signals. Her head was light with thirst and hunger. When she ran her tongue along her lips, they were dry and cracked. Her stomach felt hollow. If she could have escaped into sleep, she would have, but shocks of terror and dread jabbed at her mind every other minute, reminding her that these hours were the last she had left.

If she slept, she'd waste them.

For another hour—or some amount of time she had no way to judge—she thought about Gifford and what he must be doing now. Likely he wasn't still in the stables, but moved somewhere more secure, now that it was night. She thought about his laugh and his jokes, the charming way he found humor in everything. Would he find humor in this situation? Tomorrow morning?

If only she could see him now. She'd apologize for the last week and a half. She'd name him king. She'd kiss him and say she trusted him. She'd— She'd—

Maybe Gifford wasn't safe to think about right now.

Jane shifted her thoughts to Edward, wondering if he'd felt

this deep unease in the face of his own death. Anxiety. Trepidation. Horror.

She tried to conjure up more synonyms, but a dim, orange light flickered beneath the door. Footfalls echoed on the steps, and a moment later the door creaked open.

Firelight shone in, blinding her. She squeaked and buried her face in the hollow of her arms and knees. Then, squinting, she looked up.

"Jane?" Lady Frances rushed in, holding a torch, which she quickly set into a holder on the wall. "The guards let me in. We have a few minutes at best. I came to ask you to reconsider Mary's offer." She knelt in front of Jane, her expression almost maternal in its concern. "I wanted you to know I'm sorry I wasn't more . . . supportive back there. Please forgive me."

Jane stared at her mother. She'd never heard an apology from Lady Frances's lips before, and she wasn't sure what to do with it.

"It doesn't matter," she said at last. "The throne changed hands very quickly, didn't it? No one resisted."

Lady Frances bowed her head. "The Privy Council turned on you. Dudley betrayed us as well. The moment Mary arrived, he declared his allegiance to her—even though it means he's not the Lord President anymore—and his loathing of Eðians. He declared himself a Verity. He made it sound like all along he was actually clearing a path for Mary to take power. But forget about Dudley for now. This is about you. Take Mary's offer. It's not too late. A life in exile is better than this."

"No."

"Jane, this is no time to display your stubbornness."

"It's not stubbornness. It's a matter of honor. I will not denounce Gifford or Eðians—you included, Mother." Jane coughed at the dryness in her throat.

Lady Frances' eyes flickered toward the door, like she was afraid someone would overhear. "Ungrateful girl. You have no idea what you're talking about. I'm no Eðian."

"I know you are. I heard you and Father discussing it years ago."

Her mother shook her head like she might deny it, but then she sighed. "And I hate it," she whispered. "I never change, not if I can help it. I push that part of me down until it's buried. It's unnatural."

"And yet it's part of you," Jane implored her. "In one of my books about Eðians, the author said that long ago, in ancient times, all people were able to change into an animal form. Everyone was Eðian. It was considered their true nature. It was considered divine."

"Nonsense." Her mother's expression grew cold. "All those books fill your head with such drivel. I should have burned them all, and then maybe we wouldn't be in this mess."

Jane closed her eyes for a moment. Then she pushed her stiff muscles until she was able to stand up. "Do not ask me to forsake Eðians again, Mother. You will not change my mind."

There were voices in the hall. Lady Frances glanced over her shoulder toward the door.

"Our time is almost up," Jane said. "I suppose we should say good-bye now."

"Please, Jane." Her mother grabbed her arm. "You don't have to die. It will bring ruin on the family. On me. I'll lose Bradgate. I'll lose everything."

"I'm sorry, I can't help that," Jane replied, and she meant it. She, too, loved Bradgate, but it wasn't worth her honor. "Do you know where Gifford is being held?"

"They took him to Beauchamp Tower after night fell. That's all I know."

"I want to see him. Can you ask for me?"

Lady Grey shook her head. "The only way to see him will be to denounce him, and then you would only see him burn."

The guards arrived. They escorted Lady Frances from the room, without another word between them, and Jane was alone again.

Her prison seemed to shrink around her. The despair she'd known earlier became a drop to an ocean. One star to the entire universe. Her mother had abandoned her, no matter what she claimed. There was only one person left in the world to think about, and that was Gifford, locked away in Beauchamp Tower, so close to the Queen's House, but it might as well have been the other side of the world.

Jane sank to the floor again, drowning in grief and misery and wretchedness and despondency and . . .

A brilliant white light flared about her, making her blink back stars.

When she could see again, everything was different. The room was bigger, for one, and she felt . . . funny. Shorter, which was saying something, but oddly long. Her spine felt strange and hunchy, and she was on all fours. And her sense of smell! There was something sour—unbathed human, probably—and musky.

The sound of voices below, the feel of the stone floor under her paws—it was incredible.

She'd changed into . . . something.

She was an Eðian.

She was an Eðian!

Jane hopped around the room in a crazy little dance, thrashing her head from side to side so hard she bashed into a wall. Unfazed, she made a soft clucky sound and danced again, an overpowering sense of joy filling her. She was an Eðian, just as she'd always hoped. What was she? It didn't matter. She was small and furry (she could easily twist herself around to see her body, but it was hard to get an idea of a whole based on just a few too-close views) and she had the best sense of smell and the best sense of hearing and the best dancing skills she'd ever possessed in her life, even if dancing sometimes meant she ran into walls. Wouldn't Gifford be so amused when he saw her?

Gifford.

The sense of elation faded as she remembered her predicament and now that she was . . . a something . . . she would likely be burned at the stake as well.

But her animal self was small, she knew that, and maybe she could do something useful now.

She hopped over to the door. There was a large crack beneath it, not quite big enough for a human fist to fit underneath. But maybe she could fit?

Jane shoved her face into the crack beneath the door. Her head went right under, followed by her shoulders, but the rest of her body stuck a little.

That was embarrassing.

She squeezed and scrambled and pushed until she popped out of the other side.

There was more light in the corridor. Twilight to her human self, but she could see quite easily now, at least within a few feet. Everything beyond that seemed fuzzy and oddly flat. Everything was shades of gray, too, except a faint red cast to some things, like the light of a lantern on the wall.

So her vision wasn't that great, but she was small and close to the floor, so what did she need with fantastic distance vision, anyway? She had other senses. Better senses.

Jane scurried to the edge of the first stair and paused, looking down. What was nothing particularly difficult in her human form suddenly appeared quite challenging. She couldn't just step down.

She pressed her belly to the stone floor and pushed her front paws ahead of her, sliding down the first stair until her paws touched the next. The rest of her body followed with an awkward flop. She repeated this process a few more times until she found a better way to control her rogue hindquarters and moved down the stairs at a quicker pace.

At the first landing, she found the guards. She was the size of their boots. She resisted the urge to smell all their interesting, earthy aromas, and instead streaked past them so quickly they didn't notice her.

Other voices below grew louder as she descended the stairs, too distant for the guards on the landing to hear, but her ears were fantastic. Amazing. Probably very cute.

One of the speakers was Dudley, she was sure of it, though in this form, the sound was overwhelming and held qualities she'd never heard as a human.

"What is it?" he asked.

"I've obtained a body," another man said. His voice was familiar, too. The royal physician? She couldn't remember his name.

"Very good." Dudley sneezed and sniffed. "Drape a shroud over it and no one will know it isn't Edward."

Jane stopped moving. It felt like all the fur on her body was standing up.

They didn't have Edward's body?

"They haven't found him yet?" asked the doctor. "The poison would have killed him by now. There's no way he could survive without an antidote."

Dudley sighed. "He was sick. Wounded. Starved. He had to have left some kind of trail."

Their voices were fading now, as though they'd been walking by the stairs.

Jane slinked down the rest of the steps, her tiny heart racing. Edward had been poisoned? Dudley had poisoned Edward? And then Edward had . . . what? Escaped?

Her heart lifted at the idea. How easily, she thought, despair could turn to hope.

At the foot of the staircase, Jane looked around the corner. The hall was enormous, but empty for now. If she kept to the shadows, she wouldn't be spotted. Hopefully. And then she could escape the Tower. Find Edward.

But first she had to rescue her horse.

EIGHTEEN
Gifford

Burned at the stake. A most unpleasant way to go, G thought. When he was just a boy of five, he'd witnessed a man being burned at the stake. It was 1538 and John Lambert had been outed as an Eðian when, after hearing Frederic Clarence had written a pamphlet denouncing Eðian magic, he turned into a dog and ate the papers, prompting Clarence to cry out, "That dog ate my scriptwork!"

Lambert was sentenced to be burned at the stake, and Lord Dudley had insisted that his children attend the execution. He later told G that nobody trusted those with the ancient magic, and the country would be safer if every Eðian suffered the same fate as Lambert. Which, at the time, G's father had seemed to truly believe.

All G remembered of that day was the scream that seemed to go on for an eternity. That and the smell.

He glanced at the lone candle his captors allowed in his locked tower room, and then looked closer at the small flame on the wick. Never had something so innocuous seemed so ominous.

He held his hand over the flame.

"God's teeth!" he exclaimed, pulling his hand back after a mere instant. He hadn't felt so much pain in his entire life, which, in the next instant, he decided was a sad statement because what nineteen-year-old man has only ever felt the pain of a candle on his skin?

One who spends most of his nights attending plays and poetry readings.

He sighed. Usually he composed stanzas in his head to calm his anxiety, but at the moment G had no desire to find a phrase that rhymed with "charred flesh."

He examined the palm of his right hand, expecting to see burned skin, but of course there was nothing. Not even a little red.

Now that the pain had subsided (not that there'd been very much of it to begin with) he turned his thoughts toward Jane, specifically the way she'd refused to denounce him as a heretic. He closed his eyes and remembered her confident posture as she stood by him, so sure in her decision, even though she could've easily sacrificed him to buy her own escape.

She wouldn't betray him.

Foolish, loyal, beautiful girl. At least her death would come much quicker than his.

He looked out the window. From this vantage point, he could

almost see the place where Jane would suffer her fate, inside the courtyard of the Tower. For G, though, he knew he would be executed on Tower Hill, where the rest of the common criminals and heretics took their last breaths. That's where he'd be burned.

It was a sad day when he yearned for a nice, tidy beheading. Instead of trying to compose morbid poetry (*to be, or not to be, that was the question . . .*), he decided to carve a name into the stone wall. Jane's name, of course.

J

Jane. He wondered if she was thinking of him, too. If he would ever see her again.

A

He'd never see a lot of people again. He'd never kiss his mother on the cheek, or make fun of Stan (who wasn't so bad, was he? Not really. It'd been unfair for him to resent Stan all this time, G thought). He'd never give Billingsly another ridiculous order, or make Tempie laugh, or try to irritate his father just to see the aggravation on the old man's face.

N

His father. G chipped harder at the stone. His father. Who had orchestrated this entire mess. Who would undoubtedly be fine, so long as he could switch to the winning side.

E

Who'd let his own son burn if it would save his life.

G decided that he couldn't think about it anymore. He put the finishing touches on the *e* of Jane's name, and then paced around the room, looking for something, anything, to get his mind off burning flesh. He found a few books, skimmed through the first few pages of each, and then tossed them one by one to the side. Maybe this had been meant to be Jane's room. She was probably locked somewhere with a barrel of apples.

A soft flutter at the door made him stop his pacing. Someone had slipped a piece of parchment underneath.

He hurried over and unfolded it and saw Jane's familiar handwriting. His heart pounded. He'd never received a love letter before, and although he knew his letter would most likely also be a good-bye letter, he felt some wild hope that she would confess some depth of feeling for him.

Dearest Edward,

I hoped to visit you this morning, but when I arrived at the palace I was informed that you are not receiving visitors. I must confess my surprise and disappointment that you would not see even me, but I know there must be a good reason, and I suspect that this self-imposed isolation means that your illness is taking its toll. For this I am so very sorry, cousin, and I wish there was something I could do to make you well again.

I'm sure you must be wondering what it is I came to see you about this morning, mere hours after my wedding. My dear cousin, the wedding is precisely the topic I wanted to discuss with you. Or rather, my newly acquired husband.

Gifford is a horse.

I'm certain you knew this, what with your referrals to "his condition" and assumptions that I would find it intriguing. What I cannot fathom is why you chose not to tell me. We've always told each other everything, have we not? I consider you to be my most trusted confidant, my dearest and most beloved friend. Why then, did you neglect this rather critical detail? It doesn't make sense.

But perhaps in this, too, I wonder now, you felt you had a good reason.

I hope that we will be able to speak more on this subject when I return from my honeymoon in the country.

All my love,

Jane

G refolded the letter, resisting the urge to crumple it up and toss it in the corner. He wasn't offended by her surprise at his condition, but did she need to sign it "all my love"? *All* her love seemed a little excessive.

It was abundantly clear to G that Jane loved Edward; he'd never forget the look on her face when she'd been told that the king was dead. But had she *loved him* loved him? Was she thinking about her cousin right now, preparing herself to join her beloved in death?

Not that it really mattered. G tried to shake his insecurity away and instead be grateful to whoever had given this to him. His wife's hand had written this letter. He could picture her face as she wrote it, her mouth pursing and brow furrowing the way it did when she concentrated. He was about to place the paper in his own coat pocket when he noticed something written in different handwriting near the corner of one of the folded edges.

It was one word.

Skunk

Well, that was a surprising word. No beauty in a word like *skunk*.

He didn't recognize the handwriting. But no matter who wrote it, it was his only connection to Jane. G placed it in his breast pocket and for a moment pressed it against his chest.

Some time later he heard a scratching coming from the door. G shook his head, chalking the noise up to random castle creaks and groans, but then he heard it again. A distinct scratching sound.

He raised the candle, which only had an inch of light left, and walked cautiously to the door, just in time to see two beady little eyes peeking in from underneath. He barely had time to register the eyes when an entire furry body snaked its way inside his chamber, flat against the ground.

G yelped and stepped back. (He definitely did not scream like a little girl.)

Once it passed the doorframe, the creature seemed to puff itself back into shape, just as G grabbed the nearest thing he could chuck at it. A pillow. He took aim and threw it, but the little rodent dodged.

It was too long to be a mouse, or a rat, but too short to be . . . what other kind of rodent was there? It looked like a cat and a snake had a baby together.

G stalked over to the thing and stomped his foot near it.

"Go away, you scruffy squirrel!"

The creature shied away from his foot, and he stomped again, in the direction of the door. "Shoo! There's nothing to see here! Go on out the way you came in."

But the rodent made no move toward the door. Instead, it scurried over to the bed, and scampered up the hanging tassels to the bedcovers and then to the head of the bed, where it nestled itself down on top of one of the pillows.

"Get off, you nasty rat!" G grabbed one of the books he had discarded and raised it above his head.

At this, the rodent sprang to attention, on all fours, long tail fluffed out. G waved the book as a threatening move, and the rodent did the strangest thing. It moved its head in a side-to-side motion, mirroring the motion of the book, its beady eyes wide and fixated on the tome.

G jerked the book forward about an inch, and the rodent flinched.

"All right, let's come to an agreement." G gently lowered the book to the bed, and that's when the rodent did something even stranger. It scurried over to the book and nestled on top of it, like a mama bird would nestle over her eggs.

"Wait. Jane?" G said.

The rodent made a nodding motion.

"*Jane?*" he said again.

The rodent nodded again, this time in a more exaggerated way.

"Jane. You're a . . . a . . . rat."

Jane froze, and then darted frantically around the bed, then around the room, then scaled the bedpost and darted in and out of the tassels. G was worried she would do something crazy like hurl herself off the bed to her death.

"Wait! Wait. You're not a rat. I only said rat because . . . well, I wasn't thinking. But you're not a rat."

She froze on top of the bedposts, waiting expectantly.

She wanted him to tell her what she was.

"You're a . . . a . . . well, it's actually something I've not seen maybe ever. But you have fur—beautiful fur," he added when she started shaking. "And two lovely eyes, four strong, if tiny, legs— but not too tiny," he added again. "Can you please come down from there before I continue?"

She stamped her foot before climbing down the poster. He could almost hear her huffing. Lord, it was so obvious she was Jane. How had he not known the second her beady eyes appeared under the door?

She settled herself on the bed and he sat down next to her. He was tempted to pet her as he would a dog, but he resisted. She might find that demeaning.

He faced her.

"Okay, so you are a . . . a . . . an E∂ian," he said, opting for the safest reference to her appearance. "I don't suppose you're a typical E∂ian who can change back and forth at will; otherwise, you would've changed back to tell me who you were yourself." He paused. "I know that sounded very roundabout, but my meaning is, you can't control the change, can you?"

She nodded.

"Yes, you can't control the change? Or yes, you can?" He realized how stupid the questions were. "Never mind. I'll phrase it this way. Can you control the change?"

She shook her head.

"All right. We are getting somewhere. Although, very slowly, and I worry about how quickly the sun will soon be rising. So what are we going to do?" He sighed. "If only we had a horse."

If hedgehogs or badgers could look exasperated, Jane did. She jumped off the bed and scurried to the door and went under it and out, then under it and back in.

G smacked his head. "Right! We have something better than a horse. We have a . . . weasel?"

Jane rolled over and played dead.

"Not a weasel, my lady, but whatever you are, I am catching your meaning. You can sneak in and out and around the tower. And possibly steal a key?"

She nodded.

"And bring the key here, and we'll unlock the door, descend the stairs, take the guard at the bottom by surprise, knock him out, steal his sword to dispatch any other guards we may come across, go to the stables, steal a horse, and head for the hills."

She nodded again, and this time did a scurry about the bed that sort of resembled a happy dance.

"Well, why didn't you say so in the first place? The way you explain it, I must say, it sounds very convoluted."

Jane didn't stick around to argue. She scampered out the door (which involved flattening herself in a move that defied physics) and left G pacing and waiting. And waiting and pacing. And then pacing and waiting some more. All the while, looking out the window for signs of dawn. If Jane didn't return in time, escape would be impossible. He wouldn't be able to fit out the door.

Maybe his captors didn't know about the daylight curse, and if Jane's plan didn't work, the sheer bulkiness of his physique would delay the whole burning-at-the-stake thing. Or maybe they did know, and they would come to fetch him sooner than the sunrise.

"Hurry, my lady," he whispered as he paced and waited. "Please hurry."

Eventually, he heard the soft clinging of metal far away, and it got closer and closer and G imagined a badger carrying a set of keys up a flight of stone stairs. He went and stood by the door, and soon enough, Jane appeared underneath.

She dropped a set of keys at his feet and nudged them as if she were in a hurry.

He snatched them up and wondered if her getaway wasn't exactly clean.

It wasn't. He heard footsteps charging up the stairwell.

Only, there were at least ten keys on the ring.

"Which one?" he muttered. He shoved the first one in the lock and jangled it about. No luck.

As he tried the second, Jane climbed up his pants and shirt and traversed across his arm as if to add urgency to the situation.

"I'm going as fast as I can!"

Third key. The lock didn't budge.

The footsteps got closer and closer.

Fourth key. Nothing.

Jane dug her tiny claws into his wrist.

"You're not helping," G pointed out.

The guard was just outside the door. "Where are you, ye little rat!"

Jane dug her claws in again.

"Don't worry, my sweet. He didn't mean it."

The fifth key did the trick. The lock clicked. All three of them heard it. Just as the guard charged the heavy wooden door, G pulled it wide open. The guard fell in and G struck him on the head with the bedpost. The guard crumpled to the floor, unmoving, but breathing.

"Quick!" G whisked Jane up to his shoulder and grabbed the guard's sword.

As he crept down the stairs, it occurred to him that as a weasel, she could've saved herself and left him to die. Again.

But when the time came, she didn't. Again.

This was the perfect time of night to escape the Tower of London, mostly because it was the time with the fewest number of guards, and the ones on duty were either exhausted or sneaking sips from a hidden flask.

Nevertheless, G and Jane ran into three guards. After all, they were royal prisoners. They couldn't expect to make it to the stables completely unhindered.

The first guard G dispatched quickly in a move that Jane would probably describe as elegant swordsmanship, but he knew was really the result of the sword slipping from his sweaty hand. As he lunged to retrieve it before it hit the ground, he plunged the sword through the heart of a guard who was just rounding the corner.

The second encounter was not so graceful. The guard raised his sword and his other hand in a fighting stance, and G did the same, hoping it wasn't obvious he'd skipped out on half of his childhood fencing lessons in favor of playing his favorite rhyming game with one of his nannies.

The two stood there for a long time, staring, preparing for what? G wondered. Attack/counterattack? Someone to give the go-ahead?

Jane, impatient with the stare down, scampered off G's shoulder, across the floor to the guard, up his leg, and inside his shirt.

The guard did some strange jerky motions, not unlike a young child learning the famed estampie dance from Spain. G used the distraction to dispatch the man, making sure to aim his sword away from any bulky parts where Jane might be.

The third guard came along, saw the bleeding second guard, looked at Gifford with his sword raised (a formidable sight, if one wasn't aware of his sword skills), and took off running.

G scooped Jane up and sprinted away as well. He started toward the stables where he'd first been held.

"We must hurry," he said, trying not to imagine what he looked like, talking to the hedgehog on his shoulder. "That one will probably sound an alarm. We need a horse."

The little rodent dug her claws into his shoulder.

"Yes, yes, but we need one that stays a horse. Especially if soldiers will be chasing us soon."

He opened the stable door as quietly as possible, backed inside, looking for any pursuers, and when there were none, he shut the door, turned around, and nearly ran into the pointy end of a man's sword.

The sword's owner was a tall man with a beard and a uniform, but not the soldier kind of uniform. More like the hired-help kind.

G put his hand on his rat in an automatic protective motion.

"Please," he said. But before he could go on, the man lowered his sword.

"Are you Gifford?"

G didn't know if he should try to deny his identity, but there was no point. He nodded.

"Where's the queen?" the man said.

"I'm sorry, who are you?"

The man pushed by him and opened the door a crack, peeked out, and then shut it again.

"Where's the queen?" he said again.

"I'm afraid you won't believe me if I tell you," G responded.

"Try me."

G took Jane off his shoulder—she was trembling—and cradled her in his arms. "She's here."

The man's scowl softened, and he leaned forward with a smile. "Ah! She's a wee ferret. She's a beau'iful thing."

"Ferret!" G exclaimed. "That's what you are, my dear, a ferret." He'd heard of the creatures, but he'd never seen one. "See? So much better than a rat."

The man grabbed G's arm and pulled him toward the stables. "We'd best be getting you on your way, if you have any hope of escaping."

"Who are you?" G asked again. "Are you the one who slid the letter under my door?"

The man nodded. "Name's Peter Bannister. I'm the royal kennel master. I was loyal to King Edward. Sent my daughter to protect him, but a lot of good that did."

"Protect him? From what? 'The Affliction'?"

Peter opened one of the stalls and hoisted a saddle onto the steed inside. "From the likes of your dirty father. The king never had 'the Affliction.'"

G stood still with his mouth open in surprise.

"There's no time to explain. Get on yer horse. Follow my daughter. She'll lead you safely away."

While G mounted the horse (with Jane on his shoulder), Peter disappeared down toward the end of the stables and out the door that led to the kennels. He returned moments later with a beautiful Afghan hound.

"There's a good girl," he said, ruffling the dog's fur. "Follow Petunia, my lord. She'll help you."

"I thought you said we were to follow your daughter."

Just then a horn blew, and then another. Peter's eyes went wide. "Go!"

He threw open the stable doors and then G and Jane and their horse and Petunia-the-dog galloped away into the night.

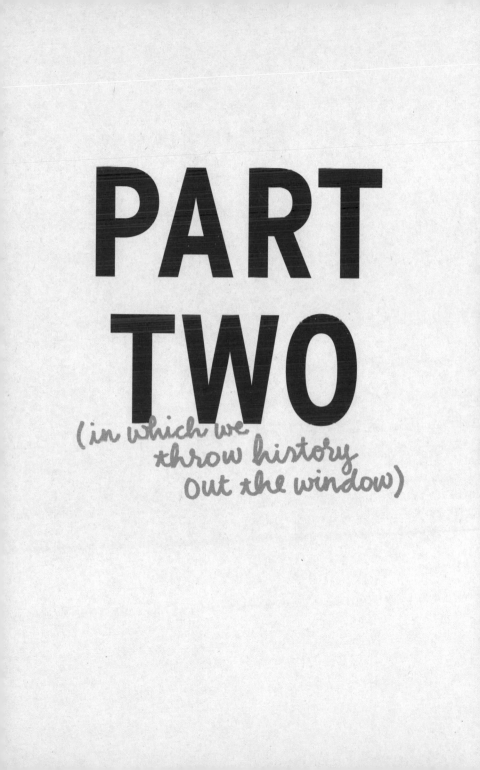

PART TWO

(in which we throw history out the window)

PART

TWO

Midlogue

Hey, there! It's us, your friendly neighborhood narrators. We just wanted to take a break for a minute to tell you something important: up until now, what we've shown you has been loosely based on what we've been able to uncover in our research, filling in the blanks where needed.

But from this point on, dear reader, we are going to go deep, deep, abyss-to-the-inner-crust-of-the-earth deep into the stuff the historians don't want you to know about, the stuff they will go to extreme lengths to hide. (Because can you imagine the cost and hassle of rewriting all of the history books?) We've traversed the great plains of Hertfordshire, spelunked the dark tunnels of Piccadilly, hiked the rolling hills of the Cotswolds searching for the descendants of our lovers and the poisoned king, and we have compiled what we so delicately refer to as . . . THE TRUTH. (Because of the danger, we considered changing our names. But we didn't. Still, we sleep with swords under our pillows.)

If the truth of what happened to our heroes and heroine scares you—and God's teeth, it should scare you—do not venture past this point.

But if you are a bucker of the system, a friend of truth, an ally of love, and a believer in magic, then read on.

NINETEEN

Edward

"Take that, you lily-livered scut!" Gracie shouted, swinging her sword.

Edward sidestepped the blow in the nick of time. He puffed out his chest. "That's King Lily-Livered Scut to you."

She laughed. "Yes, Sire," she said. "Of course. How could I forget?"

His heart was pounding from more than just the exertion of the fight. This whole sparring-with-a-girl situation made him wildly uncomfortable. It wasn't proper, of course. What if he were to hurt her? But Gran had said that was nonsense and sent them outside to "work up a sweat."

Right. Edward was definitely sweating now. Gracie was making sure of that, what with the distracting trousers that hugged her in all the right places as she parried and thrust at him, her eyes bright and cheeks flushed, the sheen of her own perspiration on her forehead and what glimpses of her neck he could see around the tumble of black curls. It was outright unfair, he thought. How could he be expected to concentrate?

"Your Majesty." She grinned and swiped at him again. He struck back at her lightly, a series of moves designed to impress her with his vast knowledge of swordplay, and she retreated.

"You're not bad. For a girl," he said.

Her next blow glanced off his shoulder, not hard but certainly unexpected. Somehow she'd made it past his superior defense techniques, but it must have been blind luck. He darted away, regained his footing, then advanced on her again. She retreated. She was open; she left him all kinds of vulnerable places to strike. Still, he could not bring himself to really hit her.

"Come on, Sire," she scoffed as his broom gently grazed her leg. "Enough with the chivalry."

"My lady," he said gallantly, "I'm willing to stop whenever you are. Perhaps you'd be better off sticking to more womanly pursuits, like embroidery or music or—"

She bashed him in the ribs. If it'd been a real sword in her hand, instead of half of a broken broomstick, he would have been done for. As it was, he went to his knees, the wind knocked out of him. She rapped his hand then, hard enough that he dropped his broom, and she kicked it out of the way. Before he could reach for it, she lifted her foot and sent him sprawling into the grass. When he looked up, the blunt end of her broomstick was at his throat.

Beaten. By a girl.

Inconceivable.

His mind whirled with excuses. He was still getting over the effects of the poison, of course. His twisted ankle remained a bit tender, not to mention the dog bite on his leg. A broom was not the same as a good sword in your hand—it was a poor replacement, in fact, different to balance, difficult to hold. The sun was in his eyes.

"Do you yield?" she asked.

He laughed up at her and rubbed his knuckles where she'd struck him. "Hey, that hurt."

"Oh, I'm so sorry, Sire," Gracie said, but she didn't look sorry. "Now, does England yield?"

"To Scotland?"

"Aye."

"Never." He grabbed her broom, a move he'd never be able to pull off with a real sword, and pulled her down to him. They wrestled, which gave Edward some lovely opportunities to touch her, to feel the gentle curves of her body against his. But Gracie was a wild thing is his arms, and not in the good way (although it certainly wasn't in a bad way, either). Within moments she'd somehow managed to flip him and was sitting on his chest, pinning his arms.

Inconceivable.

"Do you yield?" she asked breathlessly.

He was going to say no again, but then he got looking at her eyelashes, which were so long that they cast shadows on her rosy cheeks. And he knew he'd say yes to just about anything she asked of him.

"Yes," he conceded. "I yield." He looked up at her, panting. "I'm a bit rusty, I'm afraid." That and, before now, people usually had let him win.

She got off him and picked up her broom. He tried not to look disappointed.

"You're getting better," she said, although he knew she wasn't referring to his fighting, but his condition in general. He *was* getting better. Even after a mere two days at the abandoned castle under Gran's torturous but effective care, his body felt stronger, his thoughts clearer. He hardly coughed anymore.

He was going to live.

Gracie reached down to offer to help him to his feet. "Do you want to make a real go of it now, Sire? Are we done playing with our dolls?"

"Call me Edward," he said, scrambling up without her help.

She dropped back into fighting stance. Edward grabbed his broom out of the grass. He wiped sweat off his brow and smiled.

"Take that, you beef-witted varlet!" He made an honest try at hitting her this time. She dodged easily, almost skipped out of his way. Edward had the sudden suspicion that up to now she'd been going easy on him.

"Who are you calling beef-witted?" she laughed at him. "Your mother was a hamster, and your father stank of elderberries!" And away they went, whirling and stabbing with their brooms, almost dancing as they moved about the field.

She was good. Really good.

"Where did you learn to fight like this?" he panted as she nearly disarmed him again. Not for the first time it occurred to him that in spite of the hours he'd spent in Gracie's company, he still knew next to nothing about her.

She tossed her hair out of her face, then brought her broom down hard against his. He only just managed to push her off.

"It was just something I picked up along the way," she answered, as slippery as ever when it came to this type of question. "I prefer knives, though. Nothing beats a sharp knife in your boot."

"Along your way to where?" he pressed. "Why are you in England?"

"Mind your own business!" She jabbed at him with her broom, but he parried. "You beetle-headed, flap-ear'd knave!"

A laugh burst from him. "You cankerblossom!" he cried, aiming a blow that made her duck. "But seriously, Gracie. Don't you think it's about time you told me something about yourself?"

"What you see is what you get, Sire." She gave him a quick bow, then swung at him again. "You poisonous bunch-backed toad!"

Sire, again. He might have preferred *toad*.

"Enough." He sighed, then suddenly threw his broomstick to the ground. "I don't want to play games anymore."

Gracie lowered her own broomstick uncertainly. "Sire?"

"Perhaps you'd better be on your way, Gracie. I appreciate all you've done for me, but I'm sure you have better things to do than play at swords. You said you would see me to my grandmother, and you did. You don't have to stay."

His heart was beating fast again. He was taking a gamble, he knew. Calling her bluff.

Her eyebrows came together. "You don't trust me? After everything?"

"I want to trust you, really I do, but I don't know you," he said. "I'm grateful for what you've done to help me, but I don't understand your reasons for doing so. You could be a spy for Mary Queen of Scots, for all I know." He shuddered at the thought.

Gracie stared at him for a few tense heartbeats, her brow still furrowed, and then she let the broomstick drop to the ground.

"Fine," she said irritably. "Come on."

She walked to the edge of the grounds where the forest began, away from the ruins of the castle and out of earshot of anyone who might hear them. He followed. She spent a few minutes picking up pieces of wood from the forest floor and then throwing them down again, as if she was searching for something. (He hoped that she hadn't at long last decided that he wasn't worth all this aggravation, and was choosing a branch to club him with.) Finally, she seemed to find one she liked. She sat down against an elm tree. Edward lowered himself to the ground a few feet away. He waited for her to speak.

"You asked me once when it was that I knew I was a fox." She drew her knife out of her boot and started stripping down the piece of wood in her hand. "I was seven."

She was going to tell him a sad story; he could tell by the way the light had gone out of her remarkable eyes. He was tempted to stop her, because he hated sad stories, and he had no right to demand something so personal from her, but then again, there was truth to what he'd just told her. He needed to know who she was.

Gracie was deftly shaping the wood with her knife, her gaze fixed on her work so she didn't have to look at him as she talked. "That night I woke to our cottage burning. We were all inside, my ma and da and brothers—I had two brothers—and they'd blocked the door from the outside, boarded the windows, too."

"The English," he said, and she didn't answer, but if it'd been anyone else, he knew she would have corrected him.

"My family was all Eθians, as I told you. My da was a beautiful red stag, and my mum a doe, which is why they got on so well. My brother Fergus was a black horse with a white star on his forehead." She laughed softly. "My brother Daniel was a big, lumbering hound. Myself, I'd never changed before. That night was the first time."

She fell silent. Edward shifted uncomfortably.

"The rest of my family were too big to get out of the cottage," she continued after a moment. "Only I could squeeze out. My da told me I had to go. He said I should make my way south, to a convent in France where I had an aunt. He even drew me a kind of map, as the house was filling with smoke, and tied it to my neck with my mum's handkerchief."

She closed her eyes.

"Why?" Edward asked softly. "The English soldiers just . . . burned houses with people inside them?"

"They burned any place that housed Eðians." With her knife she stabbed at the piece of wood fiercely, chips littering the ground near her feet. The carving was taking on a shape now, but Edward couldn't tell what. "And they burned the homes of those who would protect them."

He wasn't so naive as to deny that such things had happened. Under his father's orders, undoubtedly. Edward wanted to believe that, as king, he wouldn't have authorized this kind of abuse. But even in that, he wasn't entirely sure. He'd been awfully hands-off in the running of the country. He'd signed the papers his advisors had thrust at him. He'd trusted them to do what was best for the kingdom.

The world felt different to him now. He felt different.

"Did you ever make it to France?" he asked.

She gave a bitter laugh. "I tried. I lost the map after the first week, so after that I just ran south until my paws bled. I nearly starved, because I hadn't yet learned to hunt or steal. I would have died if . . ."

She stopped whittling momentarily and swallowed hard, like this next part pained her to speak of even more than losing her family.

"If . . . ?" Edward prompted gently, when she didn't finish her thought.

She looked up and met his eyes. "If the Pack hadn't found me."

Edward sucked in a breath. "Oh," he said, trying to sound like this was no big deal. "The Pack."

"They weren't always so bad as they are now," Gracie explained. "In the beginning, the Pack was about securing safety for the Eðian people. Yes, we stole and we plundered and occasionally we got into unfortunate scrapes with certain soldiers, but for the most part we kept to the shadows. We survived. We helped one another."

She brushed an errant curl from her face. "The leader was like a father to me. He took me in when I had no one else. He taught me everything I know, and not just how to get by. He taught me to read and write. Mend a shirt. Figure numbers. Handle a bow, a sword, a knife. Carve and whittle. And he also taught me history and philosophy and the like."

"What happened to him?" he asked, because he knew from her clouded expression that something had. Not long ago, he thought.

"He got old." Gracie resumed her whittling. "Another man—Thomas Archer is his name—challenged him for the leadership, and won. After that things were different. Archer believes that Eðians should do more than simply survive. He believes that we are one with nature, and therefore we should dominate it. Take what we want. Punish anyone who would challenge or harm Eðians. Archer gathered up a group of men who become wolves, and they started to go about making trouble."

"So you left," Edward assumed.

"Yes." She frowned in concentration as she began working on the finer details of her carving. "I went off one night and didn't return. Which didn't sit well with Archer. I was useful to him."

"So that's why you were so keen to avoid them."

She coughed lightly. "Er, yes. Archer put a price on my head."

"How much?" Edward asked.

She glanced at him. "Why do you want to know?"

"We're short of money, of course. Every little bit helps."

She caught on that he was joking. Her dimples appeared. "Ten sovereigns."

His eyes widened. "Ten sovereigns! How fast can we get to this Archer fellow?"

"The Pack uses a tavern as their headquarters," she said matter-of-factly, as if turning her in was a real possibility. "The Shaggy Dog. It's about half a day's ride from here, I'd say."

She was finished with her carving. She wiped her knife and slid it gently back into her boot. Edward leaned forward to look at the figure. It was fox, which actually bore a remarkable resemblance to Gracie in her Eðian form, gracefully suspended in the act of running.

"Is there anything you can't do?" he asked.

"Needlepoint," she said, smiling. She put the fox into his hand. "I can only carve foxes. Everything else I try ends up looking like a lumpy dog."

Together they gazed down at the little wooden fox. "It's nice," he murmured. "Thank you."

"You're welcome."

"I only have one more question, then," he said.

She nodded. "Ask it."

"If the English killed your family, forced you from your home, hunted you, hurt you at every turn, then why did you help me? And don't give me that rot about being a friend to the pathetic creatures of the world. Tell me why."

It was the first time he'd ever seen her look embarrassed. She gave a little sigh. "The truth?"

"The truth."

"I liked the look of you."

He sat back, amazed. He thought (although he wasn't entirely sure) that she meant that she'd found him good-looking. "You liked—"

"You had kind eyes. A nice smile." She was blushing.

This was wonderful, wonderful news. "Have you seen your own eyes?" he said impulsively. "Green like . . . forest moss."

"Moss?"

"Like pools of . . ." He cursed himself that he was not more of a poet.

"Yes?" Her lips twitched as she clearly tried not to laugh at him.

"Beautiful eyes," he stumbled on.

"Pools of beautiful eyes?"

"Yes. Exactly. And your hair. And your smile, as well, is so . . . And you're funny and clever. And brave. I've never met a girl like you."

"Oh, I'm not so very brave." She was looking at him. *That way.* He could smell her, the lavender soap from Gran's bathtub mixed with a woodsy smell that never seemed to leave her.

He glanced down at her mouth. He couldn't help it.

And (miracle of all miracles) she looked down at his.

He wet his lips nervously. What if he didn't do it correctly? What if their noses bumped? What if she found his lips chapped? What if his breath was foul?

"Gracie," he murmured, her name a kind of music on his lips. "Grace." Their faces were close. Almost close enough.

His heart started to beat like a war drum. He inched even closer.

"Sire," she breathed. "I—"

"Please call me Edward," he said. "Things don't have to be so formal between us."

Before he lost his nerve he reached out and tucked one of her wild curls behind her ear.

He leaned in. This was it. His first kiss. His first k—

"BOY!" yelled a distant voice. "WHERE ARE YOU, BOY!"

Grace drew back abruptly. "Your granny is calling you."

"She can wait," he said.

"IT'S TIME FOR YOUR MEDICINE!" Gran called out.

Gracie jumped to her feet. "You should go in."

"BOY!"

She hastily brushed off her trousers. "Besides, I just remembered some chores your sister wanted me to get done. Some very important chores. Full of . . . tasks."

"Tasks?" Edward said, doubtful.

"Yes, tasks. Lots of them."

"Gracie," he started as she backed away from him. "Wait."

"GET IN HERE, BOY!"

He watched helplessly as Gracie set off toward the keep, almost at a run.

"BOY!"

At that moment we should confess that Edward briefly considered murdering his dear sweet grandmother. And he might have gotten away with it, too, on account of the rest of the world thinking the old lady was already dead.

When he entered the keep, Gran was waiting for him with one of her nasty potions.

"Ah, there you are, boy. Drink up."

"I wish you'd stop calling me boy," he muttered.

"And what would you have me call you?"

"I'm a man," he said.

She threw back her grizzled head and laughed heartily. "That's cute. Tell me another one."

She handed him a steaming goblet. He protested—*How much of this stuff are you going to make me drink, anyway? The poison is gone, isn't it? This tastes like rotten apples*—but she made him choke it down. Gran had made him suffer through many terrible things in the name of ridding his body of the poison. The first day, in addition to the rotten apple brew she made him guzzle by the jugful, she'd forced him to stand for twenty minutes under the spray of an icy waterfall, then bathe in a tub of boiled milk. On the second day she'd wrapped a chicken gizzard around his neck, stuck a lump of charcoal under his tongue, and made him say the alphabet backward.

"What was the alphabet part for?" he'd asked after he finally reached *a*.

"Nothing," Gran had chortled. "I just wanted to hear you say it."

Gran delighted in torturing him.

"And when you're done with that, go see your sister. If you're not feeling too manly to speak with a woman," Gran chortled now as he gulped down the last of the potion.

He did what she told him, but only because he'd been wanting to talk to Bess anyway. Not because he was a little boy who was scared of his grandmother.

He found his sister waiting for him in his chamber. "Come. Sit," she said, and pointed him to a chair. Edward sat. On the table in front of him there was a map of Europe with several wooden figures placed upon it in strategic positions. The figures all resembled lumpy dogs.

One of the ways Gracie was making herself useful.

His gaze fell on London, and he turned his thoughts to Jane. Bess had a network of Eðian raven spies at the Tower of London, and occasionally a raven made its way to Helmsley with news, the most recent of which being that the new Queen Mary had rounded up all the known Eðians on the staff and meant to make an example of them in a large bonfire at the end of the month. And after that she was planning to send soldiers into London to gather up the Eðians from there, as well.

Mary's purge of Eðians was already well under way.

But, in spite of Bess's best efforts, there had strangely been no word of what had become of his cousin. It was as if Jane and Gifford had simply up and vanished from London the same day that Mary had arrived there. Edward assumed that Mary probably had Jane secretly locked up in a tower somewhere, if he knew his sister. But he also knew Jane, and he knew Jane could be . . . spirited . . . when challenged, and Mary taking away her throne would be the biggest challenge of all. His cousin had a troublesome habit of speaking her mind in tense situations.

And Mary was easily offended and rather too fond of saying, "Off with her head!"

In other words, Edward was worried.

But they couldn't rescue Jane or stop the Eðian bonfire—not yet. They weren't ready to take on Mary's considerable forces, i.e., the English army. At least, not according to Bess, who seemed to be working out a plan.

Edward looked over the map and the wooden figures on the

table before him. "These are parts of an army?" he asked Bess incredulously. "Whose?"

Her lips turned up in what was not quite a smile. "Mine. I have my contacts, my favors owed. When I found out that you were being poisoned and Mary was building a secret army to make herself queen, I thought I might put together a secret army of my own." She smoothed her hand over the map, and her smile vanished. "But it's not enough men, Edward. Mary's army is greater by half. She has the support of both the Spanish and the Holy Roman Emperor. The Spanish armada is formidable. Unbeatable, they say. I don't know yet how we're going to overcome them."

He glanced up at his sister. Her face was drawn in concentration. She was staring at a line of ships in the English Channel.

"Who do these belong to?" he asked, picking up a ship and turning it over in his hand.

"France. I believe their King Henry will support you, not Mary, as the rightful monarch, once he sees that you're alive. He's got to be afraid of a woman usurping the throne the way she did. It's the only solution I can think of."

Edward had underestimated Bess. He knew that now. She knew the world in a way that Edward himself didn't fully understand.

"If we could get ships and troops from France," Bess continued, almost to herself, "and perhaps at the same time seek the support of Mary Queen of Scots, reinforcements from Scotland, then we might stand a chance. . . ."

He felt his face drain of color. "Did you say . . . Mary Queen of Scots?"

Bess didn't seem to notice his dismay. "Of course, who knows the state of the Scottish army? And help from the French king won't come cheap. He'll want something from you in return, probably, and you'll forever be in his debt if you succeed, but it's the only way."

The only way. To regain his throne. To save Jane.

Edward swallowed. "Sounds like I'm going to France," he said lightly, but his heart was beating fast. "When do I leave?"

Bess bit her lip. "I want you to rest a few days more. Gather your strength. You're going to need it."

"Can't we send someone to retrieve Jane?"

"Who would we send? Gran?" Bess shook her head.

"Gran's not a terrible idea."

"I know Jane is dear to you," Bess said. "I also know that she's in danger. But Jane is one person, Edward. There are thousands of lives at stake. There's a kingdom on the edge of a knife. We must tread carefully."

He sighed. On the map, London was just a finger's length from Helmsley. But Jane was very far away.

"Very well," he said tersely. "A few more days, and I'll depart for France." He rose from the chair, crossed to the window, and slung his leg up onto the sill. He wanted to be a bird now. Then he could fly away to Jane. To at least tell her that he hadn't forgotten her. That he was coming for her, even if it took longer than he meant to.

Bess slipped out of the room behind him, closing the door.

"I'm sorry," he whispered. The sky overhead was blue and beckoning, but he resisted its call. "I'm sorry, Jane." A wave of melancholy overtook him. "Oh, Janey, where are you?"

Jane ↳TWENTY

Jane, as it happened, was fleeing for her life.

After escaping the city, they'd started in . . . some direction. Still in her ferret state, Jane clung to Gifford's shoulder while he rode their stolen horse out of London as fast as they could go. Pet ran on ahead of them, leading the way. To where, Jane couldn't tell.

It was away from Mary's soldiers; that was all that mattered.

The roads would be the first place anyone would look, so they diverted into the forest. The hooves of their stolen steed beat the ground in a relentless tempo. Hounds bayed in the distance, making Pet lift her nose to the wind. It seemed their pursuers gained on them. Jane huddled in the curve of Gifford's neck, terrified and exhausted, as they veered here and there, lost in the dark, dark night.

Gifford hunched lower over the horse. Jane scrambled to adjust her weight, but he scooped her up and held her against his chest. "I have a plan," he said.

Wonderful. Jane loved plans.

He glanced down at her. "It's a good plan. I think."

Jane bit him—not hard—urging him to just get it out.

"Shortly, the sun will rise and I will begin my daily departure from my two-legged self to my four-legged self, and then we will be able to move more quickly. I'll send my equine friend here off on another path to create a diversion. Meanwhile, you will remain in your ferrety form and I will carry you . . . somewhere safe."

Jane cocked her head. It wasn't a terrible plan (although it was a tad vague), but what about Horse Rule 3? (No riding the horse.)

Gifford shook his head. "I know what you're thinking, dear, but now's not the time for such rules. We need to be fast. You weigh next to nothing in this form. As long as we can find a way to secure you to me without the use of those magnificent claws, I'll be able to run at top speed."

That sounded good to Jane.

"Excellent," said Gifford. "I'm glad we're agreed."

They careened down a narrow deer trail. The minutes stretched like hours. With the trees growing tall and ancient all around them, it was difficult to track the moon and stars. But eventually the woods lightened to a soft purple, and birds began to sing, and Jane felt herself breathe more easily. This terrible night was almost over, and she'd survived it. They were still being hunted down like dogs, sure. But things never seemed as bad in the light of day.

Gifford called to Pet and reined in the horse.

They were just slowing to a trot when Jane changed.

One instant, she was a ferret, cupped in Gifford's hand and pressed against his chest. The next, she was engulfed in a blinding white light and then she was a girl, sitting sideways on the saddle with her legs hanging off one side, and she was most definitely naked.

Their stolen horse snorted and stopped, disgusted with the sudden weight of two people.

"Jane! This wasn't part of the plan!" Gifford untied his cloak and threw it around her shoulders. "You didn't bite me when I explained it, so I assumed we were in agreement."

Jane scrambled off the saddle and landed in an undignified heap on the ground. She tried to get up, but her legs were wobbly after the sudden transformation.

Gifford dismounted and knelt beside her. "Are you all right?"
She nodded.

There'd been so much she'd wanted to tell him before, when she'd been locked in the Tower, but now (possibly for the first time in her life) Jane felt tongue-tied.

Gifford looked like he wanted to say something, too. He took her hands in his, fingers grazing the rings of cuts and bruises on her wrists from the shackles, and she sucked in a sharp breath. Her wrists hadn't hurt so much as a ferret, though there'd been a shadow of pain. Now they felt like they were on fire.

"You're wounded," Gifford observed.

"It's nothing." She tried to smile at him. "So, I suppose I can't control the change yet."

He arched an eyebrow at her. "What's that, you say? You can't *control the change*? How's that possible, when you've read so very many books on Eðians?"

Her face felt hot. She sat up straighter. "Well, these are just less-than-ideal conditions. I will be able to perfect the change with a bit of practice, I'm sure."

"Oh, I'm sure you will. You should try. Change back, and we'll go," he said.

He was teasing her. She wasn't sure if she liked it. She took a deep breath and concentrated on the idea of becoming a ferret again, because that was the plan, but nothing happened. She tried again. Nothing.

Gifford's gaze dropped to her collarbone. Then the shape of her under the cloth. "Wait. Never mind. Stay just like that."

Jane yanked the cloak more tightly around her and jumped to her feet. "Gifford Dudley! Eyes to yourself."

He laughed and began taking off his boots. And then his socks. And then his belt.

"What are you doing?"

"It's morning," he explained as he continued undressing. "These are my only clothes—the guards gave them to me when I was moved from the stables to the Tower—so it would be a real shame to ruin them in my transformation."

His shirt went next, revealing the contours of his chest. Jane tried not to stare. When he began tugging at his trousers, she *meeped*, clapped her hands over her eyes, and spun away. "Have you no shame?"

"None at all."

"And I don't suppose you brought clothes for me?"

He whinnied in reply.

Jane turned around. "No clothes for me?" she repeated to her husband, the horse.

Gifford didn't answer.

She bit her lip and eyed the clothing strewn over the ground. Trousers. How degrading. But less degrading, possibly, than spending the day wrapped in a thin cloak and nothing else.

A sharp bark pierced the air, startling her. Pet had circled back to find them all just standing around doing nothing. She barked again, and Jane remembered the soldiers still pursuing them.

They had to hurry.

Gifford's plan had been all well and good, but what kind of plan was *go somewhere safe*? Now that she was the sole human of the group, the decisions were up to her, she supposed. Because no one here was capable of talking back.

First, she decided, she would get dressed.

"Gifford." She cleared her throat. "I don't want to question your honor, but that's exactly what I'm doing." She threw the cloak over his head so that he couldn't peek at her while she put on the clothes he'd just discarded.

Gifford-the-horse made a huffing sound, but held still as she dressed. His clothes were warm and slightly sweaty. They smelled of horse. Everything was much too big, but she tightened the belt as small as it would go and rolled the hems of her pants and sleeves. Then she tied her hair into a quick braid and freed Gifford of his blind.

"So I'm to ride on *your* back?" she asked nervously. "And break Horse Rule three?"

He tossed his head in the affirmative.

She tromped over in too-large boots to inspect the other horse's saddle.

She'd read about saddles in *The Great Saddle Controversy: Pros and Cons of Various Saddles and the Best Choice for a Patriotic Englishman.* This saddle only vaguely resembled the ones she'd seen sketched in the book, but how hard could it be? Seat, saddle tree, girth, blanket. There was a small saddlebag as well, but Jane didn't open it to inspect its contents. No time.

Pet let out a yip. *Hurry,* she seemed to say.

"Hold your horses," Jane muttered as she began to unsaddle the borrowed horse. This proved to be a challenge, since the horse was much taller than she, and the saddle weighed at least half what she did, but finally she managed to haul it off and dump it on the ground.

The pad of blanket underneath was damp with sweat, but she didn't have a choice except to drape it over Gifford's back with an apology. Still, she was wearing his clothes. He could wear their horse's blanket.

Next came the saddle again. Gifford was at least kind enough to walk over to a large rock, flat enough for Jane to stand on. But his movement had gotten the blanket all out of place, so she had to drop the saddle, fix the blanket, and urge Gifford to stay still while she adjusted the saddle into place. With some difficulty, she fitted the girth strap into its buckle and tugged as tight as she dared. When she hopped off the rock to inspect her work, she realized horse-Gifford looked a lot . . . rounder than normal. "Are you holding your breath?"

Gifford blew out and resumed his normal proportions while Jane tried again to tighten the girth.

By now, Pet was running circles around the group. Jane gave the girth strap one more good yank—Gifford dramatically heaved a breath—and then reached for the other horse's bridle.

Gifford shied away from her, snorting. The message was clear: she might be able to break Horse Rules 1 and 3, but Horse Rule 2 still stood. No bridling the horse.

"Fine, but at least let me take this off. I don't want him to trip on the reins." She unbuckled the other horse's bridle and let it slide to the ground. Then she grabbed the saddlebag and strapped it onto Gifford.

Pet whined and barked and circled again, tighter. Both horses' ears flickered backward. Even Jane could hear the pounding of hooves now. Mary's men were catching up.

She threw herself onto Gifford's back and tried not to fall off as he launched himself like an arrow in the direction they'd been heading before, the other horse following close behind.

Jane tried to keep her head down. Twigs and brush snapped around her as Gifford ran tirelessly on. He leapt and swerved and pounded through the trees and close underbrush, sure-footed and strong, and even when the forest became too thick for speed, he stubbornly continued forward.

They'd been going for a while when, as abruptly as he'd started, Gifford stopped. The other horse stopped, too, and Pet, who sat down a few feet away. For a minute they all just stood there, breathing hard.

"What are we doing?" Jane hissed.

The other horse began ripping up bites of grass. Gifford bobbed his head, as if acknowledging a good idea, and nibbled on his own patch of greenery.

"Gifford, this is not the ideal time to take a break," Jane admonished him, leaning over his neck. "The soldiers are still close."

Gifford shook his head so his mane rubbed across her face. She spat out horsehair, straining to hear anything under the wind rustling trees and the horse teeth grinding grass into a gross, green pulp.

"This is stupid," she commented.

Then, without warning, Gifford turned on the other horse and bit the air close to his nose.

The horse—previously believing Gifford to be a friendly man-horse—reared up and screamed. Jane shrieked and clutched the pommel as tightly as she could while Gifford pushed forward, snapping and lunging at the other horse. He circled around him, blocking the jagged path of the way they'd come until the poor creature had no choice but to peel off into the woods.

They listened to the horse crash through the underbrush. Then Jane, Gifford, and Pet were alone.

Jane pressed her hands against her chest and dropped her forehead against Gifford's neck. "That was mean," she said, and reached forward to flick his ear. "He was a nice horse."

Gifford blew out a breath and immediately began picking his way through the woods, doubling back to the deer trail.

So as to leave less of a trail, Jane realized. Now anyone who followed them here would likely follow the new trail the other horse had left, not expecting Jane and Gifford to go back the way they'd come.

"I see now," Jane said. "I guess I forgot the plan. That was still mean, though. You should try to be nicer to the other horses. You're herd animals. Who will you run with if he goes back to tell the others of your two-faced personality? Who will you compare apple notes with? Soon you won't have any friends but me."

They ran on and on until the sky turned a fiery red. They'd lost their pursuers hours ago, no baying dogs or thundering horses behind them now, but they still kept up a steady pace through the woods.

She was just about to suggest that they make camp when they came upon a small, abandoned farm. Gifford paused at the edge of the trees, giving Jane a chance to appraise the tumbledown cottage and the barn tucked behind it.

"This seems a good place to spend the night, doesn't it?"

Gifford made a noise that sounded like assent and she slid from his back to look around. Pet ran with her, tail flagged with canine joy, stopping every few feet to check for danger. They found none. The cottage was in bad shape, the thatched roof caved in and the rooms full of birds and mouse nests, but the barn still seemed intact. They could take shelter there.

Jane's legs were shaky from riding so long, and her whole body felt weak with hunger, but she was able to haul open the barn door just wide enough for a saddled horse to fit through, and then Gifford trotted inside, pausing to nose at her shoulder as he passed.

"I'm so hungry I could eat a horse. Oh. Sorry, G. Not you, of course." She pulled the door closed. There was a rusty lantern hanging on the wall, and she moved to light it. Then she turned to Gifford. "Now let me take that saddle before you ruin it when you change."

Pet zipped around the barn, sniffing here and there. Then, just as Jane was about to get to work, Pet ran back to the door and scratched to be let out. She looked decidedly uncomfortable.

"You should have gone before we came inside," Jane muttered and opened the door a crack. Alone with her horse husband, Jane set about unbuckling the girth and relieving him of his humiliation.

He shook and stretched at the sudden freedom, then—to Jane's horror—rolled on to his back and rubbed himself against the dirt floor.

"Now that's just ridiculous." Jane snapped the blanket, making drops of sweat fly off, and laid it over a post to dry. The saddle followed.

It wasn't long before sundown, so she dropped the cloak near him and dug through the saddlebag to search for additional clothing. Nothing.

Instead she found a bag of cured meat and two containers of water. She'd drunk an entire flask of water and wolfed down nearly half the meat before she realized she ought to wait for Gifford to change, and give him the bigger share. Surely he was as hungry and thirsty as she was. He'd been on his feet all day.

"It seems we're going to have to fight for the clothes," Jane said. "One of us should get the shirt and trousers, and the other the cloak. As for the boots, they don't fit me anyway, so you'll just have to keep carrying me."

A burst of light filled the barn, and then Gifford said, "As you wish."

"G!" Jane spun around to find Gifford just pulling the cloak around himself. Impetuously she ran to embrace him, in spite of their awkward (and scandalous, though they were married, so did it really count as scandalous?) clothing situation.

"Jane." He wrapped his arms around her and kissed the top of her head.

It surprised her, this sudden gesture of affection, but she welcomed it.

"We survived the day," she said against his chest. "We both kept our heads. Hoorah for us."

A laugh rumbled through him. "So we did. Hoorah."

She pulled away to smile up at him, and felt a paper crinkle in her breast pocket.

"What's this?" She vaguely remembered feeling a folded parchment in the shirt earlier, but she'd been too busy fleeing for her life to give it any attention. She took it out and instantly recognized her own handwriting.

It was the letter she'd sent to Edward before she'd left for her honeymoon.

"Peter Bannister slid that under my door in Beauchamp Tower." Almost hesitantly, Gifford brushed Jane's face and smoothed back her hair. "I thought you might want to keep it."

"Thank you." All at once she felt safe, for the first time since their last night in the country house. She was tempted to snuggle back into the circle of his arms, but the letter seemed important. "Why would Peter Bannister want you to have this?" she asked.

"I don't know. I thought he was just giving me something of yours. To comfort me."

She turned the paper over. On the back there was a single word scrawled: *skunk*.

Her breath caught. "This is Edward's handwriting."

Gifford frowned. "Edward's?"

"Edward's! I'd know his writing anywhere. You see how he shapes the *s*? When we were younger we had this one terrible tutor—Richard Cox was his name—and he was always going on about Edward's ghastly penmanship. 'You should write like a king,' he always chided him. He made the king copy pages and pages of the letter *s*." She smiled at the memory. "Poor, dear Edward."

"Yes, poor, dear Edward," Gifford agreed faintly. "So what does *skunk* mean?"

"I don't know. I—" She gasped. "Our gran—my great grandmother, his grandmother—turned into a skunk. She was banished to an old abandoned castle in the north years ago. I've visited her there. It's called Helmsley."

"Does that mean Edward is alive?"

"I think it does." She hugged Gifford again, elated by the idea of seeing her cousin. "If Edward's alive, then he's heading to Gran's and we can go there, too, and then everything will be all right, you'll see, and you and I can—"

Jane turned into a ferret.

TWENTY-ONE

Before G had time to be surprised about Jane's transformation, something scratched at the barn door. G partly drew his sword from its sheath. (Not that he was really any good with a sword, but G was masterful at this particular bluff—to act like he could fight. Sometimes the act was all that was needed.)

"Who's there?" he called out, his heart hammering.

There was an urgent whine in response.

G opened the door and Pet flew in. She let out a couple of shrill barks, ran out the door, ran back to Gifford, ran outside, and then stared out into the night, one paw lifted, frozen.

"What's she trying to say?" G asked Jane-the-ferret. Jane responded by scurrying up G's leg, then up his shirt, then snaking around his neck and ending up on top of his head.

At this point, G realized he'd just asked a ferret what the dog said.

With his Jane hat in place, G squinted into the darkness, trying to figure out what had gotten Pet in such a fluster. Pet ran a few yards out, turned, and panted at G. She leaned even farther away from the barn as if she would take off in that direction if only G would follow.

"Pet," G said. "Remember the bad soldiers. Right now is not a good time to travel, especially when I'm not a horse, and therefore we have no speed."

Pet darted back inside the barn, and with a flash of light, suddenly she was a girl.

A naked girl with long, tangled blond hair.

Naked.

With no clothes on.

"I caught His Majesty's scent!" she exclaimed.

A soft tail swept across G's cheeks and came to rest right in front of his eyes, but G could still see the flash of light as Pet transformed back into a dog.

He stood there for a long moment, flummoxed.

"Did you see the . . . less formally attired girl who was just here?" he asked Jane. She dug her claws into his head. "Did you have any idea Pet was a girl? Although she didn't look very comfortable as a girl. She didn't make any motion to cover herself." This time, Jane scratched his face. "Not that I noticed."

Pet emitted a high-pitched bark again and pointed her nose

outside the barn, and it wasn't until that moment that G remembered she had said words. While standing there. Naked.

"You caught King Edward's scent?" G said.

Pet barked twice and ran back to the door.

"We can't go now," G argued. "It's too dangerous."

With another flash, she was the naked girl. "We have to go now! It's already faint, and the rain will make it worse." She flashed to the dog again. This time, Jane hadn't had a chance to cover his eyes. How did Pet switch forms so easily, when G, and now Jane apparently, were governed by the sun?

He'd have to focus on that later.

"Pet, we have no supplies."

The dog growled.

"All right, all right. We go now."

G grabbed his cloak and saddlebag, removed his lady from his head to set her on his shoulder, and they followed Pet out into the night.

Pet was a fast tracker. With her nose to the ground, she slipped along, somehow maintaining a swift pace without breaking contact between her nostrils and the dirt. G tried to keep up. At least the moon was especially bright tonight, making it easier for G to keep from stumbling.

They had to stop often so that G could catch his breath. During one of these rests, with ferret-Jane asleep around his neck, Pet flashed into a girl and stood before him. "Why can't you just change?"

G averted his eyes from her southern hemisphere, and then from her northern hemisphere, and then decided the only safe place to look was the stars.

"I can't control it. It's a curse. When the sun's down, I'm human. When it's up, I'm a steed." Okay, *steed* was probably pushing it.

Pet groaned. "Get yer house in order."

"My house? I have no house."

"Not the one over there," she said, pointing in the direction of London. (He could see her pointing out of the corner of his eye, even though his gaze was still averted.) "Your house in here." She poked his forehead and then his chest.

"Ow," G said. Her fingers were incredibly strong. "Ow. How am I supposed to—"

But she flashed back to her dog form and began running again before he could finish his question.

They ran and rested and ran again. Breathless and panting, G longed for the sunrise, partly because it would give his human feet a break, and partly because Pet seemed thoroughly unimpressed by his long-distance running, and she refused to hide it.

Then Pet stopped and looked around, confused. She sniffed in one direction, then the other, then the other . . . and didn't pick one. She sniffed out every possible path, and even up the trunks of a few trees, and then she lay down and whimpered, her brown eyes drooping at the corners.

"What's the matter, girl?" G crouched down and stroked Pet's head.

A flash of light, and Pet was a girl, and G was still crouched over her, stroking her hair. It was a move that definitely breached the boundaries of propriety. He leapt back so quickly he almost threw Jane-the-ferret into the trees.

Pet-the-girl looked like she might cry. "His Majesty was traveling with one other person. I was tracking both of their scents." Her nose wrinkled as if she found the smell of this mystery person unpleasant. "But His Majesty's scent, it . . . it stops. Something bad happened here."

Before G could ask her to explain, she flashed back into a dog. She seemed more comfortable that way, as if she could better manage her despair in that form.

G felt his little ferret shaking on his shoulder, and knew that Jane must be fearing the worst for Edward.

"He's okay," G whispered, then faced the dog. "Pet, we'll follow the second scent. If it doesn't lead us to Edward, it will certainly lead us to answers." His wife trembled again. "But I'm sure it will lead us to Edward."

Jane gave a ferrety nod and flattened herself, ready for him to start running once more.

G wasn't nearly as excited to be reunited with Poor, Dear Edward as Jane was, though.

He wondered if that made him a bad person.

Several hours later, and after a too-brief nap, G became a horse, and Jane became a girl.

He wondered what they were going to do with no saddle (which they'd left in their rush from the barn), but Jane didn't hesitate to climb up on his back.

(At this particular era in time, it was scandalous for a woman to ride with no saddle. It would be considered reprehensible—and possibly justification for a prison sentence—for a woman to ride with no saddle on a horse who is really a man. Even if that man were her husband.)

No one had ever ridden G before. It was a strange, but not entirely unpleasant sensation to feel Jane's weight on his back, her legs gripping him around the middle.

"Do you mind if I hold on to your mane?" she asked, in as proper a voice as she would've used at a dinner party when asking, "Would you mind passing the butter?"

G held his head back toward her in response.

She took a handful, but she didn't hold too tightly.

"Let's go find Edward, Pet," she said to the waiting dog. "This scent must lead us to Helmsley."

Yes, G thought a bit glumly. *Let's find Edward.*

They walked for hours, until he felt Jane slump against his neck and then slip dangerously to the side. G lurched the opposite way to counterbalance, and she was able to right herself.

"I'm sorry," Jane said. "I'll hold on tighter."

They needed food, G thought. Neither of them had eaten more than a few bites of dried meat for almost two days. Everything from the saddlebag was gone now, and the bag itself left behind because even that small weight would slow them.

"We need food," Jane said, as if she'd read his mind.

But in order to get food, they would have to forage (none of them had experience), or they would have to hunt (none of them had ever killed an animal), or they would have to head closer to civilization (where there might be soldiers who wanted to kill them). And he couldn't do any of these things in his current state. All he could do as a horse was try to walk evenly.

"I'll find something," she announced. G stopped, and she slid from his back. He waited as she wandered off, returning a few minutes later with a small handful of dark purple berries. "I gathered all I could find. They're Dorset berries. They're safe. I read about them in *Poisonous and Nonpoisonous Berries of the Wild: the Joys of Surviving England on a Budget*. At least, I think they're the safe ones. The pictures in the book weren't very clear."

With that shining endorsement, she laid the berries out on a piece of cloth, divided them up into three even groups, placed one pile in front of Pet and another in the palm of her hand. She lifted it to G's mouth, and he ate them, trying desperately not to chomp off one of her fingers in his excitement over food.

Jane looked at her hands, now covered with horse slobber. "Gross." She wiped her palms down G's flank. "You can have that back."

Then she ate the other pile.

"We'll need to go to a village," she said, her lips stained purple.

Again, exactly what G had been thinking.

*   *   *

Soon enough they hit a road, and it was only a little while after that they came upon a small town, centered around a giant tavern with a wooden sign above its door that bore the silhouette of a mangy-looking dog. It was nearly dusk and the three weary travelers had no money and nothing to trade with, so they stayed at the edge of the forest to come up with a plan.

Jane loved coming up with plans.

She climbed down from G and put the cloak over his back, anticipating the change. Then, she crept up behind a tree and peeked around the edge of the trunk to survey the village.

The sun touched the horizon. In a flash, G was a man. He held the cloak around him and jogged over to Jane.

There was a brightness in her eyes and a smile on her face that made his heart lift.

"There's a storehouse in the back of the tavern," she said excitedly. "I saw a man loading dead rabbits and cured beef inside."

"Oh. I'm sure they lock it up. We'd have better luck if I broke into a house."

"We're not going to steal it!" She shook her head, as though she couldn't believe he would suggest such a thing. "I just meant they have food. And we can get some. By we, I mean you. You'll have to go in there and do something in trade."

G imagined standing in the corner, reading poetry for a different group of strangers, a ferret riding on his shoulder. He imagined the ferret biting him if she didn't like the poem. Not that he'd had a chance to prepare anything. Or bring a page with anything. The first time he'd read for a crowd, he'd meant to recite the poem from memory—he'd gotten to "all the world's a blah" before his mind went blank—and he'd mumbled a few words that vaguely rhymed and then fled.

"I'm not sure that's the best course," he said. "My skills are somewhat limited, thanks to my daily horse diversion, and I haven't— In a while— I mean—"

Jane blushed bright red. "Anyway, we're married. And do you think anyone would really pay you for that?"

G blinked a few times before it hit him. She meant—ah—consummation. And that no one would pay him for it sounded something like an insult, but there was no time for offended feelings now. "Oh, ah, I don't— Rather, I haven't—"

"Never mind that." Jane waved the topic away. "Don't do whatever you were thinking about doing. Just clean some tables or scrub the floor. Taverns always have dirty floors, don't they? What with the sloshing ale and the vomiting."

Jane seemed rather overcritical of taverns in general.

"I see. I can do that." He started down the hill, but she stopped him. Probably good. He was wearing only the cloak, he realized.

"Wait! I'm going with you."

"But you're about to change," he pointed out.

"I'll go as a ferret. In your boot."

"Jane," he protested. "This could be dangerous. We don't

know what to expect in there. I won't be able to concentrate if I'm worrying about you."

"But—"

"Please. Stay here and stay safe."

She frowned and looked like she was about to protest, but then with a flash of light, her clothes fell to the ground and she was a ferret.

G took the clothes and dressed. They were still warm from the heat of her body, and still smelled of her faint perfume. He was tempted to take a moment to breathe it in, but Jane-the-ferret was edging toward his boot. "No, darling. Stay here. I'll come right back. I promise."

She stopped, let out a long ferret sigh, and deflated until she was lying flat on the ground. She looked unbearably bored.

"Consider taking a nap," he said. "You've earned it."

The inside of the tavern was well lit and filled with men and women in plain but sturdy clothes, most covered with some kind of fur, as though everyone worked with animals. They didn't have the look of farmers. An odd stink rode under the scents of roasted meat and bread, but the food made his stomach grumble loudly. It was all he could do to keep from launching himself onto the nearest plate.

Conversation died as everyone stopped what they were doing and turned to look at him.

"Ah, hello." He gathered his courage. This was just like reading poetry, but subtract poems and add people casually placing hunting knives and daggers on their tables. One of the women was filing her fingernails into sharp points, like claws.

Just like reading poetry.

G regathered his courage and strode to the far end of the room, toward the bar. He had to squeeze in between two burly men with tear-shaped scars on their faces. They all smelled vaguely like wet dog. A young man at the end of the bar leaned forward and smirked at him in a decidedly unpleasant manner.

The bartender eyed him. "What do you want?"

"I—" G had never needed to admit to not having money before. "I don't suppose you have any work that needs doing around here?"

"Work?" This fellow clearly had not so much brain as ear wax.

"I could clean the tables or scrub the floor."

The bartender pointed to a haggard-looking serving wench, who scowled at him. "Nell here does that."

"Or I could peel potatoes. Or carrots. Or onions. Or any root vegetable, really." G had never peeled anything before, but how hard could it be?

"We have someone who does that, too," the man said. "Why don't you push off. This isn't the place for you."

G would have suggested yet more menial tasks he'd never attempted, but at that moment, he put together the hints: the wet-dog smell; the fur on everyone's clothes; the defensive/protective behavior when he, a stranger, entered.

That, and they were eating beef.

Cow.

Possibly that village's only cow.

All at once, he knew. This was the Pack.

"Er, yes, perhaps I should be pushing off, as you suggest—" he started to say.

"Rat!" Someone near the door lurched from his chair, making it topple over behind him. "There's a rat!"

It couldn't be Jane, he thought. He'd told her to stay put.

"It's not a rat, you daft idiot," cried another. "It's a squirrel!"

"It's some kind of weasel!"

Bollocks. It was his wife.

"It's dinner, that's what it is." That was the man directly to G's right. "And he's a spy. Asking all those questions about vegetables."

"She's clearly a *ferret*!" G yelled as he lunged toward the dear little creature dashing about on the floor. But Jane was too far away and everyone was suddenly moving, weapons in hand as they rushed toward G. He tried to dart to one side, but the man who wanted to eat Jane for supper threw out his arm and caught G in the throat. G immediately dropped and gagged.

Over the thunder of footfalls on hardwood and shouts of "Get the rat!" Gifford heard the most terrifying sound of all: a loud shriek, followed by silence.

Someone had stepped on Jane.

G shoved himself up and pushed through the group until he reached his wife, who looked like she was preparing for another good scurry. Nothing broken, then. Probably. Hopefully. G grabbed her up in his arms.

From the exit, a series of loud barks sounded: Pet.

G tucked the ferret against his chest and turned to flee. There were a half dozen people in the way. He curled his shoulders around Jane and ran head-on into them, barreling through the press of people and—after a few bright bursts of light—dogs and wolves. If there'd been any doubt before that this was the Pack, it was gone now. But somehow, in spite of the various daggers and swords they slashed at him, G finally made it to the door.

Pet was on the other side, snarling and biting at those who would follow (gosh, we love that dog), and she stayed back to give G time to escape. He ran as fast as he could as a man, and after a few minutes he found himself alone in the forest, just a shuddering Jane against his chest. He let himself slow down. It was then that he finally registered the stabs of pain in his arms and legs. He must have been cut during the scuffle.

G dropped to one knee to catch his breath, and relaxed his hold on Jane. "Well, at least no one will ever say that our married life has not been exciting, right, my dear? But I thought we agreed that it would be for the best if you stayed in the woods."

She didn't respond.

All at once he became aware of the blood soaking the front of his shirt and how unusually quiet she was.

Jane was never quiet.

She was hurt.

G threw off his cloak, laid it on the ground, and placed the ferret on top. It was too dark for him to see anything besides the outline of her small body and her breath coming in fast, short gasps. He ran his fingers down her side and discovered a long, deep gash. He tore a piece from his shirt and wrapped the cloth around her, hoping to stanch the flow of blood.

"Jane?" His voice shook. "Tell me you're all right."

Of course, ferret-Jane couldn't answer. She just looked up at him, limp in the bundle of the cloak. A tiny whimper escaped her.

Brush crackled and G whirled, but it was Pet.

In a flash of light, she was a naked girl. "The other dogs won't follow." She flashed into a dog again, came over, sniffed at Jane, and whined. G closed his eyes and bowed his head.

"Jane. Jane, you stubborn girl." He carefully picked her up and cradled her against him. "I'm going to get you to Helmsley. Don't leave me before then, Jane. Don't leave me. Go, Pet!"

The dog took off and G followed her, running like he'd never run before. He ran flat out for at least ten minutes, and then he kept on running, because Jane was depending on him, and now it was his turn to save her life.

TWENTY-TWO

Edward →

A dog was barking. Stupid dog.

Edward had been lying awake for hours, trying to sleep, but he found his bed uncomfortable, and his head full of women: Mary with her great velvet-encased rear end upon his throne, which irked him. Jane shut up inside a cold, dark room somewhere, weeping because she thought he was dead, which—okay, well, Edward liked the idea of Jane mourning him more than he would have admitted out loud. It did seem appropriate that she would grieve for him; she was his best friend, after all. But the idea of Jane locked away in London and him here, helpless to go to her, nettled him. And then there was Bess with her complicated plans that all seemed to come down to Edward entreating the King of France—one of his least favorite people—for help, which felt an awful lot like begging, and kings did not beg. Plus Gran with her disgusting tonics and her razor tongue and the infuriating way she had of making him feel like a boy who had only played as king.

And Gracie. Gracie, Gracie.

The way she'd said she liked his smile.

The surprising roughness of her hand against his when she'd given him the little wooden fox.

Her trousers, because she was too stubborn to wear skirts like a proper female.

Her finger against his lips back in the barn, her eyes full of danger and fun.

Her untamable hair.

Her laugh.

Of course she was always laughing at him, it seemed. Mocking him. Knocking him onto his backside. Disobeying his commands, even the simple ones like, *Call me Edward*. How hard could it be to call him Edward?

Edward was vexed.

The dog was still barking, a sound that bounced off the stone walls of the old keep, loud and constant. Edward turned over onto his side and yanked at the tangled covers. The mattress was lumpy, stuffed with a combination of wool and straw. In the palace, he'd slept on a feather bed with fine sheets and the softest of furs. He'd never had to clean his own shirt. Or see to his own chamber pot. Or subsist on rabbit stew for three nights in a row.

Bark, bark, bark, went the dog.

And let's not forget the women. He found himself suddenly overtaken by women, and not the demure and silent young ladies that fawned over him at court. Oh, no. He had to be surrounded by opinionated women who delighted in bossing him around.

Aggravating, unkissable women.

And still the blasted dog would not stop barking!

Even the dogs here are ill-mannered, he thought as he crammed a pillow over his head and pressed it to his ear. In the palace, the dogs never barked all night. That was not allowed. Pet certainly never barked, unless there was something wrong. Something urgent. Pet never—

Edward sat up.

Of course at that exact moment the barking stopped. The night fell so silent that he was afraid that his eardrums would burst, he was straining so hard to listen. Then he heard a door bang somewhere in the keep, and muffled voices in the hallway. Alarmed voices.

Edward got out of bed and quickly put on his pants and boots. More doors were slamming downstairs, and there was the scrape of heavy furniture being dragged across the floor. The castle could be under attack—it wasn't outside the realm of possibility. If Mary caught on that he was alive, she'd send soldiers to dispatch him straight away.

Edward looked around for a sword, but all he could find was a butter knife and his half of the broken broomstick, which would have to do. He stuck the knife in his boot, tightened his grip on the broom, threw open his chamber door, and stepped out into the hall.

Immediately he was hit with an invisible wall of Gran's skunk stench, so strong it could have knocked him over. Another ominous sign.

Edward crept down the stairs, his heart thundering, his hair practically standing on end. The entire population of the castle added up to seven people: Edward, Gracie, Bess, Gran, a cook, an old lady-in-waiting who served as a housekeeper, and an ancient man-at-arms who could hardly lift his sword. If they were set upon by soldiers, they were done for. His head would be delivered to Mary in a basket, come morning.

The main hall was deserted, not even the fireplace flickering, but Edward could hear voices. He followed the sound to the kitchens. Banging. Yelling. Carefully, he pushed open the door a crack.

What he saw through the crack was Gran. The old lady was moving with uncharacteristic swiftness around the kitchen, lighting candles, followed closely by a drawn and grim-faced Bess.

"Yarrow, that's what I need," Gran said to Bess. "It's a purple star-shaped flower. It should be in my storeroom hanging from the rafters. And horsetail, if you can find it. Go!"

Bess darted out of the room through the back door, which led out into the ruined courtyard. Then Gran put her foot up on a chair and hiked up her gown, showing a purple-veined leg. She started to hack at her underskirt with a kitchen knife. Edward must have made a sound then, because Gran looked up.

"Get in here, boy," she barked.

Edward obeyed. No one else was in the kitchen. The long table in the center had been cleared off, and in the middle there was a cloak, and something on it—something dark and furry. An animal of some kind.

"Are you cooking something?" Edward asked stupidly. "What's happening?"

Gran tossed him what was left of her undergarments. "Here. Tear this into strips."

Before he could form a coherent protest, the door to the courtyard burst open, and Gracie and a stranger came in, lugging a large bucket of water between them. They went straight to the fire and poured the water into the cauldron that hung over the flames.

"Good. Now go to Elizabeth in the storeroom and help her find what I need. You know something of plants, I think?" Gran said to Gracie, who nodded and slipped out again.

"You," Gran said to the man who'd helped Gracie bring in the bucket. "Sit down before you fall down. I don't want to be stitching up your head tonight, as well."

The man swallowed like it would hurt him to attempt to speak. He was sweat-stained and unwashed, and he looked exhausted. He pulled a chair over to the table and sank into it, gazing down at the tiny creature. It was a mink, Edward thought, similar to a pelt his sister Mary wore as a scarf around her neck in the winter months. Beautiful, soft fur. But why all this fuss over a mink?

The man reached out a hand to stroke the small head, with

such tenderness that Edward's breath caught. But the creature didn't stir.

The man's lips moved, a word that resembled *please*.

"Edward. The linens," Gran snapped.

The man looked up at Edward and met his eyes.

It was Gifford Dudley.

Jane's husband. Here. The look on his face like his heart was being rent in two. Like the little mink on the table meant more to him than anything else in the world. Like it was him dying.

Edward's breath left his lungs.

"Is that Jane?" he gasped. "Jane! Is that Jane?"

Gran grabbed him by the collar and dragged him away from the table. "Yes, it's Jane, and she's hurt, and I'm really going to need those linens, boy."

Immediately Edward set to tearing up the linens, all the while watching Gifford, who kept his eyes on the table—Jane! Jane!—his expression so miserable and so lost that it was no wonder Edward hadn't recognized him at first.

What had happened to them?

The water in the cauldron was hot. Edward finished tearing up Gran's underskirt, and Bess and Gracie returned with the herbs. Gran brought a candlestick over to the table and peeled the bandages back to reveal the mink's long, blood-streaked body. Edward's heart was in his throat as Gran peered at the small form.

"She was wounded in this form, not as a human?" she asked Gifford gruffly.

Gifford nodded. "We were trying to . . . I don't know what happened, really." His voice faded. "It was so fast."

Bess handed Gran a bowl of the paste she'd made from the herbs, and a basin of hot water. Gran began to clean Jane's wounds. Within moments, the water was pink.

Edward felt light-headed. And also like he might lose his rabbit-stew dinner.

"Edward," Gran said quietly, her eyes never leaving her work. "You sit down, too."

He sat and took some deep breaths until he felt marginally less queasy. "Jane's an E∂ian," he whispered as he watched Gran tend to the little creature.

"So it would seem," Gran said.

"All this time, it's all she ever wanted, to be an E∂ian. What . . . what is she, exactly?" Edward asked.

"A ferret," Gifford answered tonelessly. "She's a ferret."

"She'd be better off a girl, right now," Gran said. "If you're hurt as a human, the wound will be less in your E∂ian form—not gone, mind you, but less. If you're in the animal form when you come to harm . . ." Her lips tightened as she stared down at ferret-Jane. "It would be better if she were human. I could see her wounds more clearly without the fur, for one thing."

"Can't we get her to change somehow?" Edward asked, his voice cracking.

Gran shook her head. "The body will stay in whatever shape it feels safest, which is typically the animal. There has to be a conscious decision to overcome the fear, and prompt the change. No. We must wait for her to wake up." She drew the cloak up over the ferret's body like she was tucking a child into bed. "We must wait," she said again.

But what if she doesn't wake up? thought Edward, but he didn't say it. He couldn't.

Gran put one hand on Edward's shoulder and the other on Gifford's. "It's late. I don't suppose I'm going to convince either of you to get some rest?"

They both shook their heads.

She sighed. "All right. You watch over her, then. Come wake me if anything happens."

It was morning, the sun not yet visible but lighting the eastern sky, when Jane changed. Edward would not have believed it if he hadn't seen it—the ferret one moment, his cousin the next, lying curled under the cloak. He jumped to his feet and ran to fetch Gran, but he'd only gone a few steps when he heard Jane moan a name.

"G," she said.

Gifford. Her husband, he remembered with a pang. Gifford was her husband because Edward had asked her to marry the young lord, even though she'd begged him not to make her go through with it. She'd listened to Edward. Which was why she was lying there now in bandages.

It was all his fault. He was a terrible best friend.

He turned. Gifford was holding Jane's hand. He brought it to his face and pressed it to his cheek, then kissed her palm. "Jane," he whispered. "Wake up."

Her eyes moved behind her eyelids, then fluttered open. "G," she said again, and the corner of her mouth lifted in a smile. "I thought I might not see you again. . . ."

"You'll have to work harder than that to be rid of me," Gifford said.

Edward suddenly felt like he was intruding on something intimate. He took a step backward toward the exit, and his foot shuffled against the rough stone floor.

Jane looked over Gifford's shoulder and saw him.

"Edward," she breathed, her brown eyes widening. "EDWARD."

She gave a choked cry and reached out. Of course he went to her. Gifford straightened and moved out of his way so that Edward could sit beside her and clasp her hand in his.

"You're alive," Jane said. "I kept asking to see your body, but they wouldn't let me, and I thought that perhaps it was all a ruse and you weren't really gone, that they were lying to me, that you were out there somewhere, and that meant that I wasn't really the queen and I shouldn't be there, but it felt like wishful thinking."

All of those words seemed to exhaust her, and she whimpered and sank back on the table. He noticed, then, that there was blood seeping through the cloak. He turned to ask Gifford to go get Gran, but Gifford had already gone. Gran came hustling through the door, rolling up her sleeves.

"Gran," Jane said, "We found you, after all."

"Be quiet, dear," Gran said. "Rest now."

Jane sighed and closed her eyes. Gran smoothed the red hair back from Jane's forehead and started to draw the cloak away from her. Then she stopped and glared at Edward.

"Out with you," she ordered. "You, too, horse boy."

Edward turned to see Gifford standing in the doorway, his expression tight. They went outside together, where the first rays of sun were touching the highest stones of the keep.

"I have to go," Gifford said. "Will you . . . ?"

"I'll stay with her," Edward offered.

Gifford lowered his head and nodded stiffly toward his chest. "Thank you."

Then he was moving away from Edward in long strides across the grass, shedding his clothes as he went, until a light flashed and he was no longer walking, but galloping across the field.

Edward sat down on the ground next to the door and leaned against the wall, drawing his knees up to his chest. He was cold, and he was tired, but he didn't care. He'd be there for Jane the minute Gran allowed him back into the room.

"Sire," said a soft voice. He glanced up. Gracie was holding a cup of something out to him. He took it. It was hot, steam curling off the top. It warmed his hands.

"Please say this isn't one of Gran's potions," he said.

"Only one way to find out," she replied.

He took a sip.

Tea. No milk or sugar, but tea, all the same.

"Thank you," he said. "You're perfect—I mean, it's perfect. Thank you."

"Well, that's what the English drink in times of crisis, I hear." She lifted her arms over her head and stretched, then yawned, then smiled. "We Scots prefer whisky."

He was too tired to smile back properly. He drank the tea slowly, savoring the heat that filled his belly. He felt his shoulders start to relax.

"You really love her, don't you?" Gracie asked him as she took the empty cup from his hand. "Jane."

"Yes, I love her," he said. "We've known each other all our lives."

He was about to say something more, about how Jane was like a sister to him, that kind of affection between them, but then he heard a mad, joyful little bark, and Pet was on him.

The dog wiggled and danced all over him, whining and whimpering and yipping, her tail wagging like mad. He grinned and tried to pet her, but she wouldn't hold still. It was only when she started to lick his face that he remembered that there was a girl someone in there, a person, and he sobered and tried to get to his feet.

"Someone's happy to see you," Gracie remarked.

"Uh . . . yes," he said. "Down, Pet. Down."

There was a flash, and she was a naked girl.

"Your Majesty," she said earnestly. "I am so glad to see you. I followed your scent all the way here, and I thought I'd lost it once, but I found it again. I would have come more quickly, but you told me to protect Jane, so I stayed with them."

He resisted the urge to say "good girl" and pat her on the head. "Well done, Pet," he said instead. "You did well to stay with Jane."

He would never get used to Pet being a naked girl. Her hair was long and thick and it fell over her in all the needed places, but it still shocked him every single time.

He wasn't the only one. Gracie was standing there with her mouth open. It was the most taken aback he'd ever seen her. He would have laughed if the whole situation weren't so completely uncomfortable.

"So, Pet," he said, and cleared his throat. "I'd like you to meet Gracie MacTavish. Gracie, this is Petunia Bannister, my . . . er . . ." *Bodyguard* felt like the wrong word. *Protector* seemed unmanly. *Companion* could be taken the wrong way. "Watch . . . person," he settled on finally.

Pet cocked her head to one side and stared at Gracie. Then she sniffed the air. "Fox," she deduced, her nose wrinkling in disgust. "So you're the one I smelled."

"Charmed, I'm sure," Gracie said wryly.

In a flash, Pet was a dog again. She crouched next to Edward's feet, gave Gracie a baleful stare, and then growled low in her throat.

"I'm sorry," Edward said, mortified on so many levels. "She's never been too fond of strangers." He bent to admonish the hound. "Gracie saved my life, Pet. She's my friend."

Pet laid her head down on her paws and sighed heavily.

He glanced up to find Gracie staring at him. "What?" he asked. "I know it's a bit unconventional, but her family has been serving the royal line for generations, apparently, and I only knew she was an Eðian a few weeks ago, I swear."

"Is that what I am? Your friend?" Gracie asked.

"Of course," he said.

"Because I saved your life?"

"Yes. I mean, no. I mean—" He didn't know which answer she wanted. He paused to collect himself. "Do you consider me your friend?"

Gracie shook her head. "I don't know what to consider you, Sire."

His teeth came together. "Edward," he corrected.

Pet growled again. He frowned at her, and she fell silent.

"Is there anything else I don't know about you?" Gracie asked. "Any more surprises we have in store?"

There was so much she didn't know about him, he thought, that he would like her to know. But he answered, "No. I think that's it."

"All right, then." She gave a little bow. "Your Majesty. Pet. I must take my leave for now. Your granny has asked me to procure some items for her, and I cannot refuse the old lady."

"Procure, as in steal?" Edward asked.

Dimples. "It's best not to ask too many questions, Sire. You worry yourself about your Jane. Leave me to my own devices."

Your Jane. He settled back into his spot against the wall. *Your Jane,* like Jane belonged to him somehow, and had that been an edge in Gracie's voice when she said it? Like she was jealous? Like she wished that she could be his Gracie?

He could only hope.

"She's going to live," Gran announced sometime later, startling Edward from where he was most definitely not sleeping. "She's asking for you. I've put her in your bed, as it's the most comfortable in the keep. Don't wear her out with talking. She'll heal quickly, but she needs rest."

He told Pet to stay, and ran all the way up the stairs.

Jane was sitting propped up with pillows. She looked tired, and vaguely ill, with lavender circles under her eyes and her lips pale as chalk, but she smiled at him bravely.

"You're alive," she felt compelled to point out again.

"So are you," he replied, sitting down carefully next to her. "We're miracles, you and I."

"I'm a ferret," she said like she was confessing a great sin that she wasn't sorry for.

"I noticed that, too. I'm a kestrel. Pleased to make your acquaintance. And it would be rather splendid, except that when I fly I seem to lose my brain. I'm working on it. Flying should be useful, when I can control it more. I can fly ahead and scout. Spy on people. I can't wait to spy on people. Just think of all the dirt I'll dig up."

She fingered the edge of the scratchy linen sheet. "That's wonderful."

"So we're Eϑians," he said jubilantly. "At last!"

She smiled again, but her heart wasn't in it. She was still hurting, he thought. He took her hand. "Janey. You're going to be all right now. Gran says so, and you dare not defy Gran."

"I'm fine," she said. "Well, I'm going to be fine. I promise."

He glanced out the window, where the sun was making its descent in the sky. "It will be dusk soon, and your husband will return. Promise him, too."

"How is he?" she asked in a wavering voice. "Is he very angry with me?"

"Why would Gifford be angry?"

"He told me to stay behind when he went into the tavern. But I went in anyway."

Now there was a big surprise.

"He's not angry. He's worried about you, of course," Edward answered. "Does his breath smell of hay? I often wondered."

Jane smacked him, then winced. "We had a fight, when I became queen. Dudley wanted me to make him king, as an equal, but I refused."

"Smart girl, I'd say. I think he's forgiven you," Edward said.

It was undeniable, the way Gifford felt about Jane. The man had been in agony at the thought of losing her. His love had been like a light burning in the room last night, clear to anyone who saw it, from the look on his face when he thought she might be dying, to how he'd paced the room and fretted about her those long hours before she'd become a girl again. Edward had not been able to stop thinking about the way Gifford had held Jane's hand to his cheek and kissed it. Edward hadn't ever known that depth of feeling. Not romantically, anyway.

Gifford loved Jane. And judging by her face when she talked about her husband, Jane loved Gifford, too. They loved each other. Even if they hadn't admitted it to themselves yet.

Edward smiled.

Maybe there was going to be a happy ending to this story, after all.

Jane

TWENTY-THREE

"The key to changing to your animal form," Gran said, "is to know your heart's desire."

Right, Jane thought. *My heart's desire.*

It was late afternoon, and Jane, Edward, and Gifford were standing just off the worn path that ran around the ruins. The keep lifted high above them, blocking the worst of the sun's glare and casting heavy shadows over the piles of fallen stone and the thick green grass. Gran stood opposite them, while Gracie circled the group with a stern expression on her face, her arms crossed over her chest.

Jane had a headache.

"Be honest with yourself," continued Gran. "If, in the moment you want to change, you do not know why you want to become a bird or ferret or horse—"

Gifford snorted. He was a horse already.

"—or human, then you will stay exactly as you are."

"What about curses?" Jane asked.

"What about curses?" A pungent, garbage odor slipped into the air, making Jane cough at the sour taste in the back of her throat. Gran had never been very patient, and the more annoyed she became, the worse she smelled.

"How are we supposed to control our changes if we're cursed?"

"What makes you think you're cursed?"

"Gifford spends his days as a horse and his nights as a man. Every day, without fail, he changes." Jane used to blame him for his struggles. She'd thought of him as undisciplined. Now she had a bit more sympathy. "And, for the time being, anyway, I spend my nights as a ferret."

At least she had every night since the Tower. The sun went down, and flash—Jane was a ferret, whether she wanted to change or not. It was a problem. The first step, she thought, was admitting it.

"That's why we're here." Gran's odor grew stronger. "Because you lot need to learn to control yourselves."

"Isn't the point of a curse that it can't be controlled?" Jane gestured toward Gifford, who'd bent his head to nip at the grass. "We need to break the curses first, and then learn how to control the change."

"That sounds reasonable," Edward said. "Good thinking, Janey."

"That sounds stupid, if you ask me," Gracie said, staring flatly at Jane. "You're not cursed. You're just stubborn."

"Gracie's right." Gran let out an aggravated sigh. "You're not cursed. There's something in you making you want to change when you do."

"Well, changing because of the position of the sun definitely sounds like a curse to me," Jane argued.

"Me too." Edward frowned. "I think it's likely that Gifford was cursed, and Jane, you got this curse because you married him. Which means this is partially my fault. I'm so sorry."

Jane touched Edward's arm, consolingly. "It's not your fault."

Gifford gave another loud snort, and something large and ploppy dropped from his hindquarters. He never had the best manners in his horse form.

Jane smoothed down the edges of her borrowed dress. The cut and colors were decades out of fashion, but that sort of thing had never bothered her. She was just grateful to have something more dignified than trousers. Then again, Gracie had made trousers look like the most fashionable things a woman had ever worn. Edward certainly seemed to appreciate the view, from the way he kept gazing at her with his mouth open.

She was almost embarrassed for him. Really.

"You both must have a reason to change with the sun," Gracie said.

"That's right," Gran agreed. "It's a matter of the heart, like I was saying. When you truly want to control your forms, you will."

This was all feeling very judgmental to Jane. "How can you say that? No one wants to control their change more than I!"

Gran clucked disapprovingly. "Tell me about when you first changed."

"It was in my time of great emotional need," Jane said with a lift of her chin. "Just like in the stories. I wanted to avoid getting my head chopped off. And I wanted to save Gifford from being burned at the stake. So I became a ferret and rescued him."

"A very noble first change." Edward smiled her way. "And mine, of course, was wanting to avoid being murdered in my bed. I needed to escape, so I did."

Gran glanced at Gifford as though she expected him to tell the story of his first change, but he just blew out a breath and gazed toward the field surrounding the old castle, like there were places he'd rather be.

"What about your first change, Gran?" Jane asked.

"One of my maids forgot the fruit with my breakfast. I became a skunk and sprayed her."

Gracie laughed. "That isn't true, is it?"

Gran lifted an eyebrow. "Are you calling me a liar?"

"I'm calling you a storyteller."

"Fine. The gardener killed a rosebush and I found myself agitated."

"Gran!" Edward said. "Tell us the truth."

"Ah, the truth is a slippery thing," Gran said, but then she sighed. "Very well. One of my ladies-in-waiting spent the night with my husband." She waited a beat to make sure they understood what that meant. "I didn't find out until court, and there in front of everyone, I transformed into a skunk and sprayed in every direction. I was aiming for my cheating husband, you see, and my traitorous lady. But skunks have poor vision, so I had to guess. I guessed incorrectly a few times."

Jane choked back a laugh. It was an amusing idea, but that had been a time when being an Eðian was punishable by death.

That was the time Mary wanted to resurrect. Which was a sobering thought.

"It took me some time to control it, too, at first, if you want to know," Gran admitted gruffly. "I don't think I understood my heart's desire back then. I was ruled by baser things."

Jane gazed down at her feet for a minute. Was she not being honest with herself? What did her heart want?

"All right," Edward said. "I'm ready to try."

"Good." Gran gave two sharp claps. "No more talk of curses."

"Close your eyes," Gracie advised. "Sometimes that helps. Think of what you like about your other form. Think about what you want to do in that form."

Jane had always been a fantastic student. She immediately closed her eyes and recalled what it was like being a ferret. She'd loved being so useful. The way she could hear and smell everything. And she was quite portable, easily draped over Gifford's shoulder.

There wasn't a better creature to be.

"I want to be a ferret," she whispered. "I want to be a ferret."

"Silently, Jane." Edward sounded vaguely annoyed. "You're not the only one trying to concentrate."

She glanced over at her cousin. He was still too thin, too pale with his recent illness—poisoning, she reminded herself—but he did look better. Stronger. Very much alive.

As she watched, the tension around his shoulders eased. His eyes were closed, and he was smiling as if he were picturing something wonderful.

"Sky," he murmured.

His light flashed so bright that Jane had to squeeze her eyes shut. She heard the flap of wings. Feathers rustling. When she looked up again, Edward was in the air.

She put her hands on her hips. "How did he do that?"

"Just how we said." Gracie looked from Jane to Gifford, who was still eating grass. "He wanted to become a kestrel enough. It was his heart's desire."

Jane was pretty sure that her heart's desire was to be a ferret, but here she was. Two legs. Upright. Not enough fur. Eyes decidedly not beady.

She poked Gifford. "What about you? Did you even try?"

He lifted his head and angled for ear scratches.

"Unbelievable!" She stepped back and folded her arms. "Don't you want to be a man during the day? If it's all about desire, why do you not desire to be a man?"

He ignored her and wandered away, seemingly satisfied to be a horse.

Meanwhile, Edward was soaring and diving with abandon back and forth above them, and soon he gave a great hawk-like cry, and vanished over the trees.

"I'd better go after him," Gracie said. "Looks like he's caught up in that bird joy again." Then right there in front of Jane, Gran, and Gifford—who was aiming for a field to run in, not even noticing the ladies anymore—Gracie shimmied out of her trousers and turned into a fox so quickly Jane didn't have time to protest.

Jane turned to Gran. "Now what?" Edward was a bird and loved it too much. Gifford was a horse and wouldn't try to fix it. Gracie and Gran could change at will and didn't see why Jane couldn't.

Jane didn't see why she couldn't change, either.

"Now you try again," Gran said. "Or I'll turn into a skunk and spray you."

She closed her eyes. She imagined herself being a ferret. She put her whole heart into it.

"You're just making your nose twitch," Gran said.

"Shh." Jane pictured being ferret-like.

"Now you're just crouching."

Jane sighed, frustrated.

"Did you just meow?" Gran said.

Jane made fists and stomped her feet. She wanted to scream, but she refrained from saying anything except an earnest whisper.

"I desperately, desperately want to be a ferret right now."

But every time she checked, she was still a girl.

Jane was still a ferret when she awakened the following morning.

Because she *had* turned into a ferret . . . eventually. When the sun fell below the horizon. Just like before.

Gran and Gracie could ignore the evidence all they wanted, but Jane knew better. A curse was a curse.

She was curled up on the pillow next to Gifford's head. He was snoring a little, so quietly it would have been nothing to her human ears, but her ferret ears were much better and he sounded like a thunderstorm. With a mind to make him stop, she stretched and bumped her nose against his eyelid.

He groaned and waved her away.

She bumped his eyelid again.

"That's cold," he grumbled.

She nipped his nose lightly.

He sat up with a start, definitely awake now. "My lady! If you wanted to wake me, you've succeeded. But you don't have to take off my nose." He was grinning, though.

Jane made a low chuckling noise and danced across the bed, the mattress giving an extra spring to her jumping.

"Most undignified, my darling. But quite charming." Gifford laughed and excused himself from the room. "I'll return once you've changed."

A few minutes later she became a girl again. Just like that: the sun was coming up, and she changed without even trying. It was mystifying that she was still, after all this time, completely unable to control her Eðian self.

She'd only just managed to get all the pieces of her second-hand dress in their proper places when Gifford knocked and came back into the chamber.

"Need help with the laces?" he asked.

"Yes. Thank you." She turned so he could access the ribbons along the back of her gown.

He swept her tumble of red hair over her shoulder, his hand lingering there for a moment before he saw to the fastening of her gown. "Anything for my wife."

She was coming to like that word—*wife*. Especially the way he said it.

"So what's the plan for today?" he asked as he fastened a hook at the top of the gown, his fingers brushing the skin between her shoulder blades. Jane shivered. "Are we storming any castles?"

"No, but we're starting our long journey to France tomorrow. So we need to pack."

"I wasn't aware that we had any possessions that would need packing." He pulled the laces tight, but not too tight. She appreciated that.

"Bess is arranging for a finer gown for me to wear," Jane explained. "For the French court. Edward says he wants me with him when he makes his appeal to the king."

Gifford cleared his throat. "Ah. I see. Edward wants you

with him." He finished with her dress quickly and stepped back. "There."

"It makes sense that I should be there, in case I'm needed to validate Edward's story."

"Yes, of course," he said stiffly. His expression was suddenly blank. "The sun's almost up. I should go."

She followed him as he made his way outside. "Wait, G—"

"Have a good day, my lady," he said, and jogged off, pulling at his clothes.

"Have a good day," she called after him lamely.

Then he was a horse. She watched him trot through the gardens and jump a low section of the crumbling wall.

She sighed.

Gifford had been acting strangely since they'd escaped London. For the most part, he was warm and affectionate with her. He teased her, but never with an intent to hurt her feelings. He often held her hand. He called her pet names, like "my darling" and "my sweet." Those things shouldn't have had such an effect on her, but they did. Being with him made her breath come quicker and her heart pound and her palms get all clammy. It made her wish she could remain human all the time so that they could stay together.

But then there were other times, especially when they were around Edward and Bess and Gran, when Gifford retreated behind a wall of silence, his jaw set in a way she recognized as anger. She wondered if he blamed her for all that had happened.

They had no home now, no safe place to go except for this

broken-down abbey. No title or position. No possessions, as he'd pointed out.

That was hardly her fault, but still. She'd been awful to him in London. They'd had an actual fight. She'd thrown pillows at his head.

No wonder he hadn't even been trying during their training session with Gran and Gracie. He was probably happy to avoid her company.

Jane watched him canter across the field, his head high, mane streaming. He seemed so content as a horse. And it wasn't as though she'd given him much of a reason to try to be a man.

Her chin lifted. They had so little time together now—just a few minutes at the start and end of every day. She'd have to use those precious minutes wisely.

She'd have to try harder to win back his trust.

When she came into the kitchen later, Gracie, Bess, and Edward were discussing the best routes to take to France.

Bess unfolded a map and spread it across the table. "If we want to move quickly—"

"And we do," said Edward.

"—then we need to take the most direct route with the best roads," Bess finished.

Jane stood on tiptoe to peek around Edward's shoulder. "Let's do that."

"But there are a few problems with this route," Gracie said.

"Mary's men will be looking for all of you, and this road"—she dragged her finger over a line—"takes us dangerously close to the Shaggy Dog."

"The Shaggy Dog?" repeated Jane.

"From the description that Gifford gave us," Edward said, "that's the tavern you were attacked in. The headquarters of the Pack."

Jane shivered. "What are our other options?"

"Longer paths on poorer roads." Edward pointed out a few. They did look rather out of the way.

"So what will we do?" Jane asked.

"I . . ." Edward drummed his fingers on the map. "Speed is of the essence. But so is safety. What do the rest of you think?"

"Long way," Gracie replied immediately. "The Pack is bad news."

"Short way," Bess said. "We're taking back a kingdom. We should be bold. And swift."

Everyone looked at Jane, who consoled herself with the reminder that, though she was a tiebreaker, this would still be Edward's decision. He was the king. "Short way," she said. "I agree with Bess."

Gracie glared. Edward looked uncomfortable. Bess gave a faint smile.

"Furthermore," Jane said, "I think we should recruit the Pack to our side."

"Are you daft?" cried Gracie. "They almost killed you."

"I'm aware of that."

"They're not just some random bandits, you know," Gracie said. "They're a well-run organization. And they see themselves as superior to humans. They certainly don't answer to any king. They'll use your pretty feathers to stuff their pillows, Sire."

"Right. Recruiting the Pack sounds like a terrible idea," agreed Edward.

"But we need anyone who isn't already on Mary's side," Jane argued. "We could use all the help we can get."

"Not their kind of help!" Gracie shook her head. "Tell her, Edward."

"What do you think, sister?" Edward turned to Bess, who looked thoughtful.

"I have my army, of course, and France will hopefully agree to loan us some of theirs once you ask King Henry. But that still might not be enough men to take back your crown." Bess tapped the place on the map where the Shaggy Dog was located. "Besides, I've been thinking that perhaps it's not enough to simply take back your crown."

Edward stared at her. "What do you mean?"

"This country is divided. Eðians and Verities are at each other's throats. The people are caught in the middle, and they are suffering for it. It's one thing to win back your crown, Edward. It's quite another to win back your country. Your people. You will need both sides to do that. Verities *and* Eðians. You must unite them. And to do that, you'll need the Pack."

"You're right," Edward said.

"You're crazy, is what you are." Gracie's green eyes were filled with worry—though that worry was masked with a practiced expression of annoyance. "If you go to the Pack, you'll die." She turned to Jane. "I don't want to hear a rumor about Thomas Archer wearing a ferret stole come this winter."

Jane shivered. She didn't want to be a ferret stole, either. She remembered the danger of the Pack well enough. The gash in her side was still stitched and healing. And she remembered the villagers and their poor cow.

That was just the kind of thing that had to stop if things were going to get better for England. Which meant that Bess was right. *I was right,* Jane thought, silently congratulating herself for having the idea.

"Thank you very much for your concern," she said to Gracie, "but I think we should go."

"What do you mean 'we'?" Edward turned to Jane, his eyebrows raised in alarm. "You're staying here to recover from your injuries."

"My injuries? I'm quite recovered now, really." Mostly.

"Even so, you're not going. The Pack is too dangerous."

Gracie straightened. "That's right, Your Majesty. The key word here is *dangerous.*"

"Why are you so afraid of them?" Edward turned on Gracie. "I've never known you to balk at danger before."

"I am not afraid!" Gracie bristled. "I just don't want to . . . see Archer again."

"Why not?" Bess folded her hands in front of her.

"Because he's my ex," Gracie blurted out.

"Ex?" Jane had no idea what that meant.

Bess leaned toward Jane, keeping her voice low. "Former paramour."

"Oh!" Jane nodded, finally understanding. "They had a romantic relationship."

"What?" Edward's face turned bright red as he looked at Gracie. "You had a relationship with him? Archer?"

"My affairs are my own business, Sire." Gracie tugged a hand through her mess of black curls. "But it does mean I know far more about the Pack than any of you, so you'd best take my advice. Stay away from them. They're trouble. Especially Archer."

"Especially." Edward frowned and turned back to Jane. "All right. I've made my decision. I'm going to recruit the Pack. But you're staying here. So are Bess and Gracie."

Bess lifted an eyebrow. "I'm not staying here."

"If you're going to .insist on this fool's errand of yours, I should go with you, too." Gracie stalked forward, her hands in fists at her sides. "Archer won't be reasonable. It's not in his nature to do anything unless it directly benefits himself. But perhaps I can keep you from getting yourselves killed."

"No," Edward protested. "You're staying here, too. To— uh—guard Jane."

The Scot's green eyes shot daggers at Edward. Jane almost felt bad for her cousin. "Oh, and I suppose you'll let Gifford go with you?" Gracie huffed.

"He's a strong young man—"

"He's a horse!" Jane and Gracie yelled at exactly the same time. They paused, glanced at each other, and Jane understood immediately that they were now on the same side. "Allow us to tell you exactly why we're going with you." With a quick nod, she indicated Gracie go first.

"I know the Pack, for one. I know their tricks and hideouts. And furthermore, when you lot get hungry and start looking for bugs to eat, I'll be the one to find something you'll actually want to eat. Not to mention I'm quick with weapons and the king needs all the protecting he can get."

"Now stop right there—"

But Jane was ready now. "To complement Gracie's considerable skills with violence and illegal activities, I have read at least twice as many books as you, Edward. Likely three or four times, which means I'm quite knowledgeable on an assortment of subjects that might come in handy."

"Just because we're girls doesn't mean you have to coddle us," Gracie said. "The truth is, you need us. You need me, especially, if you want to face the Pack."

"It's not because you're girls." Edward's face was red again. "All right, fine. I suppose you'd just follow us anyway and then we'd have to rescue you in addition to everything else that awaits us. I guess you can come."

"Fine," said Gracie. "Then it's settled."

But Jane had a feeling that it was still anything but.

The group's mood was somber as they approached the Shaggy Dog—Gracie had told them over and over that this was a bad idea. That it wasn't going to work. That they were all going to die and become pillows and stoles.

"Well," Bess said as they were finally making their way down the main street of the village toward the tavern. "If anyone's inclined toward prayer, now might be the time."

"Yes. Last chance to call it off," Gracie said.

"You can still wait with the horses," Edward said. "I can do this on my own."

"Shut up, bird boy."

There were five horses with them—four normal and one very special, in Jane's opinion—and they tied the four real horses to a post. Then they were standing at the tavern steps. The sign over the door squeaked on its post—the image of a dog with vague scratches in the paint to signal shagginess. It looked different in the daylight. And smaller, now that she wasn't a tiny ferret with blurry vision.

Still, Jane shivered. This was where she'd almost died just days ago.

Edward said, "Gifford—"

The fifth horse snorted.

"Call him G," Jane translated.

"G, watch our mounts."

Gracie began changing the knots on the horses' leads. "This is a better knot for our situation. If we run out screaming, we—or G—can just pull the ends of these and flee."

The whites around Gifford's eyes shone.

"I agree," Jane said to him, and turned to Gracie. "Do you think fleeing will be necessary?"

Gracie nodded toward a corner on the far side of the street where a man disappeared behind a butcher shop. Then to the rooftop of an apothecary. The streets were eerily empty for this time of day. "They know we're here. Maybe they haven't done anything yet, but they know."

Jane petted Gifford's soft cheek. He blew out a breath and dropped his chin on her shoulder, pulling her into what might have been a horse version of a hug. She put her arms around his neck for a moment and breathed in the warm scent of his fur.

"I'll be fine," she whispered by his ear. "They won't recognize me. But if anything bad happens, you have my permission to kick down the door." She rubbed his forehead before hurrying after the others into the tavern.

"I'm here to speak with Thomas Archer," Edward called as the door swung shut behind them.

There were seven people in the taproom—five drinking at tables, one working at the bar, and one in deep conversation with the bartender—and all of them stopped what they were doing and turned to stare at Edward.

"Who are you?" asked the bartender.

"I'm the King of England," Edward announced. "And I want to speak to Thomas Archer."

One of the drinkers laughed. "The king is dead. So is the new queen. The new new queen sits on the throne now. Mary."

"She is *not* the rightful queen," Jane objected.

Bess bumped Jane's arm in warning. Then, subtly, she nodded toward Gracie, whose gaze was fixed on the man sitting at the bar. The Scot's hands were clenched into fists at her sides.

No question about it: that man was Archer.

His back was turned to them, but there was enough to reveal him as a young man. His form was slender and straight. Strands of black hair curled over his collar.

"He is the king," Gracie said to him alone. "He's telling the truth."

Slowly, the young man at the bar turned around. He had a striking face, with sharp cheekbones and a strong jaw. He looked Gracie up and down. "So, the little fox returns. With a king, no less. You're looking fine, Gracie. Did you miss me?"

"Not even a little."

"Aw, now." Archer grinned and pressed a hand to his chest. "You wound me, lass. Do it again."

Edward reddened and strode up to the bar, pulling out a handful of coins, which he slapped down in front of Archer. "Ten sovereigns. To pay off the bounty on her head."

Archer looked from Edward to the coins, and back. "Bounty? Is that what she told you?"

Edward pushed the coins toward Archer. "And now with that matter out of the way, I wish to recruit you to my cause."

Archer remained sitting. "And what cause is that?"

"I want to get my kingdom back."

Another drinker laughed. "Mary has an army, from what I hear. You have a fox, a grand lady"— he nodded respectfully at Bess—"and a redhead."

"Hey, Jane's hair isn't that bad." Edward ceased the truly inspiring defense of her hair and composed himself. "What I mean to say is, I intend to take back the throne, and as citizens of England, the Pack should be with me."

Archer scoffed. "What has England done for us?"

"You're E∂ians," Edward said.

"Guilty as charged. But I don't see why that means we need to side with you, boy king."

"Mary is Verity, through and through. Even now she is hunting down E∂ians with the intent of purging them from England."

"I know," said Archer grimly. "Haven't you heard that the royal servants have already been interrogated, and anyone thought to be an E∂ian has been jailed? They'll be burned in less than a fortnight, I hear." He took a deep drink from his mug of ale. "But we E∂ians have survived hundreds of years of persecution. What does it matter to us if the reigning monarch is E∂ian or Verity?"

Bess stepped forward. Everyone looked to her—there was just something about Bess that commanded a room. "Freedom," she said to answer his question. "*Real* freedom, Mister Archer. You'll be equals to Verities. No longer persecuted."

"Begging your pardon, my lady, but King Henry made the same promise when he transformed into a lion, and that didn't change much for us." Archer shook his head. "Be king or don't. It doesn't matter to me."

This wasn't going well.

"But I am your king!" Edward said. He was saying that a lot lately. Too much.

"Nope," said Archer. "But if you leave now, I might let you walk out of here with your lives. Because I'm feeling generous today."

Like we mentioned earlier, there were seven people in the tavern, and now six of them had some sort of weapon drawn.

The members of Edward's party exchanged anxious glances. Well, they'd tried and failed. Gracie had been right: there was no reasoning with Archer. Perhaps they'd just have to consider it a victory if they got out of there alive.

Edward sighed. "All right. Come on."

He turned to go.

Jane stepped forward. "Wait. You'll join us," she said to Archer. "And it will be for one very simple reason."

Everyone was looking at her now.

"Times are hard." Jane hid her trembling hands behind her back and moved to stand before Archer. "You're a powerful band, but that doesn't make you immune to the world's problems. The

378

Pack is being hunted. You say you're not concerned about the mass burnings Mary has scheduled for the Eðians, but I heard your voice catch when you talked about it. Likely some of those palace servants work for you, and you know there's nothing that you can do to help them. But Edward could help them. He could stop the huntings. The burnings. The endless circle of killing and being killed. If you align yourself with the king, it will benefit the entire Pack. Are you so full of pride that you don't see that?"

Archer lifted an eyebrow in Edward's direction, and Edward took the opportunity to puff out his chest. "If I regain my throne, the Pack will be pardoned, on the condition all illegal activities cease. And I will make this country safe for Eðians. I swear it on my life."

"Right. But why do you care so much about Eðians?" Archer challenged.

"Because he *is* an Eðian," Jane said.

Archer's gaze swung appraisingly to Edward. "You? You're an Eðian?"

"Yes." Edward met the Pack leader's stare. "I am."

"What creature?"

Edward looked down at his hands. "A type of bird. Like a falcon."

The side of Archer's mouth curled up. "Interesting."

"We do not make these promises lightly, Mister Archer," Bess cut in, before the man could ask them to prove their Eðian status and they'd all have to get naked. "A pardon, food, medical supplies, coin, whatever you need: all will be made available to you."

Archer's eyes flashed greedily. They'd done it, Jane thought. He would agree to fight alongside them.

"No, I don't think so," he said after a long moment. "I just don't believe you're the kind of king I want to fight for."

Edward was flabbergasted. "Why?"

"Let's be honest." Archer leaned back in his chair. "The kingdom wasn't in the greatest shape before you allegedly died. Verities still hunted Eðians. The authorities were corrupt. Even a shilling isn't worth what it used to be. You never did anything to help us then. You may be an Eðian, and you act like you're the one in charge, but your ladies have been the ones making all the compelling arguments." Archer gestured at the others in the tavern. "We have a decent life here. None of us want to risk our skins for someone who hasn't proven he's worth the effort."

Edward took a deep breath. "How would you have me prove my worth?"

"There's something I want," Archer said, and Jane suspected he'd had this in mind all along, maybe even before they'd made their initial plea. "If you can deliver this item, I will join you."

"What is it?" Bess asked.

Archer looked at Gracie. "I want Gracie to return the item she stole from me."

After a moment of surprise, Jane and Edward both turned to Gracie.

"Well?" said Jane.

"Go jump in a river," Gracie said to Archer. "You're not getting it."

"It belongs to the leader of the Pack," he argued.

"It was Ben's, and he'd have wanted me to have it."

"Er, Gracie, the fate of the kingdom is at stake," Edward murmured, but she ignored him.

"I offered you ten sovereigns for it," Archer said. "You could buy a hundred knives with that."

"A knife?" Edward gaped at Gracie. "The bounty was over a knife?"

"*My* knife." Gracie's hand went to the pearl-handled knife strapped to her hip. "I can't give it up. I won't."

Jane thought all this fuss over a knife was a bit excessive, even if it was an attractive weapon, to be sure. But then Edward sighed and touched Gracie's shoulder. "All right." He turned to Archer. "There must be something else I can give you."

Archer's eyes went back and forth from Edward to Gracie, stopping at where Edward's hand rested on the girl's shoulder. He scowled. "I want the knife. There is nothing else I desire."

"The knife is not mine to give. It's Gracie's," Edward said. "But there must be something else. A task, perhaps. Something *I* could do for you."

There was a heavy silence throughout the room. Finally, Archer laughed and said, "All right, then. Kill the Great White Bear of Rhyl."

Jane scoffed. "That's an absurd demand. The Great White

Bear is a myth. I've read every book on the subject, and all the experts agree that the beast is nothing more than a fiction." Legend had it that the Great White Bear was tall as the Cliffs of Dover. As wide as the English Channel. Mothers and fathers often told their children the Bear would come after them if they didn't go to bed on time or do their chores, but that was all. An old wives' tale. A fable.

"Oh, the bear is real, all right." One of the men at a table pointed to a set of long scars that ran down the side of his face. Claw marks. "It doesn't live but a few miles from here. It attacks this village regularly. Steals food. Plunders far more than the Pack does."

Archer gave a rueful grin. "That's my condition. Kill the bear. Take it or leave it."

"Excuse us for a moment." Edward gestured for Bess, Gracie, and Jane to join him in the corner. They huddled together and spoke in low voices. "What do you think?"

"The GWBR?" Jane shook her head. "I don't believe it exists."

"Or it does exist, and Archer's just trying to get me killed for his own amusement," Edward said grimly.

"Either way, it's a diversion." Bess frowned. "We have France to see to. A country to regain. We don't have time for a goose chase—or a bear hunt."

Edward nodded. "I know. But if it's the only way to get the Pack on our side . . ."

"What about the knife?" Jane snapped. "Let's just give him the stupid knife."

Grace straightened. "My knife is not stupid. It's the only thing I have left of Ben. Archer only wants it because he knows that."

"You're not giving him the knife." Edward reassured Gracie. Of course. He liked her. He was showing off. And Archer was competition. But this was *not* the time to go around proving his dominance.

"The question remains." Bess kept her eyes on her brother. "Do we do it?"

"You said before—we probably don't have enough men to take on Mary's army," Edward's jaw tightened. "We need them. Whatever it takes."

He stepped out of the huddle and faced Archer once more. "Very well. I'll do it."

Archer glanced from Gracie to Jane to Bess to Edward, and at last gave a slow, easy nod. "Fine. We have a deal." He slammed a fist down on the bar. "Time to celebrate!"

While the others passed drinks all around, Jane went outside to move the horses into the stable, and to tell Gifford the news.

They were going to fight a mythic bear.

TWENTY-FOUR

↖ *Gifford*

As soon as the sun touched the horizon, G flashed into a human, and Jane hurried him inside and started talking. Fast.

"You heard me tell you we're going to kill the GWBR?" He nodded, and she embraced him quickly, for their time was short. "Good. Now, I've saved all my bear knowledge for when you're human so you'll remember easier. Firstly, bears are always hungry. So when you encounter the bear, don't act like food."

"Huh?"

"I read it in a book last summer, called—"

G held up a hand. "Don't tell me the name! No time."

"Right. As I was saying, bears are always hungry. Try not to act like food."

"How does one act like food?"

"I'm simply telling you what I know." Anticipating her change, she adjusted her skirt underneath her cloak, and in her haste, she flashed G the briefest of glimpses of the milky white skin of her leg.

G stopped breathing.

"The next thing you should do is try to make yourself appear bigger than you are."

G didn't say anything; he still wasn't breathing. Because, soft skin.

"Maybe hold your cloak above your head. Or puff out your chest. G, are you listening?"

G squeezed his eyes shut and scratched his forehead and tried to focus on bears and not skin. "Yes. Don't act like food, make myself look bigger. Anything else to add?"

"Yes. Use anything at your disposal to defend yourself. Rocks, sticks, anything. Only don't bend down to pick it up, because then you'll appear smaller and more vulnerable."

G sighed. "So, grab any weapons that happen to be at shoulder level."

There was a knock at the door and Edward stuck his head in, Gracie and Bess standing just behind him. G waved them in.

Jane kept talking. "And if worse comes to worst, play dead. But if the bear starts licking your wounds, that means he's planning on eating you, and you should do something else."

"So, play dead unless he starts eating me."

She shrugged helplessly. "I'll do whatever I can, of course. I'll distract him and then run up a tree to safety."

G shot a look toward Edward, surprised that the king had let her believe she would be accompanying them. Edward smiled in a she's-not-my-wife-I-shouldn't-have-to-tell-her-no kind of way.

Should G inform her that she wasn't coming? The last time he'd told her that, she'd come anyway, and she'd gotten hurt.

He wasn't about to let that happen again.

Jane didn't notice the exchange of glances. "I have the perfect way to distract the bear," she said. "I read in a book once that bears can't turn their heads very far in either direction, so I was thinking I could climb up onto his back and pull his fur, and he'll spin about trying to get me, and that's when you and Edward can go in for the kill."

It was almost dark. They had only seconds before Jane would change. G had to tell her. "You won't be there."

"How will I not be there?" She narrowed her eyes at him.

"How? Because you're not coming."

"Oh, I'm going with you. I won't have it any other way. Tell him, Edward."

Edward scratched the back of his neck, but he didn't answer. When she realized she would be getting no help from her cousin, she turned back to G. "You are my husband, not my master."

"Yes, my lady," he said. "You will always get your way. Except for right in this instance. And any others which may endanger your life."

"Gifford Dudley, you do not get to decide when my life may or may not be in danger."

G bowed his head. "Of course, Jane. And in the future, I will most definitely keep that in mind. But not tonight."

Jane pressed her lips together in a thin line. "You can't stop me."

His eyes happened upon an empty birdcage in the corner of the room. "And I would never dream of it. Except tonight, when I will do whatever it takes to stop you, even if it means locking you up."

"You wouldn't dare!"

"Not even if a hundred Carpathian bulls threatened to trample me. Except tonight, of course, I'm going to have to lock you up unless you promise not to come with us."

She gasped in outrage. "You can't treat me like this! You can't catch me!" she said with enough force that the air around her trembled. With a flash, she was a ferret, but G was ready to pounce. Before she could shake off the disorienting haze of the transformation, he had her by the scruff.

"I would never treat you like this," he whispered in her ear. "Except tonight."

Then he placed the squirming ferret inside the cage and latched it.

"Are you sure you want to do that?" Gracie remarked. She and Bess had been silent up to then, but they looked tense.

"I'm sure," G said, and he was. "I want you to promise me that you won't let her out. That you'll protect her."

The princess nodded and settled into a chair beside Jane's

cage. "I suppose this time we're actually staying behind to guard Jane. I'd object, but I don't know how I'd be useful in a bear hunt."

"I won't let her out," Gracie agreed. "But she is going to murder you later, I think."

She sat down at the edge of the bed.

"Wait, Bess *and Gracie* are both going to stay behind?" Edward looked startled. "Why shouldn't Gracie come? She'd be useful."

"I don't trust the Pack," said Gracie. "Especially Archer. I should stick around here in case he's up to something while you're gone. Keep an eye on him. And Bess can stay with Jane to make sure she doesn't ferret her way out of that cage."

"Can you use *ferret* as a verb?" G asked.

She shrugged. "You can now."

Edward's eyebrows were furrowed.

"Sire?" G said. "Are you troubled?"

"No. Everything is fine. With Gracie. Staying behind. With the Pack. And . . . Archer. That's fine."

"Right," G said slowly. He picked up his sword. "We are off, then?"

"Without hesitation," Edward said.

And for a few moments, they hesitated. Then they were off.

It was just G and the king, then, alone on this quest, and as the dirt path passed beneath them, G could not help the niggling memory that had been pricking at the back of his brain ever since they'd arrived at Helmsley. It was the image of his half-conscious wife pushing him out of the way so she could get to Edward. Yes, she had believed her cousin was dead, and it must have come as a happy shock to see him alive.

And yet, the niggling thought . . . well . . . niggled.

G remembered how close he'd been to losing her. How weak she'd been. How much blood she'd lost. It wasn't until her eyes had fluttered open that G realized the hold she had on his heart.

But then she had stopped just short of shoving him out of the way because she'd seen Edward. It turned out that the most important person to her, the one she wanted to embrace upon defying death, was Edward. Her dearest and most beloved friend—wasn't that how she'd phrased it in the letter?

Maybe hunting a legendary bear would be a welcome distraction from his thoughts, which he was sure were irrational. After all, Jane had never come right out and said that she was in love with Edward, and she was the type to tell him how things stood. And Gifford knew she was fond of him—he did. She smiled at him. She always hugged him after the change. She tried to translate his horse-thoughts to the others.

But she'd signed that letter to Edward with "all my love."

Yes. Hunting bears. Right. Here they were.

But that niggling thought still niggled.

And of course he was happy that her dear cousin was alive, but it was also a bit troubling. After all, G knew from Edward's pre-wedding talk, the one that went something like, "Hurt my cousin and I'll kill you, even if I'm dead," that Edward loved Jane, and maybe in more than a cousin kind of way. Perhaps he'd only betrothed Jane to G because he was dying, and now that he wasn't dying, perhaps he regretted the arranged marriage, and perhaps Jane was thinking the same thing.

Oh Lord. Too many *perhaps*es. Perhaps he should focus on how to kill a giant bear.

But then G wanted to ask Edward about his feelings toward Jane, and, more specifically, what the two of them did while he was a horse and they were alone and human.

G did not like to entertain the thought of all the hours they'd had to spend together while he was a horse. But he was the one who was actually married to Jane, he reminded himself. Not only that, but kestrels were hunting birds, and would no sooner hesitate to eat a ferret than they would a squirrel. There. G was her husband, and Edward might eat her. Those were two very good reasons why Jane should stay with G. And hair! G couldn't believe he'd forgotten about his full and rich locks that outshone the sad ponytails of most other men in the kingdom. Even the king's.

So, he was her husband, Edward might eat her, and no one's hair could rival his.

G sighed. None of that could really compete with the King of England.

So instead of asking Edward those questions, he said, "Did Jane tell you all she knows about bears?"

"Yes," the king replied. "Don't act like food, inexplicably double your height and weight, and play dead unless it doesn't work."

"She didn't, perhaps, mention how we might kill the beast?"

"No," Edward said. "Her information was more the useless type."

They traveled onward in silence for a while, until—

"Sire, you love Jane." G hadn't meant to blurt it out, but there it was.

"Of course I do. She's family."

"But you, Your Majesty, I think, *love* her love her."

Edward didn't protest, although he looked a little confused, possibly due to the phrasing.

G let the rest spill out. "And I know you arranged for our marriage at a time when you thought you would die, and now you're not going to die, and if you want her for yourself, I will step aside. I will do the honorable thing." His voice cracked in an embarrassing way at the end.

"Gifford," the king said.

"Call me G," G said.

The king ignored him. "Your wife loves you."

G looked at the king and raised an eyebrow.

"She does. She leaves your favorite apples in the stables, even though she has to walk over a mile to get them. She brushes your mane, and is meticulous about picking the burrs out of your coat."

"That's all just logical horse maintenance." G lowered his eyes. "She didn't want me to be her king. She didn't want me ruling by her side."

"That was when she didn't know who to trust. Believe me, Gifford, Jane loves you."

G was silent for a moment, hoping it was true.

"At least, she loved you before you threw her in a cage."

And there was that.

Edward was quiet for a moment and then sighed. G thought he might be about to confess something. Like how even though yes, Jane loved G (or so Edward claimed), that was just too bad because the king was in love with Jane, too, and now it was going to be G's duty as a citizen of England to give her up to the king. For the sake of the country.

"What did you think of Gracie?" Edward said, while at the same time G blurted out, "You can't have her!"

"Sorry, who?" G said.

"Gracie."

"Oh. I like her."

Edward pressed his lips together and nodded. "And that whole thing with Thomas Archer . . . You don't suppose that there's anything between them?"

"Jane said Gracie wouldn't give up the knife."

"No, I mean romantically."

"Ah. Romantically. Well, Jane mentioned Archer was Gracie's ex, so I suppose there used to be something romantic between them."

Edward's shoulders slumped.

G added, "As for whether it's still there, I don't know. But then, I wasn't actually *inside* the tavern when they were in the same room."

Edward sighed again. "I wish I knew what to say to her. Every time I try to tell her how I feel, I end up looking stupid."

G literally sighed in relief. Praise the heavens above—Edward fancied Gracie! Of course he did! Gracie was very fetching, if you liked that kind of beauty. G preferred redheads, of course. Warm brown eyes. Soft skin. Bookish. Opinionated. But Gracie was lovely; yes, he could concede that.

G wanted to sing, he was so happy. And he knew just what Edward meant about looking stupid. "Yes, well, love looks not with the eyes, but with the mind, and therefore is winged Cupid painted blind," he said.

"What?" Edward gazed at him blankly.

"I mean to say, the course of true love never did run smooth," G clarified. That was good, he thought. He'd have to write that down later.

"Is that from a play?" Edward asked.

"No, it's . . . um . . . just a thought I had."

"Hmm. You're a bit of a poet, aren't you?" the king said.

G felt heat rise in his face. "I dabble."

"I like poetry," said the king. "And plays. I used to put on little theatricals at the palace. If we survive this, and if I get my crown back, and if there's time, I'd like to open a theater someday."

"If we survive this, you totally should," G agreed.

They both tightened their grips on their swords and coughed

in a manly way that meant that they weren't scared of a silly old bear. "Do you know any poems about courage?" Edward asked after a moment.

G didn't. He endeavored to make something up. "Um . . . cowards die many times before their deaths," he said. "The valiant never taste of death but once. Screw your courage to the sticking-place, and we'll not fail."

"The sticking-place?"

G shrugged. "It's the best I could do on such short notice."

"That's good," commented Edward. "You should write that down."

The map Archer had given them was easy to follow, and the journey was short, but G couldn't figure out if it was really short or it only seemed short because he was dreading killing a giant bear. They had packed up weapons of all sorts: broadswords, battle-axes, a mace. Jane had even made them a "tincture" she'd told Edward would burn the bear's eyes.

The map didn't lead them to an exact location, just a valley near Rhyl in which the bear had most frequently been seen. Of course, that information was based on rumors and reports. As they got closer, G began hoping the reports were wrong, but soon realized they weren't, because the ground was dotted with bear droppings. G knew they were bear droppings, because the only other animal capable of such sizable droppings in this part of the world was a horse, and G knew the droppings weren't of a horse, because he was sort of an expert.

"We're getting close," he said to the king.

"You remember our plan?" Edward said.

G nodded.

The two wound their way through trees and brush until Edward came to a jolting halt. And then G did, too. And then Edward said to G, "I think we're going to need a bigger sword."

The beast was huge. This was one of those times when the English language was inadequate to fully describe the bear's girth. The thing was eating fruit from a tree, and to get the fruit, he didn't even have to stand on his hind legs. And he didn't just eat the fruit, he ate the leaves and the branch as well, because his mouth was huge and he could.

The ground trembled as he walked to the next tree.

G turned toward Edward and bowed. "It's been a pleasure, Sire, but this is where I leave you." He was jesting only in part.

"What about your talk of courage?"

"Fiction, Your Majesty."

Edward sighed. "Stop playing. We stick to the plan."

"What about giving him a chance to surrender?"

"Shut up." Edward let out a war cry. The bear turned, roared so loudly G thought his eardrums would burst, and charged after the king, who turned and ran back into the forest.

G was alone. He let out a breath and climbed a tree. Because that was the plan. Minutes later, or maybe seconds, or hours, Edward came running back to him, shouting, "Gifford! Be ready!"

G lit the torch he'd been holding.

The bear had been chasing Edward, but now he followed the light and placed his front paws on the tree, which gave G the perfect angle to pour Jane's tincture into his eyes.

The bear let out a terrible growl and a cry, and then with a whimper, he let his front paws scrape down the bark.

Now was the time Edward was going to go in for the kill, except the bear began to run around in circles, frantic, roaring. And then, with the force of a battering ram, he collided with the trunk of a tree.

G's tree.

He fell through the air.

The brunt of the impact was softened by landing on the bear's back, a fact that G would have celebrated, had it not been the case that he had just fallen onto the world's most giant bear.

Thankfully the collision with the tree had stunned the bear, and G was able to gather his brain and climb off the beast. Where was Edward with his sword? But of course, it was pitch-dark now, because G's torch had gone out on the way down from the tree, and Edward couldn't very well stab the bear without risking stabbing G at the same time.

"Gifford?" Edward called.

The sound seemed to rouse the beast. G thought quickly. He didn't have a weapon with him (because he was supposed to watch from the tree as Edward killed the bear) and he couldn't very well kill a bear with his own hands, so he did the only thing he could.

He played dead. And acted like he wasn't food.

"I'm dead, Sire," G said. He didn't know why he didn't say, "I'm playing dead," except on the off chance the bear understood English. He wouldn't have said anything at all, but he wanted Edward to know that G would be on the ground, and so aim his sword anywhere but at the ground.

There was no reply.

Gifford tried to think of what his lady told him to do in this situation, but then he was thinking of his lady, and that flash of flesh, and the possibility that she might love him, and then the possibility that he might never see her again, which got him thinking about the bear again.

G closed his eyes and tried to still his labored breathing. The bear growled and whined and sniffed and pawed at the ground—and then pawed at G.

It was all he could do not to move. Or scream. Where was Edward? Had he left G here to die?

The bear sniffed G's leg. G tried to make his leg look less like food. The bear pushed G's shoulder, and pushed again as though trying to turn him over. G wasn't sure whether complying would make him seem more dead or less dead. But then again, if he were actually dead, he wouldn't fight being turned over.

When the bear pushed again, G turned over onto his stomach.

The bear pawed at G's back again, and then did something that made G's blood run cold. He sniffed the back of G's head, and licked.

Licking means eating, G thought. *Licking means eating!*

Jane had told him to play dead, unless the bear was about to eat him, but she didn't say how he was supposed to get out of such a vulnerable position. The bear licked the back of G's neck, and G was just about to try to spring to his feet and run for it, when suddenly the bear reared his head, let out a roar, and collapsed against G.

And just as suddenly, G realized he would most likely not die of a bear bite, but of being smothered by a bear. When his lady received the news, he hoped the king would tell her he died of a bear bite. Not because the bear essentially sat on him. He felt a hand grasp his own, and Edward was pulling him out from under the dead bear, who'd not once acted un-bearlike. The Great White Bear of Rhyl was definitely not an Eðian. Which comforted G.

"I used the broadsword and stabbed the base of the bear's neck. That did the trick."

"Wonderful," G said. "But never forget, I weakened him in the first place by falling on him."

"You're right," Edward said good-naturedly.

They both stood there panting for a while. "You know, Sire, with you being king, and also now a legendary bear killer, I'd say you will be able to woo any woman you desire."

"And your wife might fall in love with you all over again."

"If she ever forgives me for putting her in a cage."

Edward didn't respond. Then something seemed to occur to him. "Oh, bollocks," he said. "Now there's nothing left on our to-do list but go talk to the King of France."

"I've never been to France," G said, "but I enjoy cheese."

"I like cheese, too," agreed Edward, as if they had just found yet another thing they had in common.

The sun rose during their trip back, and G arrived at the Shaggy Dog as a horse. Gracie, Bess, and Jane were standing in the doorway of the tavern waiting for them, although Jane's expression quickly turned from relief to anger. She glared at him. Said no words. Spoke only with her narrowed eyes.

Suddenly, G wanted to go back to the bear.

She took a deep breath and turned to Edward, her expression softening as she touched a scratch on his face. "Darling cousin, you're hurt."

Edward smiled. "It's just a flesh wound."

"Come inside. I will tend to it myself."

G snorted and threw his head back. Jane raised her eyebrows. "And you."

He sheepishly nudged her shoulder with his nose. She seemed unmoved.

"I would sooner face a thousand Carpathian bulls than banish you from the tavern." She scowled. "Except in this instance." She pointed to the forest. "Go to your room."

It was going to be an awkward trip to France.

TWENTY-FIVE

Edward

It took them four days to get to Paris. And now Gracie was wearing a dress.

"What are you staring at?" she asked when Edward could not stop ogling her.

"You," he replied. "You're a girl. I mean, a woman. I'm amazed at the transformation."

"I clean up nicely when the situation calls for it." She tugged at the bodice of her gown to cover more of her cleavage. "But it doesn't suit me, I find."

The gown was gray velvet, and it cinched her in at the waist and exposed the upper swell of her chest, a side of her that Edward had never seen before, and it made his eyes wander to places they shouldn't. She was beautiful, but she was right; the finery didn't suit her. The gown diminished her somehow, pushed and squeezed and swallowed her in yards of fabric.

"Thank you for doing this," he murmured.

"You're welcome." Her hand rose self-consciously to touch the back of her pinned-up hair. "But I don't really know how I'll be any help to you with the King of France."

"Not with the king," Edward said. "With Mary Queen of Scots. Who lives with the King of France."

He couldn't help the shudder that passed through him.

Gracie's eyebrows lifted in surprise. "Why, because we're both Scottish?"

"Because she hates me, and I need her to like me. I think that if anyone can get her to like me, Gracie, it's you. Because you're Scottish, yes. And because you're you."

Her cheeks colored slightly. She nodded. "So she hates you. Why?"

"Because she was supposed to be my wife."

"What?" Gracie exclaimed. "When was this?"

"When I was three."

Yes, Edward had been a lad of three tender years when his father betrothed him to Mary, who'd been a baby at the time but a queen already, since her father had died when she was six days old. Such a match would have unified England and Scotland for good, in the Lion King's way of thinking. Henry had even wanted Mary to live with them at the palace, so he would oversee her upbringing and teach her to think like a proper Englishwoman.

Mary's legal guardians had other ideas. They'd signed a treaty approving the engagement, but they didn't honor it. So later, when King Henry received word that Mary's regents had accepted another offer of marriage, this one from the King of France, pairing her with the French dauphin, Francis, King Henry had eaten the messenger immediately and remained a roaring lion for days.

Then he'd invaded Scotland.

For years Henry's soldiers had chased the fledgling queen from place to place all around the Scottish countryside, but they never managed to capture her. It was believed to be Eðian magic that enabled her to escape them. She had a habit of vanishing like smoke from the tightest of spaces. And so Henry, who was usually more tolerant of Eðians, since he himself had proved to be one, had punished the Scottish Eðians for harboring her. This was most likely why, Edward knew, the cottage belonging to Gracie's family had been burned. Because his father had been angry with a toddler.

The people called it the Rough Wooing. Emphasis on *rough*.

Edward had been a child through all of this, but he remembered being told that he was going to marry a queen, and he remembered staring up at a portrait of Mary Queen of Scots that hung in one of the palace hallways. The girl couldn't have been older than four years old when the portrait had been commissioned, yet she still held herself like a queen. She accused Edward with her dark eyes. *I loathe you,* the painting almost seemed to sneer at him. *I will always hate you. You'd better hope that we don't get married. I will make your life a living nightmare.*

That was the one bit of relief Edward had experienced after his father died. He no longer needed to pursue Mary Queen of Scots. She slipped away to the custody of the French king and his family at the Louvre Palace, where she'd been residing ever since.

They'd met once, he and Mary, a few years back. He'd been traveling to Paris to craft a peace treaty with the French king. Mary had been eight. She'd been presented to him as the intended of Francis, the dauphin (which Edward kept thinking sounded like the word *dolphin*, which seemed an odd term for a prince). Mary had curtsied. Edward had bowed. She'd glared at him, every bit as vengeful as her portrait. He'd tried to ease the tension by complimenting her shoes.

She'd responded by stamping on his foot

Hard.

She'd been sent straightaway to her chambers, because young ladies should not assault kings, but Edward hadn't truly minded. He'd been overjoyed, in fact, by the idea that he wouldn't be expected to talk to her, and that he wasn't likely ever to see her again. Ever.

But now here he was, back in the Louvre Palace, here to plead his case before the king, and of course it would be wise for him to draw Scotland to his cause as well. At least that's what Bess said, and Edward always believed what Bess said.

None of this he felt like explaining to Gracie, of course. "Just talk to her, if you get the opportunity," he said. "You don't have to sing my praises. Just tell her what you know of my situation. See if she'll be amenable to helping us, in whatever she has the power to do, which may not be much, really, not from here, and she's only a young girl, but—"

"All right," Gracie said, holding up her hand. "I'll talk to her."

"Thank you." She owed him that much, he felt, after the lengths he'd gone to ensuring that she could keep her pretty knife.

There was a tap on the door, and Jane and Bess entered, both appearing fatigued after the week's activities with the Pack and the bear and their most recent stealthy boat ride across the English Channel. Jane, especially, looked peaked, like she hadn't slept.

"Edward," she greeted him. "You're like a proper king again."

Yes, he was once again wearing tights, gold-embroidered pumpkin pants, a silk undershirt, a gold-and-cream brocaded doublet with puffy sleeves, and a fur-trimmed velvet robe to top it off. He had forgotten how heavy all these layers of clothing were, when he'd been dressing like a peasant for weeks. He could feel the weight like the physical manifestation of all that he was responsible for, pulling him downward.

"You ladies are quite splendid, as well," he said, looking from Gracie to Jane to Bess and back to Gracie.

Jane stood in front of him and smoothed down the fur at the edge of his robe. "This isn't ferret, I hope."

"White-spotted ermine," he answered. "Although I believe I shall give up fur, when all of this is done. I would hate to be wearing some unfortunate Eðian by mistake."

"I feel the same," she said.

"How's Gifford?" Edward asked, because suddenly he felt the young lord's absence keenly. If Jane was like a sister to him, then perhaps Gifford would be his brother now. His friend. Nothing says friendship like staring down into the jaws of angry death together, he reasoned. "Is he still in the doghouse for locking you up?"

"He's in the stables," Jane said stiffly.

"Don't punish him too long, Janey," Edward entreated on Gifford's behalf. "He only did it to keep you from harm."

"But that's the problem." She settled with a sigh onto one of the parlor chairs. "I just don't know how to talk him about it. Every time I try, I feel like I say something shrewish and high-pitched and stupid. Which is unlike me."

He stifled a smile. "Anyway, I'm glad to have you along," he said. "I'd rather face a giant mythical bear, I think, than have this meeting."

Gracie seemed surprised at this. "This will be nothing, won't it, after all the other trouble you've had? All you have to do is talk to the man."

"I have to be the King of England," he said, rubbing at the back of his neck. "I will have to speak to Henry as one king to another." A task that frightened him, in some ways, much more than facing any beast.

"You are the king," said Bess quietly. "It's as simple as that, Edward. Be yourself."

"So the King of France is named Henry. That won't be

confusing, will it?" said Gracie, fidgeting again with the neckline of her dress.

"It's easy to remember this king," Edward mused. "He is King Henry, and his wife is Queen Catherine. Like my father without all his extra wives."

The door to the parlor opened, and an opulently dressed steward entered and bowed low to Edward. "His Majesty will see you now, Your Majesty."

"No, not confusing at all," muttered Gracie. She turned to address the steward. "Can you find me an audience with the young Queen Mary? I'm a Scot, you see, and I have some news for her from home. Nothing important, of course, but something that she'll find entertaining."

The steward looked slightly put out by the informal nature of her request. "I'll see if the queen is receiving visitors," he said. "Wait here."

Jane stood on tiptoe to kiss his cheek. "Good luck, cousin."

Gracie was frowning, he noticed. He delighted in the thought that she might be jealous of Jane kissing him. And he also knew a perfect opportunity when he saw it. He turned to Gracie. "Don't I get a good luck kiss from you as well? I'm going to need as much luck as I can get."

Her green eyes narrowed as she looked at him. "I'm not sure I'm terribly lucky."

"You're lucky for me."

"Oh, all right." Her lips were a quick, warm brush against his cheek. "Good luck, Sire."

"Your Majesty?" the steward prompted.

It was time.

He tried not to think too hard about how this one meeting would make or break them. They needed soldiers. And ships. And steel. Without the French king's help, they could not hope to overcome Mary. Everything was riding on this single encounter. On his words.

His knees were trembling, he realized, ever so slightly. Even a kiss from Gracie was not enough to overcome his nerves.

"Remember what we talked about," Bess told him as they moved forward through the door.

He nodded.

"Stay with that and you'll be fine," she said. "Stick to the plan. Play to the king's weaknesses and your strengths."

"I'll do my best," Edward said. That was all that he could do.

The King of France was nothing like Edward's father had been. This particular Henry was a cool, collected sort of man with a well-trimmed beard who liked to wear white fur and heels that elevated his height. He was fond of dogs, but he was not an Eðian or a supporter of their cause. He was quite vocal, instead, about how distasteful he found those people who became animals, like such a thing was a matter of rude behavior. This made Edward's position a bit precarious, under the circumstances.

Still, King Henry was proving to be sympathetic to Edward's

plight. He wanted to hear all about how Edward had lost his throne, like it was the best kind of royal gossip.

"So this Mary herself took part in the plot to poison you?" the king asked in horror when Edward reached that part of his story.

"She put the fork to my lips," Edward answered. "But I wouldn't take it."

"Such brazenness," King Henry exclaimed. "This woman attempting to murder a king, her own brother, no less. Such audacity. And however did you escape?"

Edward took a deep breath. *Be yourself,* Bess had told him, but what she really meant was, *Be yourself unless you sometimes find yourself turning into a bird, in which case, don't be that—don't admit that, ever. Be a respectable Verity, for heaven's sake.*

"One of my servants smuggled me out," he lied smoothly. "In the back of a hay cart. It was quite the terrible ordeal."

"Ha!" The king was greatly amused by this. "A hay cart. Imagine."

He laughed, and the members of the court laughed with him.

"So you see," Edward continued delicately when the merriment died down. "If my sister is allowed to sit unchallenged on my throne, it will send a dangerous message to rest of the world: that any grasping, covetous woman of royal blood can reach for the crown and succeed in taking it, even from a rightful, ruling king. Then queens will start popping up all over Europe like rabbits in a garden. It will be chaos."

He tried to sound supremely confident. Bess had coached him

to say all of this about the awful precedent Mary would set and the terrifying anarchy of women, but for some reason he felt unsettled when he spoke the words, especially with Jane and Bess standing behind him, these two women who he now held in the highest possible regard.

King Henry leaned forward on his throne. "Well, that makes sense. Yes, they're always reaching, aren't they?" He cast a quick accusatory glance at Queen Catherine beside him. She was a notorious schemer, Edward knew from Bess, and the French king often worried that his own wife would be the end of him someday, so his son would end up on the throne and she could rule as regent.

"Yes, they reach far above their station," Edward agreed. "And you and I both know that it is a man's place, not a woman's, to rule a country. Women are ill designed for such a task."

"But you yourself put a woman on the throne, did you not?" King Henry asked, gesturing to Jane.

The court fell silent.

Edward glanced at his cousin. Her eyes were closed. Her lips moved like she was counting backward from ten.

Edward turned quickly back to the king.

"My desire was for my crown to pass to my cousin's male heirs," Edward explained. "Naturally. Of course I couldn't have considered Jane a queen on her own merits."

Oh, she was going to stab him in his sleep. At least she was being mercifully silent. For now. Edward cleared his throat. "But unfortunately, I became ill so quickly that there simply wasn't time for Jane to produce a male heir. And in the absence of a boy to inherit the throne, Dudley persuaded me to amend the line of succession to name Jane as the ruler, to be followed by her sons, of course. A decision I regret, but there wasn't much of a choice at that point."

"Hmm. Well, it doesn't matter," King Henry said thoughtfully. "If they'd succeeded in poisoning you without such an amendment, Mary would still be sitting on your throne now, wouldn't she?"

"Correct." Edward raised his hands, palms up, like, *What's a fellow to do?*

"And so you are here, asking for my help," King Henry said, a gleam in his eyes as if Edward were kneeling before him in supplication.

Edward was not going to do any kneeling, of course. He straightened his shoulders. "Mary cannot be allowed to get away with such treason," he said, meeting the king eye to eye. "I have some ships and armies of my own, of course, but Mary needs her comeuppance. I thought it would please you, perhaps, to stand with me on this matter. We could send a different message to the world: that a king will not be cowed by some conniving, middle-aged female suffering from delusions of grandeur. We are men. We are kings. We will not yield on such matters."

Queen Catherine was shooting daggers at him with her eyes, but he forced himself to concentrate on the French king.

And the king was feeling generous.

"Very well," Henry said after a long, dramatic pause. "You

shall have French ships at your disposal, and you shall have French soldiers, as well, as many as I can spare. Get rid of that ridiculous cow who dares to call herself a queen."

It took an effort for Edward not to sway on his feet, so great was the relief he felt in this moment. "I will," he promised. "You have my thanks."

"And I will expect that in the future, our countries will be better friends," the king said.

He was indebting himself to France, Edward knew. The man would have more than just his thanks. But that was the price of his crown. He must be willing to pay it.

"Undoubtedly," he said.

"And if I may give you some advice," King Henry added. "From one king to another."

"Of course. I'd be thankful for any wisdom you could offer me."

"The thing for you do, young man, is to find yourself a wife. As soon as possible, I should think. Produce a son of your own. I have three sons, myself, and a number of bastards. It's very comforting for me to know that I will find never myself in your predicament. My bloodline is secure. You should see to yours."

Edward tried to thaw himself quickly, because at the word *wife*, his chest seemed to have frozen over. He couldn't get proper air in his lungs.

A wife.

King Henry was right.

Edward could marry. He would have to marry. And soon.

"A wise prescription," he managed to get out. "Again, I thank you."

"Perhaps you will consider my daughter, Elisabeth," Henry said, and Queen Catherine roughly pushed a young girl forward. The girl had been dressed extravagantly in an attempt to disguise the fact that she was quite plain. She curtseyed deeply before him.

"Uh . . . yes, I shall consider her," he said. "Mademoiselle."

"Votre Altesse." (Which means, for those of you who don't speak French, *Your Highness*.) The little princess didn't meet his eyes.

He was in a bit of daze as he took his leave. He had not been considering all that was going to be expected from him, if indeed he took back his throne.

He had forgotten that, as the ruler of England, he would never truly be free.

King Henry held a celebration that night in Edward's honor, so of course Edward had to attend, even though he would have liked to have spent some time alone to sort out his thoughts. This discussion of women and their merit had left him confused about how he actually felt on the subject. He wished that Jane was there to talk to (and possibly apologize to, but why would he need to apologize? He'd only said what Bess had told him to say, and besides, it was true, wasn't it? Women were the weaker sex, were they not? Wasn't that even written in the Holy Book?). But Jane was in her ferret state now. Gifford hadn't made an appearance. Bess had returned to her chamber to strategize their next move. And he hadn't seen Gracie since before he'd spoken with the king.

He wandered among the music and dancing and fancy French pastries. All this was a blatant over-expenditure of the French king's wealth, it seemed to Edward. The Louvre Palace was huge, easily three times the size of Edward's largest palace, and lavishly furnished. Under normal circumstances it would have given Edward a serious case of palace envy, but now he found the entire building rather vulgar.

His old life felt like a lifetime ago.

How was it possible, he thought, to be so lonely when he was surrounded by so many people? There was a throng of admirers about him, many of them women who had no doubt paid attention when the king had advised Edward to find himself a bride *toute suite*, but when they spoke to him, he found himself nodding blandly and not listening to their words, just staring into his goblet of wine.

A wife, he kept thinking. *Such an intimidating word.*

Bollocks.

But he'd be the king again, and he could decide for himself who and when he would marry. There was that to comfort him. No one could force his hand.

"Your Majesty," came a high, sweet voice at his side. "I was wondering if you might honor me with a dance."

He looked up.

It was Mary Queen of Scots. Of course he would have recognized her anywhere, with those eyes so dark they were almost black, those eyes that had haunted him from her portrait for all those years. But she looked different from the girl who'd stamped on his foot. Older, of course. She'd been eight then. She must be close to thirteen now. She wore a red satin gown and her black hair was braided and pinned in a complex pattern that must have taken hours. There was even a spot of rouge on her cheeks.

She looked quite grown-up.

"Your Majesty?" she queried.

"Your Majesty," he answered, and bowed stiffly. "Of course I will dance with you."

They moved to the center of the floor. The dance was long and complicated and held little opportunity for talking, a series of seemingly endless turns and whirls that left him breathless. Mary was light on her feet, an experienced dancer. She smiled at him often, which Edward didn't know what to do with. Did she have a dagger meant for him tucked in the folds of her dress somewhere? Part of him expected to feel it pierce his side at any moment.

The dance ended. He thanked her. He turned to flee.

"Will you walk with me?" she asked, before he could. She held out a small hand.

He nodded and tucked her hand into his arm.

"I spent the afternoon with your lady, Grace," Mary informed him as they strolled along the outer edge of the room. "I found her stories quite amusing."

God's teeth, what had Gracie told her? "Yes, she's an amusing woman," he said.

"Quite. It made me miss Scotland, to hear her brogue." Mary herself had no Scottish accent that Edward could discern. Too many years away from home.

They walked in awkward silence. Edward found himself tongue-tied. He could feel the gaze of others on them, keen and speculative, especially that of the French queen and her dour-looking daughter, Elisabeth.

"You're taller than I remember," Mary Queen of Scots said at last.

"Yes, I find you changed as well."

She flushed. "Forgive me, regarding your foot last time."

He smiled. "Forgiven," he said. "I hope we can put all that past ugliness behind us and be friends."

"Yes. Friends. It's just, I didn't like to be told what to do, or to whom I should be married," she said, her voice lifting a little. "It made me cross to look at you."

"Believe me, I understand."

She stopped and pulled her hand from his arm. Her dark eyes were earnest when she gazed up at him, but not naive. "I still don't like to be told." He followed her gaze when she peered out into the center of the room, where Edward spotted a sulky-faced blond boy in splendid clothing.

Ah, the dauphin, he assumed. Prince Francis.

"He seems all right," Edward observed as they watched the boy grab a handful of sweets from a passing tray and stuff them into his mouth. Then the crown prince picked his nose, and ate that, too. "Oh. That's unfortunate."

Mary Queen of Scots pursed her lips unhappily. "Sometimes he pulls my hair or calls me names."

"He'll grow out of that, I think," Edward said. And hopefully the nose picking, as well.

The little queen turned to regard Edward with a carefully blank expression that made him feel sad for them both, that they would have learned to wear such masks at their young age. "I think I would like England better than France, don't you?" she said quietly.

He lowered his voice to match hers. "Definitely. Apart from the food."

"Oh yes," Mary agreed. "The food here is good. But the king is quite mad sometimes. And the queen is horrid to me, she hates me, and . . . and this is not a friendly place for people like us."

Edward was intrigued. Gracie had done her work well on Mary, obviously. She wanted to confide in him. To trust him. "Like us?" he repeated.

She pulled on his shoulder to make him lean toward her, so she could whisper in his ear. "I hear you're a kestrel."

His heart beat faster in spite of himself. This was a country still in the hands of the Verities. It was dangerous, even for him, to admit to being an Eðian here.

But this journey was about taking risks.

He turned Mary so he could whisper, "I am. What are you?"

She smiled conspiratorially, her dark head close to his, her breath on his cheek. "I'm a mouse. That's how I get away if people chase me—I turn into a little black mouse that nobody ever notices. I'm very good at hiding. And listening. I hear such things, you wouldn't believe them if I told you." She leaned even closer. "I have a secret army, you know, back in Scotland. All of them Eðians. Isn't that marvelous?"

"Marvelous," Edward agreed.

She bit her lip. "I will send my army to help you. But I think someday I might turn into a mouse, and run away from France and never return. Will you help me then?"

His breath caught. "Of course," he said. "You'll always be welcome in England, Your Majesty."

She took his hand and squeezed it. Her fingers were soft, her nails perfectly cut and rounded. "Call me Mary."

"Mary," he said, and he became aware of an ache in his chest. He pushed past it. "And you should call me Edward."

"Edward." She smiled. "I'm glad we understand each other."

Yes, he thought, and the ache bloomed into something larger. He understood her. Maybe a little too well.

Mary looked pleased. "And here's your lady," she said, glancing past him. "Hello, again."

"My lady?" Edward turned to see Gracie approaching them in the gray velvet gown. His chest swelled at the sight of her.

"I'm not his lady," Gracie corrected. "I'm just his friend."

Queen Catherine was calling for Mary to dance with the dauphin. "He always steps on my feet," the little queen said with a scowl, becoming once again the furious girl from her portrait. She swept away to join her betrothed. Edward felt a weight lift at her departure. He offered his hand to Gracie.

"Shall we?"

She shook her head so hard a curl came loose from its pin and tumbled into her face. "I don't know how to dance."

"There's something you don't know how to do?" he said incredulously. "How can that be?"

She laughed and considered the couples whirling around them. "It is a different world that you live in, Sire. So full of color and music. So very grand. I can see why you'd miss it."

He didn't miss it, he thought. Not really.

"Let's walk along the river," he suggested. "It's stuffy in here."

"If that's what you command." She took his arm and he led her outside, where the stars were bright and the palace seemed to stretch on and on against the Seine.

"Let me teach you to dance," he said when they'd found a quiet place.

"I'm not sure that would be wise," she answered wryly. "I'd hate for you to die now, after all this trouble I've gone to keep you alive."

"It's largely a matter of bowing and curtseying." He dropped into a bow. "Now you."

Grace stood still for a moment, considering, then slowly and awkwardly curtsied.

"See, that wasn't so bad. Take my hand," he directed.

She did.

"Now I'll draw you toward me, and we'll bow, and then we'll step away, and bow."

They practiced for a while, moving in time to the music that was still spilling from inside the palace.

"You're quite good at this," she admitted as he guided her through the steps.

"I've had years of lessons. My instructors often said that the key to a successful dance is to make it seem like you can't help yourself. You look into your partner's eyes, as if that gaze binds you while your body moves to the music."

They both seemed to be holding their breath as they looked into each other's eyes. He put his hands on her waist, and lifted her in a slow circle. Her arms went around his neck as he lowered her to her feet.

"Can I kiss you?" he asked impulsively. "I've never kissed a girl before, and I want it to be you. Will you?" It was terribly inappropriate, what he was asking her, and he knew it. There were rules for people like him. The future could go two ways: he could fight and die in this endeavor to take back his crown, or he could fight and win, and then he'd be the King of England and he'd marry some foreign princess to strengthen the ties between their countries, or one of these days a little black mouse was going to show up at his palace door, and he knew what she'd expect of him, and he knew that he should probably comply. And Gracie would still be a Scottish pickpocket, and he'd have no business kissing her.

But he didn't care.

"I won't pretend that I'm a fine lady," Gracie said, lifting her chin. "It doesn't matter what dress you put me in. I don't belong in a palace."

"I know. Kiss me."

She gave a little laugh. "You're a forward one, aren't you?"

"Grace. I've wanted to kiss you from the moment I clapped eyes on you. It's been agony not kissing you all this time."

"Agony?" She sounded doubtful.

He cupped her face in his hands. "Poison was less painful, believe me. I nearly strangled Gran that day you carved me the wooden fox at Helmsley. Please put me out of my misery."

She laughed again, nervously. "All right, then. It's only a kiss."

Only a kiss, he told himself.

A kiss. Nothing more.

And then he could surrender to being a grown-up and being a king and doing all the things that were expected of him.

She shivered and wet her bottom lip with her teeth, and Edward thought he would burst into flames. He leaned closer to her. Fell into those green, green . . . pools of beautiful eyes. He prayed he wouldn't mess this up. It felt important, as big as winning his country back. Bigger. His eyes closed.

"Wait," Gracie said. "Sire."

"Dammit," he breathed. "Call me Edward."

"I can't," she said, her voice wavering. "I know you want me to. But I can't forget who you are. You will always be the king."

The words were like cold water splashing him. He opened his eyes and drew himself away from her abruptly. "All right. I understand."

"I like you. I do. But I can't—"

He rubbed his hand down the front of his face. "I should go."

She frowned. "Sire . . ."

"Dammit!" The word burst out of him. Light flared. He was a kestrel. He was flying away. He gave a great cry that pierced the still night air, and then he flew higher, and faster, until Gracie was a speck he could leave behind.

"So. You have all you asked for," Bess said, much later.

"Right," he said sarcastically. He leaned against the rail of the fine French ship that was carrying them back to England. The sun was rising. The wind ruffled his hair.

"What's the matter with you?" Bess wanted to know.

"Nothing. Yes. I have my army." He was watching Jane and Gifford, who were standing close farther up the bow, spending their few minutes together, that precious and brief window of time before Gifford would change into a horse. How easy it was for them. How simple.

"It's the strangest army to ever walk this earth," Bess said with that quiet, almost smug smile of hers. "Made up of Frenchmen and Scots and thousands of Eðians rallying behind you, brother. We're going to win, Edward. If we play our cards right."

"And then I'll be the King of England again," he said.

"You never stopped being the king, in my opinion. But now you'll get to truly rule," she continued. "You'll be able to right all of the wrongs of this country. It was true, all that you said to Archer. You can see to it that Eðians and Verities live side by side in peace. You can change the way things are done, rein in the wild spending and live modestly, see that there's gold in our coffers again, restructure the taxes to take the burden from the common people, ease their suffering, yet still see to the needs of the nobles. You could be a better king than Father. Wise and just and even-tempered."

"Better than Father?" He could not conceive of such a thing.

"Yes. England can be prosperous once again. I long to see that day," his sister said passionately.

He stared off into the horizon, lost in thought. He'd spent the better part of the night flying, and thinking while he flew. It had been the first time he hadn't lost himself to the bird joy. He supposed that was something of an accomplishment.

"Did you know," he said after a moment, "that Mary Queen of Scots is a mouse?"

"Of course."

He glanced up at her, startled. "You knew that? How is it that you know absolutely everything?"

"I'm a cat," she confessed. "She smelled tasty."

That drew a startled laugh out from him. "Kestrels eat mice, too." He remembered the one mouse he'd killed, the night he first became a bird. He wanted to fly again, to stretch his wings.

"We'll have to practice restraint, if we encounter her again," Bess remarked.

"We will," he said softly.

Bess was scrutinizing his face. "What's troubling you, Edward? Are you afraid? Of this battle to come?"

"No," he said without hesitation. His hand curled into a fist on the railing. He looked up at her, his gray eyes fierce and shining. "I am ready to fight."

But it occurred to Edward, not for the first time since our story began, that he had been a poor excuse for a king before. That he did not deserve to be king now. That someone else (anyone else, really, except for Mary) might be better suited for the job.

Jane TWENTY-SIX

The E∂ian encampment was quiet save for the crackle of campfires and the muted voices of soldiers, who were huddled in groups around the fires, discussing tactics or telling stories they'd never told anyone else, but needed to be told. In case they died in the morning.

The sunlight was fading from the sky. From the opening of her tent, Jane couldn't see London—that was hidden by hundreds of other tents. But she knew it was there. Looming large on the landscape of her destiny.

A chestnut horse trotted toward her through the camp.

Gifford.

Jane breathed out a sigh. Many E∂ians had been sent to scout earlier, including Gifford, and she'd worried the whole time he was gone.

She pulled the tent flap wide to let him in and save him the indignity of transforming into a naked man outside. Gifford squeezed past her, carefully avoiding stomping on the lone sleeping pallet, and held still while Jane slung a cloak over his back.

It was the same evening ritual they'd performed since leaving Helmsley, an attempt to hold on to as much of their overlapping human time as possible. Sure, there was the usual scramble for clothes and the impending second change, but they'd made it work so far. Same for a similar morning routine, which was sometimes shortened when neither of them wanted to wake up. Ferrets and young men were both notoriously late sleepers.

But things had been awkward between them since the bear hunt. For obvious reasons.

"I hope your horse time was productive," Jane said. The tent was dim, lit by a single lantern hanging from the topmost pole. "If we can't pull this off, we'll be right back in the Tower waiting for our executions."

Light flared inside the tent. "Don't talk like that." Gifford quickly adjusted the cloak and found the clothes Jane had laid out for him. "We're going to live tomorrow, and for long after. We'll have years and years to fight about everything you want to fight about."

He made it sound like it was a desirable thing.

"I hope so," Jane said. "I've been making a list."

"I don't doubt it. What shall we fight about first?"

"I think you know."

"Uh . . ." He was more or less dressed now, the cloak a crescent moon around his feet. She turned to him and crossed her arms.

"You locked me up. In a *cage*." How could he not understand what a problem that was?

"I was trying to keep you safe!" he countered.

Jane threw up her hands. "I don't want to be kept safe! And I definitely don't want you to be the one to decide whether or not I need to be kept safe! That's not your duty."

For a few moments, they just stared at each other.

"I'm your husband," he said at last. "If keeping you safe isn't my duty, what is?"

For the first time, Jane realized that maybe he was just as uncertain in this relationship as she was. Maybe he wasn't as sure of himself as she'd always assumed.

"As my husband," she said softly, "your duty is to respect me. To trust me. If I say I want to do something, you can't stop me just because I might get hurt. That's not living. I need to make my own decisions."

"When you came after me at the tavern, you nearly died." He looked wrecked at the memory. "You nearly *died*, and then who would I have argued with?"

"You'd have found someone."

"No." He stepped toward her. "I only want to argue with you."

She met his eyes and saw that he meant it. "And I only want to argue with you."

"I *do* respect you," he said earnestly. "And I trust you." He spoke more hurriedly now; it was almost dark. "I'm sorry, Jane. I shouldn't have locked you in a cage without your consent, and I shouldn't have made you believe that what you want isn't the most important thing to me. I just couldn't stand the thought of losing you. But I am sorry. Deeply, madly, truly sorry."

Jane spent a moment untangling that. "So you're apologizing for locking me in a cage?"

He nodded. "And I'll apologize every day for the rest of our potentially short lives, if that will help."

"Quite unnecessary." She closed the distance between them and looked up (and up and up) to meet his eyes. She shook her index finger at his nose. "But if you ever even think about locking me in a cage again, I will stab you with a knitting needle."

"It's as though you've reached right into my worst nightmares, my lady." He grinned.

"And I suppose I'll try to be less rash when it comes to putting myself in danger. After all, if I died, who would you argue with?"

"I'm glad you're finally seeing reason."

She laid her head against his chest. Gifford's warm breath stirred against her hair, making sparks ignite in her stomach. "Now," he said. "I want to hear about your day. Did you read any new books?"

"I've read all the books we have." She wrinkled her nose. "Armies aren't very good about carrying libraries with them. I can't imagine why. We'd fight so much less if everyone would just sit down and read."

Gifford's laugh rumbled through him, loud against her ear. "A question I often ask myself. Imagine how much money the realm would save if the rulers focused their finances on libraries, rather than wars."

"Not if I were allowed to shop for books."

"England would go bankrupt," he said gravely. "Thank God for wars."

She pushed him away, playful. "You can't switch sides like that."

The corner of his mouth quirked up. "It's too late. I've switched already, and since you've forbidden switching that quickly again, I'm stuck opposing you."

"Congratulations," she said. "You've just described our entire relationship." She took his hand, her eyes going serious again. "I'm not sorry we got married. About the way it happened, maybe, and all the discomfort we've put each other through. But not that we got married."

The way Gifford smiled was so full of hope and relief, it made Jane's breath catch, and she had the strongest urge to stand on her toes and press her lips to his. But then he glanced toward the tent flap. "It's almost ferret time."

He tried to pull away, but Jane held tighter to his hands and shook her head.

"I don't want to change tonight." She hugged him, burying her face against his shoulder. "I want more than these few minutes, Gifford. G."

"I know," he whispered. He held her tight. "Me too."

Jane clung to him like he was her anchor. Some nights she was resigned to the change, and others she fought and knew she would not win. But right now she resisted the flickers of light with all her will.

She felt the magic fill her. Then it drained away, and Jane opened her eyes, expecting to be small and furry and cupped against Gifford's chest.

Only the last part was true.

Gifford held her against him, but it was her human hair that he stroked, and her human legs that she stood upon, and her human eyes that met his.

Awe filled his face. "You . . . broke your curse."

She was still trembling with the anticipation of the change. Maybe they'd been wrong about the time. After weeks of living half lives with short times at sunrise and sunset, they'd both learned how long they typically had together, but maybe they'd been wrong.

"You didn't want to become a ferret," Gifford continued, "so you stayed human."

"It wasn't that," she breathed. "I wanted to stay with you. That was my heart's desire."

Wonder and disbelief warred on his face, but finally a wide smile won as he cupped her face in his hands.

Heart pounding, Jane leaned forward. They were close. So close.

Cloth rippled and torchlight shone in. "G—" Edward stopped halfway into the tent. "Oh. I'm sorry, Jane, I thought you were a ferret."

For a moment, Jane wished she were a ferret. It'd be less embarrassing than her cousin walking in on . . . something. A kiss that didn't happen.

She leaned back and caught her breath, resigned. The kingdom had to come first. "It's all right. I learned how to control it at last. I think I'll remain a girl tonight."

"Good. That's good." Edward flashed a tense smile and turned to Gifford. "We're having a strategical meeting in my tent."

Gifford turned to look at Jane. "You should come with us."

Jane froze. Go with them? To plan? To strategize?

Edward stared at Gifford. "We'll be planning a *battle*, G. The men, I mean. Well, and Bess, of course."

"Which is exactly why Jane should join us," Gifford said. "She's excellent at planning."

Jane looked back and forth between them.

"All right," she said. "Let's go. I have lots of ideas."

The three of them walked to the tent where the leaders of their assembled forces—Archer, Bess, the commanders of the French and Scottish armies—were standing around a table that bore a map of London. Gifford spent a few minutes pointing out different places of interest—what might be a useful hill and where they might focus their attempts to enter the city.

"*That's* the plan?" Jane asked after a few minutes of listening to Edward and Archer bicker over the best place to attack the city wall. "To besiege London?"

Edward shrugged. "We have to take London somehow."

"London has never crumbled under siege, not in all of recorded history," Jane pointed out.

"But it's not as though Mary will meet us on the battlefield." Edward coughed lightly. "She won't send out her army when she doesn't think she needs to. The rules of engagement mean nothing to her."

Jane had a sudden idea.

"Then the rules of engagement must mean nothing to us," she announced. All the men in the room frowned. "London cannot be taken. And it doesn't need to be taken."

Mary hadn't needed an army to take London. Yes, she'd had one, but they'd just sat around the wall being scary while Mary intimidated the Privy Council into submission and seized the throne.

"What do you propose, Jane?" Bess gave her an encouraging smile.

"We take Mary."

"Take her where?" asked the French commander.

"Take her *how* is probably the better question," G said.

"Take Mary. Yes, that's clever," Bess said, ignoring G's concern. "All Edward needs to do is show up to confront Mary. When everyone sees that the rightful King of England is alive, they won't be able to deny his claim to the throne. But it must be in the proper place, where there can be no question about his identity. And we must not give Mary any time to prepare."

"Mary will be holed up in the Tower of London, won't she?"

G asked. "In the royal apartments at the top of the White Tower?"

Jane slammed her palm on the table. "Then we break into the Tower."

"The Tower that . . . also hasn't been breached, ever?" Edward eyed Jane.

"Right, but we have advantages others haven't." Jane counted on her fingers. "One: an intimate knowledge of the layout and inner workings of the Tower of London. Two: a kestrel."

Everyone looked at Edward. (Even the French commander, though he wasn't sure why everyone was looking at Edward. In spite of all the hints, he hadn't figured it out yet.)

"I can't go in there alone," Edward protested.

"I'd volunteer," boasted Archer. "But I can't fly over the walls."

(Here, the French commander's eyes narrowed with suspicion. France was still a country run by Verities, after all.)

Edward glared at Archer. "The problem isn't the walls. It's that I'd be naked. And unarmed. I'd have to land and change on the Tower Green, conveniently in the very same place Mary executes people like me, and I'd rather not make it that easy for her."

(Everyone definitely knew what they were talking about now.)

"It's fine with me if you want to send the bird in." Archer smirked at Edward. "But we have these armies, you see. Are they for nothing?"

The Scottish and French commanders looked at each other in a moment of mutual solidarity.

"The armies *are* useful." Jane wished the others would all

just hurry up and understand. "They will be a *diversion*. Imagine her panic when Mary looks out and sees several thousand soldiers assembled outside the city. Here." She touched a spot on the map. "On the opposite side of London from the Tower." She leaned forward over the table eagerly. "Mary doesn't even know you're alive, Edward. As far as she's aware, *I'm* the one preparing to attack London. And we'll let her continue thinking that."

"Which doesn't change the problem of a naked bird king standing on the Tower Green," Archer said. "Do you have a plan to keep him from getting killed before he surprises Mary?"

"Yes." Jane grinned. "I do."

Edward had been planning to attack the city at dawn, but with Jane's new and improved plan, they were going to hold off until night fell, so that it'd be easier to sneak into the Tower unseen. Which would give them the entire day to prepare.

"I'm going to practice," Jane announced when she and Gifford returned to their tent together to get some much-needed sleep. She hung a cloak from one of the tent poles to act as a curtain, then took off her clothes. Light flared as she changed from girl to ferret to girl again. It was surprising how easy she found the change now that she knew she could do it. Now that she knew what she truly wanted.

"Show-off," Gifford said from the other side of the cloak curtain. "You're probably keeping our neighbors awake with that light."

She just wished G would want it, too. He'd be much more useful in the morning in his human form. And there were so many other reasons that she wanted him to be with her tomorrow.

Jane turned into a ferret and ran up his leg and side until she perched on his shoulder.

Gifford stroked her fur. "Nicely done, my dear. Now can we go to sleep?"

She considered asking him to practice, too. But if he wanted to, he would suggest it. He would try. But since he didn't offer to try, she became a girl again, dressed, and together they squeezed onto the narrow sleeping pallet.

"This is nice," G said against her hair, pulling her back against his chest. "Thank you for not making me sleep on the floor."

"You're welcome," she murmured. It was more than nice, she thought as she closed her eyes and tried to quiet her mind. She'd go to bed like this every night, if she could. But this could be their last night together.

It was starting to feel terribly familiar, this feeling that tomorrow they could die.

The sounds of birds singing woke her a few hours later. She stretched her arms and wiggled her toes; she was still a girl.

"Did you sleep?" Gifford's voice behind her was deep and groggy.

Jane nodded and pulled herself out of their makeshift bed. "Not well, but it was better than nothing." In truth, she'd tossed and turned for hours. There was much riding on her today.

Gifford sat up and smoothed back his hair. "I didn't sleep. I kept thinking about you breaking your curse."

Jane looked over at him, hopeful.

"Your heart's desire, you said." He rose to his feet, his clothes all sleep-tousled and a pressure mark running the length of his face. He was beautiful, she thought, if one could call a man beautiful. There was a question in his eyes, and she knew the answer.

"Gifford, I—" The word balanced on her tongue. Was it so difficult to say? It couldn't be wrong. The feeling had been gathering in her since those days in the country house, growing and deepening ever since. And now that she knew the secret to controlling her form, they could actually have a future together.

She desperately wanted a future together.

"Jane." He glanced at the tent flap. "It's almost time. The sun."

"Don't change," she whispered. "Stay with me."

"I want to, but—" He began tugging at his clothes, loosening his shirt collar and picking at the buttons.

"Don't change!" Jane went to him and took his shoulder, like her touch could break his curse. "Want to stay with me more than you want to do anything else."

"I'm sorry, Jane. I wish—"

She grabbed his face and kissed him, shoving her fingers through his hair to draw him closer. "Stay with me," she pleaded against his lips. "Don't change."

Gifford pulled back for a heartbeat, his eyes wide with surprise. "Jane," he breathed. "I—"

"Don't change." She lifted her gaze to his. "Please."

"Oh, Jane." He kissed her. Softly at first, but then she pulled him close and pressed her lips harder to his. And that was it. She could feel him giving in by the way his body pressed against hers, the way one of his hands cupped her cheek, and the way the other slid down her arm. She could feel his desire to stay human in the fevered, desperate way he kissed her. Like he wanted this to last, to make this moment stretch on.

But then he jerked back and threw his shirt free, bright white light enveloping him.

"No!" Jane's eyes stung with tears.

The light faded, and Gifford stood there as a horse.

Jane pressed her hands to her mouth to hold in a faint sob.

His head dropped.

"It's all right," she said tremulously after a long moment. "It's very difficult to master the change. Even Gran said she had a hard time with it, remember? You can try again. When you're better rested."

She went to lift the flap for him to step out of the tent.

"I'll see you later," she said. "Tonight."

He didn't look at her as he passed. He just went. Then she was alone in the dim space that still smelled faintly of horse.

She stared down at the tangled blankets they'd shared, trying not to cry. Perhaps she'd put too much hope in his feelings for her.

What if he didn't care about her as much as she cared about him? What if that was why he hadn't stayed human? She'd *tried*. Oh, she'd tried, and they'd *kissed*. But it hadn't been enough.

She hadn't been enough.

Jane spent the day waiting for dusk.

She didn't see Gifford, except the occasional glimpse of him running with other horses, or resting in the shade. It was impossible to tell what he was thinking. Not that she had time to dwell on him. There was so much to do to prepare for nightfall.

When the sun was almost down she made her way to Edward's command tent. Gifford trotted toward her, chestnut coat shining in the honey light, and then he vanished into the tent without pausing to acknowledge her whatsoever.

Her heart sank.

She watched as the camp readied itself for battle. The men put on their armor and strapped on shields and swords. The archers tested their bows. The cavalry saddled their horses. And the noncombatants pinned open their tent flaps, preparing to receive the wounded.

There would be wounded. There would be dead.

"All they have to do is look scary." Edward came outside his tent and saw Jane brooding over the infirmaries. "It's like you said. They'll distract Mary from us."

"I know." Jane hugged herself. "But some will inevitably be injured. They're here to draw fire." Archer was out there among the assembling troops, ready to lead the Pack into battle. Gracie, she knew, had insisted on joining him in the fight. What if Gracie was hurt? What would it mean to Edward if she were killed?

A chill ran through her. What if Edward himself was killed? Her plan wasn't perfect. There were variables she couldn't possibly account for. He could die.

She didn't know if she could survive his death a second time. Or Gifford's.

Gifford.

(At this point we as the narrators would just like to say something about the true danger of this entire situation. We should remind you now that we only promised to tell you an alternate story to what the history books record. You'll be lucky if you can find a history book that mentions Jane at all—since she's often skipped over in the line of English monarchs—but if you do, that book will say that Lady Jane Grey ruled England for nine days, was deposed by Mary, and then had her head chopped off. Well. We already know that didn't happen in our tale. Our Jane still has her head.

But we can't promise that Jane's always going to be safe in the part that's coming up, or Gifford, or Edward, or any of the other characters you've come to know and love. The truth is, any of them could die at any moment, and then, well, Queen Mary would undoubtedly spend the next five years living up to the nickname Bloody Mary by having hundreds of poor Eðians burned at the stake. So keep that in mind as you read onward.

Anyway, back to Jane and her worrying.)

"We're all doing this for the same reason," Edward said gently. "The soldiers know it. They're willing to sacrifice everything for that reason, if sacrifice is what they must do."

"What reason is that?"

"To make England the kind of place that we would have it be: a land of peace and prosperity, a kingdom where we are permitted to be our true selves without fear."

"That's worth maybe dying for." Gifford's voice came from behind her.

She turned. At seeing him as a man again, a shiver ran through her, both delight and sorrow. She'd *begged* him not to change this morning, and he had anyway.

"See?" Edward nudged Gifford with his elbow. "Even the horse agrees."

Gifford bowed.

"Screw your courage to the sticking-place, right, G?" Edward said. He clapped Gifford on the shoulder and leaned to kiss Jane's cheek. "Now I'd better change. To make sure I have time to get hold of the bird joy."

He'd better *get hold of the bird joy,* Jane thought. And truly, he'd improved, as far as she'd seen. But if he wasn't there when she was ready . . .

Her cousin became a kestrel and flew into the starry sky. She watched him go.

"You don't have to be the one to do this, Jane," Gifford said, when they were alone. "There are others who could."

She smiled at him sadly. "I must do this. I was queen for only nine days, and I don't wish to be queen again, but I do love England. I want to fight for it. For Eðians. For us."

Gifford searched her eyes, stepping close, but he didn't touch her. Didn't kiss her. His change this morning was still too thick between them.

"Then let's go, my lady."

They returned to the tent and found Pet sitting with her chin on Edward's chair.

"Come on, Pet." Jane kept her voice soft. "I know you want to help Edward. We'll do it just like I told you earlier. Come on."

Pet whined like maybe she found this whole thing a very dumb idea, but she followed Jane and Gifford out of the camp.

"Don't worry, Pet," Gifford said as they walked. "I can defend us, should the need arise."

Pet whined again, and Jane agreed. She wasn't totally confident in her husband's skills as a swordsman. Although she supposed he'd managed well enough with the giant bear.

Trumpets sounded in the distance—the attack on the city had begun. Jane, Gifford, and Pet moved swiftly in the opposite direction, moving parallel to the old Roman wall that protected the city.

"Here." Jane guided the group to a wide ditch that ran alongside the wall. The high weeds would provide the perfect cover, as long as they stayed quiet. "Keep low."

Gifford snorted. "That's easy for you to say."

She arched her neck to look up at him. "No one asked you to

be so tall." But she was pleased her demure stature was finally good for something. It was an advantage at last. A boon. An asset. A virtue— She stopped herself from continuing her synonym spiral. There was work to do. "We'll head for Saint Katherine's."

The three of them sneaked as quickly as they dared. Every shout from beyond the wall made the two (at the moment) humans duck. Pet always turned her ear toward the sound, growing statue still, and then wagged her tail when she was sure that all was clear.

It had been a last-minute idea to send Pet with Jane and Gifford, and Jane was glad for the companionship, even if Pet was sometimes a naked girl and that made everyone uncomfortable. Pet was always good to have in a scrape.

She hoped tonight wouldn't be too much of a scrape.

Ahead of them, a large priory stood against the darkening sky. Jane knew this land well—she and Edward had sometimes played near here as children. There were several abbeys in this part just outside of London, and a church, gardens, and a hospital. She could already see the Tower and its many structures before them, rising against the night. Torches shone along the walls. She wondered where Edward was—if he was circling overhead already, waiting for her. But she didn't see him. It was too dark.

"Look here," Gifford said, glancing around. "We're on Tower Hill."

Jane shuddered. They were standing on the ground where Gifford was to have been executed not so long ago. A huge, newly built pyre stood nearby, stacked with brush just waiting to be lit.

Awaiting the Eðians Mary had been rounding up over the last few weeks. Jane had never seen a burning, but one of her books—*The Persecution of Eðians Throughout the Ages: A Detailed Account of Animal Form Downfall*—had indeed given detailed accounts of the way one died when burned at stake. A terrible, painful death.

That was meant to be Gifford. Her Gifford. Her stupid horse husband who didn't even try to control his form. Who didn't love her, not the way she loved him. But Jane would fight any war if it meant keeping him safe.

She reached for Gifford's hand and found him already reaching for hers. If they failed tonight, this pyre would be waiting for both of them by dawn.

They hurried by the Aldgate and farther south down East Smithfield Road, until they reached Saint Katherine's Abbey. The three of them aimed for the gardens, keeping to the heavy brush and weeds that grew on the river's edge.

"This is as far as you go," Jane said as they settled behind a low wall near the abbey. She pointed across a dark field, toward a small bridge that crossed the moat and led straight into the Tower of London. The Iron Gate—Jane's destination—stood on the other side, a lowered portcullis blocking the way in. There were four guards on the bridge; it didn't require much in the way of sentries, which was why she'd chosen it.

She took a moment to catch her breath. The Thames rushed by not twenty feet away, but Jane could hardly hear the noise over the pounding of her own heartbeat as she watched the guards, analyzing their movements, trying to find a pattern.

"I don't like this," Gifford glanced at her worriedly. "It's not safe."

"It's not your choice," she snapped, but softened when he winced. "I must. And you know I must. I'm the only one who can. A horse would get caught. Even a dog. But not me."

"My darling, I don't think ferrets are as stealthy as you imagine."

Jane pinched his arm. "I'm as stealthy as I need to be. I rescued you from Beauchamp Tower, didn't I?"

"Yes, but—"

"And I could hold perfectly still if I wanted."

"Not even while you sleep, my sweet."

"And I could vanish for hours and you'd never find me."

"Only because you'd have fallen asleep in the fold of some forgotten blanket." But he looked terrified. "Please reconsider."

"It's the only way," she said, lifting her eyes to his. Waiting. Hoping. Wanting him to say something more. Hadn't she proved her feelings last night when she didn't change? If he'd just say something now, that might help ease the knot of emotions and anxiety.

Pet sighed and rolled onto the ground, bored.

Jane turned into a ferret.

The light from her change must have alerted the guards, because even as Gifford dumped Jane over the low wall they'd been hiding behind—and she crashed and rolled into the weeds on the other side—she heard a shout, and then Pet began barking and

Gifford shuffled to another hiding place.

There was no time to worry about them now. Jane took off at a speedy walk—because running ferrets were very bouncy and not stealthy at all. Gifford did have a point about that.

As she sped through the high grass, what had been a short walk suddenly became much longer now that she was tiny. She missed her human sight, too, though as a ferret the darkness wasn't quite so impenetrable. And also, she could hear the guards far better.

"Look for an E∂ian," one guard called from the middle of the bridge.

"Kill any animal you see!"

Jane's tail felt huge and prickly. Instinct urged her to run in the opposite direction. (She had read somewhere that ferrets were fearless creatures, but she didn't believe that, even if she was a ferret with a human mind. Ferrets wanted to live as much as anyone else.)

"Look, a dog! Get it!"

Boots struck the ground. She couldn't tell how many went away from the bridge. Surely not all of them—they wouldn't leave this entrance to the Tower completely unguarded.

She lifted her head, and looked around. *Sniffed* around, we should say, now that she had such an excellent nose.

First, she smelled the foul odor of sewage from the moat, and she immediately regretted her excellent nose. Then she tried to block out the stink and search for different notes in the air. Plants. Mold. Sweat.

There were two humans still here, she surmised after a moment of smelling and listening, both with their weapons drawn, ready to kill any animal they saw.

Ready to kill her.

Jane pressed her furry belly to the ground and considered her journey across the bridge. It was a narrow bridge, at least for a human. As a ferret, she had much more room. She just had to get past the men, squeeze through the closed portcullis, and find the correct tower.

Piece of cake. Right.

Behind her, toward the church where she'd left Gifford and Pet, a dog howled and suddenly went silent. "I got one!" called a guard.

A fresh wave of adrenaline rolled over Jane.

(Okay, so we told you that anybody could die at any time, and you seem like you're getting worried, but Pet's fine. Jane had foreseen that the guards would spot the flash of her Eðian change, so she'd recruited Pet to draw away the guards. Which would, in turn, give Gifford time to hide elsewhere while he waited for her to open the gate. Pet was meant to lead the guards into an ambush with some Pack members on the other side of the field, but whether she would accomplish that—or the guards would give up the chase— remains to be seen. But trust us: we're not the type of narrators who would kill a dog.)

The dog howling was Jane's signal to go.

Jane scampered onto the wooden bridge and darted down it as

fast as her tiny legs could carry her.

"Watch out!" Boots came thumping toward her. "A rat!"

I am not *a* rat, Jane thought, and dashed straight for the nearest guard. She jumped onto his leg, climbed up to the top of his high boots, and bit hard into the soft flesh behind his knee. Her claws dug into the leather of his boot. *Can a rat do* this? she thought smugly.

The guard howled and swatted her off, knocking Jane's tiny body toward the edge of the bridge.

"Get that rat!"

Her anger fueled her. Jane jumped to all four feet, ignoring the shocks of pain from her tumble, and kept running, darting to and fro. The guards were after her, but she was quick enough that they could never quite catch her. Finally she swerved so that when they bent to scoop her up, they crashed into each other—and Jane was across the bridge, through a hole in the portcullis, and running into the Tower of London at full tilt.

The stone walls rose above her, huge and imposing. Even more so as a ferret.

But, of course, Jane had spent the day memorizing maps of the Tower of London and figuring out how long it would take her to get from place to place in her Eðian form. So it was with reasonable certainty that she hastened across the green, squeezed beneath a door, scurried through a few halls, and finally faced an endless set of stairs that would take her to the top of the Constable Tower— the building in the Tower of London that they'd decided would make the best place for their little invasion.

The steps were each as tall as she was.

Speed was important.

But so was stealth.

But so was speed.

Edward was waiting.

She listened hard for anyone moving nearby, but there were no sounds here. Not yet. But the guards she'd evaded on the bridge would soon be after her.

Which meant she needed speed more than stealth right now.

Jane turned into a girl.

She was a naked girl, but there weren't any options for clothing. As quickly as she could, she hurried up the stone stairs, her bare feet growing more and more chilled with every turn around the narrow stairwell. It was the right decision, because she reached the top more quickly as a human than she would have as a ferret.

The room with the biggest windows was at the top. Hurriedly, Jane grabbed a fire poker from next to the hearth and crossed to the south-facing window. The windows of the Tower were made of cloudy, ancient glass, and they didn't open. She felt guilty, but she had no choice. She hit the glass with the poker using all her strength, over and over until it cracked and then shattered, leaving a large gaping hole that opened into the night sky.

That should do it.

Jane dropped the poker and scanned for anything useful. The room was crammed with wardrobes and cabinets and crates, which was part of the reason they'd chosen this particular part of the Tower of London.

First, they needed clothes. Most of the clothes in the wardrobes were military uniforms, which were all too big for Jane. (Not to mention the indignity of pants.) But since nudity was out of the question, she pulled on the smallest set she could find and laid out another uniform next to the broken window.

"Come on, birdbrain." She glanced out, but all she saw was dark. From this angle, she couldn't see much of anything—not the battle where Bess and Archer led their attack on the city wall, not even the place nearby where Gifford was hopefully unharmed and waiting for her. But she could hear the guards calling to each other in the courtyard below. They probably hadn't seen where she'd gone (although surely they'd heard the window bashing, so they might have a general idea), but they knew someone had infiltrated the tower. At some point they'd get organized and search it structure by structure. If she stayed here much longer, she'd be caught.

But Edward wasn't here yet.

What would she do if he didn't come?

Jane tried to ignore the wild thudding of her heart and moved on to search the cabinets, looking for weapons, but they were all filled with stockings, boots, and hats. Further inspection only turned up a few vaguely weapon-like items. A frying pan. A rolling pin. Oh, and the fire poker.

Jane snatched it up from where she'd dropped it on the floor and smiled at the pointed tip. That could work.

But *where* was Edward?

As if on cue (or maybe a bit late on his cue), a kestrel flew through the window.

"Edward!" At least, she hoped the bird was Edward. It'd be embarrassing to just start talking with a strange bird.

At the flash of light, Jane turned away and covered her eyes.

"Jane!" the king greeted her happily. "Sorry, but it was harder to tell which window I should come to. I know you said the south-facing window, but I don't have the best sense of direction as a bird."

"No time for conversation, cousin," Jane said. "Gifford's waiting."

"Right." He sounded uncharacteristically nervous. "Let's go."

"But I did set out some clothes for you."

"Oh, right. How thoughtful." He shuffled around and hurried into his clothes. From the courtyard below Jane suddenly heard a shout: a soldier had come upon the broken glass from the window. They only had a few moments before they'd be discovered.

Edward looked at her grimly. "So what do we have in the way of weapons?"

Jane tossed him the fire poker.

He held it like a sword, so maybe it would be useful after all. "Good enough. And for you?"

Jane picked up the frying pan.

TWENTY-SEVEN

↖ *Gifford*

Where was she? G paced back and forth on the other side of the Iron Gate, squinting into the darkness past the portcullis, hoping for a sign of his Jane. The minutes felt like hours, and the seconds felt like days. Every violent sound that pierced the night air (and there'd been a few violent sounds since he'd hoisted ferret-Jane over the abbey wall earlier) could be the harbinger of her death. The death of his wife. His beloved.

G loved her. But he hadn't told her he loved her.

She had begged him to stay, and he'd wanted to, especially given the way she had kissed him. How had a girl like Jane kissed him like that? With her whole heart and her whole body? She'd probably read a dozen books with titles like *The Kiss: It's Not Just About the Lips.*

The way Jane kissed, it was an art. She kissed by the book.

And yet, he'd still changed into a horse. And he hadn't told her he loved her. Now she might die without knowing that she'd become his day and his night, and his sun and his moon. He adored Jane—he loved her! he loved her!—and he should have worn that for all to see. He shouldn't have hidden his heart.

He closed his eyes and sent a quick prayer to the heavens that he would see her again.

He prayed Edward would keep her from harm.

He prayed if Edward failed, she would turn into a ferret and hide.

He prayed if she was discovered, she would slip from the soldier's clumsy fingers.

And that if she couldn't escape, they would kill her quickly.

G squeezed his eyes shut and tried to forget that last plea to heaven. Instead he composed a line of prose in his head.

If I may but see you again, my dearest, I will wear my heart upon my sleeve. . . .

He remembered Jane's face right before she'd kissed him. He glanced at the flicker of the torches that framed the heavy gate, their flames weak and faint against the wind. Jane's face could have taught those torches to burn bright. Last night, she was the sun, and all of the flowers in all of the counties turned toward her for warmth.

G pulled his quill, ink, and notebook from his pocket and fumbled as he tried to uncork the jar without spilling its contents.

(Unfortunately, reader, the much more portable pencil would

not be invented until the late sixteenth century, and the closest thing to the pen we are all familiar with now was not invented until the nineteenth century, so G was left to fumble with ink and quill. The first people to read of our tale wondered why he bothered to bring a quill, ink jar, and notebook into battle at all, considering he was already carrying three swords—one for himself, Edward, and Jane, when they needed them—but G would argue that he was more familiar and comfortable with a quill in his hand rather than a sword, and if he had to choose one or the other to bring into battle, he'd bring the quill. Because when it came right down to it, he would probably have a better chance of defending himself with a quill.)

When G let his swords drop to the ground, he was finally able to put quill to paper.

Oh how she could teach the torches to burn bright. She was the sun—

Before he could finish his thought, he heard footfalls on the cobblestones inside the Tower, and then a hushed voice.

"Gifford?"

It was Edward. G pressed closer to the gate and could barely make out the silhouettes of two figures rushing toward him, but they didn't come within a stone's throw of G's position before two other figures, with the distinct silhouettes of the Tower guards, intercepted them.

"Jane!" G called out in a loud whisper.

As G's eyes adjusted to the scene before him, he saw Edward raise a . . . fire poker? . . . and Jane pull out . . . a frying pan?

Whose cockamamie idea were these weapons? Probably

Jane's. They seemed like Jane's idea of weapons.

No one paid attention to her frying pan, though. Jane, by virtue of being a lady, was allowed to slide into the background. No one else so much as glanced in her direction as she retreated against the wall. She didn't pose a threat.

Good, G thought. But part of him was grieved that she'd barely seemed to notice him at all.

The guards drew their swords and faced the king.

"Gentlemen," Edward said. "Sheathe your weapons. I am King Edward the Sixth, by the grace of God, ruler of England, France, and Ireland. In earth, the supreme head. I am your rightful sovereign."

"King Edward is dead," one of the men responded. "And besides, doesn't France have its own, separate king?"

"I am *not* dead," argued Edward. "There are nefarious villains who would have you believe I died. But any accounts of my demise have been grossly exaggerated, I assure you, for here I am, very much alive."

The guards exchanged looks.

"He speaks the truth," G called from his position beyond the gate. "He is our true king. I have traveled with him to France to gather troops. I have fought alongside him as he killed the Great White Bear of Rhyl. Long live King Edward!"

The guard on the right began to lower his sword, until the guard on the left said, "Hold on. There's no such thing as the GWBR. He obviously lies."

The first guard scratched his head. "But what if he speaks the truth?"

"If he's not speaking the truth, and we let him go, we'll be hanged for treason. But if he is speaking the truth, we could kill him here, and no one would ever be the wiser."

"No!" G said. "Bad decision!"

The guard on the right re-raised his sword and took a deep breath as if to speak, but he didn't get a sound out before a loud *bong* rang out and he dropped like a stone. Jane stood behind the guard, her frying pan raised to where the man's head had been.

"Wonderful, Jane!" G grinned. Frying pans. Who knew?

Edward, with his excellent mastery of fencing and his years of training and his newfound strength, swiftly dispatched the other guard with two flicks of his fire poker.

"Well done, Sire," G said. For a moment, he wondered if it was indeed the best choice to skip those fencing lessons in favor of writing poetry. But that worry would have to wait until later. After the sword fight.

Edward sprinted to the gate, and soon Jane was there, too, and they used their combined weight to activate the pulley-and-counterweight system that raised the portcullis.

It didn't lift fast enough for G. His gaze held Jane's through the bars. The sound of paws against gravel announced Pet's sudden arrival, and the dog scrambled under the portcullis and ran to Edward. As soon as G could, he crawled underneath and took his wife in his arms. "Jane."

"Gifford."

"I . . . we . . . There are so many things I should've told you—"

"We should get going," Edward said.

(Now, we, as narrators, feel the need to inform you, dear reader, that we do not know how Edward always managed to thwart kisses. All we do know is that it was a gift he demonstrated throughout his life, most notably when his third cousin the Lady Dalrymple of Cheshire was about to kiss her new husband over their wedding altar, just after the priest pronounced them man and wife, and Edward stepped forward from his place of honor by the priest and said, "I hate to interrupt, but I thought now would be an excellent time to remind the wedding party not to throw rice, on account of the fact that birds, even kestrels, can choke on it.")

Back to the scene at hand. Edward said to G and Jane, "Now we must get to the White Tower. And Mary."

They all turned toward the huge stone structure that stood in the exact center of the Tower of London. The White Tower—the most ancient and well fortified of the castle buildings. Where Mary would be sitting on Edward's throne.

"Did you bring the swords?" Edward asked G.

G ran back to the other side of the gate and tried to act like he hadn't just left the swords sitting there. Jane kept her frying pan, but G and Edward each took a sword.

They were coming into the Tower of London as thieves in the night, and G was struck by the difference from the last time, when Jane was to be crowned queen, with royal guards escorting them in ceremony and deference. But before they could even start toward the White Tower, three more figures blocked the way. The first was a man G didn't know. The second was G's brother, Stan. The third was the owner of one giant eagle nose.

Edward raised his sword immediately. "Bash," he said.

"I'm sorry, what?" G was confused.

Edward tilted his head to indicate the first man with the sword. "That's Bash, the weapons master. He taught me everything I know about swordplay."

"Oh, excellent," G said faintly. "Bash. Is that short for something?"

The man called Bash just glowered at them and dropped into a fighting stance. G moved in front of Jane and held his arm across her, feeling the urge to protect her, although he knew when it came down to it, there'd be no stopping her.

Dudley sneered at them. "How quaint. A sickly boy, a useless man-horse, and a girl. This should be easy."

G had to admit his father had a point. Perhaps Edward could compete with Bash, but there was no way G could take on both Stan and his father.

"John Dudley," spat out Edward. "You treacherous snake. You are a traitor to your country and your king. I will see your head on a pike."

Bash made an offensive move—"Watch out!" Jane cried—and Edward reacted quickly. He lunged toward Bash as if he'd been waiting his whole life to duel the fencing master. The two of them almost danced to and fro, their swords flashing in the moonlight. Edward looked brilliant in G's opinion—strong and quick on his feet. He fought like the king he was.

G turned to his brother, who lifted his own impressive blade.

"Stan," G entreated. "Come to your senses. The king is alive. This will all come down to two sides: the righteous and the imposters. Right now, you stand with the latter."

Stan's sword wobbled, and he glanced sideways at his father.

"You're wrong," Lord Dudley said. "You've always been a fool."

"The fool thinks he is wise," G retorted. "But the wise man knows himself to be a fool."

That was a great line, he thought. He tried to remember where he'd stashed the quill and paper.

His father looked annoyed. He cleared his throat. "Whatever. Bash will dispatch the boy, and we all know that you're no skilled swordsman."

Everyone glanced at Edward and Bash. The weapons master was, at the moment, on the offensive. Edward retreated gracefully behind a tree to buy himself some time and rest before he began his own offense. But for the moment, it appeared that Bash had the upper hand.

"You see, Gifford?" his father crowed. "You see how your king cowers?"

"Edward does not cower!" Jane banged her frying pan against her hand. Stan and Dudley didn't seem impressed by her threatening display, but G knew she'd fight them, too, if it came to that.

Though his wife was little, she was fierce.

Bash advanced, and Edward continued to retreat. Advance. Retreat. Advance. But just as Bash looked ready to deliver a stunning blow, Edward's feet flicked and he was out from behind the tree and driving his opponent backward.

"Unexpected, yes?" Edward said, breathing hard. "Just like you taught me."

Jane whooped in a way that would have seemed unladylike if anyone had been paying proper attention.

Both men went back to the dance of two expert swordsmen, and G turned to his father, the clang of blades in the background.

"Perhaps, Father," he said, "you will change your mind about who win will this scuffle in light of some recent news. The first is this: King Edward is fully recovered from your poison. I watched him kill the Great White Bear of Rhyl without even breaking a sweat. He's no sickly boy. The second, which might be even more disconcerting to you: your beloved firstborn has fled."

G jerked his head toward the spot where Stan had stood only moments before. Indeed, between the far buildings, Stan's retreating form could be seen careening around a corner. He always did have the courage of a flea.

"I could go after him," Jane suggested. "With my frying pan."

"He's not worth it, my dear. Save your frying pan for someone who matters."

Jane *hmphed* but stayed where she was.

"And the final piece of news . . ." G suddenly swung the

tip of his sword closer to that eagle nose. "Since you last saw me, I have spent every waking hour sharpening my fencing skills. I have sliced candlesticks and skewered straw dummies and sparred with some of the finest blades of France. I might not be able to beat a weapons master, but I can easily best an old, top-heavy, pusillanimous, two-faced, paltry, odious excuse for a man." He pushed his sword forward until it was against his father's coat. "Drop your sword."

Lord Dudley, lacking in grace and honor—and at this point in time, any sort of backup—dropped his sword and fell to his knees, just as Edward disarmed Bash of his blade.

Bash put his hands together. "I will give you anything you ask of me, Sire," he panted, and bowed his head.

"Fealty. Swear your fealty," Edward demanded.

"My king, my sovereign, your smallest wish is my soul's desire. Kill me if you need, but if you deign to let me live, I will be your humble servant, in whatever capacity you deem fit."

Edward wiped sweat off his brow and looked to G. "Do what you will," he said, nodding at Lord Dudley.

Now this was a matter between father and son.

G turned and placed the tip of his sword on his father's chest. He pressed it with enough force to break through the topmost layer of fabric.

"Now, Gifford, think about what you're doing." Dudley's voice was unnaturally high.

"Shut it, Father." G spat the word in disgust.

"My son, please. I only did what I did for the good of the kingdom."

"A kingdom you destroyed? Even now, at this very moment, men are fighting out there behind the walls, fighting and dying because of what you did. You're a most notable coward, an infinite and endless liar, an hourly promise breaker, the owner of not one good quality."

Lord Dudley held out his hand. "You just don't understand politics. Have you learned nothing? Everyone involved in the running of a kingdom deserves to die at some point. It's how the game is played. You win or you die."

"You deserve to die." G looked at his father's outstretched hand and it made him sick that he shared the same blood as this man. (Or maybe not, because he didn't have the nose.) With a flick of his sword, he cut a gash in Lord Dudley's palm.

Behind him, Jane gasped.

Dudley fell to his knees. "My son. My boy. I understand you are angry. What can I do to make you spare my life? I'll do anything. Anything!"

"Anything?" G said. "Will you give me your estate?"

"Yes! I will give you all that I have and more!"

"Will you stop telling people that I'm a half-wit and admit publicly that I'm an Eðian?"

"Yes!"

"Will you tell me that I'm just as good as Stan?"

Dudley hesitated. "Well, Stan's exceptional." He looked again at

G's sword. "But . . . yes. You are quite . . . good. Please don't kill me."

Jane's small hand crept to his shoulder. G reached up to place his hand over hers. He let out a breath and looked up at the night sky. He already knew what he was going to do with his father. Yes, some would say that Lord Dudley deserved to die, but G was not the king, nor was he a judge, nor was he an executioner.

"I will leave you, Father, to the will of the people, who by this time tomorrow will all know of your treachery."

Jane used rope to tie Bash and Dudley to the iron lattice of the portcullis (she had, after all, once read a book on the proper securing of captives), and once the prisoners were bound, the three of them made their way into the White Tower. To the throne room.

(You're probably thinking the same thing we were: where did Jane get the rope to tie the prisoners? We researched this very conundrum thoroughly, and after two weeks we can say, without a doubt: nobody knows. It's a question that has baffled historians and archaeologists alike. Professor Herbert Halprin explains: "Ropes have been a mystery to scholars throughout the ages. The first ropes were thought to appear as far back as 17,000 BC and made of vines. Unfortunately, being made of vines, none of those early examples survived. Later, da Vinci drew sketches for a rope-making machine, but it was never built. In medieval times, there were secret societies, called Rope Guilds, whose rope-twisting practices were protected via a complicated series of handshakes and pass-words—" Okay. Your narrators are interrupting the dear professor, for reasons of boredom. Plus, his English accent sounded sketchy and forced. We asked him where Jane could've gotten the rope, but maybe he thought we asked him where *anyone* could've gotten *any* rope at *any* given point in history. Trust us, we are as frustrated as you must be about the lack of a definitive answer.)

Anyway. It was time for our heroes to do what they'd come to do. It was time to face Mary. Finally.

"We should make this quick, like in and out," said G as they approached the throne room. He nodded his head toward the windows, where the shades of approaching dawn filtered through. A few more minutes and he'd be a horse again, stuck in the White Tower. And he'd been there and done that already.

But as they reached the door to the throne room, Edward paused.

"You really think this will work?" he asked suddenly. "Because there are probably loads of people on the other side of this door." He glanced down at his ill-fitting uniform. "Maybe they won't recognize me."

"They'll recognize you," assured Jane. "This will work."

"Either that or we're all about to die," G added. "But it's for a good cause."

Edward nodded and put his hand on the door.

"Wait!" G stopped him. He turned to Jane. "There's something I have to tell you."

"Now?"

"I don't know if I'll get another chance." He took a deep breath. "I've been weak. I've been a horse, when I should have stayed a man. But I can't go in there and face whatever we're about to face without you knowing that I am yours. Flesh, man, fur, horse, I am yours, Jane."

He glanced again at the window. The sun was almost up. "At least for a few more seconds."

Jane stood on tiptoe so she could look into his eyes. "Stay with me, G."

He sighed. "I have never wanted so much in my life to stay human."

"But you didn't even try before. Why wouldn't you try?"

G shook his head, ashamed. "For most of my life, it's been easier to run. What if my heart's true desire is to keep running? What if I can't get my house in order, and be the man you want? But Jane." He took her hand and kissed it. "Dear Jane. You are my house. My home. I may have only half a life, but what I have, I pledge to you. I . . . I love you."

"You love me?" she whispered.

"The very instant I saw you, my heart flew to your service," he said.

"Really?"

"No," he admitted. "Not exactly. But it's a good line, am I right?"

"G." She sighed. "Talk sense, please."

"When I first saw you, I thought you were so beautiful that you couldn't possibly love me. I never saw true beauty until that night." He stroked her cheek with the back of his hand. "But I didn't know you then. I didn't know how clever you were, how courageous, how kindhearted, how true to yourself you always are. My lady. Jane. I would not wish any companion in the world but you."

Her eyes were shining. "I love you, too."

"You do?"

She smiled. "I do. But I have one question."

"What is it, my lady?"

"Do you see the light through yonder window?"

G blinked, confused. "What?"

Jane took his face in her hands. "The sun is up," she whispered. "See?"

"It can't be the sun. I am still a man," G said.

"The sun is up, and you are still a man," Jane confirmed.

G closed his eyes, and for the first time in six years, eight months, and twenty-two days, he felt the sunlight on his skin. He breathed in its rays and absorbed its glow, and there rose a peace in his heart, the kind of calm that comes from the feeling of arriving home after a long journey. His curse was broken.

The two lovers embraced, while Edward and your narrators turned their heads to give the lovebirds their moment of blessed union.

"Ahem. Are you quite done?" Edward asked, when lips finally parted long enough for them to take a breath.

"Not quite." G pressed one last soft kiss to Jane's poetry-inspiring mouth. "Now we're ready."

"Good," said Edward. "Because there's still something *I* have to do."

TWENTY-EIGHT
Edward

Edward threw open the door and strode into the throne room.

He'd done it. He'd gotten into the Tower, a nigh-impossible feat. He'd fought bravely and well. He'd dispatched the guards, confronted Dudley, even beaten Bash at swords. And now he was about to reclaim his crown. Everything had gone according to Jane's plan. He was nearly there—he could practically taste his victory.

His first surprise was that the throne room was almost empty. He'd supposed it would be bustling with courtiers and members of the Privy Council there to advise Mary and show the queen their support during the attack on the city wall. But at best there were a dozen people present. Not exactly the boisterous crowd he'd been hoping to witness his glorious return.

Still, the room fell silent when he entered, all eyes turning to him, mouths opening in shock. Because even though he was streaked with sweat and stained with blood and not wearing any shoes, he was undoubtedly King Edward, back from the grave.

This was going to be good.

He turned to the steward stationed next to the door, whom he'd known since he was a young boy. "Announce me, Robert," Edward commanded.

The man looked like he was seeing a ghost (which he kind of was) but he obeyed without question. "His Majesty Edward Tudor."

Edward padded toward the throne to stand before Mary.

"You're sitting in his chair," piped up Jane from behind him.

Mary fidgeted with her handkerchief. "Oh, Eddie. I'm so glad to see you're alive. My heart was simply broken when they told me you were dead."

"How dare you," Edward said to her, his voice so dark with fury that he didn't sound like himself. "How dare you steal what is mine. You poisonous bunch-back'd toad!"

"Ooh, that's a good one." There was a rustle of paper behind him as Gifford wrote the line down.

His sister's face paled. "Now, brother—"

"You have the audacity to call me *brother* after what you've done? I should have you drawn and quartered. Or would you prefer to be burned at the stake? Purified—isn't that what you called it? Isn't that what you had planned—a great burning of traitors?"

"It was Dudley's doing," Mary said softly. "He took your throne because he wanted it for his son. I simply took it back."

Edward laughed, but it was not a merry sound. "Oh, am I supposed to thank you for keeping my chair warm?"

She stared at him mutely.

"No more lies, sister," Edward said. "Let us speak plainly now, about what's to be done."

This would be the part where she'd beg for her life, he thought, where she'd cry and plead and grovel before him. He wondered if he could ever find it in his heart to forgive her.

Probably not.

But in this he was surprised again, because Mary did not beg. She stood up slowly, her back straight and unyielding before him. Still wearing his crown. "You're only a foolish boy," she said at last. "How could you possibly know what to do with this great kingdom?"

"I've been ruling this great kingdom for years," he pointed out.

She scoffed. "You call that ruling? You were a puppet of the council, nothing more. And look what we've come to. Eðians running about freely, causing havoc at every turn, savaging the land, defiling our very way of life. You have let this country slide to the edge of ruin. The Eðians are determined to bring us into an age of darkness and perversity, and you are helping them."

"I am an Eðian," he said. "Like my father before me. I am my father's son."

"And I am my father's daughter," Mary replied hotly. "I am his firstborn child, his only true heir. He may have played at marriage

467

with a bunch of Eðian harlots, but my mother was his only legitimate wife. Which makes me, and not you, who are basically a bastard, the rightful ruler of England."

Huh, thought Edward. He hadn't been expecting her to argue. His mouth opened, then closed again. He wanted to say, *Wait, no, that's not right at all. I'm the rightful ruler. Mary can't be. Because she's a woman.*

But that logic didn't make sense to him anymore. He didn't believe it.

He couldn't think of what to say. He was, quite literally, speechless.

At his silence, a triumphant gleam appeared in Mary's eyes.

"I am the queen," she said, drawing herself up still further. "All my life I've watched you wrest that title from me, you a flagrant heretic, a pathetic, trifling boy. You talk of stealing, but it's you who are the thief here. *You* are the usurper."

"No," a voice called out from the back of the room. An authoritative voice.

Bess.

Edward spun around to watch his other sister come up the aisle.

Bess's gray eyes narrowed as she looked at Mary. "Edward is the rightful heir to the throne of England, because our father named him as his heir. The king can name whoever he wishes to succeed him."

"But Father only named him because he was deceived by the

foul Edians into casting aside his good and virtuous wife." Mary pressed. "And only because Edward was a boy."

Bess smiled knowingly. "Wrong, sister. Father left his throne to Edward because he knew, even then, that Edward had the heart of a king. Father knew that Edward would be generous and thoughtful when it came to the welfare of his people, and wise in his decisions. Father knew that Edward would be the best choice for this country."

Huh, Edward thought again, frowning. He might have been flattered at these words, but deep down he knew that they weren't true. When he'd "ruled" before, he hadn't given much thought at all to the well-being of his people. In truth, he'd known nothing about his people. And he certainly hadn't been wise. He'd done what he was told, signed what they'd put before him, agreed to the course of action the men around him informed him was the correct one. He had been a puppet, a king in name only. And his father *had* chosen Edward solely because he'd been born a son and not a daughter.

Bess came to stand beside him. "Edward is the true king," she said. "It's Edward who will lead England to peace and prosperity. He will make England great."

She turned to address Mary. "You would have led us all to ruin. You who conspired to kill your own brother and pilfer his crown. You who threaten to tear the very fabric of our nation in two. You're a disgrace to the royal blood that runs through your veins."

"Arrest her!" Mary shouted at the guards. "Off with her head!"

The guards didn't move. They looked to Edward. He said nothing.

"The game is up, Mary," Bess continued smoothly. "You've lost."

"No!" The word echoed in the room. Then Mary let out a bellow of rage and barreled toward Bess with outstretched hands, as if she would choke the life from her sister.

But before she could reach Bess, a light flashed.

The onlookers gave a collective gasp.

Where Mary had been standing, there was now a chubby gray mule.

The first person to laugh was an elderly woman near the front of the room—a stranger to court, people would later remark, but a distinctive figure who gave everyone who played at card games a peculiar sense of déjà vu.

"Oh dear. What an ass!" the old lady cackled, and then everybody began to giggle while the old mule brayed and stood there looking generally miserable at the turn of events that had befallen her. (As narrators, we'd like to inform you now that Mary was never seen as a human again. She remained an ass, all the rest of her days. As asses typically do.)

Edward didn't laugh at her with the others. He turned to the guards. "Take her away."

A man—it was Peter Bannister, actually—slung a rope around the former queen's neck and led her from the room.

Edward approached the throne. It was just a glorified chair, he thought. It wasn't even that comfortable. Nevertheless, he sat down on it carefully and surveyed the room. Because that was what was expected of him.

The people quieted once more. Then slowly, in a rustle of fabric and a shuffle of shoes, they kneeled before Edward. "Long live King Edward," they said in one voice. "Long live the king."

A lump rose in his throat. He didn't feel the way he'd expected to feel in this moment. He didn't feel triumphant, or victorious, or righteously entitled to the throne. He felt much the way he did the first time he'd been told that he was king. A sinking in his stomach. A dread.

Bess bent to pick up the crown from where it had clattered to the floor when Mary had showed the world her true self. She walked slowly and purposefully to stand beside Edward. She smiled. Then she raised the crown above his head and . . .

Edward caught her wrist. "Wait."

She froze. "Edward, what are you doing?"

"What Mary said is true," he whispered. "I'm not the rightful ruler."

"Of course you are," she said.

"Why, because I'm a boy?"

"Did you not hear what I said before? About why Father chose you?"

He looked down at his feet and smiled wistfully. "You're the generous one, sister. I never really considered the welfare of my people. I'm not wise. I'm just a boy."

471

"You've never been just a boy," she said.

"I don't have the heart of a king, but you do," he said earnestly.

She stared at him. "Me?"

"You're the one who's going to make England great." He took the crown gently from her hands and stood. Jane and Gifford and Gran were all standing near the front, mouths open in shock—even Gran, who he'd always thought unshockable. He wished that Gracie were here. He'd been trying not to dwell too much on Gracie, as she was probably still fighting alongside his soldiers at the city wall, and he couldn't afford to be distracted by the thought of what was happening with her. But he would have liked to have seen her face when he did what he was about to do.

"Listen well," he announced to the people assembled. "I, King Edward the Sixth, do hereby abdicate my crown to my sister Elizabeth Tudor, who I find, by both her birthright and her immeasurable good qualities, to be the rightful heir to the throne of England. Any rights and privileges I have heretofore enjoyed as monarch of this fine land, I bestow upon her."

Silence.

He met Jane's eyes. She closed her mouth and tried to smile. Then she nodded slightly.

"Long live Queen Elizabeth!" she called out, her voice small but strong. She turned to Gifford, who had been clasping her hand all the while, and nudged him.

"Oh. Long live Queen Elizabeth!" he added, and then the other voices began to join in, louder and louder.

"Come, sister," he said to Bess. He took her hand and led her to the throne.

"Are you sure?" she whispered as she sat carefully in his chair. (King or not, it was going to be a while before he stopped thinking of it as his chair.) "Consider what you're giving up."

He knew what he was giving up. Power. Prestige. Wealth beyond measure. A life of leisure and luxury. A person always standing by to make sure he didn't choke. And, most of all, his future. Edward couldn't honestly imagine who he would turn out to be if he wasn't king. By stepping down he was relinquishing his very identity.

But his country needed a ruler who was worthy and capable. England needed Bess.

"I've never been more certain of anything in my life," he said. "You're going to be a fine queen, Bess. The best. Even better than Father. Trust me."

She gave him that subtle, thoughtful smile at his familiar words before she bowed her head for a moment, her eyes closed, her face as pale as chalk. He could see all twenty-two of her freckles. Then she looked up to address the people. "Very well. If that's my fate, I will be as good to you as ever a queen was to her people."

"Long live Queen Elizabeth!" they answered unanimously. "Long live the queen!"

Edward placed the crown upon her head.

* * *

Let's pause for a moment. We know, we know, we're so close to the end now that you can practically taste the happily ever after. And who would have seen that coming, right? I mean, who could have predicted that Edward would stand up then, and right there in front of the Privy Council and all of his adoring fans, he'd say that she—Elizabeth I—should be the Queen of England?

Because obviously she was the most qualified for the position. At long last Edward had arrived at the enlightened state of knowing that a woman could do a job just as well as a man.

Yep. That's how it happened. Edward abdicated his throne. Elizabeth would be crowned queen at Westminster Abbey that same week, and we all know she'd be the best ruler of England ever. And now history can more or less pick up along the same path where we left it.

But what happened to Edward, you ask? Well. We still have a little bit of the story left to tell.

Edward spent the better part of the next few days thinking about (what else?) Gracie McTavish. Because he still wanted to tell her that he'd stepped down from the throne and see that surprised look on her face. And because (let's be honest) he still very much wanted to kiss her. He thought about it embarrassingly often.

But the charming Scot was nowhere to be found.

"She'll turn up eventually," Bess said as he anxiously paced the throne room. She picked at a stray thread on the red velvet cushion of the throne. "You needn't worry, Edward."

Bess was right. Bess was always right, even more so now that she was queen; it was getting annoying. Gracie was alive. There'd been exaggerated tales of a valiant black-haired woman leading the Pack during the false attack on the city walls—but then where had Archer been? And where was Archer now?

The entire Pack had not yet made an appearance in London. They'd retreated back to the Shaggy Dog the moment the fighting was done. Gracie, he figured, must be among them.

With Archer, probably, Edward thought miserably. Burned bright in his memory was the way Archer had told Gracie that she was looking very fine. And the way that flea-bitten man had ogled her like she was a piece of meat.

He couldn't stand the idea of Gracie with Archer. And why wouldn't she have come to see him? Their last moment together in France had ended badly, but so badly that she wouldn't want to see him again?

"Edward, sit down," Bess said. "You're making me queasy."

He sank into a chair. Pet lumbered up to him, tail wagging. He scratched behind her ear, and she gave a happy dog sigh and collapsed at his feet. Pet had asked to remain a guardian to the queen, and after all she'd done for their cause, Bess had agreed (even though she wasn't too fond of dogs—remember, cat person). It was a little awkward at times, but the least they could do—well, that and give her a scratch and the scraps from the table every now and then.

"Um, Your Majesty," came a voice from the doorway. A

frightened voice. "About your crown."

"What about my crown?" Bess asked the trembling servant who came to cower before her—Hobbs, Edward remembered the man's name was.

"Have you . . . moved it?" asked Hobbs.

"Moved my crown?" Bess frowned. "Where would I move it?"

"Normally it's kept on a velvet cushion in the king's—I mean the queen's—chamber."

"Right." Edward and Bess exchanged worried glances. The citizens of England seemed to unilaterally accept Bess as the official ruler of the country now, but if someone had literally stolen her crown, it could mean trouble. Not to mention that the crown was virtually priceless.

"Speak, Hobbs," Bess commanded. "Tell us what's happened."

Hobbs shifted from one foot to the other nervously. "It's gone, Your Majesty."

"Gone."

"Yes, Your Majesty."

"Gone where?" Bess's voice rose, and the servant flinched.

"Gone missing!" Hobbs cried. "My job is to polish it. That's what I do, every Thursday—I polish the crown, only today when I went to retrieve it, I found . . ." He started to cry. "I found . . ." He hiccupped. "I found . . ."

Hobbs held out his fist, which was clasped around something

very small —much too small to be a crown. Maybe a crown jewel. But it meant bad news all the same.

"What is it?" Edward and Bess both leaned forward to look. "Show us," Bess said.

Hobbs opened his hand. He was sure he was going to lose his head for this. So he was shocked when both the former king and the current queen broke into broad smiles.

"Your Majesty?"

"It's all right, Hobbs," Bess said.

Edward started taking off his clothes.

"Um, Your Majesty . . ." Hobbs was very confused now.

"You don't still need me here, do you?" Edward asked Bess as he pulled his shirt over his head.

"I can manage," Bess said. "Go."

"Thanks." He gave her a grateful smile and turned toward the window, shuffling off his pants. Then there was a flash of blinding light, and when Hobbs could see again, the boy who had been king had simply vanished.

Hobbs stared down his hand, at the item he'd found resting in place of Bess's crown.

A tiny wooden fox.

When Edward came down to rest on the roof of the Shaggy Dog, he saw, with his magnificent kestrel eyes, that one of the back doors had been left open a crack. This door turned out to be the entrance to a small storeroom, which was currently crammed to the gills with all manner of freshly delivered food and supplies.

A gift, compliments of Queen Elizabeth, as a promise that she would honor Edward's agreement with the Pack.

In the center of the floor was something Bess hadn't sent: a stack of clean, neatly folded clothes. Nothing fancy, of course. A simple linen shirt, black pants, and a pair of boots in exactly his size. Edward put this on so fast that he got the shirt backward at first.

When he came out of the storeroom there was a man waiting for him. The man grunted something like, "She's up thar," and pointed to the hill behind the inn.

Edward ran.

He came upon Gracie standing at the top of the hill under a large, spreading oak. She didn't see him at first. She was staring out at the setting sun.

Edward stopped and drank in the sight of her. She was wearing a long gray skirt and a white blouse, her hair loose and spilling all over her shoulders. She had a small satchel slung across her back, and the pearl-handled knife strapped to her belt.

He cleared his throat, heart hammering.

She turned. "Sire."

"I'm not the king anymore," he blurted out stupidly.

"I'm the leader of the Pack," she said at the same time.

He wasn't sure he heard her correctly. "Wait, what?"

"Archer's dead," she informed him. "He took an arrow to the

chest in the first ten minutes of the siege."

"Oh, I'm sorry." A minute ago, Edward could have wished a pox on Archer. But now he felt rather bad for him. "Did you . . . hear the part where I said I'm not the king?"

"It's all anyone can talk about around here. You didn't do that . . . for me, did you?" Her green eyes were genuinely worried.

"No, I didn't do it for you," he answered quickly. (Although if we're being totally honest here, there was a teeny tiny bit of Edward that really had wanted to give up the throne of England so he'd be free to kiss a Scottish pickpocket as often as he liked.) "I wasn't thinking of you at all!"

She looked down. "Oh. I see."

"What I mean to say is, I don't want to be king," Edward continued in a rush. "All my life the crown's been forced upon my head. But when I had a choice in the matter, I found I didn't want it."

She bit her lip to keep from smiling. Dimples. And that was all it took.

Edward closed the space between them in two strides. He didn't really know what he was doing, only that he had to do something right now or he'd explode. Her warm heart-shaped face was in his hands, his fingers caught in her curls. She opened her mouth to say something, and he kissed her.

He kissed her!

He knew he must be doing it right because after a few stampeding heartbeats her eyes closed and her hands reached up to grasp at his shoulders and she kissed him back.

Edward felt like he was flying, only his feet were firmly on the ground.

He kissed her and kissed her.

With tongue, it must be noted.

She pulled away, green eyes wide. "Good Lord," she breathed.

He considered that a compliment.

"You have no idea how long I've wanted to do that." He tucked a glossy black curl behind her ear, then dragged his thumb gently over her chin.

She leaned in until her lips were nearly touching his. "I have some idea."

He kissed her again.

Of course this whole kissing Gracie thing didn't mean that Edward was going to marry her, and that they were going to live happily ever after. (But if he played his cards right, who knows?) The happily ever after of this book belongs to Gifford and Jane. Naturally. But for now, Edward just kissed Gracie. More slowly this time. An explorer of new worlds.

Some time later he said, "Now give me Bess's crown back, imp."

She laughed and pulled the crown out of the satchel. "Fine. Have it. But I thought you said you didn't want it."

"I don't want it. I'm not a gyrfalcon, am I? I'm a kestrel," he said against her ear. "Not a king."

She turned her head and kissed him, a teasing brush of her lips on his. "All right, then," she said in her charming brogue. "But just so you know, Edward . . ."

He kissed her again. "You called me Edward!"

"Yes. Edward." She grinned up at him. "You'll always be a king to me."

TWENTY-NINE _{& Jane}

Okay, we're almost to the happily ever after. But before that, we have to talk about the wedding. Oh, we know there was already a wedding. We mean a *second* wedding.

Jane and Gifford's second wedding was very much like their first wedding.

Except this wedding took place outside.

During the day.

And the bride and groom actually liked each other.

And they were both human at the time of the nuptials, which was indeed the case at their first blessed union, but given the daytime nature of this one, we thought we should make that clear.

Jane and Gifford stood below an arch laced with flowers, a field spreading all around them. There were only a handful of chairs for guests, but every one of them was full. Lady Dudley and G's younger sister, Temperance, were seated in the front row. Edward and Gracie (holding hands, of course), Bess, and Gran sat on the opposite row. Peter Bannister and Pet had also come, both in their human states (and this was the first time anybody ever saw Pet wearing actual clothes). Notably absent were those who'd conspired to set up the first wedding: Lady Frances had gone into exile when it became clear she wouldn't be able to manipulate (or pinch or poke) Jane any longer (she ran off with the Grey Estates' master of horse, which was quite the scandal); the Privy Council was certainly not invited; and Lord Dudley—well.

Lord Dudley was never heard from again. As far as we know, he lived, sentenced to finish out his days near a sulfur mine. It was that or death, and he chose sulfur. Whether or not he was happy with that decision, we may never know.

Anyway, back to the wedding.

On everyone's lap rested a book. Any book. In case the wedding got boring. As the priest droned on in the same manner as last time, Jane was both pleased and annoyed that no one was taking advantage of her thoughtfulness.

"And now," said the priest, "let us declare the miracles of holy matrimony."

First, true love.

With her free hand, Jane squeezed Gifford's, smiling up at him. Love, they definitely had. It felt true. Her heart pounded as the priest extolled the wonders of love and finding one's perfect match.

"I love you," Gifford whispered, and Jane warmed all over.

"We're not to the vows yet," the priest muttered out of the side of his mouth.

"Sorry."

Second, virtue.

Gifford's gaze dropped to peer down her bodice.

Jane snorted and laughed, drawing Looks from everyone. But she didn't care. Not this time.

Third, progeny.

Well, that was under discussion. Maybe one day.

"Now you may give your vows," said the priest.

"I'm going first," Jane said. Gifford had gone first at their previous wedding, and it was only fair that Jane got to lead this time. "I, Jane Grey-Dudley, hereby declare my devotion to you. I swear to love you faithfully and forever, rescue you when you're in mortal peril, and keep a pantry stocked with apples so that you never go hungry. To illustrate the depth of my emotions, I've written a list of things you outrank."

Jane took a moment to unfold the paper flowers she'd been carrying. Gifford shifted nervously, trying to get a look at the writing. She flicked the papers toward her so he couldn't see.

"Gifford, I love you more than knitting, though to be honest, I love a lot of things more than I love knitting.

"I also love you more than being queen, which admittedly, I didn't love a lot.

"I know I'm not inspiring much confidence at this point, but there's something else I thought I'd bring up." She lifted her eyes to him. "I love you more than I love books."

Gifford laughed and leaned down to kiss her, but the priest cleared his throat. "Ring. Then more vows. Kissing comes last."

Gifford heaved a melodramatic sigh and offered his hand. "Very well."

Jane pulled a ring from the pocket sewn into her gown—the same ring she'd put on his finger during their first wedding, stashed in a drawer since that night. Now, she slipped it onto his finger and held her hand over his. "I give myself to you."

"I receive you," he whispered. And then, louder: "I know I said this last time, but this time, I mean it with my whole heart. I, Gifford Dudley, hereby declare my devotion to you. I swear to love you, protect you, be faithful to you, and make you the happiest woman in the world. My love for you is as deep as the ocean and as bright as the sun. I will protect you from every danger. I am blind to every woman but you. Your happiness is paramount in my heart." He retrieved the matching ring and pushed it onto her finger. "I give myself to you, my Lady Jane."

"I receive you." Jane didn't wait for instructions to kiss. She stood on her toes and wrapped her arms around her husband's shoulders and kissed him as the guests clapped and clapped.

THIRTY
Gifford

What's a wedding without the wedding night? Considering that their first wedding night ended with a heap of horse dung in the corner of their room, it wasn't difficult to hope for something better this time.

And better it was, for G loved his lady, and his lady loved him.

And there were no secrets between them anymore, save one. G wanted to confess it to his lady before they commenced with the very special hug.

He asked Jane to sit next to him on the bed. "There's something I need to tell you."

"Go on," Jane said.

G took her hand in his and traced his finger over the delicate skin of her arm. What she didn't realize was that he was scrawling the words of a poem he had recently written. It was inspired by his lady and he had spent many long hours trying to find the words that adequately conveyed the feelings of his heart.

There were many false starts, because at first he tried to capture the moment a horse fell in love with a ferret.

Shall I compare thee to a barrel of apples?
Thou art more hairy, but sweeter inside.
Rough winds couldn't keep me from taking you to chapel,
Where finally a horse would take a bride. . . .

And then he tried to wax poetic about the ferret alone. . . .

Shall I compare thee to a really large rat?
Thou art more longer, with less disease.
One would never mistake you for a listless cat . . .
Nor a filthy dog, because my dog has fleas.

He could never confess his passion for poetry with those paltry examples.

And then, at the second wedding, as G basked in the glow of Jane's radiant smile, inspiration finally hit him, and after the feast he put quill to paper and wrote and wrote until he had it right.

"Tell me, my love."

"You remember how I had a reputation? With . . . ladies?"

"Yes," she said, eyeing him warily.

"The truth is, there were never any ladies, nor late night romps at houses of ill repute."

His Jane looked confused. "Then where did all the stories come from?"

"There were late nights, but those nights consisted of . . ." His voice trailed off as his heart raced.

"Of what?" Jane said, her mind racing to all sorts of unsavory conclusions.

"P—" He started to say the word, but paused.

"Perversion?" Jane said.

"No."

"Peculiar habits?"

"No. Well, one."

"If you don't tell me right away what it is, I will knit all of your clothes from now on," she said, and she fully intended to follow through on her threat.

"Poetry," G blurted out.

"Pardon me?" Jane said.

G climbed out of bed and stood at the foot. He pulled out the paper and began his recitation.

"My Lady Jane . . .

Shall I compare thee to a summer's day?

Thou art more lovely and more temperate:

Rough winds do shake the darling buds of May,

And summer's lease hath all too short a date;

Sometime too hot the eye of heaven shines,

And often is his gold complexion dimm'd;

And every fair from fair sometime declines,

By chance or nature's changing course untrimm'd;

But thy eternal summer shall not fade,

Nor lose possession of that fair thou ow'st;

Nor shall Death brag thou wander'st in his shade,

When in eternal lines to time thou grow'st:

So long as men can breathe or eyes can see,

So long lives this, and this gives life to thee."

With a deep breath, G tore his eyes away from the paper to assess his lady's reaction.

"That was . . . lovely," Jane said.

"You really think so?"

"Yes. I mean, I'm glad we will not be forced to live by your quill, because I am rather used to having food on the table. But, I appreciate the effort behind those words."

(Now, some of you might recognize these words as belonging to a certain Mr. Shakespeare, the likes of whom hadn't actually been born yet in the year 1553. But you should also know that there are all kinds of conspiracy theories about who actually wrote Shakespeare's plays and sonnets, and we contend that the real writer was a very old and very happy Gifford Dudley—assisted by Jane and the immeasurable knowledge she drew from books—who went on writing not to make himself famous or rich, but to make a certain lady happy.)

G smiled and fell back onto the bed. "You have no idea what

a relief it is to hear you say that."

Jane lay down next to him, on her side, her head propped up by her hand. "Do you have any other confessions, my lord?"

"Hmmm," G said. "You heard the one about how much I love you?"

Jane put her hand on his chest, and slowly pulled on the tie that held his undershirt closed. G's breath caught.

"Yes, I remember that one."

The knot fell open.

"And, you know the one where I don't know much about swordsmanship?" Gifford's voice was low and soft.

"Yes, I remember that one as well."

Jane tugged at the top button of his vest. G clasped her hand in his. "Kiss me, Jane."

Lips met lips, soft and questioning at first, and then, quite suddenly, desperate and wanting. And where at their first wedding, their wedding-night chamber seemed full of the echoes of strangers eager to have their say, tonight, they were very much alone. G lost himself in Jane's kiss. He pulled back for a moment. "I have to tell you, Jane, the way you kiss is a work of art—"

"Shut up and kiss me," Jane said.

They kissed again, lips exploring and asking and answering, and then eager fingers fumbled at buttons and untied ribbons and never did their lips part except for a moment here and there to say it again.

"I love you."

"I love you."

They collapsed into each other, and although it would be indelicate to detail what happened next, these narrators will tell you that a "very special hug" does not begin to describe it.

P.S. They totally consummated.

And now, dear reader, there isn't much more to say on the matter except this: Gifford and Jane lived happily ever after, their destinies colliding quite often. Which pleaseth them both.

The End

Acknowledgments

Hi! Lady Janies here. This is the part where we're supposed to tip our hats to all the wonderful people who helped make this book into what it is, but there are three of us and we each have an extensive support team, so we'll try to be brief (ha-ha). After all, you just read a five-hundred-page book. You're tired. So are we.

Here's a (totally incomplete) list of people we think are pretty awesome:

First off, our readers, both old and new. Every time we mentioned writing a book about Lady Jane Grey (a comedy?!), you always responded with such enthusiasm. It made the idea seem a little less crazy and a little more doable. Thanks for that. You rock.

Our agents, of course: Katherine Fausset, Lauren MacLeod, and Michael Bourret. "The three of us want to write a book together" was probably the most logistically nightmarish thing you've ever heard us say, but you ran with it. Thank you for your unwavering belief in us and our funny little story.

Our fantastic editors, Erica Sussman and Stephanie Stein, who just *got* this book from the very beginning—the humor, the characters, the playfulness in the telling. One of the best parts of writing *MLJ* was getting to make you laugh. Also, thanks to Kristin Rens and Laurel Symonds for not minding when Brodi and Jodi ran off to play with a different book for a little while.

Our publicist, Rosanne Romanello, who read this book so quickly we got whiplash. Pterodactyl E∂ians are totally a thing.

Our jacket designer, Jenna Stempel, for not killing us for how picky we were this time around, and for giving us a jacket with pearls and lace and Jane looking mischievous.

Our families, for their patience and support while we ran off for weeks at a time to write and play in England. (That's Jeff for Jodi; John, Will, and Maddie for Cynthia; and Carter and Beckham for Brodi.)

Our pets: Todd and Katniss and Kippy and Walter Fishop III and Stella and Frank and Pidge and Jewels and Fred the Pigeon we found on our balcony in London, who may or may not be a girl. You're our E∂ian inspiration.

And the yeoman at the Tower of London who talked to us about Jane and ran up Beauchamp Tower to make sure we saw both places where Guildford had carved Jane's name.

And that's it. We'll stop now. Bye.

READ EVERY NOVEL
IN THE CAPTIVATING
UNEARTHLY SERIES
by CYNTHIA HAND

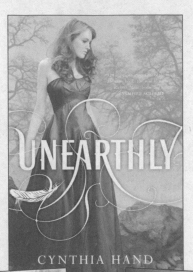

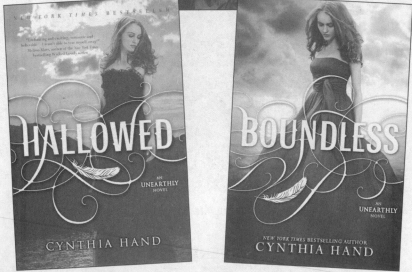

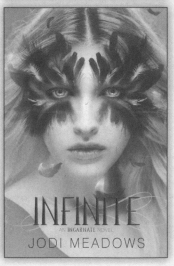